I0661310

The Chronicles of John Zebedee

Elizabeth Schechter

Published by Elizabeth Schechter, 2023.

The Chronicles of John Zebedee

Copyright © 2023 Elizabeth Schechter

All rights reserved, including the right to reproduce this book, or portion thereof, in any form.

This is a work of fiction. Any references to historical events, real people, or real locales are used fictitiously. Other names, characters, places, and incidents are the product of the author's imagination, and any resemblance to actual events or locales or persons, living or dead, is entirely coincidental.

Published by Ravens Wing Books

Previously published on Kindle Vella as:

John Zebedee and the Heir of the Elvenlands (2022)

John Zebedee and the Monstrous Town (2022)

John Zebedee Meets the Witch-Queen of the Elvenlands (2022)

Editor: Michael Schechter

Cover design by GetCovers

Ravens Wing Books

ravens-wing-books.com

ISBN: 9781952598494

Table of Contents

Author's Note:

A MULTITUDE OF THANKS to Valerie Willis of 4 Horsemen Press. These stories were originally written for a shared world project that she created, and which included both the setting of Wraithtown and the character of Jacob Wraith. The project had to be cancelled, but my contribution was already complete, and she graciously allowed me to continue to use both the place and the character that she created.

John Zebedee and the Heir of the Elvenlands

CHAPTER ONE
Fireflies

1870 — SKULLYVILLE, ARKANSAS

There was something about the sparkle of sunlight on water. Something nostalgic. Something familiar. Even though these weren't the waters of his childhood, the sparkles were the same, and they brought with them a sense of peace that John had found hard to come by since he'd last come this way.

He leaned on the rail of the topmost deck of the steamboat, listening to the creak and groan of the great paddle-wheels at the stern, looking out at the bank of the Arkansas River. There were ruins on the bank, ruins that shouldn't have been there. The last time he'd been here, those ruins had been a decommissioned fort and a thriving town. Fort Coffee had housed a school for Choctaw boys, and there was a sister school, an hour ride further down the river in Choctaw Agency. The people here lived in peace with the Choctaw tribes that made their homes on the far side of the river.

That had been before the war, though. How much else had changed? His destination was some three hours ride south of the fort — would the dugout still be there? He hadn't considered that it might be gone. He hadn't realized the fighting had come this far west. What would he do if the place was gone? Where would he go then?

"Now, if you keep staring like that, son, you're liable to break something."

The voice was slightly accented, very pleasant, and entirely unexpected; John jumped, reaching for the gun that he wasn't wearing. It took him a moment to remember that the war was over. That he wasn't under attack. The old man who had startled him raised his empty hands. "Easy, son. I apologize. I gave you a fright. I should have realized you were a soldier, and I shouldn't have snuck up on you like that."

John swallowed, trying to slow his heartbeat. He forced a smile. "Old habits die hard. I'm sorry, sir—"

"No, it was entirely my fault," the old man protested. "You have nothing to apologize for. Now, you're over here scowling like you're mad at the world." He leaned on the rail next to John. "I've been watching you. And thinking that's a fine-looking young man. A nice young fellow like him certainly should have no reason to be looking so fierce that we should be praying for the fish down there."

John chuckled. "The fish are perfectly safe from me. Until I get back to my nets. Then they're in trouble."

"Oh, you're a fisherman?"

John nodded. "Once. Maybe I will be so again."

"Maybe so, maybe so." The old man spat into the water, then smiled. "Going home, then? Not many other reasons to be coming out here."

"In a manner of speaking, yes," John answered. "My father had a place out here, near Fort Coffee and Choctaw Agency. He left it to me, and I'm hoping it's still there."

"Because you have no place else to go?"

"And a long time to get there," John added. "A very long time."

The old man nodded. "Those of us who travel the river have seen a lot of that since the fighting ended. Plenty of young men with that same fierce look. They can't settle, can't be still. They've seen too much. Done too much. Or had too much done to them. They come this way, looking for a place with no memories. Someplace entirely new. And you can't get more new than Skullyville."

"Skullyville?"

"What used to be Choctaw Agency," the man answered. "They changed the name of the town, back in '60."

John nodded. "Did they? Well, then, it is new." He turned and offered his hand. "John. John Zebedee."

The old man chuckled and shook John's hand. "Nice meeting you, Zebedee. I'm Ben Parsons." He pulled a flask from an inside pocket of his coat and offered it to John. "Now, let me make that fright up to you. Have a nip of something that's good for what ails you."

John shook his head. "Thank you, but no. I don't drink."

Parson's brows rose. "And you a soldier?" he asked. "I'm an old man, and I've never once met a soldier who didn't drink." He pulled the cork out of the flask and took a swallow.

"Now you have," John said, leaning back on the rail. They'd be arriving in Choctaw Agency... no. Skullyville. They'd be docking soon. Would anyone still be there who would remember him?

He hoped not. That could be awkward. And that was something he should have thought of before he set out. What would happen if someone recognized him?

"Do you smoke?" Parsons asked. "I don't, usually. But I carry some, for trading."

"No I don't." John smiled. "Or chew."

Parsons snorted. "You don't drink *or* smoke? You must be trying hard to get into Heaven, son. You've got no vices!"

The words stabbed John through the heart, feeling like rough iron nails being hammered home. He forced a laugh. "Well, I'm trying hard."

"I can't imagine why," Parsons muttered, taking another pull from his flask. "From what I hear, it's a boring place. No drink, no chew, no horizontal refreshment—"

John burst out laughing. "What?"

"You know!" Parsons insisted. "As young as you are, and looking like you do? You probably have the public women paying you for the privilege."

John shook his head. "I prefer to sleep alone. Less disease that way."

"Definitely heading for Heaven, then," Parsons declared. "One foot there already."

John swallowed and watched the docks coming closer. "Eventually, maybe I'll get the other foot in."

JOHN EXCUSED HIMSELF to return to his cabin and pack, leaving Parsons to wonder about the rarity of a soldier who neither drank nor whored. In truth, John had packed his few belongings before going on deck, but the lie gave him a completely plausible reason to leave the conversation. He let himself into the cabin, closed the door, then leaned on it and sighed.

"This was a mistake," he muttered. "Coming back here was a mistake. It hasn't been long enough. They'll know me." He crossed to the plush couch, where his hat, his rucksack and the long case that held his clothes and his rifle were waiting. The price of the steamship cabin had been more than what he'd gotten for selling his horse, but it was only money, and he'd wanted his privacy. He wanted to be sure no one would be able to sneak up on him, and startle him into reacting without thinking, the way that Parsons had at the rail. He didn't regret the choice, but now he was wondering what it would have been like to make the trip by train. Or to have kept going. "I should have gone to the frontier. No one would know me there. I could have spent years alone..."

His voice trailed off. That was it. That was what had made him decide to come back here. He knew this place. He'd been as close to happy as he ever got here. He'd lived in the little dugout near the floodplains of Deadman's Slough for years — long enough that the people in Fort Coffee and Choctaw Agency had started looking curiously at him when he came into town for supplies. So in 1845, he'd regretfully made the decision to leave, starting the rumor that he was leaving to go east and marry. He had no intentions of ever returning.

Then the war happened. And Camp Sumter had happened.

Now, he desperately needed the peace he had found at Deadman's Slough. He needed to escape the horrors he'd seen in the war, and the memories that followed him like locusts. He'd tried to find escape at the bottom of a bottle, and when that failed, he'd tried to find it in a bullet. Only to be reminded yet again of words said in love so long ago, words that cursed him to walk the world. Words that bid him to wait until the first man he had ever loved came back for him.

No matter what Parsons said, there was no Heaven for him. Nor Hell neither.

There was nothing but the waiting.

He sighed, and swung the rucksack onto his back. He picked the case up, put on his hat, and looked around the cabin. There was nothing left here. It was time to move on. Time to go back to Deadman's Slough and see if he could find something there that he couldn't find anywhere else.

And besides, he reasoned, twenty-five years was a long enough time that if anyone did find him familiar, he should be able to convince them that they were mistaken. That he wasn't the man they thought he was — that the John Zebedee who was arriving in Deadman's Slough was the twenty-year-old son of the John Zebedee who they remembered, and who had left to go east and marry.

At least, that was what he kept telling himself.

He let himself out of the cabin, and followed the line of other passengers who were disembarking in Skullyville. He made his way down to the lower deck, and watched as the ship drew up to the landing. The town looked as if it had fared only a little better than Fort Coffee — it wasn't a ruin, but there were few buildings standing that were undamaged. Several looked abandoned, and for a moment, John was tempted to just stay on board. To keep going west.

No. If he was going to head west, he needed more planning. Supplies. He needed things he simply didn't have, and that he would have no chance to obtain. He'd consider it, if he didn't find what he was looking for at Deadman's Slough. He resettled the rucksack on his shoulders, and waited for the planks to be laid so that passengers and cargo could go ashore.

WALKING THROUGH THE streets of Skullyville reminded John painfully of walking through the streets of other towns, following in the wake of troops that had gone through like the plagues of Egypt. Windows were boarded up and broken, and the people peering out from behind them were equally as broken. He could feel eyes on him as he walked down the middle of the street, making a show of looking at the buildings on each side as if he didn't know exactly where he was going already. He stopped, turned to look around, then started toward the building that had been his destination the entire time — the mercantile.

A bell chimed merrily as he opened the door, and he stepped into the cool shop and let the door close behind him. He heard a familiar muffled voice from somewhere behind a closed door, calling, "Just a moment!"

The inner door opened, and an older man came out of what John knew was a stockroom. He saw John standing there and stared, his face gone stark white.

"Excuse me," John said, trying to sound hesitant. "I'm looking for Nathaniel Miller. Might you be him?"

"I... I am," Miller stammered. "And I think I should know you. You're very familiar."

"I'm told I look very much like my father," John said. "It was he who told me that if I came this way, I was to look for you. His name—"

"Zebedee?" Miller interrupted. "John Zebedee?"

"Yes, sir. I'm John Zebedee as well, after my father."

"And you're the very image of him," Miller said. He came around the counter and held his hand out. "Good to meet you, son. What brings you here? Last I heard from your father, he was heading to... Baltimore, was it?"

"New York," John corrected. "And I came..." he paused, looking around. "Looking for something new. Someplace to settle. He used to tell me about his claim out on Deadman's Slough. I was hoping it might still be there."

"I haven't been out that way in ten years or more," Miller said slowly. "Not since before those blasted Yanks came through. Might not be anything there but ashes."

John nodded slowly, trying to hide his disappointment. Damn it. He hadn't been sure which side of the war Skullyville would have taken, but he'd hoped... now he needed to make sure no one figured out that he'd been a Union soldier, not a Johnny Reb. "I'll have to see. Which means I might be back in town looking for a place to sleep tomorrow."

Miller chuckled. "If you end up coming back, you come spend the night with me and Mrs. Miller. We can spare a place for the son of John Zebedee. How is he?"

"Gone to his rest, I'm afraid," John said. "Before the war started."

Miller's face crumpled, and he shook his head. "I'm very sorry to hear that. He was a good man," he said slowly. "Now, you're just in off the *Cavalier*?"

"Yes, sir," John answered. "And I'm in need of some supplies, and a horse. Is there a livery, or someone who has a horse to sell?"

Miller frowned slightly, then nodded. "Maybe. Maybe. Judge Hoskins might have something. You need a rig, too?"

"I hadn't hoped to be that lucky," John answered, being completely honest. "I thought I might have to order something from a wainwright."

"You'd have to send to Fort Gibson for something like that. We haven't had a wainwright for years now. But the one out in Fort Gibson is a good one, does good work. The Judge, he might be willing to part with his, though. I'll take you over, introduce you. He came here around the same time your father left. Not sure they ever met, but I'll vouch for you."

"I appreciate that," John said. "Your kindness... I appreciate it more than you can understand."

Miller looked oddly at John for a moment. Then his brows rose. "You got a haunted look to you, son. You fought in the war?"

John nodded. "I did. That's why I'm here." He tapped his temple. "Up here, I'm still fighting. I need to be alone. I need the quiet. I need to stop jumping at shadows."

Miller nodded slowly. Then he frowned. "What side?"

"Excuse me?"

Miller's frown deepened. "What side did you fight for?" he asked. "You fight for the South, or did you fight for the Yanks?"

John nodded slowly. "Mister Miller, I can honestly say that I fought on the side of the angels."

The non-answer seemed to satisfy Miller. He nodded once. "Come on, then. Tuck your case back behind the counter. No one will touch it. I'll introduce you to the Judge. Then we can come back and see what I have in stock."

John followed Miller out of the shop and down the street. He was fairly certain he knew who Judge Hoskins was — he remembered a young lawyer by the name of Hoskins who had come to town not long before he left. Surprising that Hoskins stayed on.

There had never seemed to be much need for a lawyer in Choctaw Agency — there hadn't been much here when he'd left. Maybe in Fort Coffee, but not Choctaw Agency. But then again, John had never spent much time in either place. He'd come in to town — first making the longer ride out to Fort Coffee, then coming to Choctaw Agency — once every other month or so to buy supplies and sell dried fish. Occasionally he would make the long drive west to Fort Gibson. Perhaps there had been more legal goings-on than he'd been aware of.

"Good morning, Mister Miller!"

The voice sounded pleasant enough, but something about it still set John's nerves on edge. He turned, seeing a tall, thin man dressed all in black coming toward them. As he got closer, John saw the clerical collar around the man's throat.

"Reverend Kerry, good morning!" Miller called back. "Reverend, this is John Zebedee. His father used to live in the area, and young John has just arrived."

The Reverend stopped and bowed his head. He arched a brow. "Zebedee. An interesting name. Where is your family from?"

John forced a smile. "I'm just in from New York. But I think you mean originally? A place called Kinneret. It's about a hundred miles north of Jerusalem, on the Sea of Galilee. I don't expect you to have heard of it. No one ever has. And the name was Zavdi, once. There were too many misspellings and mispronunciations."

"Well, then," Reverend Kerry said, apparently satisfied. Which only reaffirmed what side of the War Skullyville had favored. John might have darker skin, but he wasn't a former slave, nor was he a freed one. Therefore, they would be somewhat polite to him. "Welcome to Skullyville, Mister Zebedee."

"Thank you," John answered. He forced himself not to fidget. He'd met many a man of God in his years walking the world. He had never met one before who made him want to run. But this man... there was something about him. John wasn't sure what, and he didn't want to know. "My father used to speak fondly of the Reverend here in town. Reverend Black, I think?"

"My predecessor," Reverend Kerry replied. "He was a dear man, but he died in his sleep a few months ago. I took on his duties a month back, and we've had a time of it. Haven't we, Miller?"

Miller chuckled. "Been a job of work. Reverend Black had only just reopened the school."

Reverend Kerry nodded and looked at John. "Did you know about the school here?"

"The school for Choctaw girls?" John asked. "Yes. And the one in Fort Coffee for boys. My father said they did good work at these schools. I saw the ruins of the Fort as we came down river. What happened there?"

"The Yanks happened," Miller grumbled. "Never mind the school, nor the people who lived there. Blue-jacketed vultures—"

"Now, Mister Miller," Reverend Kerry chided. "Mind your language." He turned and smiled at John. "Thank you. It's good to know that our work is known outside of Skullyville. There was good work done at the schools, yes. And we'll continue to do good work, now that we're reopened. For the girls, at least." Reverend Kerry nodded, then cleared his throat. "Now tell me, Mister Zebedee. What's your business here in Skullyville?"

"Passing through," John answered. "Going to go out and see if the place my father left me is still standing. If it is, then I'll be setting up housekeeping. If it isn't..." He let his voice trail off, then snorted. "Well, I don't know yet what I'll do if the place is gone."

The Reverend nodded. Then he looked up. "We've been having some odd weather recently. Terrible storms. It might be best if you stayed the night in town. The Zebedee place... that's a fair distance out of town, isn't it?."

"It is. You know my father's land?" John asked.

"When I first arrived, I studied the old maps of the area. It's labeled on them." He looked up again. "As I said, we've had frightful weather recently, and those storms start rolling in at midday, or a little after. You won't be anywhere near shelter if you don't set out now."

"Which you won't be doing, seeing as you need supplies," Miller said. "Maybe you should stay in town tonight? You'd be welcome with us. We'll get things ready, and you can head out tomorrow morning early."

"Or you'd be welcome to spend the night at the school," Kerry added. "We've a guest house. It's small, but comfortable."

John looked up at the clear sky. "Thank you. Thank you both. But I'd like to be on my way." He looked around. "Being around too many people... it's unsettling." He gave an uneasy laugh, wondering if either man would see through his pantomime. "I've not had an easy time of it, since the war. I prefer to be away from others."

Miller made soft, consoling noises. "We'll get you squared away, John. Get you set up right. Let's get you over to see the Judge." He smiled at Kerry. "Reverend, you'll come for coffee? Mrs. Miller always appreciates your visits."

"I'll be happy to come and sit a spell," Kerry answered. "Mister Zebedee, will I see you on Sunday?"

"No, sir," John answered. "Thank you, but I'm not of your creed."

Kerry looked startled. "Is that so?" he asked. "And what—?"

Miller started laughing. "Forgot about that!" he said. "Your father was the first Jew I ever knew! The only one I ever knew, I think."

"Ah, I see. Of course," Kerry murmured. "Well, if you feel the need to talk, Mister Zebedee, I'd be happy to listen. And perhaps you might come to see things from a different perspective. After all, you do tend to find the most interesting things when you're not looking for them." He nodded to them, then continued on down the street. John watched him go.

"That was odd," he murmured softly.

"He is a touch strange at times," Miller agreed. "But he preaches a good sermon. And he's good with the children. Come on, now. Let's go see the Judge."

CHAPTER TWO

Lightning

Judge Hoskins was indeed willing to sell his wagon, along with the harness, a saddle and bridle, and a horse that was both harness and saddle trained. He insisted on more than twice what they were worth, pointing out that there wasn't another wagon for sale anywhere in the town, let alone anywhere outside of Fort Gibson. John gave him the pleasure of dickering, reminded of the markets he'd passed through in his travels. They both came away satisfied — John because of the well-built wagon that would hold up well, and the Judge because he clearly thought he'd gotten the better of the deal.

"You know he cheated you?" Miller whispered as they harnessed the horse to the wagon.

"He didn't," John answered, keeping his voice low. "Because I'm well aware that I paid more than I should have. But I have the money to spare, and I need the horse. I wasn't expecting him to offer the wagon, too, or the tack. I need both, so I let him have what he wanted." He looked up and smiled. "It's worth it to me. And it made him happy."

"You're an odd man, Zebedee," Miller said.

John laughed, remembering Nathaniel telling him much the same thing as a young man, so many years before. "My father used to say that people said the same thing about him."

"Honestly, I think I did. Often." Miller laughed. "To be completely honest, I think your entire family tree is odd, Zebedee. It's in your blood!"

John smiled. He had no idea. "This is ready. Want a ride?"

He drove the wagon back to the mercantile, and went inside with Miller, taking a list from his pocket. They went through the store and the storeroom, and John started transporting supplies out to the wagon. A barrel of flour. Another of oats, and a third of rice. Bags of barley, dried beans, and dried fruit. Plenty of salt. Coffee, tea and sugar. A few packets of spices. A crock of honey and another of butter. Seed corn, and other seeds for a garden. A basket of eggs, and did anyone by chance have laying hens to sell? Or perhaps a goat?

"Check the livery when you go past. They might know, and you need feed for the horse. And I'll put the word out that you're looking for livestock," Miller said. "We'll see what we can find for you. Bacon? No... wait. Your father didn't eat bacon. You don't either, I suppose?"

"Not if I have a choice, no."

"Right. We'll leave it alone. I've got some dried beef. Yes? Good. Now, what else?"

Tools and hardware. Pots and pans. A coffee grinder. Cloth, needles and thread. Blankets, both for John and for his horse. Soap. Buckets.

"You wouldn't happen to have towels you'd like to sell?" John asked. "Or bed-sheets? It will take me time to make them, and I'd like to sleep in a bed tonight."

"I'll ask my wife," Miller said. "Anything else?"

"Cord, if you have it?" John suggested. "I'll be making nets."

"Going to fish, like your father did?" Miller asked. "I've got cord. Come back to the storeroom." He led the way, and took out several balls of heavy cord out of a box. "This is the stuff, if I remember correctly. Now, let me see...I wonder..." He looked around, then went to a corner and opened a box. "I thought they might still be here," he declared, and took out a bundle of candles. "You'll want a lamp, and oil, but I seem to remember your father also wanting candles, for whatever it is you do on Fridays instead of church."

John stared at him. "You remember that?"

Miller nodded. "Your father was a good man. Never did spend much time in town, but when he did, I enjoyed his company. I was fond of him, and I valued his friendship, for all that he never really let anyone get close enough that I think he'd call them a friend. And I missed him when he went east. So yes, I remember."

John swallowed, feeling a lump in his throat. He honestly had no idea that Nathaniel had felt so. "My father spoke very fondly of you. He did consider you a friend. The closest he'd had for a long time. I don't think he knew that you felt the same. Thank you."

Miller passed him a bundle of candles, slender ones that John remembered vividly from another life. Nathaniel's father had special ordered them for John, bringing them in monthly so that John would have them for the Sabbath.

"I'm surprised that you still have these," he said, following Miller back out to the counter. He turned the bundle over in his hands. "There can't have been much call for them once... once Father was gone."

"There wasn't," Miller admitted. "That bundle might just have been there since your father's day. I'll start ordering them again."

John smiled. "Thank you. I appreciate that you remembered that you had them. It's been a long time since I last had a chance to light them."

"Since before the War, I warrant? I don't imagine the other soldiers were all that welcoming to a Jew?"

"Not at all," John agreed, but didn't explain further. Explaining would have revealed the lie – Grant had outlawed Jews from serving the Union at first, until he was overruled. But it had made John a bit more circumspect than he usually would have been.

Miller didn't seem to notice. "It's Friday. Are you going to be able to light them tonight?"

"Not tonight, no," John answered. "I doubt I'll be finished unloading before sunset. Next week will be soon enough. God understands."

"He does. Now, when you do, say a word for me and Mrs. Miller? It's always a good thing to have someone thinking of you." The shopkeeper turned around, studying the shelves behind the counter. Then he looked at John. "You've got a rifle?"

"Yes."

"You need powder? Lead?"

John shook his head. "I have a Henry. It uses cartridges."

Miller's brows rose. "A Henry? One of the fancy ones, like I've read about? Load it on Sunday and fire all week?"

John grinned. "Yes, that one."

Miller whistled. "You must have spent a pretty penny on that," he said.

"Actually, I won it in a game of cards," John admitted. "From a Yank who thought I looked too innocent to be cheating."

Miller burst out laughing. "Good for you! What sorts of cartridges?"

".44 caliber. I have some—"

"Probably not nearly enough. I'll see what I can order for you. I'll have to send to Fort Gibson." Miller scrawled a note.

"They're made by New Haven Arms, from Connecticut," John offered. "I'll prepay you for them, if you like."

Miller nodded. "Half down, for the special order," he said as he started to tally the list of supplies.

John walked out to the wagon to tuck the candles in with the rest of the supplies. He looked up at the clear blue sky then shook his head. Storms? He doubted it. He walked back inside. "Mister Miller, what do I owe you?"

"Let me add this up again," Miller said. "I want to be sure I have my sums right." He went over the column of numbers again, then nodded and looked up. "Do you want to take a look?"

"I trust you, Mister Miller," John said. "What do I owe you?"

"Fifty-seven dollars and eighty-six cents."

John blinked. "Mister Miller, are you joking?"

Miller looked up. "I'm sorry?"

"The supplies I loaded into that wagon must be worth at least twice what you just quoted me. At the very least. So I think you missed carrying a number in your addition." John looked out the window at the loaded wagon. "I figure... a hundred and fifty? At least? Not counting the half down for the cartridges?"

"John, I am not going to let the first thing you do in Skullyville be beggar yourself," Miller said. "You paid far too much for the wagon and horse—"

John sighed. "Nathaniel, please. I appreciate your kindness, but you can't give me these supplies at your cost! Your wife wouldn't thank you for taking food off your table."

Miller looked shocked. "You even sound like John. Like your father." He frowned slightly. "It's frightening how much like him you are."

John looked down. Damn it! He should have gone to Fort Gibson for supplies! And he never should have called Nathaniel by his name! He shook his head. "No. I pay my way, Mister Miller. So please, what do I really owe you?"

Miller came out from around the counter. He leaned on it and folded his arms over his chest. "John, your father would know not to argue with me when I've set a price."

"I'm not him," John protested. He looked up. "Mister Miller —"

"Call it one hundred dollars even, then," Miller said, and held out his hand. "And that includes the deposit on the cartridges. Is that enough to satisfy you?"

"No," John grumbled. "But I don't think you'll let me give you more." He took Miller's hand and shook it, then let his hand fall and looked around. "May I step into your storeroom? I've a money-belt—"

"Of course," Miller said. He led John back to the storeroom and opened the door. John stepped inside and closed the door, then took off his coat and waistcoat. He tossed down his braces and opened his shirt, shifting the money-belt that he wore around so that he could unbutton it. He took out a small stack of banknotes, counted out two hundred dollars, and put the rest away. He put his clothes back to rights, and slipped one hundred dollars into the inner pocket of his coat. He looked around, smiled, and tucked the second hundred dollars into a basket of eggs. Then he walked back out into the shop. Miller was standing near the counter, talking to a handsome older woman.

"Ah, here he is," Miller said, looking over at John. "John Zebedee, I'd like to introduce you to my wife, Abigail."

John came toward them, and bowed over Abigail Miller's hand. "Mrs. Miller, it's a pleasure."

"My, he does have lovely manners," she said with a laugh. She had a light, lilting accent that he couldn't place. "Did his father have such lovely manners?"

Miller laughed. "John Zebedee was as proper as the day is long," he declared. "Except for when he wasn't."

John blinked. "Are we talking about the same John Zebedee?" he asked. "My father? When was he ever not proper?"

"Nothing I'd be willing to say in front of a lady," Miller said. Then he winked at John. "But I'll walk you out to the wagon."

Abigail laughed. "Nathaniel, you're likely to frighten him. Now, Nathaniel says you're looking for bedding and towels. I have some that are a mite threadbare, but still serviceable. Will that suit?"

"That will be perfect," John answered. "Until I have time to make my own."

"You sew, as well? My, you're well-rounded," Abigail said with a smile. "Now, John, the next time you're in town, I expect you to stay for supper."

"It would be an honor, Mrs. Miller," John said. "Thank you."

"Goodness," she murmured. "Do you think we can have him give Jeremiah etiquette lessons?" She smiled and turned away, leaving through the door that John knew led to the house behind the shop. She came back with a neatly folded pile of linens, which she laid on the counter. Then she went back into the house.

"Jeremiah?" John asked.

"Our son," Miller answered. "Fourteen and incorrigible. But then, we were all incorrigible at fourteen."

"I certainly was," John agreed. He took the money from his coat pocket. "One hundred dollars. Not a penny less."

Miller took the money and went behind the counter, tucking the money into a cash-box before coming back around, picking up the linens as he passed them. "I'll walk you out to the wagon," he said. "Don't forget your things."

"Will you tell me that story, too?" John asked, retrieving his case and rucksack from behind the counter. He could not, for the undying life of him, remember just what Miller was talking about!

They walked outside, and John put his case and rucksack into the wagon. He took the linens from Miller, tucked them away, and tugged the canvas up to cover them. Then he turned to face Miller.

Miller looked up and down the street before pitching his voice low. "Your father was a good man. A fine man. One of the finest I think I've ever known. He was true to the bone. And... if he had a little too much to drink, he didn't mind the company of a lady..." He paused, then shook his head. "Or a gentleman. Preferably the gentleman. Your father... had more than a small streak of lavender when it suited him."

"Mister Miller," John said, his voice equally low. "Are you saying that you and my father...?" He let his voice trail off, uncertain of how the question would be taken. There had been a certain number of men he'd served with during the war who weren't fussy about their bed partners. Soldiers always seemed to be more pragmatic that way. But Miller wasn't a soldier, and in civilian life, men loving men was a capital offense. John's mind raced. What was the penalty for sodomy in Arkansas? He wasn't sure. It was a capital offense in almost every other state where he'd spent time. It was overlooked in the army, but he wasn't a soldier anymore.

Miller just smiled. "Never so far as that, John. Never so far as that. But there was a trip to Fort Gibson, and a bottle of whiskey, and... well, there might have been a bit of spooning. But then, we were young, and incorrigible, searching for excitement. The pair of us calmed down and grew up." He winked, then laughed again. "You should see your face, son!"

"I'm not sure if I'm more surprised at the story, or at the admission," John said. "I'm not surprised about my father. I knew. He told me. But really, this is not the sort of thing that a man speaks of openly."

"Considering that if you're caught, you face hanging? You'd be right. Better to keep things quiet. But you're a soldier. You understand a man's needs. And, you're John's son. As I said, I was more than a little fond of him," Miller said. He slipped his hands into his pockets. "That was part of why I was so shocked when you walked into the store. You're the image of him. Shocked me to the core."

"I apologize for that—"

"Don't be ridiculous, John," Miller scoffed. "You can't help what you look like." He looked oddly at John. "He actually *told* you?"

"When I came to him with questions," John answered, and let the words hang. Let Miller assume what he would. He probably wouldn't be wrong.

Miller nodded. "I see. Like father, like son, I suppose. I wish he was still alive, so I could send a letter to him. But I lost track of him when he went east. I'd have liked to speak to him one more time. Introduce him to Abigail. She would like him, I think."

"I think he would have liked her. And I can honestly say he remembered you fondly, Nathaniel," John said. He looked up. "Not a cloud in the sky," he added. "Storms? Really?"

"Every day for nearly a month now," Miller answered. "It's been the oddest thing. It's not the season for them, but they've been rolling in every afternoon." He looked up. "John, you're more than welcome here tonight. We've a spare room, and we'll leave you be if you want... and you even have his sour look!" Miller laughed and shook his head. "He'd look at me the same way when I pushed too hard. If I didn't know better, I'd think you were him!" He smiled. "If you were staying, I'd want to hear all about your mother. Any woman who could make that man settle and marry must have been extraordinary."

John nodded. "She was that, Mister Miller. Her name was Mary."

"And it was just you?"

"You mean children?" John shook his head. "No. I had an older brother. Jacob. He's gone now, too."

Miller looked surprised. "So young? Was it in the war?"

John swallowed and looked up. "No," he said. "Jacob had... something of a temper. He died in a fight."

"Oh, that's horrible," Miller murmured. "And here I am, bringing up old wounds. John, I am sorry." He looked up again. "And I'm keeping you. You're determined to ride out?"

"Yes, I am."

"If the old place is gone, then you come back here," Miller said. "I don't care how late it is. You're always welcome. And if by some chance it's still standing... then you come to supper next week."

"No promises," John said. He checked the canvas covering his purchases, then swung into the driver's seat and unwound the reins from the brake. "I will try, though."

Miller nodded. "That's all I can ask. Good luck. Remember, you come back here if anything is amiss."

"I will do that," John said.

Miller turned back to the door, then stopped. "So, where did you hide the rest of the money I wouldn't take from you?"

John laughed aloud. "It's in the eggs," he admitted.

"Thought it might be. Your father would do the same thing if he thought my father was undercharging him. See you at supper in a week."

John clucked to the horse and snapped the reins, still laughing as he drove away. He stopped briefly at the livery stable to buy feed and hay for the horse, straw to stuff his mattress, and to ask about livestock, but it wasn't long before he'd left Skullyville behind him. And before he was alone with his thoughts.

He hadn't gone to Fort Gibson with Nathaniel Miller more than two or three times. He'd owed a debt to Miller's father, who loaned him the money to buy materials to build a barn after his own burned down from a lightning strike. They'd agreed that he could work the loan off in dried fish, in manual labor, and occasionally, in transporting goods. If there had been a bottle of whiskey... that had to have been the last time they went...

"Oh," he breathed. "Oh, yes." It had been years since he'd last thought of that night. He remembered buying the whiskey to celebrate the debt being paid. He remembered them stopping because of a summer storm, taking shelter under the wagon. He'd opened the bottle and they'd passed it back and forth. He remembered lying huddled underneath the wagon, sharing a blanket with Nathaniel. Talking about girls. Then, talking about boys. John was drunk enough to admit that he'd once had a lover, and Nathaniel to admit to being curious.

That tryst had ended with considerably more than just spooning. Afterward, Nathaniel had turned cold toward him. Which didn't make sense with him saying how fond he'd been of John now. Or of bringing that one night up in the first place. Granted, he hadn't said much. Nathaniel must not have wanted to shock him too much. Which completely discounted the shock of him sharing even that much information! John shook his head. "It doesn't make much sense," he told the horse. "But things stopped making sense for me a long time ago." He watched the horse's ears flick back toward him. "You're going to have to get used to me talking to you, you know," he added. "If there's no one around, I talk to my animals. And there's never anyone around." The horse snorted, making John smile. "I'm certain that you'll have a much higher opinion of my conversational skills once you know me better. Now, I never did find out what he named you. Or if he named you. So I'll have to give you a name." He considered the question — the horse was a dark bay with one white sock, and a jagged, narrow stripe that zigzagged from his forehead to the tip of his nose. "Hrm... Barak. I think I'll call you Barak. It means Lightning."

As if on cue, he heard a distant rumble of thunder. Turning in his seat, he studied the clear, blue sky. Then he turned back and considered the horse.

"Maybe I should name you Blaze, instead?" he called. There was another rumble of thunder, and he shook his head. "Fine. Barak it is. Let's see how soon you can get us out of the weather, Barak."

CHAPTER THREE

Embers

The thunder grew louder the further they got from town. John could feel the rumbling in his bones, like enough to the rumble of artillery to set his nerves on edge. The sky above him was still clear, but he could see the clouds building on the horizon, dark and seething with occasional flashes of fire. He snapped the reins, urging Barak on faster. They'd be caught in it, and a storm like this meant twisters. He wanted to be safe under cover if that happened.

Another rumble, this one loud enough that Barak shied and danced, and John had to struggle to keep him under control.

"It's all right," he called. "It's all right. It's just a noise. It's not going to eat you." Ears swiveled back at the sound of his voice, and the horse shivered, the harness jingling wildly. "It's all right. We're almost there." He glanced up, then fished his pocket-watch out and looked at it. The old place was two hours south and east of Skullyville. They still had just over an hour to go. He tucked the watch away and snapped the reins again. "We're almost there," he repeated.

The skies overhead darkened, casting the day into an artificial gloaming punctuated by flares of lightning that arched and crackled above them like Yahweh's own fury. The rain started as they forded the stream, the landmark for the final stretch of trail, and John cursed in Aramaic, tugging the collar of his coat up higher. The rain was cold, heavy fat drops that felt like thrown pebbles when they hit skin. But they were almost there. John could see the standing stones that marked the edge of the land he once called his own. Which meant he needed to stop. He drew back on the reins, and jumped down, going forward and taking hold of Barak's harness, leading the horse forward.

He rested his hand on the rock. As old as he was, he'd learned more than a few things over the years. Some of them occasionally came in useful. This, for example. Magic like this wasn't supposed to exist, and if it did, it wasn't something that any religion known hereabouts would ever have sanctioned. But John reasoned that his very existence wasn't something that any religion hereabouts would sanction, and he could think of several that would remove it from him completely if they could, so he didn't worry overly much about the two bits of magic that he knew. And besides, what he was about to do was something that had been taught to him by an archbishop. He was fairly certain that the person who taught him this hadn't *actually* been an Archbishop. He had been a very holy man, a very old acquaintance, a mage, and the only other immortal being that John had ever come across. The last time John had seen him, it had been in France. John wasn't even sure how many years it had been. Five hundred? More? Was he even still walking the world, the way that John was? He wasn't sure. But one night in France, over many flagons of wine, Turpin had taught John a few things. Not a lot — John hadn't been capable of learning much. He just didn't have the knack for it. But what little he'd learned, he'd learned well.

Like how to set a barrier to keep the curious away. He usually took the barriers down when he left an area. He was never really sure why he'd left this one standing. Perhaps that was why he'd decided on coming back here — he knew it would be safe for him, at least for a little while. He rested his hand on the rock and closed his eyes, trying not to shiver as the rain soaked into his clothes.

"It's me," he whispered. "I've come back. Let me in." He felt a tingle, as the old barrier tested him. Tasted him, it felt like. It recognized him, and parted to let him pass. John walked the horse forward, through the opening, then went back and touched the rock again. "Thank you. Close up."

The barrier closed with unusual alacrity and an almost audible snap, which took John by surprise. That had never happened before, not any time he'd used this particular trick.

Was something out there?

He turned, squinting out into the rain trying to make sense of the gray shapes and shadows that might be rocks and trees. Or might be soldiers in Confederate gray. Nothing moved, but just to be on the safe side, he went to the wagon and reached under the canvas, opening his case and sliding out the Henry. Working by touch, he opened the magazine and loaded a dozen cartridges, then slid the cartridge-follower back into place. He climbed carefully back into the driver's seat and slid the rifle down behind him on the seat. He'd learned the hard way that if he dropped the loaded rifle, the impact would fire the gun. Thankfully, no one had been hurt when he'd learned that lesson, but it was a serious flaw in the design, and one about which he'd written to the New Haven Arms Company. It was the reason that he kept the rifle unloaded most of the time. As for the rest of the time? Well, he tried damned hard not to be in a position where he would need to shoot something. Or someone.

He'd had enough of that for several lifetimes.

He peered into the gloom, then shook his head, scattering water off his hat. He still couldn't see if there was anything moving out there. Best to keep moving. There shouldn't be anyone inside the barrier, anyway, he told himself. The barrier would have warned him otherwise.

At least, it was supposed to warn him, if he was inside of it. He'd never tested it from outside.

He snapped the reins, and the wagon lurched forward.

He knew this not-quite-a-road, knew where to turn, and finally drew the wagon to a stop. The dugout cabin was still there, and he could see the dark bulk of the barn. He'd offload quickly, then see to Barak; he wound the reins around the brake and jumped down, splashing through the mud to the door set into the side of the hill. There was a second barrier on this door, but it was the work of a moment to have it recognize him and unlock. He opened the door and whispered the other spell he'd mastered — the one to call light. A small lamp that hung from the ceiling started to glow, revealing surfaces thick with dust and dirt that had been untouched for a quarter of a century.

John grimaced as he looked at the furry surface of the table. From the looks of things, he'd be spending the first week here just cleaning! He took a sodden handkerchief from his coat pocket, wiped down the table, then went back out into the rain. He lost count of the trips, carrying supplies from the wagon into the house, then making trips from the pump to the house with a bucket, refilling the water barrel. But finally, he was done. He set the bucket down and looked around. The Henry was laying on the worktable, so he picked that up, unloaded it, and set the empty rifle on the pegs over the door, dropping the cartridges into an empty bowl. Then he stood for a moment, hearing the steady dripping of water as it ran off his clothes. What next? Oh, yes. He had to see to Barak and offload the supplies that needed to be in the barn. Then he could come back and light a fire in the stove. Undress. Dry off.

Figure out what he might want to do with the rest of his immortal life.

But first, the horse. He headed back out into the rain, taking hold of Barak's bridle. "Come on. Let's see you dry and fed." He had to raise his voice to be heard over the rain. Barak let him lead him to the barn, only to shy away as John swung the door open.

"What is it?" John asked. "There's nothing here. Nothing inside." He repeated the spell to bring light, and another lantern started to glow inside the barn.

The light reflected off of the wet imprints of someone's bare feet. John stared for a minute, then cursed softly.

"Whoever is in there, I'm not going to hurt you," he called. "So... ah... no hurting me. Do we have a deal?" He heard nothing, so he led Barak in out of the rain. The barn and the hayloft both looked empty. There wasn't even any hay left. That wasn't a surprise — there hadn't been a barrier set on the barn, so every mouse, squirrel and crow in the area had been well supplied with bedding for generations. He'd have to mow the grass in the paddock tomorrow, once it was dry. For now, he took a bale of hay from the livery and spread it around in one of the stalls, adding more to the manger. Then he went back to the wagon and started unfastening buckles, releasing the horse from its harness. He heard no one moving, but he was certain he could feel eyes on him. "If you can be patient, I'll offer a hot meal," he said. "I've only just come home, and it'll take a while to fire the stove."

Still, no answer. John carefully brushed Barak down, and threw the new horse-blanket over him before leading him into a stall. He tried not to look around as he worked, the better to show he wasn't a threat to whoever was in the barn with him. He fetched a bucket of water, filled another with grain, and left both where Barak could reach them. He cleaned and dried the harness, hanging it neatly, then leaned into the wagon to move it out of the way. Then, and only then, did he start to search the barn. The only other living thing he found on the first level was a cat, nursing her kittens in the back of the last stall. He smiled down at her.

"Well, you're welcome to stay as long as you like," he murmured to the young mother. "I don't have any milk at the moment, but I can offer you a steady diet of fish once I get the nets made."

The cat studied him for a moment, then turned back to her babies; John smiled and looked up. Whoever was still watching him must be up in the hayloft.

"I'm coming up," he called. "Remember. Don't hurt me, and I won't hurt you."

He climbed slowly up the ladder, expecting at any minute for someone to attack. But there was no one — the hayloft was empty.

At least, it appeared empty. But John could still feel someone watching him. And he thought he could hear a faint clink of chain.

"Well," he said, coming the rest of the way up the ladder and kneeling on the boards. "You're better at hiding than I am at finding. So I'll leave you be. You can stay as long as you like. I'll leave the light. But no stealing my horse." He climbed slowly back down the ladder and went to check on Barak. The horse was nose-first in the grain, and ignored John completely. John smiled as he reached out to scratch the horse behind the ear.

"You stay put, Barak," he said. "I'll be back."

He left the barn, closing the door behind him, and trudged back through the rain to the house. He hung his sodden coat and hat on pegs to dry, and turned to look around. There had never been much to the dugout — it was a large space divided into two "rooms" by a canvas curtain, and he could walk from one side to the other in about ten steps. The dirt walls had been plastered with a mix of crushed gyprock and water to keep the dirt down, and John had set river stone into the rear wall to reflect heat from the stove. The smaller room held a rope-frame bed, which at the moment was draped with a large canvas bag that would soon be a mattress. Besides the pot-bellied stove, the larger room boasted a large table, and a collection of goods-boxes placed on their sides to form shelves which still held dust-covered pots, pans, and other cooking implements. There was a painstakingly-laid wooden floor, two windows that looked out the front, and a solid door. It was warm in the winter, cool in the summer, and comfortable in ways that had never made any real sense to John. He'd lived in fancier places, and in larger ones — he'd gone from this dugout to a comparatively palatial townhouse in New York. But this place...

It was home. In a way that he had never expected when he'd settled here. He hadn't really had a home in more years than he cared to think about. He took a deep breath, let it out, and turned to the stove to start a fire. Once there was a blaze going in the pot-bellied stove, he filled a pot with water so that he could make something to eat and wash up. He properly washed down the table, then started to unpack his supplies. Casks and baskets went on top of the goods boxes, while bags were hung from the ceiling. By the time everything was cleared away, and ingredients for a pottage were measured, the water was steaming. John filled the water pitcher by the door with warm water, then poured the bowl of ingredients into the rest of the water to cook. Then he dragged one of the bales of straw to the smaller room, and started the messy, dusty process of stuffing the mattress. Better to do it now, before he cleaned the rest of the dugout. Three bales of straw later, the mattress was lumpy, but full, and roughly stitched closed. John wrestled it into place on the ropes, draped threadbare sheets and a blanket over the top, and took a long breath.

Finally, finally, he had time to stop and think. The footprints in the barn. They had to be recent — perhaps only a quarter of an hour old when he'd seen them. If even that much. And he could have sworn he was being watched. But there hadn't been anyone else in the barn... unless the reason they were better at hiding was that they could hide themselves completely, something that he knew was possible, even though he couldn't do it.

John frowned as he went to fetch his case, bringing it to the bedroom side of the curtain. There wasn't much in the case – he'd cut all ties in New York, left behind anything he couldn't sell, so what he had left was here. He opened the case, looking at the few things he'd brought with him. He took out the box of cartridges. Two clean shirts. A second pair of trousers. Clean socks. A nightshirt. A rucksack that contained his medical supplies — some simples, bandages and salve. And at the very bottom, wrapped in oilcloth...

He sat down on the lumpy mattress and considered the rifle-green kepi. It marked him as one of Berdan's Sharpshooters – two regiments of elite marksmen who had served under the command of a brilliant Colonel. In the early years of the war, they had become the stuff of legend. Then came the Battle of Cold Harbor. The disaster at Cold Harbor — John had been wounded and taken prisoner. He'd been charged as an enemy combatant, and sent to Camp Sumter. Sent to Hell was more like it. The only reason he'd survived was that when he died, he wouldn't stay dead, and there had been many miserable nights when he roundly cursed the man who had unknowingly cursed him. Cursed him, only to beg forgiveness with the dawn — *Joshua, I'm sorry. I didn't mean it. Any of it. Please come back. Don't leave me here alone.*

The hat was the only piece of his uniform he'd managed to save, stubbornly hiding it, stealing it back from thieves, and once, killing a man for it. It had made him both a target to the Confederate jailers, and a touchstone to the other Union prisoners. He'd been their hope — one of their own, one of the best of them. And he'd survived, and he kept on surviving. He'd sat by so many of them as they'd died. Too many to remember all their names. There was a list, he knew. The lonely graves were marked, finally, and the dead were being remembered. But he'd never gone back to see.

He couldn't go back.

He swallowed and put the hat back into his case. He slid the case under the bed, then got up and went to check on the pottage. He stirred it, tasted it, added a touch more salt. Then he wrapped the pot handle in a rag and carried it to the table. He scooped some of the thick stew into a bowl, then stopped and looked at the door.

How many nights in Camp Sumter would he have killed someone for a meal like this? For a meal, or for a blanket? Was that why he'd promised the phantom in the barn a hot meal?

He swallowed again, and reached over to pick up a spoon. He dropped it into the bowl, and went to fetch the second blanket and his coat and hat. He managed to make it to the barn without getting too much rain in the bowl, and without the blanket getting too wet. He set both down on the back of the wagon.

"A hot meal, as I promised. And a blanket," he called. He turned, and nearly fell backwards in shock.

The man was a few inches shorter than he was, skeletally thin, and pale enough to be a ghost. For a moment, John thought he might actually be seeing the ghost of one of the poor souls from Camp Sumter, one who'd been drawn here by John's memories. But no, this man was real, real and barely standing on his feet in front of John. He'd clearly been someone's prisoner — there were fading bruises on his face and neck, and the jingling sound that John was hearing came from the chain that connected the manacles on his wrists. He looked exhausted, sick and terrified, his brilliant green eyes wide and frightened. There was something strange about his eyes....

John held his hands out to the sides. "I won't hurt you," he said softly. "Let me help." He took a step forward, and the man flinched away, raising his chained wrists to defend himself as he turned. The flinch became a fall, and he collapsed into a motionless heap at John's feet.

CHAPTER FOUR
Sunbeams

John stared for a moment. Then he lunged forward, dropping to his knees next to the man. He was still breathing, and the pulse at his throat hammered against John's fingertips like the heartbeat of a bird. John examined him quickly, hissing at the raw skin beneath the manacles. How long had this man been a prisoner? And... a prisoner of who? Someone had beaten him and starved him, and they had to be somewhere close. There was no way this man could have gone far on foot, not in this condition.

John looked further, brushing back long, filthy hair to check for head wounds. He didn't see any blood, but...

Pointed ears?

The something strange about his eyes finally became clear — they'd been slitted like a cat's eyes. Pointed ears, and cat's eyes... something teased at the edges of John's mind. A story, perhaps? A song? He wasn't sure. It didn't matter. What mattered was that he had to do something now. He had an injured man to care for. Perhaps sick as well. He got up, grabbed the blanket off the wagon, and bundled the man up in it. He left the bowl — the cat would appreciate the meal, and it might convince her to stay. He headed back out into the rain, carrying his patient back to the dugout. He kicked the door closed behind him, and laid his burden down on the floor near the stove before stripping off his sodden coat and hat. But the floor was no place for a sick man. He needed to put him to bed. He scooped the unconscious man back up, marveling for a moment at how little he weighed. He shoved the thought to the side and carried him past the curtain to the bed, calling the light spell out to the lamp that hung from the ceiling so that it started to glow. The new-stuffed mattress hadn't settled yet — John had been planning to jump on it to break up the fresh straw. But there wasn't time for that. He laid his guest down, covering him with the dry blanket. Then he frowned. Now what?

The chains needed to come off. And then he needed to get some food into this starving bastard. He turned away, heading back to the other side of the curtain, hunting for the toolbox he could have sworn he'd left here. All the while his mind was racing — what had they fed to the survivors at Camp Sumter? Some of those poor souls hadn't been strong enough to even eat, and had died while the nurses had spooned gruel into their mouths. He didn't think this fellow was that far gone, but what could he feed him? The stew was too heavy for a starving man.

He found the tool chest in a corner, and hauled it up onto the table, looking through it. What did he have? And what did he have, among his supplies? Rice? That was easy. Light. He could make rice. And what else?

Unbidden, he suddenly remembered a bit of lore. Saint John of the Cross, kidnapped and starved. He'd been nursed back to health by nuns, who'd fed him warm pears and cinnamon. John looked around, then grabbed another pot. Water. Rice. Dried pears cut small. Cinnamon. Honey. He set the mixture to boil, and went back to the tools. Hammer. Chisel. And for a hard surface, a box.

When he went back through the curtain, his guest was awake, struggling to sit up.

"No," John said. "It's all right. You're safe." There was terror in those green eyes, as plain as day. And he hadn't been wrong — they weren't human eyes. But it didn't matter. John put the box down and held his hands up. "It's all right," he repeated. He held his hand out. "Let me help." He stepped forward, then realized something. "Do you understand me?"

The young man frowned. When he spoke, his voice was weak and raspy, and he spoke in a language that John didn't recognize. It was something liquid and musical, and completely strange.

"I don't understand," John said. He repeated himself in Spanish. In French. In German. In Hebrew, in Latin, in broken Choctaw, and finally, in Aramaic. Each was met by a headshake. Finally, John huffed.

"Well, we'll start from the beginning," he said. He tapped himself on the chest. "John. I'm John." He held his hand out to the man in his bed.

The man frowned slightly. Then he raised one hand, the chain jingling as he pointed at John. "John," he repeated. He pointed to himself. "Ethriel."

John smiled. His guest had a name. An odd name, but a name. "Ethriel. Well, it's very nice to meet you." He stepped closer, and reached out to tap one of the manacles. Then he stooped and picked up the hammer, showing it to Ethriel.

Ethriel looked puzzled. Then he touched the manacle, and made a gesture like he was throwing it away.

John smiled and nodded. "Yes." He repeated the gesture. "Off with them."

Ethriel nodded. He held his hand out, biting his lip. John laid the hammer aside, helped him to sit up, then examined the manacle. It was like nothing he'd ever seen before — some kind of light metal, and the keyhole was triangular. But the important part was that the hinge was on the opposite side from the chain — knocking the chain free should open the manacle. He nodded, then looked at Ethriel.

"Right. Ready?" John picked up the box and set it on the bed, then took out the chisel. He turned the box over, and Ethriel slowly laid his wrist down on the box. John nodded and set the chisel in place at the spot where the lock and chain met the manacle. He glanced up to see that Ethriel had his eyes squeezed closed. Too bad John couldn't do the same. He took a deep breath, and struck.

The light metal was incredibly strong, but the steel chisel was stronger — the chain sheared away after the third blow. John laid the tools aside and took Ethriel's hand, easing the manacle open and grimacing at the raw and bleeding skin underneath. He looked up to see tears on Ethriel's face.

"Ethriel?" he breathed. "Did I hurt you?" He reached out and brushed the tears off Ethriel's cheek with his thumb. "I'm sorry."

To his shock, Ethriel reached up and grabbed his hand. He turned and pressed a kiss into John's palm, the heat of his lips burning John's skin like a brand. Then he offered his other wrist.

Breaking the second manacle took five blows, and the chisel shattered along with the lock. John took the broken manacles, the hammer, and the pieces of the chisel and dropped them into the box. Then he went and fetched his rucksack. He laid that on the bed, and opened the curtain, leaving it drawn so that Ethriel could see him. He stirred the rice in the pot, added more water, then filled a bowl with warm water and picked up a clean towel. He came back to the bed, got the towel wet, then held out his hand. Ethriel immediately put his hand into John's, only to wince and pull away when John started to bathe the wounds.

"I know it hurts," John said gently. "But I have to clean the wounds or they will putrefy." He held his hand out again. Ethriel scowled. Then he held out his own hand, reaching for the towel. John handed it to him, and held the bowl while Ethriel washed his own wrists. He examined them when Ethriel was done, then reached into his rucksack for the pot of salve and the rolls of bandages. He handed the pot to Ethriel, who opened it, sniffed it, then raised one eyebrow.

"It will help the wounds heal," John said. He took the pot, scooped some of the salve out, and took Ethriel's left hand. He smeared the salve over the tortured skin, then picked up a roll of bandages. By the time he was finished, Ethriel was looking pale.

"Food next," John said. He put the salve and the extra bandages away, and carried the bowl back to the table. The rice-and-pear mixture was bubbling nicely when he checked it, and it tasted good, so he took the pot off the stove and scooped some of the rice porridge into a bowl. He carried that back to the bed with a spoon, sitting down facing Ethriel. He filled the spoon, blew on it, and offered it to Ethriel. Ethriel made a face, said something in that liquid language, and reached for the spoon. His hand was shaking hard enough that John drew the spoon away.

"I want this in you," he said. "Not all down your front. Open." Dimly, he remembered saying those same words to a child, but in Aramaic. Was it Sarai? If it was Aramaic, then it had to have been Sarai. Which made it a very, very long time ago. He offered the spoon again, and Ethriel rolled his eyes. Then he opened his mouth. He smiled at the taste of the porridge, and let John feed him the rest. They went slowly — John didn't want to have to clean up used rice porridge if Ethriel gorged and purged. So by the time they were done, the porridge had cooled completely, and Ethriel was nodding.

"You need to sleep," John said gently. He set the bowl into the box, then helped Ethriel lay down, pulling the blankets up. He pointed to himself, then the other side of the curtain. "I will be right there."

Ethriel frowned slightly, then turned his head and looked at the wide mattress. He gestured toward the other side, and John felt his pulse quicken. Oh, he couldn't mean... could he? No, no... even if he did, he was in no condition. He shook his head.

"No," he said, and reached out to pull the blanket up further. "Go to sleep, Ethriel." He murmured the spell to cancel the light, and the lamp dimmed. Ethriel sighed, but didn't protest, and John stepped out, carrying the box. He left the curtain partially open as he sat down to eat his now-cold supper. Then he covered over the rest of the rice porridge and the last of the pottage, washed the bowls and spoons, and put away his tools. When he was done, he glanced at the curtain.

Ethriel was sound asleep, his breathing soft and even.

"Good," John murmured. "Who are you, I wonder? And where did you come from?"

There would be no answers there. Not for a while. Not until he could teach Ethriel some English, or found a language they had in common. He'd worry about it later. For now, he fetched the still-slightly damp blanket, then turned to the stove, banking the fire for the night. He stripped, and hung his still-sodden clothes by the stove to dry. He wrapped himself up in the blanket and lay down on the floor. At some point, he'd sleep in his own bed, but not yet. For now, the floor was bed enough. The blanket was warm, and he'd slept in worse places.

He fell asleep listening to the hiss of the rain, the distant rumble of thunder, and the soft, even breathing from the other side of the curtain.

JOHN WOKE UP WITH THE sun in his eyes — he'd forgotten to close the interior shutters, and the outer ones must have either been open or had fallen off. It didn't matter. He was awake. He sat up and rolled his shoulders, hearing his muscles crackle and pop. The sun was out. That meant that he needed to get to work. He had hay to mow, and cleaning to do, both inside and out. He had a sick man to care for. And laying about did none of that. But he had to do one thing first. He got to his feet, leaving the blanket where it fell, and walked outside. The air was cool against his naked skin, and he walked out into the sun and stretched, throwing his head back and letting the sun warm his face.

"I miss you, Joshua," he murmured in the language of his birth, as he had every morning for so many years. "Now and forever. So if you could maybe hurry up a little?" No answer, except for the whisper of the wind. Or maybe that was the answer. He sighed, imagining he could still remember the sound of laughter. He'd had the most wonderful laugh. John remembered that much. But he couldn't remember exactly what it sounded like. It had been too long.

Maybe now, that sound was the whisper of the wind.

He chuckled. "If that's the case," he said to the air. "I wonder what you're laughing at?"

He turned and headed back into the house. He dressed in yesterday's clothes, ate the last of the pottage that he'd made for himself. He raked the coals in the stove, cleaning out the ashes and laying a fresh fire that he left waiting. Then he looked across through the open curtain, and saw that Ethriel was awake. How long had he been awake, watching?

John smiled and walked over to the bed. "How are you feeling?" he asked.

Ethriel smiled and sat up. Then he winced and shook his head. John nodded.

"I'll fetch something for you to eat," he said, and turned away. He heard movement, and turned back, seeing Ethriel trying to get out from under the blanket. "No," he said. "You stay in bed." He held his hand up, and Ethriel flinched. John immediately dropped his hands. "No," he said softly. "I'm not going to hurt you. I'm not going to hit you." He stepped closer, and pulled the blanket back up. Then he rested his hand on Ethriel's chest and gently pushed him down. "Stay here."

Ethriel frowned. "Stay... here," he repeated. He pointed at the bed.

"Bed," John supplied the word.

"Stay... bed?" Ethriel asked. Then he smiled. "Stay bed." He laced his fingers together and rested them on his chest.

"Yes," John said with a laugh. "You stay in bed."

Ethriel nodded. "Stay bed," he repeated. Then he looked thoughtful. "John... stay bed?" He smiled, his brows raised in a hopeful expression, and John was suddenly sure in his bones that there was more to that smile than just being friendly. That he'd known exactly what he'd meant when he'd tried to invite John to the bed the night before.

John felt warm. His throat felt tight. So did his trousers. It was tempting. So tempting. But Ethriel wasn't hale. And John might not be understanding him properly. This could end badly.

But it was still tempting.

"You're quick," he answered. "No." He shook his head. "I have things to do. You stay in bed." He fetched the pot of rice porridge, portioned it out, then brought it back. "It's cold, so you can eat it straight away. Slowly."

Ethriel sat up again, taking the bowl from John. He took a cautious bite, then another, and John nodded.

"When you are done, sleep," he said. Then he closed his eyes and made a snoring sound, and Ethriel nearly spit out his porridge laughing. He had a good laugh.

No, he had a *wonderful* laugh.

John swallowed again, pushing lust back into a mental lock-box and slamming the lid. Then he smiled, patted Ethriel's leg through the blanket, and headed out of the dugout.

THE BARN DOORS CREAKED as he swung them open, and John laughed as Barak whinnied at him, clearly wanting his breakfast. He went past the horse to the wall and took down a rope, which he fastened to Barak's halter so he could lead the horse outside. He tied the other end of the rope to the paddock fence, and Barak immediately started to graze. John went back to the barn, where the tools that he'd left here still hung on their pegs. He took down the scythe, a pitchfork, and the whetstone, and carried them all out of the barn. In the bright sunlight, he examined the scythe blade — he'd oiled it after he'd last used it, so there was only a touch of rust. It just needed to be cleaned a bit, and the edge honed.

There was a rhythm to using a scythe, one that John found similar to using a great sword. Once you got the movement going, and the momentum, it was relatively easy to keep going. It took John only a few minutes to work from one side of the small paddock to the other, mowing down grass that came to his hips. He stopped at the far side of the paddock, already sweating, and leaned the scythe against the fence so that he could go and fluff and spread the new-mown hay to dry. Then he sharpened the scythe again, and went back for another turn.

He did half of the paddock, then looked up. If those storms were going to come through again today, he needed to leave the rest of the paddock alone — he needed to get the hay he'd mown into the barn, or it would get soaked through and ruined. He left the scythe and the pitchfork where they were, and weighed his options. There was a wheelbarrow, or he could hitch Barak to the wagon so he could move all the hay at once. That would be more work, but it would be faster than using a wheelbarrow. "All right, Barak," he called as he headed for the picket line. "You're going to earn your keep."

Even with the time it took to harness Barak, hitch him to the wagon, and load all the hay, it was still under an hour before he drove the wagon back into the barn. He removed the harness and took Barak back out to the paddock, stopping to scrub out the water trough and fill it before leaving the horse to graze again. He brought the pitchfork and the scythe back to the barn and sighed. Now, he had to get the hay up into the loft. He got into the bed of the wagon, and looked up. considering using the pitchfork to throw the hay up into the loft. Then he laughed.

"That didn't work the last time you tried it, Yohanan," he said aloud. "You're not tall enough for that to work." He laughed again, and started making bundles. He could manage three bundles at a time on his back going up the ladder, but it still took him ages before he made the last trip. Then he had to fetch the pitchfork and spread and fluff the sweet-smelling hay to dry. Finally, finally, he was done, and wiped his sweaty face off on his sleeve. He looked at the mounds and nodded.

"A good day of work," he murmured. "And one that's not done yet." He climbed down, once more, and cleaned out Barak's stall, using the last of his purchased straw to replace the soiled bedding. The new hay would be ready to use tomorrow morning, he hoped, and if it didn't rain, he could leave Barak in the paddock until sunset.

John walked out of the barn, leaving the door open. What next? He was already dirty, so cleaning the house out, he decided. He'd need to light the fire in the stove so he could heat up water, open both windows—

He stopped, staring. Ethriel was standing in the doorway, holding onto the doorframe with both hands and looking around with wide, wonder-filled eyes. He smiled when he saw John, and his smile lit the world like a bonfire.

"John," he called. He stepped out of the doorway, stumbled, then grabbed the doorframe again. He laughed, steadying himself.

"What are you doing out of bed?" John asked. He hurried over and gently put one arm around Ethriel. He intended to help Ethriel back to bed. Or to the midden, which was probably the reason Ethriel was out of bed in the first place.

Ethriel had other ideas. As soon as John's arm was around him, he turned, putting his arms around John's neck and pressing his body against John's. He met John's eyes, smiled slightly, then kissed him lightly on the lips. He drew back, biting his lower lip.

John shivered. There was no doubt now what Ethriel wanted. Proof positive was jabbing him in the hip, and his answer, damn it all, was tenting his own trousers. He *shouldn't*. He knew he shouldn't.

"John?" Ethriel asked slowly. "John, Ethriel, bed?"

John thought he heard a whimper. Maybe it was his own voice. He wasn't sure.

He didn't care. He stooped, scooping Ethriel up in his arms, hearing that wonderful laugh.

"Yes," he said. "John and Ethriel are going to bed. Right now."

CHAPTER FIVE
Reflections

John woke up with straw poking him in the back and a warm weight on his chest. Ethriel was still asleep, and John ran his fingers through long, auburn hair that felt like tangled silk, wondering what had just happened.

Ethriel had clearly been no stranger to bed-play. No stranger to men. He'd known exactly what he was doing, and took a great deal of pleasure in doing it to John. John was fairly certain that Ethriel knew more than he did. He wasn't sure how that was possible. Ethriel couldn't be old enough! Unless...

He closed his eyes, trying to remember. Pointed ears. Eyes like a cat. He knew he'd heard something...

"Beautiful, she was. You think you know what beauty is, and then you meet one of them. One of the Fair Folk. You'd never mistake her for a proper lass, a human lass. Her ears, they came to points, you ken? And she had eyes like emeralds. Cat's eye emeralds. You know what a cat's eye looks like? Like that. I have never seen such eyes, before or since."

Thomas Learmont.

He opened his eyes and stared down at the top of Ethriel's head. He hadn't thought of Thomas Learmont in two hundred years or more. They'd spent a span of drunken nights together, one winter in Scotland, and Thomas had told John about the woman he'd loved and lost. The Queen of Elvenlands, who'd stolen him away as her lover for seven years, and brought him back with the gift of prophecy and a life-long pining for her. John wouldn't have believed him, but he'd proved himself to indeed have a gift for seeing the unseen. Proved it by looking John in the eye and calling him Yohanan ben Zavdi. And telling him things that no one who hadn't been in the garden that night would ever have known. Not even Maryam had known about his failure.

He pulled himself back to the here and now, trying to remember anything True Thomas had told him about the Fair Folk, but what he'd thought were the ramblings of a drunken man were sadly lacking in details. Pointed ears, cat's eyes, and beautiful as the day is long. All of which fit Ethriel.

And, according to Thomas, they were immortal. It was possible that the very young-seeming man sleeping on John's chest was older than he was. The idea made him giddy — someone he wouldn't have to watch die? Someone who he wouldn't have to leave behind in twenty years, before they realized that they were growing older and he was not?

Someone it might be safe to care about?

He closed his eyes, running his hand down the length of Ethriel's back. What was an elf doing hiding in his barn? And who had been holding him captive?

And were they looking for him?

The train of thought derailed when Ethriel sighed and shifted, raising his head and smiling at John, then moving up John's body and kissing him. John wrapped one arm around Ethriel, slid the other hand up to catch his fingers in long hair.

When Ethriel drew back, he cocked his head to the side, then reached up and stroked one finger along John's jaw before tapping John on the chin. He waited, frowned, then tugged on one of the hairs of John's short, dark beard. John yelped.

"Stop that!" he said with a laugh. He tapped his jaw. "Beard. It's a beard."

"Beard," Ethriel repeated. He frowned, then raked his nails over John's ribs. John yelped again, grabbing Ethriel's arm, trying to avoid the bandages. Ethriel laughed. Then he tugged his hand free and gestured to John.

"You want to know... what?" John frowned, then saw Ethriel wiggling his fingers, getting closer to John's exposed ribs. "Oh!

Tickle!" he gasped, laughing. Then he tickled Ethriel, who giggled in delight.

"John beard tickle!" he declared. He reached out and stroked John's jaw, smiling. He said something in his own language, then rested his head on John's chest again. John closed his eyes, basking in the warmth.

"We should get up," he murmured. "The house needs to be cleaned, and so do we. We both need a bath."

Ethriel raised his head, looking puzzled. He shook his head, and John laughed. He slid out from underneath Ethriel, getting out of bed to hunt for his drawers, pulling them on once he found them. If it was going to rain, they should bathe first. He went to the other side of the curtain and collected soap and towels, then went back through the curtain. Ethriel was sitting on the bed; he had mirrored John, putting his trousers back on. With him sitting up, John could see that the bruises on his face and neck had already faded dramatically.

"You're looking much better this morning. Come on," he said to Ethriel. Ethriel stood up, swaying a little, then took John's hand. John smiled and led him into the other room. Just before the door, he stopped.

The Henry hung over the door. And he had no answer to the question he'd asked — was whoever had kept Ethriel prisoner looking for him?

He put down the towels and soap, took the cartridges from the bowl where he'd left them, and reached up to take down the rifle. Better to be safe.

NOT FAR FROM THE HOUSE, there was a gentle slope that led down to a gravel beach and a natural spring. The springs were the reason John had made his home here — the water was plentiful, even in the heat of the summer, and he'd been able to dig the well pumps without having to dig too deeply. This spring gradually grew deeper the further from the bank you went, and it was a pleasant place to swim. And to bathe. He stopped at the top of the slope and looked at Ethriel. Ethriel looked at the water, then at him. He pointed.

"Yes, we're going in," John said. He laid the Henry down on a rock, set the towels down with it. He held onto the soap, and started toward the water's edge. Ethriel tugged on his hand. When John turned toward him, Ethriel dropped his hand and unfastened the waist of his trousers, letting them fall.

"Oh, I see," John murmured. He handed the soap to Ethriel and stripped off his drawers, tossing them onto the gravel near the rock. He turned back to Ethriel and laughed — Ethriel was sniffing the soap. Before John could stop him, he licked it. Then he dropped it, shuddering all over before giving John a wounded look.

John laughed, picking the soap up. "It's for washing, not for eating," he said. He held it up. "Soap."

Ethriel scowled. "Soap," he repeated, and made a face.

John held his hand out, and led Ethriel down to the water. He waded into the water up to his knees, got the soap wet, and scrubbed it between his hands until there was lather. "Soap," he repeated, and scrubbed the froth over his arms. He looked up to see understanding on Ethriel's face.

"Soap!" he declared, and laughed. He splashed out to join John, taking the soap from him. They traded it back and forth, until the both of them were covered in lather. Ethriel pointed to the far side of the spring.

"It gets deeper," John said. He held his hand over his head. "So deep."

Ethriel's brows rose, and he walked further out. When the water was up to his hips, he dove in, surfacing about halfway to the rocks on the far side of the spring. He swam to the rocks, then climbed out to perch on the rocks. John watched him as he scrubbed himself all over with the soap.

"Come back," he called, waving at Ethriel. Ethriel made a face and beckoned to John to join him on the rocks. Well, John reasoned, he needed to rinse off. He put the soap onto the rocks and waded out until he was deep enough to dive in. He cut through the water easily, surfacing and shaking his head to clear water from his eyes. When he looked up at the rocks, Ethriel was nowhere to be seen.

"Ethriel?" he called, turning. "Where did you go?"

He heard the giggle, and twisted in the water, only to find himself with an armful of wet, slippery elf. Ethriel kissed him, laughing against John's lips. John chuckled, holding Ethriel close with one hand while running his other hand down the elf's side. The cool water was doing nothing to dampen the heat between them...

And a mental alarm bell started clamoring. John jerked back, hard enough that he went under. He resurfaced sputtering.

"The barrier," he gasped. "Someone's come through the barrier." He looked at Ethriel, saw the alarm on the elf's face. He pointed to the shore and started swimming, hearing Ethriel splashing behind him. He scrambled up the bank, grabbing his drawers and pulling them on without stopping to dry off. Then he grabbed the gun. Ethriel joined him, panting. He picked up his trousers.

"John?"

John looked at him, then closed his eyes. How to tell him to go back to the dugout? "Ethriel. Bed." He pointed toward the dugout. "Bed. Stay bed."

Ethriel nodded. Then, he vanished, and John felt a phantom touch on his cheek. The gravel shifted, and he knew was alone.

"That would be a useful thing to know how to do," he muttered. He picked up the towels, slung them over his shoulder, and followed Ethriel, his rifle ready. All at once, he was back in battle, stalking through the trees, looking for movement. If they were coming in on horse, they'd be visible fairly soon. How had someone gotten through the barrier?

He saw movement and raised the rifle. Only to lower it a moment later.

"Hopaii?" he called. Then he laughed. "That explains everything. What are you doing here?"

"Thought I smelled you," the rider called. He dismounted slowly, leading his horse toward John. "The wind changed, and I smelled the Hattak Falaya. Came to see for myself."

John grinned. He'd started trading with the Choctaw not long after he'd first come here, and his first meeting with the tribal chief had ended with him being named Hattak Falaya — the Long Man. The person who had done it was Hopaii — the father of the man who now stood in front of him. John still wasn't sure if Hopaii was a name or a title, and he wasn't sure how to ask. But from the first, both of the men called Hopaii had recognized him as immortal, and had been able to walk through his barriers with barely any hesitation. He should have remembered it.

"I forgot you could walk right through my guard," John said. "I thought I was under attack."

"Just me. Come to see an old friend," Hopaii answered with a laugh. "Been a long time since I was a threat to anyone. How long you planning on staying this time, John?"

"Until they start looking at me funny again, I suppose," John answered. He looked over his shoulder. Maybe he'd get some answers from Hopaii. "Come up to the house. There's someone I want you to meet."

"You take a wife?" Hopaii asked, falling in next to John.

John chuckled. "No. But since I got back, odd things have been happening. And... well, that's who I want you to meet." He held up his hand for Hopaii to wait, then went to the door. "Ethriel? It's me. It's John." He looked around the door, and saw Ethriel. He'd put his trousers on, and had his back to the wall next to the window, where he could see out. He had John's big cooking knife in one hand. John stepped the rest of the way in and nodded. "Good. Very good. It's all right. He's a friend." He pointed at the window. "You were watching?"

Ethriel looked at the window, then back at John. "Stay?"

"It's safe," John said. He held his hand out. "May I have the knife?"

Ethriel straightened. He flipped the knife neatly, then handed it to John hilt first, the blade resting along his other forearm.

John blinked in surprise and took the knife, bowing his head in an almost reflexive gesture. It took him a moment to remember why — the last time someone had handed him a blade in such a manner, he'd been in Venice, and learning to fence. It was apparently still the proper response. Ethriel bowed in reply, then sagged against the wall.

"Well, you can handle yourself with a blade," John said as he set the knife down on the table. "I'll have to teach you to shoot." He laid the Henry down next to the knife, then held his hand out. "Come with me."

Ethriel took his hand, then pulled John into a tight embrace. He was shaking, and John wrapped his arms around the smaller man, gently rubbing his back.

"It's all right," he murmured. "It's safe. You're safe."

Ethriel moaned softly, then jerked back, pulling out of John's arms, hissing something in his own language. John turned, and saw Hopaii in the door.

The Choctaw looked startled. "Well, never thought I'd meet another one of your kind," he said. He held his hand up and said something, pronouncing the words haltingly. It was clearly the same language that Ethriel spoke. Ethriel stared in shock, his eyes wide.

"You know his tongue?" John demanded. "And his people?"

"I know some of his kind. And I know just that one phrase," Hopaii answered. "So he's what the fuss is about? I'd wondered what was going on over here."

"What fuss?" John demanded. He looked at Ethriel, then pointed to Hopaii. "Hopaii," he said. "He's a friend."

"Hopaii," Ethriel repeated. "Friend?" Hopaii said a word in Ethriel's tongue, and Ethriel laughed out loud. "Friend!"

"I assume that's what that word means?" John asked. "Does what you just said mean I'm a friend?"

"Close enough," Hopaii answered. "I put my horse in your paddock. This story needs sitting down. It's some telling."

"Let me put some clothes on, first," John said. He pulled a chair out and offered it to Hopaii. Then he gestured to Ethriel and led the elf to the other side of the curtain. He tugged it closed, turned, and found Ethriel standing there. Waiting, expectantly. John was pretty sure he knew for what — he pulled the elf close and kissed him. Then he held him tightly, feeling arms closing around him.

"Ethriel," he whispered into still damp hair. He drew back slightly, looked into those emerald cat's eyes. Ethriel smiled, then reached up and kissed John on the tip of the nose. John laughed and stepped back. He handed a towel to Ethriel and started looking for clothes.

They came back out from behind the curtain to find that Hopaii had poured water into cups. He held one up.

"Nothing stronger?" he asked.

"I stopped drinking after the war," John answered. "I didn't like the man I was when I was in a bottle. I could make coffee, if you want?"

"Water is good. This would be easier if you had something stronger, but water is good," Hopaii waited until John and Ethriel were both sitting down. "You got here yesterday, in the storm. I know."

John nodded. "I found Ethriel in the storm, too."

"The storms... there are Ishkitini around. Hunting for something." He gestured toward Ethriel. "Him, I'm thinking."

John frowned. "Ishkitini," he murmured, trying to remember. "That's... witches? You mean witches?"

"Something like that," Hopaii agreed. "It's close enough. But if you hear a great horned owl at night during one of those storms, you shoot the thing. Because that isn't an owl."

"Why?" John murmured, looking at Ethriel. "He'd escaped from something when I'd found him. He was chained. Had been chained for a while, it looked like." He took Ethriel's hand, unwrapped the bandages, then held it toward Hopaii so that the man could see the healing skin.

Hopaii winced. "What are you doing to take care of that?"

"The salve you taught me to make," John answered. "It's healing very fast — this is much better than it was last night. And the bruises are almost all gone."

"They heal fast, their folk," Hopaii said. "Those bandages are wet."

John shrugged, taking Ethriel's other hand and unwrapping bandages. "We were bathing in the spring. You came through the barrier and scared the life out of me."

Hopaii burst into laughter. "There's power!" he crowed. "To scare the life out of the Hattak Falaya! I wish I had that power.

I'd scare off all the Ishkitini. These storms are scaring off the game, ruining crops. It'll be a hard winter if this doesn't stop soon."

John nodded slowly. "You said you've met someone else of Ethriel's people. Who?"

Hopaii shook his head. "Promised I wouldn't say. They're here in hiding. They're older than him. Apparently, there's some magic that can make them look like us. The other ones can do that."

John looked at Ethriel. "That would be useful to know," he said slowly. "I can't very well take him to town. And I can't leave him here alone, not if someone is hunting him." He kept Ethriel's hand in his, lacing their fingers together as Ethriel shifted his chair closer. John smiled at him, then turned back to Hopaii. "What do you know? About him?"

"About him? Nothing," Hopaii answered. "And about who is hunting him? Almost nothing. My main source isn't always in town, my other source doesn't know as much, and I don't go there much anyway, unless it's to visit my daughter—"

"Daughter?" John repeated. "How did that happen?"

"The usual way, John," Hopaii answered. "As old as you are, you don't know how it's done?"

"Don't make me be rude to you, Hopaii," John said, mock-scowling. "I know how it's done. I've been married. And, before you ask, to women. There's never been a child. Not for me."

Hopaii's brows rose. "I didn't know. I'm sorry."

"I've raised other men's children," John said slowly. "It's... it's enough." Enough to shatter his heart, to make him glad that there would never be a child of his own. It was hard enough to see other men's children grow.

Watch them grow old.

Watch them die.

The first had been Joshua's daughter, Sarai.

He shook his head, and realized that Hopaii had reached across the space between them to rest his hand on John's knee. "I am sorry, my friend. I didn't know."

John nodded. "Thank you." He took a deep breath. "All right. I'm tired of being maudlin. Tell me what I need to know to keep Ethriel safe."

"Stay inside when the storms come," Hopaii answered. "Keep your barriers tight. They let me through because they know me. Tell them not to do that again. Stay out of town. I'll go visiting in the next few days. See if my friend is there. See what I can learn. You keep your head down until I come back."

"And if I hear a great horned owl—"

"Shoot the bastard," Hopaii said firmly.

John nodded. He took a deep breath, let it out. "Right. We have more than enough to do here. And I have supplies. So... I think the next thing I'm going to do is teach Ethriel to shoot."

Hopaii nodded. "I wish I could tell you more—"

"You've told me enough to put me on guard. That's a good thing," John interrupted. "And you're going to find out more. That's better." He frowned. "Hopaii, how old do you think he is?"

"It's a little late to be asking that question, don't you think?" Hopaii asked, his voice dry. "Don't tell me you aren't sleeping with him. I know that look."

"What look? I do not have a look!" John protested.

"Sure, old man." Hopaii shook his head. "Be careful."

"With these witches? Of course."

Hopaii drained his cup, set it down, then got up. He shook his head. "No, John. You be careful with him." He nodded at Ethriel. "You're the Hattak Falaya. I know what that means. I've seen what that means. You're my friend. I don't want you hurt."

John snorted and looked down at Ethriel's hand in his. "I've been hurt before. It hasn't killed me yet."

"There's a first time for everything, John."

CHAPTER SIX

Sparks

Hopaii left, promising to bring information back as soon as he learned anything. John watched him ride away and thought about following him out to the standing stone. He needed to reinforce the barrier. He could saddle Barak, ride out, and be back before the rains came. Then he could take the rest of the afternoon and teach Ethriel to shoot. He looked up at the sky, trying to judge the weather. He fished his pocket-watch out, wound it, and checked the time. No, if the rains came at about the same time every day, then he wouldn't have time to do both. He turned back into the house, hearing Ethriel doing something behind the curtain.

"Ethriel?" he called. "What are you doing?"

Ethriel peered out from behind the curtain. He smiled, and pulled the curtain back to reveal a much tidier bedroom — the bed had been smoothed and the blankets straightened. Clothes had been picked up and folded, and all of the flat surfaces had been dusted clean with one of the damp towels. Ethriel waved one arm to encompass what he'd done, then tucked his hands behind his back and smiled shyly.

John looked at him and smiled. "Thank you," he said. "This is wonderful." He held his hand out, and when Ethriel took it, he pulled the elf close. "I wish you could understand me. I know you'll learn." He frowned. "Maybe I should learn. I should learn your tongue, too." He tried to remember the phrase that Hopaii had used. When he tried to repeat it, Ethriel burst out laughing. John made a face at him, which only made the elf laugh harder. He turned toward John, put his arms around John's waist, and said the phrase, waiting until John repeated it. John sighed and added, "I don't know what I just said!"

"John friend," Ethriel answered. Then he repeated John's name, followed by a word in his own language, one that John recognized from what he'd just said.

"That means friend?" John asked. He repeated the word, then added, "Friend?"

"Friend," Ethriel said with a nod.

John laughed. "Right. We'll trade words later. For now, come with me." He stepped back and went to pick up the Henry. He held it up. "Rifle. This is a rifle."

Ethriel frowned. "Rifle."

"You are going to learn to use this," John added. "Come with me." He gestured for Ethriel to follow, and they left the dugout and headed for the barn. In a box of assorted scraps, John found a collection of old cans, most of them pockmarked from earlier target practice. He carried them out and away from the barn, toward a large stump near the banks of the slough. He set the cans up, then led Ethriel back, away from the stump. He held the Henry up again, and fell immediately into the role of an instructor faced with a new recruit.

"This is a Henry rifle," he said. "Lever-action, breech-loading. It holds fifteen cartridges in the magazine. And I know you didn't understand a word of that." He shook his head, laughing at himself as he pointed to a spot behind him. "Old habits die hard. I suppose that means I'm an old habit. Ethriel, stand there." Ethriel frowned slightly, then moved to where John was pointing. He grinned when John nodded. John smiled in return, then turned back to the targets. In one smooth movement, he raised the rifle, aimed, ran the lever, and fired; one of the cans flew off the stump into the brush. John lowered the rifle and looked back at Ethriel, who had his hands over his ears and was staring in wide-eyed fear. He gaped at John for a moment, then gasped something.

"Yes, it's loud," John said. "Startling, the first time you hear one. I remember the first time I did. Come here." He lowered the rifle and held his hand out to Ethriel, beckoning him closer. Ethriel came closer slowly, looking askance at the rifle. He let John position him, then relaxed against John as he moved to stand at Ethriel's back. Only to freeze when John raised the rifle. Gently, John coaxed the elf into holding the rifle, left hand supporting the barrel, the butt against his right shoulder. He guided Ethriel into running the lever with a firm movement, then squeezing the trigger. To his credit, Ethriel didn't drop the rifle when it fired. He did shudder all over, like a fly-stung horse. And, John noticed, none of the cans moved. Still, it wasn't a bad first try.

"Good," he said in Ethriel's ear. "Very good. We'll try again—" He stopped when he heard thunder rumble overhead. "Or perhaps not. That's hours earlier than it started yesterday. I suppose the barrier will have to wait until morning." He took the rifle, stepped away from Ethriel, and ran the lever to eject the cartridges. He collected them off the ground, tucked them into his pocket, then looked up again. "Come on," he said. "We've got work to do before the storm comes."

He brought the rifle into the dugout, setting it on its pegs and putting the cartridges into the bowl. He set Ethriel to work filling the water barrel from the pump, then he headed to the paddock. Barak shied away from him, racing to the far edge of the paddock, and refusing to let John get close enough to catch his halter. John chased him for a moment before stopping in the middle of the paddock, panting and listening to the rumble of thunder overhead. Looking up showed the high, dark clouds overhead, and a flash of lightning.

"Barak," he called. "I'm not leaving you out here in the storm." He turned, thinking to go and get something to lure the horse into the barn. A bucket of grain, maybe? A flash of movement caught his eyes, and he looked to see Ethriel coming toward the paddock. The elf looked at him, then at Barak at the far end of the paddock. He pointed.

"That?" John asked. "Horse. That is a horse."

"Horse," Ethriel echoed, and said something in his language. Probably his word for horse. Then he tapped his chest. "Ethriel." He pointed at the horse, and cocked a brow.

John grinned. "Barak."

"Barak horse." Ethriel nodded. He looked at the barn, then pointed. "Barak?"

"Yes, but he won't come to me," John growled in his frustration. Ethriel smiled. He slipped into the paddock and walked past John. As he reached the edge of the tall grass, he started calling, soft and low. Barak started to shy away from him, the way he had from John, and John started to move to catch him. Then Ethriel's voice changed, grew more musical. More compelling. John found himself being pulled in that direction, and stopped himself, staring in wonder as Barak walked up to Ethriel and stood without balking.

"How did you do that?" John asked, watching as Ethriel took Barak by the halter and led him toward the gate. He followed them to the barn, shaking his head and trying not to laugh. Ethriel clearly knew how to care for a horse, and Barak was soon safely in his stall, his manger refilled and water in reach. Ethriel looked around, then caught John's eye and made brushing motions over Barak's neck. John went and fetched the brushes, then climbed up to the loft to check on the hay while Ethriel groomed Barak.

From the loft, John could hear the solid splatter of rain starting to hit the roof. He swore softly and looked down. "Are you nearly finished?"

In answer, Ethriel walked into view, held up the brushes, and went to put them back on the shelf. John clambered down the ladder and looked out — it was already raining hard. He glanced at Ethriel, who grinned and ran out into the rain.

"Wait for me!" John shouted. He closed and barred the barn door behind him, then followed Ethriel back to the house.

THE SHUTTERS INSIDE and outside were closed against the weather, the door was barred shut, and all of them were sealed with a barrier. John wasn't sure what sorts of witches Hopaii might have meant, but he wasn't going to take chances. He considered loading the Henry, but decided against it. It wasn't worth the risk of having a misfire if the rifle was jostled. He set the little lamp aglow, lit the fire in the stove, and set water to boil while he and Ethriel finished the last of the rice porridge he'd made the night before, eating right out of the pot and fencing with spoons for the last few bites. Then Ethriel helped John to clean the dugout, filling dirty pots with water and setting them to boil while John organized supplies and cleaned twenty-five years of dust off of surfaces, and out of cookware and dishes.

Scrubbing the pots was John's job, using a stiff bristled brush and pouring the dirty water off into a bucket to be tossed into the midden in the morning. While he worked on that, he started naming things. Pot. Stove. Fire. Ethriel absorbed it all like a sponge, pointing out things and demanding their names. Table. Chair. Coffeepot. Eggs. Dish. Cup. And the all-important word — What?

"John?" Ethriel asked as John set the last of the now-clean pots into its place on top of the goods boxes. He picked up an egg, held it to his mouth, then asked, "What?"

"Eat?" John offered. He picked up one of the clean spoons and pantomimed putting something into his mouth. "Eat."

"Eat," Ethriel nodded. "Ethriel eat egg. John eat egg?"

"Yes, John eats eggs. Is that your way of asking for eggs for dinner?" He reached out and took the egg from Ethriel, putting it back into the bowl. "I should make something to go with them. And it will pass the time." He started picking through the cookware, taking down a bowl, a dented tin cup, and a rolling pin. He put those on the table and went back for the Dutch oven. He carried that around to the stove, using the shovel to arrange coals on the stone beneath the stove. He set the Dutch oven down, and put more coals on the lid so it would start to heat.

Making beaten biscuits was oddly relaxing. Having to bludgeon the dough to prepare it did tend to leave a man feeling more at peace with the world than he had when he'd started. When he started beating the dough with the rolling pin, Ethriel had jumped in shock. When John showed no signs of stopping, he'd settled himself to watch. And, after the third or fourth time John stopped to fold the dough and change hands, he held his hand out for the rolling pin.

"Just hit it, as hard as you can," John said. Ethriel frowned, nodded, then slammed the rolling pin down. He started out with a fierce scowl on his face, one that gradually faded as he worked. By the time John waved him to a stop, he was grinning.

"What?" he demanded, handing the rolling pin to John. He pointed at the dough. "What?"

"Biscuit dough," John answered. He set the rolling pin down, folded the dough a few more times, then rolled it out and cut the biscuits. The biscuits went into the hot Dutch oven, and John replaced the lid and added more coals. He looked up to see Ethriel watching him.

"Biscuit dough," he repeated. He turned and picked up a scrap of dough that hadn't made it into the oven. "Eat?"

"Not yet," John answered. Then he grinned. "Just a minute." He got up and got a frying pan. He'd need one anyway for the eggs. He moved the burner out of the way, and set the pan in place to heat. He went to the table and picked up the scraps of dough, rolling them together into a small ball that he flattened on the bottom of the pan. Ethriel peered into the pan.

"What?" he asked.

"Pan," John answered, pointing. He waved over it. "Cooking. Cooking so we can eat."

Ethriel nodded slowly. Then he looked at the table. He frowned slightly and waved his hand, encompassing the table and the biscuit making equipment. "Clean... clean away?" he asked slowly. He looked at John. "Yes?"

John smiled. "Yes," he agreed. "You're very quick."

Ethriel laughed, a laugh that was cut off as thunder boomed, loud enough to rattle the door. He gasped and nearly threw himself at John, who caught the elf and gently shifted him so that he was standing behind him. He moved to the door and rested his hand against it, feeling the prickle of the barrier against his palm. He wasn't sure if he'd feel anything else — he'd never had one of these barriers actually attacked before. He wasn't sure if it would hold.

It would give him time, though. He reached up and took down the Henry. He loaded it, then went to the other side of the curtain and picked up the box of cartridges. He had slightly more than half a box. Not nearly enough. Why had he let himself come out here so unprepared?

Because he hadn't been thinking. He'd been reacting.

No, no, he'd been running.

Now, he had to think. He brought the box out and set it on the shelf next to the bowl. He put the Henry onto the table — where could he put it near the bed that would be both stable and within reach? Thinking, he turned to see Ethriel watching him.

"What?" he asked Ethriel. Ethriel shook his head and backed away from the door, putting his back to the stones set into the far wall. John joined him. He could smell the biscuit — it needed to be turned, but Ethriel was more important. He put himself between Ethriel and the door. "I'm not going to let them hurt you," he said softly. "I'll take care of you. You're safe."

Ethriel looked up at him, his brow slightly furrowed. "Safe?"

"Safe," John repeated. He took a deep breath. "How do I explain to you what safe means?" He turned, absently reaching out and turning the biscuit over in the pan, grimacing a little as he scorched his fingers. Ethriel gasped and grabbed his hand, looking closely. Then he looked up at John.

"I'm fine," John said. "And you're fine." He put his hands on Ethriel's shoulders. It didn't feel like enough; he pulled Ethriel closer, holding him tightly. "You're safe," he repeated, and felt Ethriel slowly relax against him.

"Safe," Ethriel murmured. "John safe. Ethriel safe." He looked up. He pointed to John, then to himself. "What?"

John frowned slightly, unsure of what Ethriel was asking. "What?"

That got a soft, frustrated growl from Ethriel. He tipped his head back, studied John for a moment, then reached up, tangled his fingers into John's hair, and pulled his head down for a kiss that John felt like fire in his blood. He moaned, and pushed the elf against the stones, pinning him there. He could feel the heat radiating from Ethriel's body, hotter than the fire in the stove.

Ethriel whimpered softly, then drew back and smiled as he met John's eyes. "What?" he asked, his voice low. He tapped John on the chest before resting his hand flat over John's heart. "What?"

This time, John understood. He just wasn't sure what to answer. Was it just lust? Just the sheer, heady elation of having someone to care for that he wouldn't eventually have to leave or watch die?

No. No, he knew what this was. It was amazing to him, just how quickly it had happened. But then, it had happened this quickly to him the first time. He'd been dizzy in love with Joshua since the heartbeat after he'd been called to follow, before he'd even put down the net he'd been mending.

"Love," John answered. "I love you. I—" He tapped his own chest, then ran his fingers down the line of Ethriel's jaw. "—love you."

Ethriel cocked his head to the side, his eyes narrowed slightly. John waited, letting him think. Hoping he understood. Ethriel bit his lower lip. Then he smiled broadly, laughed with sheer delight, and threw his arms around John's neck. John laughed with him, holding him tightly, listening as Ethriel repeated the word in an almost giddy tone.

"Love!" He stopped and kissed John firmly on the lips. He laughed again. Then he sniffed. "Fire?"

"Fire?" John repeated. He looked at the stove and laughed. "The biscuit!" He let go of Ethriel and grabbed the rag, picking up the frying pan and turning the scorched, flat biscuit out onto the table. He let it cool, then picked up a knife and scraped the burned bits off. It was still edible, mostly, so he broke it in half and handed a piece to Ethriel. "It's not my best," he apologized. "The others will be better."

Ethriel sniffed the biscuit. He licked it. Then he took a bite. His brows rose, and he ate the rest. "Good," he proclaimed. "Ver' good."

John laughed. "If you like that, you'll love the unburnt ones." He ate his own piece, then crouched down and checked the oven, adding more coals to replace the ones that had cooled. He looked up. "Are you hungry? Do you want to eat?"

Ethriel nodded. "Eat. Yes."

"Then I'll start making eggs." He picked up the bowl of eggs and the butter, and started to cook. Soon the dugout was filled with the scents of frying eggs, and Ethriel went unbidden to the cupboard and took out plates, forks and knives. He filled cups with water, then brought them to the table. Then he cocked his head to the side.

"What?" John asked. He didn't expect an answer. So he was surprised when Ethriel made a rumbling sound deep in his chest.

"What?" he asked, then repeated the rumble.

"Thunder," John answered.

"Thunder," Ethriel repeated. He looked up as thunder rumbled outside. "Thunder?"

"Thunder," John confirmed. He turned to look at the elf, and saw a bright flash through the shutters. He braced himself for another rumble... but none came.

"That's odd," he murmured. Then he turned back to the eggs. Didn't thunder always follow lightning?

A moment later, he heard another rumble, this one sounding more distant. He nodded. There. Nothing to worry about, he thought as he reached for a plate and started serving eggs.

Ethriel's enjoyment of even the simplest of food was a joy to watch — he seemed to be delighted with the properly-baked biscuits, especially when they were drizzled with honey. He ate more than John thought he would, half of the eggs, and nearly half the biscuits. Then he yawned, hard enough that John heard his jaw crack. John laughed.

"If you want to go to bed, I can clean up," he said, and gestured toward the curtain.

Ethriel smiled and shook his head. "Clean away," he replied, and stood up.

"All right. You can help," John said. He got up from his chair, and nearly fell when a crack of thunder sounded, so loud that he would swear he felt it inside his head. He grabbed onto the table and held on as the thunder rolled over him, echoing up and down his spine. He knew Ethriel was next to him, could hear his voice.

Not the words, just the frightened tone. What had happened? Lightning? Could he be struck by lightning inside the dugout?

No, it hadn't felt like lightning. That had only happened once, but he remembered what it felt like to be struck by lightning.

He took a shaking breath and shook his head, taking stock. He was... fine. He was fine. He wasn't sure what had happened, but he was fine. He straightened and looked around. There wasn't anything amiss that he could see. There wasn't a mark on the door, or on the window shutters. He wasn't even sure if lightning could penetrate—

"The barrier!" he gasped. He pushed off from the table and staggered like a drunkard toward the door, resting his hand on the wood. The prickling against his palm was reassuring — this barrier, at least, was intact.

Was what he'd felt been an attack against the other one? More importantly, was it still in place?

For a moment, the temptation to go look was overwhelming. He could get his coat and his hat, and the Henry, and walk out to the standing stone. He turned toward the peg where his coat hung, and nearly bumped into Ethriel. It was enough to stop him. He couldn't leave Ethriel here, alone and undefended. He'd go in the morning, once it was safe. Once whatever was hiding in the storm was gone.

"John?" Ethriel asked. "What?"

"I don't know," John answered, and shook his head. The movement was enough to make him sway like a sapling in a strong wind, and Ethriel caught his arm to steady him.

"John bed," he said, his voice firm. "Ethriel... I...I clean away."

John stared at him for a moment. "An almost complete sentence?" he said. "I'm impressed. Ethriel, I'm fine."

Ethriel's eyes narrowed. "John bed," he repeated, and pointed at the curtain.

John laughed. He saluted, then went to the curtain. He took off his boots and lay down, but not before pushing the curtain all the way to one side, so that he could lie on the bed and watch as Ethriel cleaned up the remains of the meal, washing dishes and the pan, and putting the rest of the biscuits into a bowl that he covered with a cloth. John found himself smiling as he watched — Ethriel had come a long way in only a day. By this time tomorrow, he might be reciting poetry.

And perhaps he'd be able to tell John what had happened to him. Who had been holding him prisoner, and why? Who was out there in the storm, looking for him. He blinked, finding himself suddenly fighting sleep.

"Ethriel, come to bed," he called. Ethriel turned and smiled at him, holding his hand up. He stacked the dishes and put them away, then looked up at the softly glowing light overhead and whistled to it. The light dimmed.

"You know that spell?" John asked. Ethriel looked quizzically at him, then came to the bed and started to take off his clothes. John made a note that he'd need to wash his clothes and Ethriel's tomorrow. Then perhaps get to sewing — he had the supplies, and enough cloth to make new trousers for both of them, and maybe another shirt for Ethriel, if he cut things right. He got up and took his own clothes off.

He turned back toward the bed. Then he stopped, listening to the storm and the wind. And...was that an owl? He walked barefoot to the door, checked the barrier once more, then took the Henry off the table. He slid the loaded rifle underneath the bed, then climbed back in and lay down. Ethriel curled up next to him, resting his head on John's shoulder. There was a distant rumble of thunder and John felt Ethriel shiver.

"Go to sleep, Ethriel," he murmured, and doused the lamp.

CHAPTER SEVEN
Flash

John woke up underneath an elf. Ethriel was stretched out over him, his mouth on John's. John wrapped his arms around him and closed his eyes, letting Ethriel assert himself, letting him explore with hands and lips in ways that left them both whimpering and wanting more. Until John growled and rolled them both over, hearing Ethriel's laughter as they traded positions. Traded kisses. Traded pleasures, until they were both spent, both sated, resting tangled in each other's arms.

It was, John decided, a most pleasurable way to wake, and one that he wouldn't object to getting used to in the future. Yes, Ethriel had come a long way in just a little over a day — from a frightened and sick escaped prisoner to a bold, almost puckish lover. A partner.

It had been a very long time since he'd had a partner.

He combed his fingers through Ethriel's hair and sighed. "We have work to do," he murmured.

"Stay bed," Ethriel mumbled. "Eat. Stay bed."

John laughed. "Eat and stay in bed? That's a lovely idea. But we have to feed Barak, and I have to mow the paddock. We have work to do, love."

Ethriel raised his head. "Love," he repeated. He stretched up and kissed John lightly on the lips. He frowned slightly, then said, "I love you."

John smiled. He reached up and ran his fingers over Ethriel's lips, over one high cheekbone. "I love you, too," he answered. He sat up, and pulled Ethriel into his arms to kiss him again. Then he slid out of bed and pulled on his trousers. The rest of his clothes he bundled up to be washed.

The washtub and the big laundry cauldron were both in the stable. He'd drag them out and get the laundry started before he mowed the paddock and mucked Barak's stall. But first, he'd need to go out to inspect the standing stone and the barrier.

"John? Biscuit?" Ethriel asked, tugging on his own trousers. He picked up his shirt, looked at John, then laid it down.

"Please," John answered, taking the shirt and putting it with the rest of the clothes. Finish the biscuits and get to work. He yawned again. Coffee would be a lovely thing, too, but he'd need a fire for that. He'd need to heat water for the laundry — he'd start a fire outside, set the coffee pot up to heat along with the wash water. He yawned and picked up the Henry, then headed for the near window, opening the shutters. He could see nothing outside, so he moved on to the door. He rested his hand on the wood, felt the prickle of magic, and dismissed the barrier spell. Then he opened the door and stepped outside.

A few steps from the house, he looked up.

"Good morning," he murmured. "I don't know if you're watching?" He looked back over his shoulder, seeing Ethriel in the doorway. "I mean, I know they say you're always watching, but I'm not sure I believe that. His name is Ethriel, and I love him. As much as I love you." He paused. Frowned. "I... really hope you don't mind. And I think you'll like him." He tipped his head back and smiled. "I love you. I miss you. I'm still waiting."

"John?" Ethriel called. "What?"

John looked back at him and smiled, holding his hand out. "Take a walk with me?"

"Walk?"

John pointed with the Henry. "That way. Not far."

Ethriel took his hand and smiled, and they started walking. They hadn't gotten far before John heard something that didn't sound like the wind in the trees.

No.

It was the creak and jingle of harness, the creak of a wagon.

Someone was coming, and there'd been no warning from the barrier.

He stopped, letting Ethriel's hand fall and raising the Henry. "Go back to the house," he said softly. "Ethriel, go back to the house."

Ethriel looked around. "What?"

"I don't know. Go!"

Ethriel took off running, disappearing before he reached the dugout. The door closed, telling John that Ethriel was safe inside. He hoped. He kept walking, moving further from the dugout, stalking through the trees. There was no cover here, and he could feel the bare skin between his shoulder blades itching. But there was no one behind him. At least, he didn't think there was anyone behind him.

The creak and jingle grew louder, and the source of the sound came into view. It was a horse-drawn gig, one being pulled by a lovely black mare. The driver, to John's shock, was Reverend Kerry.

John lowered the rifle, waiting as the gig drew closer and drew to a stop. "Reverend," John said slowly. "This is a surprise."

"I can see that," Kerry answered, looking John up and down. "Not expecting callers?"

"There's a reason I live this far out," John answered. "It does tend to discourage casual visitors. So I assume you're not."

Kerry smiled. "I came to see how you were faring."

"Faring quite busy, to be honest," John answered. "I spent my morning yesterday mowing hay and cleaning the stables. The rest of the day was spent cleaning out the house. I'll be doing the rest of the paddock today. Then laundry. And if it starts to rain, I'll start weaving my nets." He cocked his head to the side. "You drove two hours out of your way, this early in the day, just to see how I was doing? I'm flattered. And curious. Why? I'm not one of your flock."

Kerry chuckled. "That's just it. I was curious. I've seen this place on the maps, but I've never been out here."

John nodded slowly. "There isn't much to see. Especially not at the moment." He shrugged, trying to fight the urge to either fight or flee. "Give me until autumn, and I'll have something to show off."

"I will hold you to that," Kerry said. He looked around again. "A pleasant place. Might I trouble you for some water for my horse? It's a long drive here, and a long drive back."

There was no way to refuse. Not without destroying any chance he had to remain here — if he was rude to the minister, John would be snubbed in Skullyville, no matter whose son he was supposed to be. John nodded. "Of course. And for yourself?"

"If it's not too much trouble?"

John nodded. "The pump is this way," he said, gesturing. He didn't move, waiting until the gig was rolling again. Then he started walking alongside. Something was not right, but he wasn't sure. His mind felt foggy.

Kerry drew the gig to a stop again. He wrapped the reins around the brake and jumped down. "How were the storms here last night?"

"Very loud," John answered. "Thunder loud enough to rattle the windows."

"I'm not surprised," Kerry said. He led his horse to the water trough. "You're lucky it's too wet to burn. There are signs of lightning strikes along the road. Trees down back the way I came, and some toppled stones, right at the bend in the road."

John nodded slowly. That had to have been what destroyed the barrier. He went to the pump and started to draw water, filling a battered dipper and passing it to Kerry. The man sipped it and smiled.

"Thank you." He looked around. "This is a fine place," he added.

"Thank you," John answered automatically. "I've still got a great deal of work to do on it." He felt in his pocket for his pocket watch, but it wasn't there. He must have left it in the house. But it was still quite early...

Wait.

For Reverend Kerry to be here this early, he'd have to have left Skullyville before dawn. And... wait, what *day* was this?

"Reverend?" John asked slowly. "Perhaps I'm misremembering the day, but isn't it Sunday?"

Kerry glanced at him and smiled. "It is."

"You shouldn't be here."

"No, here is exactly where I should be," Kerry replied. He handed the dipper back to John. "Where is he, John?"

John frowned slightly, trying to look confused. "Who? I'm alone here, Reverend."

Kerry chuckled. "You are very good. But we know the prince is here." He cocked his head to the side. Then, to John's amazement, he changed. The somber clothing of a priest was replaced with clothing of the sort that John hadn't seen for nearly five hundred years — a brocaded tunic over breeches, with a jeweled leather belt and gauntlets. Kerry's features shifted. His hair lengthened. His ears drew to a point, and his eyes shifted to resemble cat's eyes. John stepped back, raising the Henry. Movement caught his eye, a stranger coming out from behind the barn. An armed stranger, a man carrying a crossbow. Training took over — he aimed and fired, turning the gun back on Kerry before the dead man had even hit the ground.

But Kerry was gone.

John backed slowly away from the pump, scanning the trees, listening for movement. Kerry clearly knew the same disappearing spell that Ethriel did. Which meant he could be anywhere. John needed to get into the dugout. He could set his barriers up and hold the dugout. But first he needed to get there.

There was nothing moving near the pump, so he turned to face the dugout. Nothing moving there, either, and the door was closed. Good. Hopefully, Ethriel hadn't locked it. He started toward the door, watching, ready, feeling as if every hair was tingling.

Movement, to his right. He turned and fired, and another stranger fell. He hadn't been there a moment ago — did they *all* know that spell?

How many of them were between him and the door?

He wanted to run, to get inside. To put himself and his barrier and the door between Ethriel and the fake priest and his men. Instead, he forced himself to walk, to keep looking, to listen. He heard a stick crack, to his left. Then, without warning, he was surrounded. He could only see the five men in front of him, because a force closed around him, freezing him in place. John growled softly — Kerry was right in front of him. There was no way to miss, not at this range! But he couldn't move to squeeze the trigger.

"Well," Kerry said. "I see why Ethriel ran to you. You are quite the fierce protector." He chuckled and walked forward, shifting the barrel of the Henry out of his way as he circled around John. Then he stopped and sniffed. "I smell him on you. Did you enjoy him? I expect you did. He is quite delightful. But you must realize that he is not for the likes of you. Not Ethriel." He circled around and stopped in front of John. "He is mine. And I will have him back now." He gestured. "Secure him. And the rest of you, fan out and find Ethriel. I am tired of this filthy human town. I want to go home."

Men started moving. Two of them moved to stand one on each side of John. The one on his right took hold of his arm. John held his breath. Would it work? The Henry had one flaw, one that he might be able to use in his favor. He just had to be ready...

The force holding him in place fell away, and John moved, twisting and slamming the butt of the rifle into the face of the man holding his arm. The impact was enough to fire the gun, and the man on his left fell screaming. Not dead, but not a threat. John brought the rifle up as he ran the lever, fired, hearing the spent cartridges hitting the ground. Where was Kerry? If he killed their leader, they should fall apart and run.

He killed four of the attackers before someone got behind him and hit him. John wasn't sure with what, but the entire world swam.

When they hit him again, the world went dark.

JOHN SHOOK HIS HEAD, trying to clear it. What had they hit him with? He felt strange, dizzy. He tried to move and couldn't, and only then felt the ropes at his wrists and ankles. He opened his eyes.

They had tied him spread-eagled between two saplings, his wrists lashed to the trees, his ankles spread and tied to the same trees. And even with him so bound, he was still under heavy guard — surrounded by men with crossbows ready to turn him into a poor substitute for Saint Sebastian. He couldn't see Kerry. Nor could he see Ethriel.

He could see the barn, and the door to the dugout. The door was on the ground, about ten feet from the doorway it had once occupied. The doors to the barn were open as well, albeit the usual way. Kerry came out of the barn as John watched.

"Kerry!" John shouted. "Where is he?"

To his surprise, Kerry laughed. "Oh, good," he said. "You are finally awake. I have the same question. Where is he?"

John shook his head. "I don't know. You've clearly searched the dugout. If he's not there, I don't know where he is. Miles from here, I hope."

Kerry chuckled and walked closer to John. "Oh, I doubt that. I doubt that greatly. No, I think he is here. Somewhere. Watching." He reached out and ran one hand down John's chest. "Wondering just what I am going to do to you. Meanwhile, I am wondering how far he will allow me to go before he reveals himself."

John went cold. He knew exactly what Kerry meant. He was going to be tortured, and Ethriel would reveal himself to try and stop it from happening. And there was no way for him to tell Ethriel that it didn't matter. That no matter how much Kerry hurt him, he could not die.

"He's smarter than that," John said softly. "He's not going to give himself up for me."

Kerry shook his head. "I think that perhaps you don't give yourself enough credit, John," he chided. He reached down and drew a small knife from his boot. "Shall we find out?"

John watched the knife for a moment, the glint of sunlight on the blade, and forced himself to relax.

"Go ahead," he growled. "It'll hardly be the first time this has happened. Nor will it be the worst thing that's happened to me in my life."

Kerry's brow furrowed, as John's words clearly surprised him. But he recovered quickly. "Well, then," he said. "You give me something to aspire to."

The knife was razor-sharp, enough that it wasn't actually the cut that hurt. It was the rush of air that followed, icy against the inside of his skin right before the heat as the blood started to flow. That was what made him want to scream and vomit. John closed his eyes and locked his jaw as Kerry laid open long slices on the insides of each arm. Down the length of his back on either side of his spine.

He tasted blood in his mouth when he bit his tongue, but he was not going to cry out. If he did, Ethriel would hear, and he would come to try and make it stop. John was as certain of that as Kerry seemed to be.

So he was not going to scream. He closed his eyes and let his head hang, waiting for the next cut. He felt dizzy, no doubt from blood loss.

He heard Kerry laugh. "I am very impressed," he said. "I have not yet seen a human who could withstand this much without making a sound. You really are remarkable, John. It is a shame I cannot waste any more time with you. I need to bring Ethriel out of hiding."

A hard hand grabbed John under the chin, forcing his head up. He met Kerry's eyes, took a deep breath, and spat in the elf's face. Kerry scowled at him.

"I was not enjoying this, John," he said softly. "I do not want you to think that I am some sort of monster. This was not at all pleasurable for me. Until now." He raised the knife, and tapped John's left cheek. "Left eye, or right?" he asked. "Where should I start?"

"Buach!"

John couldn't see past Kerry, but he heard Ethriel's voice ring out loud and clear. Kerry let John go and stepped back.

"There you are," he called. "I knew you would come out if I hurt him enough." Then he said something in what John assumed was the same language Ethriel spoke. John heard his name, but nothing else made sense. It didn't matter. He stared at Ethriel.

The prince, Kerry had said. Where was the *prince*? John had met royalty in his life. He never would have imagined his Ethriel as a prince. Until now. Now, Ethriel stood strong and proud. Even half-naked, there was a presence to him that hadn't been there before. He stalked toward them, pointed at John, and gave a very clear order.

Kerry just laughed. "He wants me to release you," he said. "Since I am assuming you have not learned to speak our tongue yet."

John ignored him. "Ethriel, go!"

Ethriel shook his head. "John," he said. He walked closer to the ring of men surrounding John and Kerry. They parted to let him pass. He ignored Kerry as if the man wasn't there, walked up to John, and kissed him. He rested his forehead against John's. "I love you," he whispered.

"Ethriel, run. Please." John whispered back.

Ethriel shook his head. "Clean away," he whispered, then smiled, no doubt at the confused look on John's face. There was no time to say anything else — Ethriel turned and looked at Kerry, saying something else in his own tongue.

Kerry looked surprised. "He wants me to tell you why," he said. "He wants you to understand."

"Since he also wants you to let me go, you could cut me down while you tell me," John suggested, trying to keep his voice from wobbling.

"You would like that, wouldn't you?" Kerry asked. "My name is Buach. I was the heir to the High Queen of the Elvenlands. My aunt. I was the only heir, until Ethriel was born. Now, he has the temerity to stand between me and the throne that should have been mine. And it will be mine. And he will be mine." He glanced at Ethriel. "He was mine, until he slipped past my guards and somehow managed to walk between the worlds."

"And took shelter here?" John asked. "Because you couldn't get through my barriers."

Kerry nodded once. "Now, though, it is over. He will be coming back with me, and this will all be an unpleasant memory."

He stepped closer, resting his hand on Ethriel's shoulder. Ethriel looked over his shoulder at him. Then he spun, and John saw the glint of sunlight on the long blade of his cooking knife as it became visible. Buach yowled in pain and dodged backward. John saw where his tunic had parted, and he saw the blood. Ethriel crouched in front of John, holding the cooking knife ready. He spat something, and Buach snorted. Then he waved one hand and snapped what was clearly an order to his guards.

There was only so much Ethriel could do with a single knife against armored men. John shouted and cursed, struggling against the ropes. But there was nothing he could do.

The fight didn't last long.

Buach watched as the guards bound Ethriel's arms behind him, bound his arms to his body. There was blood on Ethriel's face, in his hair. He looked up at John, and the despair in his eyes made John want to weep.

"It was a good attempt," Buach said. "Foolhardy, but that was ever Ethriel. He always was a little fool." He picked up the discarded knife and examined it. "Yours, I presume? A cooking knife?"

John glared at him. "Now what?" he demanded.

"Now? Now, I take my wayward prince home," Buach said. "We have the wedding, thereby sealing my right to the throne." He looked at Ethriel and smiled. "And on the wedding night, after I take my pleasures... he dies." He turned back to John. "But you die first."

John screamed as the knife slammed into his chest, hearing Ethriel screaming his name.

The screams faded to nothing.

CHAPTER EIGHT
Rekindled

... pull... knife...
But... dead...
...trust...

John gasped explosively as the knife was tugged from his body and life flooded back in. He took a deep, shuddering breath, feeling the warmth returning to his hands and feet. He was on the ground. Who had cut him down? He struggled to sit up, only to hear a man cry out, "Jesus, Mary and Joseph!"

"His name was Joshua," John muttered. Then he realized who was speaking. "Nathaniel?"

Nathaniel Miller knelt over him, the bloody cooking knife in his hand, his eyes as wide as saucers. "You were dead. You were dead, man!"

John nodded, and tried to sit up again. This time, he made it. He looked around, and saw Hopaii. With him were a woman, and an older man. John blinked, and looked again.

Both the woman and the older man were elves.

"John!" Nathaniel gasped, and John turned to look back at him.

"It's hard to explain, Nate," he said, and watched as Nathaniel's jaw dropped.

"It's you," he whispered. "It's... it's you. Not... you're not his son. You're *him*! You're my John!"

John nodded. "I'm sorry. I... there's no real way to tell someone—"

"I should think not!" Nathaniel blurted. Then he laughed. "For years, I've wanted to talk to you. For years, John!"

"Nathaniel, we've more pressing matters to hand," the woman said as she came to join them. Her hair was dark, and her skin was closer to John's own olive tones than to Nathaniel's ivory-with-atendency-to-burn skin. John was certain that he'd never met her before, until she spoke again, "I'll want to know how it is you cannot die, John Zebedee. But not now. Can you stand?"

"In a moment, yes. You know me? Have we met?" John asked.

She smiled, then her form shimmered slightly. Her human guise was one that he recognized.

"Abigail?" John gasped.

She laughed, and let go of the illusion. "'Tis one of the few bits of magic I have to my name. And it's Avriel, when I'm at home."

John nodded. Then he looked at Nathaniel. "I think I'm not the only one who has explaining to do. But we have no time. Where's Ethriel?"

"Think you can stand?" Nathaniel asked. He got up, held his hand out. "We can talk while you put some clothes on."

John took Nathaniel's hand, let himself be pulled up off the ground. He held onto Nathaniel for a moment, steadying himself.

"What do you need, John?" Hopaii asked.

"A moment that we don't have," John answered. "And something to eat." He blinked, then asked again, "Where's Ethriel?"

"The bastard took him," the older man answered. "But they can't take the walk between the worlds. Not yet. We have until dark. We have time, and my Avriel is a fine tracker."

Avriel smiled. "You'll make me blush, Papa."

John shook his head and growled. "Where did he take my Ethriel?"

"Oh, no," Nathaniel warned. "You're eating and getting dressed first. Then we'll go after him."

John turned and stared. "We?"

"You don't think I'm letting you go off—" Nathaniel stopped. He frowned. Then he snorted. "I was going to say and get yourself killed. But you did that before we even got here. John. How—"

"My name — my real name — is Yohanan ben Zavdi," John said. He took a deep breath, and said words he had never before spoken aloud. The truth. "I was born near the Lake of Gennesaret. You know it as the Sea of Galilee. I am..." He stopped and did the mental math. "Eighteen hundred and eighty-nine years old. When I stopped aging, I had just turned twenty." He swallowed. "You know me already. You knew of me before you met me, Nathaniel. You've read your Bible."

Nathaniel frowned, and John watching him put the pieces together. "John... what you told me about a brother... that was true?" When John nodded, understanding bloomed on Nathaniel's face. "The Beloved Disciple. You're John, the Beloved Disciple."

John nodded. "Yes."

"And... there are stories..." Nathaniel paused. "The stories are true. My God. You're... you're waiting. For... for Him."

"I wasn't given much of a choice in the matter," John said. "But yes. Joshua told me to wait. And I've been waiting."

"Joshua? Oh, you mean Jesus."

John snorted. "I mean Joshua. His name was Yeshua. Is Yeshua." He shook his head, and threw himself off balance.

"Nathaniel, you can ask your questions later," the older man said. "He needs to recover, and to prepare for the fight." He smiled and walked over to John. "When I met you on the *Cavalier*, I had no idea you were the ally that the seers said was coming."

John stared at him. "Parsons?"

He nodded. "Been up and down this river for most of one of our years, searching. The seers said that the missing prince would be found near here. But they're never very precise in time or in place."

"A year?" John echoed. "He's been Kerry's prisoner for a year?"

Parsons nodded, his face somber. "Our year. Not yours. Our time is different. And we thought he died when Buach and his witch mother overthrew the king and queen. If we'd known..." He shook his head. "Nothing we can do for it now. Except find him before Buach makes him disappear again."

"Kerry... no, Buach. Buach isn't going to make him disappear," John said. He shrugged off Nathaniel's hand. "He's going to kill Ethriel. He said he's going to marry him, and murder him. Your folk — men can marry?"

Avriel laughed. "And that's what you fix on? I can see why you're so interested in the prince, then."

"Abby, let be," Nathaniel murmured. "John, what do you need from us?"

John took a deep breath. "Food. Ah... someone needs to feed my horse. We'll need him."

"I'll take care of the horse," Parsons said. "What else?"

"My rifle," John answered. "I'll need that."

"I saw it," Avriel said. "I'll bring it. Nathaniel, can you manage?"

"I know my way around a kitchen, woman. Off with you."

Avriel laughed and trotted away. It was only then that John realized she was wearing men's clothing. He looked back at Nathaniel.

"You married an elf?"

"She's a half-blood," Nathaniel answered. "Parsons traveled between the worlds quite a bit, and he likes traveling the rivers. He had a human wife out west. Sioux, I think. When she died, Abigail started traveling with him. That's how we met." He took John's arm and steered him into the dugout. "It's been a long time since I was last here. It looks the same."

John nodded. "There were biscuits. Ethriel wrapped them up. If you can find them? I'll go dress." He tottered toward the bed and tugged the curtain closed. Then he leaned on the bed and gave in to the shaking.

He'd never told anyone before. Never had anyone he could tell. Now...

What had he done?

He shook his head. He'd have to deal with the consequences later. He needed their help to find Ethriel. Then...

He'd worry about what happened then once he had Ethriel back.

He went through the bundle of clothes, found his other trousers and his drawers. He stripped to the skin and tugged on the dirty clothes, then went and pulled out his last shirt. He put it on and buttoned it, then picked up socks.

"How long have you and Avriel been married?" he called.

"Just about two years now," Nathaniel called back. "I met her when she and her father first came through Skullyville, after the war." The curtain moved. "Did you ever meet my mother?"

John looked up from putting on his boots. "No. She died the winter before we met."

"Ah, then you don't know that she was uncanny?" Nathaniel smiled. "She never told Father. He'd have put her out if he'd known. You remember him, and his temper. But I've a bit of it, and she taught me to use it. Most important, I can see."

"See... see what?" John asked.

"In the case of the elves? I can see through their illusions. Jeremiah can, too. He knows his stepmother isn't human. He doesn't care. He loves her. I can see a touch of magic on you, too. Not much, but I can see it." He looked around. "Let me find those biscuits."

"So if you can see the elves, then you knew Kerry wasn't really human?"

Nathaniel nodded. "When you're done, come out and eat. And yes. I knew he was an elf, but I'd no idea who he was. Avriel was raised in this world, and Parsons was in Little Rock until Friday when he came in on the *Cavalier*. Abby's never seen Buach before, so she didn't know that it was him right under our noses and taking coffee in our parlor for the past month. There are... more elves than you think, especially in this area. One of the easy routes between the worlds is near here. After Buach and his mother overthrew the royal family, there's been quite the stream of elves running to find safety. They usually go west, away from the cities. I help them, when I can."

"And how do you know Hopaii?" John asked as he came out from behind the curtain.

Nathaniel handed him a pair of biscuits before answering, "His daughter and my Jeremiah are sweet on each other. I'm not the stubborn jackass my father was. I like Talula." He smiled. "I owe you an apology. I've owed you an apology for a long time."

While he chewed, John tried to think of why Nathaniel would owe him an apology. He swallowed and shook his head. "Why? And hand me the honey."

"Sit down first. Before you fall down." Nathaniel waited until John was sitting. Then he handed him the honey pot and sat down across from him. "I need to apologize for how I treated you."

John smeared honey on his second biscuit, then looked at Nathaniel. "After the trip to Fort Gibson. You never said more than good morning to me ever again. I never understood why."

"Because my father beat me half to death when he realized I'd slept with you," Nathaniel said. "And forbade me from ever speaking to you again. He... John, you bit me, and he saw the mark." He tapped his collar. "Right here. My nightshirt didn't hide it. And he didn't believe me when I told him we'd visited a brothel."

"You lied to your father?" John gasped. "Nate—"

"It didn't work. It might have made things worse," Nathaniel shrugged. "Honestly, I know I'm supposed to honor my father and all that, but I'm glad he didn't live to meet Julia or Jeremiah."

"Julia?"

"My first wife. Jeremiah's mother," Nathaniel said. He smiled. "Father would have disowned me if he'd ever met Julia. But you'd have liked her." He licked his lips, then met John's eyes. "She was Black, John. Freeborn, from a place down in Louisiana you've probably never heard of. Her folk were involved in... something uncanny. I don't know. She wouldn't tell me. But she needed to leave town, and she ended up here. Her skin was light enough to pass as white, lighter than yours, even. She told me the truth when I asked her to marry me, but I didn't care. We kept her secret. I loved her, and I protected her." He looked around. "You fought in the war. On the side of the angels, you said. And you were in New York. You fought for the North?"

John finished his biscuit and nodded. "I did."

"I hoped so. Honestly, I would never have expected anything else of you," Nathaniel said.

"You keep surprising me, Nate. You sounded like a very convincing Reb on Friday," John said slowly.

Nathaniel laughed. "I make the right noises, to protect my son. But... because of Julia, I started doing what I could to help get people to safety." He smiled sheepishly. "That's the other reason I know Hopaii. He helped us get escaped slaves out of Arkansas and down to Mexico, where they'd be safe. And we've been doing the same with the elves."

"Not Canada?" John asked.

Nathaniel shook his head. "It was too dangerous. We'd have to get them through Missouri and Iowa, and I'm told that there are places in Illinois where they would send the poor bastards right back. Safer to go south. There's a place—" He shook his head. "Not important. Do you want another biscuit?"

John shook his head. "No, I just needed something to convince my body it's still alive. Again." He turned as Avriel came into the dugout, carrying the Henry. "Oh, thank you."

"'Tis a lovely rifle, John," she said, laying it on the table. "Perhaps you'll let me try it?"

"You shoot?" John asked. He nodded. "Of course. But I've limited ammunition at the moment, so if you don't mind waiting?"

"We've more important things for you to spend your shot on," she agreed, and sat down with them.

"Abby, where are we going?" Nathaniel asked.

She drummed her fingers on the table. "The gateway is near the mounds—"

"The ones northeast of here, near the river?" John asked. "Before the bend?"

She nodded. "'Tis a sacred site, so the walls between the worlds are easier to pass through. But there are rules to such things, and one of those rules is that it cannot be done while the sun is in the sky. He must wait for the moon to rise. There will be no storms tonight, I warrant."

John nodded. He closed his eyes and took stock. He was tired. He was usually tired after he rose from the dead — it seemed to take a lot of energy to do it. But he couldn't stop to rest.

"Abby, would you put on a pot of coffee?" Nathaniel asked. "John is going to fall off his horse the way he looks right now."

"I am not!" John protested. He opened his eyes and smiled. "But coffee would be good. I'll light—"

"Don't you move," Avriel warned. "It's only a stove. I know how it works. And I see your grinder, and the water barrel. You rest. We've a job of work to do."

"John," Nathaniel asked, sounding hesitant. "Do you mind if I ask how many times you—"

"Have died?" John finished when Nathaniel's voice trailed off. "I stopped counting a long time ago. It's not an easy life. I move quite a bit. I learned the hard way that if I stay too long in one place, people get notional. But I think I've died more in the past ten years than I have in the previous hundred."

"From the war?"

John looked over at Avriel and nodded. "Twice in combat. Twice by mischance. And four times in Camp Sumter."

"John!" Nathaniel gasped. "You... you weren't *there*?"

John swallowed. "You know about Sumter?"

"I've heard. People talk to shopkeepers. Say things they might not tell their priest." Nathaniel reached across and took his hand. "Dear God, John, the thought of you in that horrible place—"

"It's the reason I came back here," John said quietly. "I couldn't stay back East. I came back because I'd been happy here, and I wasn't happy. Not anywhere. I couldn't be, with the memories chasing me. After Sumter, I turned to drink. Spent most of '69 in a bottle and I do not clearly remember a day between June and... was it October? Yes, October." He took a deep breath. "I ended '69 by putting a bullet in my own brain. And woke up sobbing like a baby on January first, 1870. That was the last time I died before today." He laced his fingers together in front of him on the table, mostly to stop his hands from shaking. "I spent the rest of the winter and the spring closing my accounts and severing my ties in New York. And as soon as I could, I came west. Came back here. Hoping to find... something."

"And you found Ethriel," Nathaniel murmured. "You found someone who will likely live as long as you will."

"Only if we get to him before moonrise," Parsons said, coming inside. "Oh, now this is a nice little rabbit warren. Cozy."

John looked up. "It is. I've lived in palaces and mansions. But this place... I like this place." He looked back at Nathaniel. "How old is Ethriel?"

"He's only just come of age," Parsons answered. "And he's not yet come into his full power."

John looked at him for a moment, feeling his throat tighten. "How old is of age?"

"Eighteen hundred of your years is of age." Parson smiled. "You say you're eighteen hundred and eighty-seven? Ethriel is exactly that old, John."

John nodded slowly. "Not come into his power. What does that mean?"

"It means he hasn't matured enough to harness the full magical potential of our people. He can vanish — the youngest child can do that spell, the better to hide from a hunter."

"Like the coloring of a fawn," Avriel added.

"Just so," Parsons agreed. "There are other spells he can do, I'm certain. But to do the greater magics, to throw fire, or lightning, he's either not yet ready or hasn't yet been taught."

"Throw lightning," John repeated. "Can Buach do that? Is that what caused the storms? Something destroyed my barrier last night—"

"The standing stones, near the turn in the road?" Avriel came back to the table with the coffeepot. "Cups are where?"

John pointed, and she walked around the table and collected four cups. She poured the coffee, and John reached for another biscuit, dunking it into the coffee before devouring it in two bites.

"Do you need something more substantial?" Avriel asked.

"Just the coffee," John answered. He blew on it, then sipped it, feeling the burn as it flowed down his throat.

"You'll scorch yourself like that," Parsons murmured. "Now, do we have a plan?"

"Not yet, no," Avriel said. "I think we need to see the lay of the land."

John nodded. "I can't plan anything without knowing what I'm against. And... Nate, Avriel, where's your son? Is he safe?"

Nathaniel nodded. "Jeremiah is spending his Sunday doing his good Christian duty of helping our neighbor, the widow Connor. He escorts her to church, and they spend the rest of the morning playing chess on her front porch. In the afternoons, she teaches him the basics of magic, which he has in abundance." He smiled. "You knew Mrs. Conner as Annabelle McCloud, John."

John blinked. "Annie? And... Connor? Matthias Connor?"

"They married in '59," Nathaniel said with a nod. "He died in the war."

John nodded slowly and finished his coffee. He closed his eyes and took a deep breath. "I'm ready."

"I'll go through your supplies, pack up something for us to take with. I don't expect us to be able to ride in and do what needs to be done without spending time planning," Avriel said. "Nathaniel, tell Hopaii that we'll be leaving? And Papa, would you saddle John's horse?"

Nathaniel nodded and stood up. "I'll bring our horses up, too," he said. He leaned down to kiss Avriel, then left the dugout. Parsons swallowed the last of his coffee and followed.

Avriel watched them go, then turned to face John. She folded her hands and rested them on the table. "He's told me about you," she said. "He missed you terribly."

"I missed him," John replied. "I didn't understand why he wanted nothing to do with me after that one night. I thought I'd done something wrong."

"Is it why you left?"

John frowned slightly. "It might have been part of it. In truth, it was time for me to go. I'd been here twenty years, and it was long past time for me to move on. I was here before the town was established. When I first went to Skullyville, it was called Choctaw Agency, because that's really all that was there. It was the Choctaw agency, a stage stop, and Miller's general store. Oh, and the jail."

He frowned. "I was close enough to Fort Coffee to ride out and trade with them once every few months. Then Choctaw Agency was founded, and I started going there — it was closer. That's when I met Nathaniel." He sniffed. "All new people, it was easy to make them believe that I was the child of settlers who had passed away. They had no way of knowing otherwise. But they started looking oddly at me when thirteen years had passed and I hadn't changed."

Avriel nodded. "I understand that. It's why I left San Francisco. I won't live nearly as long as my father, but I'm already past fifty, and people were starting to fuss."

Parsons appeared in the doorway. "The horses are ready," he said. "It's time we go."

John stood up and started toward the pegs where his coat and hat hung. Halfway there, he stopped.

"A moment," he said, more to himself than to the others. He turned and went through the curtain to the bed, reaching under the bed for his case. He opened it and took out the rifle-green kepi. He held it for a moment, then put it on. It felt strange, but right.

He'd worn this in service to his adopted country. Fighting, as he'd told Nathaniel, on the side of the angels.

He'd wear it once more in service of his heart. Fighting to save his own angel.

CHAPTER NINE
Gloaming

They were almost to the mounds when John realized how late in the day it actually was — he must have been hanging there for hours before Nathaniel and the others had arrived. The sun was dipping down toward the horizon as they stopped in a stand of trees.

"We won't have a lot of time," he said, peering off into the distance. He could just see the mounds. "Where are we going?"

"It's about a mile or so," Parsons said. "The passage is on the far side of the second largest mound." He pointed. "That one. Do you see anything?"

"Smoke. They must have a fire. No guards, and that's a good thing," John answered. "As flat as the ground is around here, if we can see them, then they can see us. There's no way to scout."

Parsons chuckled. "Avriel?"

"Yes, Papa. I'm off," she said. "John, come with me. I'll be able to hide you."

John nodded and urged Barak to follow her. As he rode up alongside her, he felt his skin tingle, as if he'd been in the sun too long.

"Was that you?"

"You felt it?" Avriel asked. "Yes. We're hidden from view now." She frowned as she looked toward the mounds. "What do you think?"

"I think I don't know yet," John answered. "I think there's no real cover, and unless you can hide all four of us, there's no way we can get to them without being seen."

"Papa can hide Nathaniel," Avriel said. "What else?"

"I don't know how many men he has," John said. "I do know that once I start shooting, he'll do something drastic. So... yes, that might be the way."

"What?"

"Find me a place where I can get a clear shot," he said. "While you and your father go in under concealment. I'll take down his men while you get Ethriel."

Avriel nodded slowly. "Perhaps. Let's see if that will work." They skirted around the mounds, and John studied the terrain. There wasn't much cover close to the mounds. Nor were there trees that he could climb for a vantage point. They grew closer and closer to the plume of smoke, until they came around the curve of the second largest mound, and Avriel gasped something. John didn't understand what she said, but he understood why.

They could see right into Buach's camp.

There was a fire, just as they'd expected. There were men milling around it — John counted a half dozen of them. He didn't see Buach, and for a moment, he didn't see Ethriel.

"Do you see him?" he whispered.

"I don't... yes. Yes, there," Avriel pointed. "On the ground. Do you see?"

John rose up in his stirrups but couldn't see what she meant. It didn't matter – he could hear them. Hear the sound of Ethriel's voice, a muffled cry of pain. He licked his lips and raised the Henry.

"There's only six," he murmured. "I could kill them all right now."

"But where's Buach?" Avriel asked.

John shook his head and looked around. "Does it matter? What can he do, if he's alone?"

"He's a mage, and he's more powerful than I am," Avriel answered. "If we're killing the snake, we've got to cut off the head."

John swallowed, feeling the anger rising. "But they're hurting him."

"Hurts mend," Avriel answered. "For him, dead is forever. If you warn Buach we're out here by shooting, he'll kill Ethriel without a blink. He doesn't need the wedding to rule. He rules already." She rested her hand on John's arm. "Have you seen what you need to see?"

John gritted his teeth and lowered the rifle. "Let's go the rest of the way around. I want to see the vantage from the larger mound."

They rode on, and John tried to convince himself that she was right. That he had to wait. That he could not afford another disaster like Cold Harbor.

If he made a mistake here, it could cost him everything.

Once they were on the far side of the mound, he drew Barak to a stop. "I'm going to the top of the mound," he said. "Do you have to come with me? Will the magic work at a distance?"

"I'm not sure how far," Avriel answered. "So I'd best come. Will your horse stay?"

"I haven't any idea," John admitted. "He's only been mine since Friday."

Avriel nodded. "I'll have a word with him, then."

John wasn't sure what she meant by that, until he dismounted. Avriel took his reins from him, and stepped up close to Barak, murmuring to him in the same musical language that Ethriel spoke. Barak nudged her with his nose and snuffled, then started to graze

"He'll stay with Meadowlark," she said. "Let's climb."

"I want to learn that trick," John murmured as they started scrambling up the steep side of the mound.

Avriel laughed. "You'll have to learn our language first."

"I've no complaints about that. I'll teach Ethriel English, and he can teach me whatever it is that you speak."

The mound grew steeper, and conversation stopped as the climb got harder. At the top, John crouched and took a moment to breathe, then crawled to the far side of the mound and lay down, looking down at the camp. He was looking straight down at

Ethriel, and he wasn't sure if the moan that he heard was from him or from Avriel.

The guards had driven two stakes into the ground, and bound Ethriel between them, stretched out flat on his back. One of the guards stopped and kicked him as John watched, and he heard another muffled cry of pain, felt it like a slap. He closed his eyes and shivered. Hurts would mend, Avriel had said. He opened his eyes and studied the scene again with the trained eye of a sharpshooter.

"This is good," he whispered, his voice sounding harsh. "This is very good." He looked at Avriel. "Go get the others. When you get back, send Nathaniel up here. When he gets here, I'll start shooting. You get in and get Ethriel."

"That's more than a bit foolhardy," Avriel murmured. Then she looked up. "But we've no time. It will be near dark by the time I get back." She looked down at the camp again. "You won't be hidden once I'm gone."

"I won't be moving once you're gone," John replied. "I'm not risking his life."

Avriel nodded. She touched his arm, then crawled back the way they'd come and vanished down the far side of the mound. As she left, the prickling sensation faded from John's skin. He ducked his head, and crawled a little closer to the downhill slope, the better to see.

The sun sank slowly, casting long shadows and revealing that John had forgotten to take one thing into account.

The sun was setting behind him. Behind the mound. The entire camp would be in shadow by the time Avriel and the others got back. He'd have to be careful not to look directly at their fire. He folded his arms around his rife, rested his chin on his hands and watched.

Buach appeared. John wasn't sure where he'd come from. Had he walked out of thin air? Had he been hidden? It didn't matter —

he started giving orders, and the men started moving around with purpose.

Striking their camp.

John raised his head and looked at the eastern horizon. No sign of the moon. What were they doing?

Then he heard a shout, and two more guards came into view, dragging someone between them.

Nathaniel?

He heard a footstep behind him and rolled, taking aim… only to relax when he saw Avriel. She nodded to him, then crept closer to stretch out next to him on the ground.

"He volunteered to act as a distraction. Papa is down there as well, under concealment," she whispered. "Hopaii is with the horses. We've not much time. Papa will signal when he's in place."

"And in the meantime, Nate's just handed himself over to Buach as another hostage," John grumbled.

"I did try to talk him out of it," Avriel whispered back. "I hate that he's putting himself in danger. He has no idea what to do in a fight."

John snorted, resettling himself, then rising up on his elbows and bringing the Henry to ready. "Can you conceal us? I don't want them to see the flash when I start shooting. And you didn't know Nate when he was eighteen."

All at once the prickling feeling was back, and John shifted for a better, more stable shooting position.

"Meaning what?" Avriel asked.

"Meaning remember what we were saying about being incorrigible at fourteen?" John glanced at her, saw her nod. "Nate carried it on until he was eighteen or so. He used to box."

"Nate?" Avriel said slowly. "My Nate? Used to box?" She sniffed. "You think you know a person. He's never said anything about it!"

John smiled, looking down at the camp. The guards had stopped what they were doing, had moved to surround Buach and Nathaniel. John could hear Buach's voice, but not what he was saying.

"What are we waiting for?" he whispered. Then he saw Ethriel react to something, saw him raise his head. The rope that bound his ankles went slack, but Ethriel didn't move. A moment later, the rope that held his wrists to the second stake was cut.

He vanished.

"Now."

John didn't need Avriel to tell him. He had no clear shot for Buach, so he aimed and fired, ran the lever, fired again, and the two guards holding Nathaniel both dropped. Nathaniel turned and ran; John didn't stop to see if he vanished, too, because he was still shooting. Another guard fell, then another. Then one who had been standing on Buach's far side. John swore softly — he'd finally had a clear shot at Buach, but the man had vanished just as John had fired.

"Scorch him!" Avriel snapped. "He's either gone after Ethriel, or he's coming for us. We need to go."

John nodded and got up, sprinting for the far side of the mound, scrambling and sliding down, hearing Avriel behind him. He could hear shouting, and knew that the remaining guards were on the hunt. At the bottom of the mound, he saw Hopaii and the horses. Saw Nathaniel running around the left side of the mound to meet them. And then, blinking back into view....

Ethriel.

John hit level ground at a run, drawn to Ethriel like a needle to a lodestone. A half breath later, Ethriel was in his arms, his still-bound wrists caught between them as he gasped out words that John didn't understand. Except for one word.

"John!"

"We need to get out of here," Nathaniel hissed, bringing the horses closer. "Parsons, cut those ropes! Abby, he can ride double with you—"

"I thought getting clear was more important," Parson grumbled, coming toward John with a knife. John kissed Ethriel quickly, then stepped back and let Parsons slice through the ropes. Ethriel winced and rubbed his wrists, then threw his arms around John; John put his free arm around Ethriel's shoulders and kissed the top of his head.

"Where are we going?" he asked. "We need to go now. Avriel, Parsons, one of you tell Ethriel."

Avriel came toward him, putting her hand on Ethriel's shoulder and speaking to him softly. Ethriel nodded and let go of John.

"What about Buach?" Nathaniel asked as he mounted his horse.

John heard... something. A twig snapping? Grass rustling? He wasn't sure. It didn't matter — he turned, ran the lever, and fired, all in a single flowing motion. One of Buach's guards appeared as he hit the ground. John looked at the ground, saw the bent grass behind the dead man. He ran the lever and fired again, and Buach howled in pain as he tumbled to the ground, his hand clasped to his bleeding left shoulder.

"Get to the horses," John said over his shoulder. He reached into his pocket and pulled out cartridges, carefully reloading as he walked toward Buach. By the time he reached the wounded elf, the Henry was fully loaded. He stopped several feet from Buach and raised the rifle, running the lever.

"John."

"Ethriel, go back to the horses," John said without turning.

"John, he wants to talk to Buach," Parsons said. "He'll be safe enough back here."

John licked his lips, then nodded. "Translate what he says for me, will you?"

"I was going to," Parsons said.

Ethriel started speaking, and Parsons translated, "Your life is forfeit, cousin. But in my mother's memory, I'm granting you mercy. Go back, and leave me here in peace—"

"He's really letting this bastard go?" John growled.

"He's the King," Parsons answered. "His word is law."

Ethriel continued, and Parsons translated the rest. "I'm not going back with you. You may hold my throne. For now. Just know that one day, I'll come for it. My John and I will come for it."

John nodded, warmed by Ethriel's declaration. My John. He liked that. "My King has spoken," he said. "Your answer, Buach?"

"How are you not dead?" Buach spat. "I killed you!"

"You'll find that I'm an impossible man to kill," John answered. "You, however, are not. Your answer?"

Buach snarled. "He's mine. Filthy human. You've no right to touch him!"

John snorted. "I had the invitation. That grants me the right. And that's not the point. He's not yours. And he's not going with you. You leave, or you die." He resettled the rifle. "Last chance."

Buach glared at him, then winced. "I will go," he growled. "But I will be back for what's mine."

"Oh, good," John said. "It will give me something to look forward to." He stepped back. "Up. Keep your hands on your head."

"I can't move my left arm!" Buach snapped.

"Then put your right hand on your head," John answered. "Up. Move."

Buach scowled, then shifted, moving onto his knees. He stopped there and shook his right hand once, a fast gesture that

John thought was to shake blood from his hands. Too late, he saw the glittering darts.

"No!" John moved, trying to put himself between Ethriel and the darts. He felt them hit... and heard Ethriel cry out.

John landed, hearing the Henry roar as it misfired. He heard Avriel and Nathaniel shouting, but couldn't make out the words over the sound of blood rushing in his ears. What had those darts been? The wounds burned... but the pain was already fading. He blinked, and opened his eyes to see Buach standing over him.

"Human," he snarled, making the word sound like a curse. "Pathetic human. If I can't have him, neither can you. Not that you'll outlive him long. Do you know what elfshot is?" He sniffed. "Maybe one of these traitors will have time to explain before you die."

He turned away. John growled softly and rolled onto his side, propping himself up on his elbow. The Henry lay nearby, and he reached for it. The burning pain had faded to a memory by the time he got to his feet. He ran the lever once more.

At the sound, Buach turned, his eyes wide. "What? How? What are you?"

"I told you," John said softly. "I'm impossible to kill."

"John!" Nathaniel came up behind him. "We need to get Ethriel back to town. Now."

"Go," John said. "Tell him I'm coming. Leave Barak and go."

"But—" Nathaniel stopped. "Right. We're taking him home. Our home. Meet us there."

John nodded and heard Nathaniel hurry away. He heard the sounds behind him, moans of pain, Avriel's soft voice, trying to offer comfort. His name, called by a broken, pain-filled voice that he prayed he'd hear again. Then the sound of horses, moving away. Good. Now all he could hear was Buach's breathing...

And the breaking of his own heart.

"What are you?" Buach demanded again. There were notes of panic in his voice.

"I am Yohanan ben Zavdi," John answered in a low voice. "The Choctaw call me the Hattak Falaya. I am the Beloved of God, blessed and cursed to walk the world and wait His coming. I'll see the world burn at the end of days, and by His holy name, you have vexed me for the last time." He ran the lever, raising the Henry and watching Buach turn pale.

"The Undying One. You're the Undying One," Buach stammered.

John snorted. "And here I just got finished saying that. You're a smart one."

Buach swayed, fell to his knees. "Mercy!" he croaked. "I cry you mercy!"

John blinked. "Mercy?" he repeated. "What mercy did you offer me? Did you offer him?" He nodded in the direction the others had taken Ethriel. "All he wanted was to be left alone."

Buach's face hardened. "He was mine," he spat. "He belonged to me!"

"You know, we just finished a war over that here," John said. "About people thinking they could own another person. They lost. You lost."

Buach whimpered, then whispered, "He... he said I could walk away."

"And you murdered him for it," John snapped.

The Henry roared.

JOHN STOOD OVER THE body for a time, until he was certain that Buach was dead. Then he mounted Barak and rode around the mounds, counting bodies. There were six dead guards, and no signs of the other two. He wasn't sure where they were, or what had happened to them. The moon had risen by the time he had made his way all the way back to where Buach's body was cooling.

"If you're still out there," he called. "Do what you want. But if you come after me, you'll join him." He turned his horse to the west and started back to Skullyville. Everything in him wanted to kick Barak into a gallop, get to town as fast as he could. But he held himself and his horse in check. It wasn't far, but he didn't want to risk Barak to a gopher hole in the dark. Still, the horse seemed to understand his urgency, and picked up his pace. The moon rose behind him, and John looked up at the stars.

"Don't take him from me," he whispered. "Not when I've only just found him. Not when I finally have hope again."

There was no answer. There was never an answer, and John turned his attention back to the ride.

When he finally reached Skullyville, the town was quiet and dark. He dismounted Barak in front of the mercantile, and lead the horse around to where he knew the stable was. There was a boy waiting there.

"Mister Zebedee?" he said. "I'm Jeremiah Miller. My father said you were coming, and that you were to give your horse to me."

"Thank you," John said. He handed the reins to the boy and looked at the house.

"He's still alive," Jeremiah said softly. "Mama says to go straight in. First room at the top of the stairs. And leave your rifle in the kitchen. The house is warded."

"So was mine," John replied. "Right. Thank you, Jeremiah. Barak, behave."

Jeremiah grinned. "He'll be fine. I have some supper for him. Go on in, sir. Papa is expecting you."

CHAPTER TEN
Evanesce

The night slowed to a crawl. John sat in an uncomfortable straight-backed chair next to the bed, and watched as Ethriel struggled to breathe. He didn't wake, didn't move, and his face was pale as milk.

Parsons leaned against the wall next to the door, his arms folded over his chest. He looked old and tired. "I never should have let him get close," he said softly. "I should have listened to you and kept him back. I should never have allowed—"

"There's no point in blaming yourself. It's done," John said. "And it's Buach's fault, from the start to the end. Now, tell me what this elfshot is. What does it do?"

Parsons sighed and nodded. "That's forbidden magic, the worst kind of forbidden magic. Outlawed long before even Ethriel's mother was born. No one is supposed to know those spells. I don't know how Buach learned them." He paused. "Elfshot. It's a relic from the last great war between the Light Elves and the Mountain Elves. Once it pierces the skin... it kills. The pain is supposed to be excruciating. There's nothing that will stop it, nothing that will dull it. It's a torturous death."

"It burned, where it hit," John said, touching his chest, where one of the darts had pierced the skin. He looked up at Parsons. "There's no cure? There's no magic to undo this? Hopaii can't do anything?"

"He tried, before you got here." Parsons shook his head. "His way... I've never seen anything like that. But it did nothing. Then he went off to see if he could find something that might help. I don't think he will. Among our healers, it's known that there's no cure. None. That's why it was outlawed. Why all record of it was erased—"

"Except that Buach knew," John said. He turned back to the bed, took Ethriel's cold hand. "And someone taught him."

"His mother, I warrant," Parsons said. "The queen's half-sister Siobhan."

"His own family did this to him?" John ran his thumb over Ethriel's knuckles. "Parsons—"

"Parciviel," Parsons murmured. "You can keep calling me Parsons. It's easier to say. But you should know that my name is Parciviel. Sir Parciviel, Knight-Commander of the Silver Thorn. I served in the court of High Queen Méabh and her consort Cathail, and in the court of her father, the High King Eiriell." He sighed. "I swore to Méabh that I would find her son. I swore it as she died. And now I've failed her. I've failed him." He shook his head.

John licked his lips. Without turning, he asked, "Buach said something right before I killed him. He said I was the Undying One. What is that, and why is it important?"

Parson pushed off the wall and crossed to stand next to John's chair. "You... you're the Undying One? I... yes. Yes, I suppose you are. You've done it twice now in front of me."

"And quite a few times when you haven't seen it," John added. "So why is it important?"

"Because there's a prophecy, involving the Shining King, and his consort, the Undying One, and how they'll bring peace to the Elven realms. Elfshot, that came from the last great war. But there have been little wars ever since then between the Light and the Mountain Elves. Border skirmishes, cattle raids. Annoyances more than anything else. We thought it done when High King Eiriell took Siobhan's mother to wife. He was of the Light elves, and her family were high born nobles from the Mountain elves, the last of the Mountain ruling family. Their marriage sealed the peace between the two kingdoms. But Lady Xanthe appeared to be barren, and turned bitter. After years of marriage, she was put aside and sent back to her family. The king married his second wife, the Lady Aoife. She died birthing Méabh." He paused, then raised his hand. "Trust me, I am getting to the prophecy."

John nodded. "I'm not arguing. Go on."

"After the period of mourning for Lady Aoife, messengers came from the Lady Xanthe. She'd given birth to a daughter, and swore the child was Eiriell's. It had been nigh unto ten of your years since their marriage had been put aside, but Eiriell took the girl in, named her his daughter. And named Méabh his heir for all that she was the younger of the two." He sighed. "He raised them both, even though it was clear that Siobhan was not his blood, not with her so close in age to Méabh. But Méabh loved her, and would hear not a word spoken against her." He paused again. "It's common, among our folk, to seek portents when there are great decisions to be made, and to ask the advice of the seers in the heart of the forest. When Méabh reached her majority, Eiriell took her to the heart of the forest, to seek guidance for her eventual reign." He smiled. "I was there, part of the entourage entrusted with the safety of our Lady Méabh and her sister. So I was there when the prophecy of the Undying One was spoken. It was said that there would come a Shining King, a prince of both bloodlines, who would take to his side a man who could not die. And together, they would bring peace."

"And that Shining King, that's Ethriel?" John asked. "It has to be, doesn't it?"

"Yes, I believe so. Many believe so. But Siobhan thought not. She returned to her mother's people after the prophecy was spoken. When we saw her next, she was a new widow, and arrived with her own child, Buach, who she said was the son of a Mountain lord. They came to court with Cathail. I believe that Eiriell chose him for Méabh, to set the seeds of the prophecy. To sire the Shining King. Cathail was a son of the same old noble line of Mountain elves as Xanthe. Her nephew, if I remember the rumors. I'm not certain – he was disowned by his kin for agreeing to the marriage. But it was a good match, a true match, for all that it was arranged. They loved each other deeply. But they were married many years before Ethriel was born, and lost several babes before him before they drew breath. It was thought by some that Méabh would die childless, that Buach would follow his aunt to the throne. There was pressure from some of the nobles for her to name him heir. And then she found she was pregnant, and bore a living son." Parsons stopped and looked around. "I need a drink. I'll be back."

"Whatever you get, bring one for me," John said, turning back to the bed.

"John—"

"I said what I said, Parsons," John said, his voice quiet. "One drink isn't going to destroy me."

"One drink? No. It's the ones that come after that are the problem." Parsons left the room, and John took Ethriel's hand again.

"You can't leave me, Ethriel," he said softly. "Not after all this. You can't."

There was a soft knock at the door, and Nathaniel slipped inside. "John, come down and eat," he said. "Abby made soup. And sourdough rolls."

John shook his head. "I'll eat later. I'm not leaving him."

Nathaniel came closer and squatted next to John's chair. "John—"

"I'm not leaving him," John repeated. "If I leave, and he—" He didn't finish. Couldn't finish. His throat closed, and he shook his head. Nathaniel nodded. He rose and rested his hand on John's shoulder.

"I'll fetch another chair," he said softly. He left the room, coming back a few minutes later with another straight-backed chair. He sat down next to John, and for several minutes, the only sound was Ethriel's rasping breath.

"What will you do?" Nathaniel asked at length.

John shook his head. "I've no idea. Go. Leave. There's nothing for me here." He paused, then looked at Nathaniel. "I'm sorry. I didn't mean—"

"No offense taken, John," Nathaniel said "I know very well that I'm not yours. You're fond of me, and I of you. That's true. But there's something in your eyes when you look at him that was never there for me. You never looked at me like that." He smiled. "Abby looks at me like that. Julia did, too. That's how I know."

"I don't know what I'm going to do," John said. He looked up as Parsons came back into the room, carrying two clear glasses filled with amber-colored liquid. John took the one offered him and studied it for a moment, then drained it, feeling the familiar burn and spreading warmth from the alcohol. For a moment, he welcomed it. Needed it. Needed the only taste of oblivion he would ever have...

No.

"I know what I'm not doing," he said, handing the empty glass back to Parsons. "That. I'm not crawling back into a bottle. Not again. I'll never come out."

"You're a stronger man than I," Parsons muttered. He drained his own glass, then asked, "You'll be leaving Skullyville? Perhaps when you go, I might join you for a time?"

John looked up in shock. "Why?"

Parsons shrugged. "It feels right. I don't know."

John sighed and took Ethriel's hand again. "I'm not good company, Parsons," he said.

"Then we'll be surly together."

Another knock on the door, and Jeremiah looked in. "Papa, Mama says that you're all to come down and eat something. I'll stay, and shout if anything."

Parsons straightened, and Nathaniel stood up. John didn't move.

"Thank you, but no. I'll stay—"

"Mama expected you'd say that," Jeremiah interjected. "So she said to tell you that if you didn't come, she'd take it as an insult against her cooking."

"I've never even had her cooking to insult it!" John protested.

"Ten minutes, John," Nathaniel said gently. "Or as long as it takes to eat a bowl of soup."

"And I will shout if he wakes up or... or anything," Jeremiah added. "The kitchen is right below us. You'll hear me through the grate." He pointed toward the floor, and a metal grate set into the boards near the wall. John could see light shining through from below. He could smell the soup and the bread.

"John, come down," Nathaniel repeated. "Come and eat something."

John closed his eyes and took a deep breath. He was tired. He'd been tired for a very long time. But there was no rest for him. And there would never again be peace.

"All right," he said. He stood up and leaned over the bed, kissing Ethriel's forehead. "You're not allowed to leave when my back is turned," he whispered. He straightened, and watched as Jeremiah took possession of his chair. The boy looked up at him, his face serious.

"I'll keep a careful watch on him, Mister Zebedee."

"Thank you, Jeremiah."

John followed Nathaniel downstairs, and into the warm, fragrant kitchen. Avriel looked up and must have seen something in his face, because she dropped the dishcloth she was holding and hurried over to embrace him tightly, murmuring, "Oh, John!"

The unexpected affection, and the warmth of her arms around him were enough to shatter the eggshell walls holding him together, and he felt his knees buckling. He ended up on the floor, his face buried in Avriel's arms, sobbing like a lost child. Another pair of arms encircled him, and he heard Nathaniel's voice, offering soft syllables meant to comfort, but which only stung like needles.

Finally, drained and dry as a bone, John pulled free of Avriel's arms and sat up. He wiped his face and looked down at his hands.

"I'm sorry," he murmured.

"You've no reason to be apologizing," Avriel answered. "And every reason to need the release. Come and drink some tea. Then you can eat. Then... well, then we'll see what comes next."

"I'm not sure I can eat," John replied, watching her as she got to her feet. She'd changed out of her mannish clothing, and now looked every bit the proper shopkeeper's wife. Albeit one with pointed ears.

"That's why I said drink tea first," she answered. "'Tis mint and chamomile. T'will calm your nerves a touch and settle your stomach." She went to the table and picked up a teapot, pouring tea into a cup as Nathaniel helped John back to his feet.

"You're welcome here," Nathaniel said. "You know that? You can stay here, as long as you like."

John nodded. "Thank you. But I can't. Once..." He looked up, seeing the grate in the ceiling.

"It's been quiet," Parsons said. John nodded again.

"Once it's done, I'll go. I'll go back out to the dugout, take what I need from there, and go. I don't know where—"

"Bandera?" Avriel said. "Come and sit. Perhaps we have an idea for you."

John went to the table and sat down, taking the teacup from Avriel. "What's a bandera?" he asked. "Other than a flag. We're not talking about flags, are we?"

"No, It's a town in Texas," Nathaniel answered. "And it's... well, it's one of the places where we've been sending the elves in exile. It's safe for them there, because it's... somewhat uncanny." He frowned. "Remember I said Julia's folk were involved in something to do with the uncanny? There was some kind of connection between that and folks in Bandera. So, she would send runaways on to Bandera, with a token to mark them as being under her guidance. I still have some of the tokens. I'll give you one. You can go there."

"Eventually, I might go there," John said, and finished his tea. He closed his eyes and took another deep breath. "What is in that soup?" he asked. "It smells wonderful."

"Beef and barley," Avriel answered. "I'll fill a bowl for you."

The first spoonful was enough to remind John's body that he hadn't eaten a real meal in over a day — he inhaled the soup, drank more tea. Ate two of the sourdough rolls, and was just finishing his second bowl of soup when he looked up to see Avriel looking past him, her eyes wide. He turned, and saw Jeremiah standing in the doorway. The food he'd eaten settled at the pit of his stomach like stones.

"Jem, what are you doing down here?" Nathaniel asked slowly.

"Hopaii is back, and he brought the doctor that John sent for," Jeremiah said. "No one told me that there was a doctor coming. And he has a funny glow to him. I've never seen anything like it. They sent me down."

John blinked. "A doctor that *I* sent for?" he repeated. "I... I never sent for anyone." He looked up at the grate, then bolted from his chair. "Ethriel!" he shouted, thundering up the stairs, hearing Nathaniel and Parsons behind him. He saw Hopaii at the top, standing outside Ethriel's door. The old man looked tired but very pleased.

"Calm down, John," he said, holding his hands up. "All of you. It's fine."

"Fine?" John gasped. "Who's in there?"

Hopaii smiled. "An old friend of yours. Who didn't look at all the way I expected him to."

"An old..." He looked at the door. Then he looked at Hopaii. "What have you done?"

"Called in a few favors for an old friend," Hopaii answered. He reached out and knocked twice on the door. "Go in."

John turned the knob and walked into the bedroom. As he crossed the threshold, the room went dark. He froze, hearing the door click closed behind him.

"Ethriel?" he called. "Who's here?"

"Ethriel is asleep," a voice he'd almost forgotten answered, speaking Aramaic. "Hello, Yohanan."

"Joshua," John breathed.

"You know, I do like that better. It's closer to what my mother calls me. She sends her love, by the way."

John closed his eyes. Mother Miryam sent her love. Why did that not surprise him? He opened his eyes again, but it was still dark. "Why can't I see?"

A breath, and a low chuckle. "Because... I wasn't as careful as I should have been," came the grudging admission. "I worded something very badly, a long time ago. I spoke rashly, and without thinking—"

"They say you're omniscient, you know."

A long pause. "I wasn't then, Yohanan. I hadn't yet gotten that part. Now let me finish. I am deeply sorry for the pain I've caused you. But you won't see me again. Not until the end of days. Because it will be your seeing me that heralds the end of days."

John blinked, wishing his vision would clear. Then he truly heard the words. "What?"

"On the day you see me again, and know me, it will be the end of your days. The end of your wait. The end of everything." Joshua sighed. "So, you can't see me now. Because it's not time yet. Just know that I watch you. Often. I hear you. Every word you say to me—"

"About that," John blurted. "I'm sorry—" Joshua laughed, that wonderful laugh that John had forgotten even in his dreams. He moaned softly, only to feel warm, familiar arms around him. He rested his head on Joshua's shoulder.

"I knew you never meant a word of it," Joshua said. "I never thought you did. I'm so sorry you suffered."

John nodded, feeling the rough weave of a shirt against his cheek, and the solid muscle underneath the shirt. "I still love you. I miss you so much."

"I love you, too. And I miss you. And I don't want you to be alone anymore." He paused, and John could almost hear him smiling. And he remembered Buach saying that he didn't know how Ethriel had escaped, or how he had slipped from the elven world into this one.

"You... you did it. You brought Ethriel here."

"I found him, and I helped him to escape, and I guided him here to you," Joshua said. "You were meant for each other, even before any of us were born. Did you know you were the same age?"

"Parsons told me that," John answered. "Is that important?"

"You were born at the same moment," Joshua answered. "You're two halves of a whole. One that I had the pleasure of sharing for a time. My mistake? My bidding you to wait until I come again? That mistake will let the both of you save his world. So perhaps I didn't make as much of a mistake as I thought." He chuckled again, and

John felt warm hands sliding up his arms, up his throat. Warm lips brushed against his.

"Joshua," John whispered. "Did you... what have you done? To Ethriel?"

That warm laugh again. "He'll wake at dawn, and be well."

John swallowed. "Thank you. And... how much longer will it be? Until the end?"

A deep sigh. "That, I don't know."

"Omniscient?"

"All right. I do know. But I can't tell you." Joshua laughed. "Now, I need to go. You're rich in your friends, Yohanan. Hiloha is quite a man."

John paused, then asked, "Hiloha? Do you mean Hopaii?"

"Yes. His name is Hiloha. His title is Hopaii."

John laughed. "I'd always wondered. I never asked. I didn't want to offend him. What did he do?"

"Ask him when you wake up," Joshua answered. He kissed John on the forehead, then on the lips. "He'll have instructions for you. Now rest, and be happy, my Yohanan. You'll see me again. Eventually."

Before John could say another word, he felt himself falling.

JOHN WOKE UP TO THE sounds of loud birdsong. The bed was warm, and there was someone warm curled up against him. He rolled toward them, pulling them into his arms. Long hair tangled in his fingers. Ethriel. There was something, some nightmare about losing him, but he didn't want to think about that. The bed was soft and warm, and it would be so easy to go back to sleep.

"Good morning."

Ethriel's voice. Strong. Lightly accented.

English.

John opened his eyes to see Ethriel leaning over him. "Good morning," he repeated. Then he smiled.

"You..." John sat up and looked around. The room in the Miller house.

It hadn't been a nightmare. Which meant...

"Joshua was here," he said. Ethriel nodded and sat up.

"He told me that I wasn't allowed to leave you yet," Ethriel said. "He brought me back. And he told me that I needed to be able to speak to you." He laughed. "I don't know how he put a language in my head, but I do like being able to talk to you." He reached out and took John's hands. "I'm sorry. I didn't mean to frighten you."

"It was none of your fault," John answered. "And I frightened you first."

"He killed you," Ethriel said softly. "I thought I'd lost you."

"I could say the same." John pulled Ethriel into his arms. "I thought I'd lost you. I thought I was going to be alone again." He closed his eyes. "I love you."

Ethriel sighed and relaxed in John's arms. "I love you," he murmured. "John, she's going to come for us. Once she knows Buach is dead."

John nodded. "We won't be here when she arrives. Joshua said that Hopaii would have instructions for me. For us. We can go find him—"

Ethriel laughed softly, and pushed John backwards onto the bed. "Later."

CHAPTER ELEVEN
Dawn

John heard voices from below as he and Ethriel made their way downstairs hand in hand. The clothes that had been left for them were, John thought, Nathaniel's — the trousers were too long, as were the shirt sleeves. With rolled up sleeves and cuffed trouser legs, he and Ethriel looked like children dressed in cast-offs. As they reached the bottom step, Jeremiah came out of the kitchen. He looked up and smiled.

"Mama!" he called. "They're awake!"

Avriel appeared in the doorway. "And so they are!" she said. "Come down and eat something, the both of you. Jeremiah, go tell your father that they're awake." She wiped her hands off on her apron, then came toward them. She embraced John warmly, then turned to Ethriel and curtsied. He looked startled, then turned to John.

"I don't get to be hugged?" he asked.

Avriel stood up. "I..." She paused. Then she smiled. "Of course you do." She embraced him, then stepped back and asked, "I'm assuming this means you don't want me to call you Your Majesty?"

Ethriel shook his head. "Until I hold the throne, it's an empty title. And I owe you and your family my life, and John's. You're never to use a title with me. Ever."

Avriel nodded. "Come and eat."

They sat down at the table, and Avriel poured coffee. Ethriel sat with his hands wrapped around his cup, looking down at it.

"Deep thoughts?" John asked.

"I'm not sure what I should do now," Ethriel answered. "I'm not strong enough to fight her. Not yet. I'm not strong enough to take the throne, or hold it. I have no men. I have no following. As far as I know, everyone thinks I died with my parents. If I go back now—"

"We're not going back now," John said. "That's the only thing I do know. Avriel, where is Hopaii? Joshua said that he'd have instructions for us."

"He's gone to the school to fetch his daughter," Avriel answered. "They're in a bit of a state over there, what with Reverend Kerry disappearing the way he did." She turned toward them and started scooping scrambled eggs and potatoes onto plates. "From what we're hearing this morning, he slipped away in the middle of the night, and took with him a good portion of their tuition funds. The matron is asking for those who can take their children home to do so. She's worried that they won't have the money to feed them all through the winter."

John frowned. "Why would he do that?" he asked. "Steal their money."

"Is there anything that can be done?" Ethriel added.

Avriel shook her head. "To lay a false trail, I imagine. And Papa has gone back out to the mounds, to see what he can find. In the light of day, it's safe enough."

"Except that two of the guards were unaccounted for," John said. "How long ago did he leave?"

"Long enough that I'm back," Parsons said as he came into the kitchen. He once again looked like the old man from the *Cavalier*. "There wasn't a thing to be found there. Not even bodies."

"She knows, then," Ethriel said softly. "We need to leave."

"We will," John said. "As soon as we hear from Hopaii. Parsons, do you still want to travel?"

"If my King allows," Parsons answered, and bowed to Ethriel.

"So long as you stop doing that," Ethriel said. "I recognized you last night, Sir Parciviel. I remember you from my mother's court."

"I'm honored, Your—" Parsons stopped. Then he laughed. "Forgive me. It will take me time to remember. Ethriel."

"You trained my grandfather," Ethriel said. "You were his master at arms."

"A very long time ago," Parsons said. "But yes."

"And you taught my mother. Would you train me?" Ethriel asked. "I don't know anything I need to know. My real training in arms and in magic should have started after I came of age. My mother talked of it. I was to go and meet with the seers to learn what my fate would be. Then there would be a celebration, and I would formally be named heir. Then my training would begin. None of that ever happened. There was never the journey. Never a celebration of my passage into adulthood." He looked down at his hands, at the scars on his wrists. "I came of age in chains."

"What?" John looked up at Parsons. "You told me that he'd only been held a year!"

"One of our years, John." Parsons sighed and sat down at the table. "Our time runs differently."

"I..." John frowned. "Thomas mentioned that. And you did. I remember now."

"Thomas?" Ethriel brightened. "Thomas the poet? He served in Mother's court! He sang the loveliest songs. And he taught me to play his harp. Do you know him?"

"He's long since died, but yes. I did know him." John frowned. "It's been... six hundred years, I think? Yes, that's about right." He looked at Parsons. "How long is your year?"

"One hundred of yours," Parsons answered. "Approximately."

John closed his eyes, swearing softly in Aramaic. He heard Ethriel cough, and opened his eyes to see a shocked look on Ethriel's face.

"You understood that?" John asked.

"I didn't know he'd put more than one language in my head," Ethriel answered with a nod. "That... what language was that?"

"Aramaic. No one speaks it anymore."

"You do," Ethriel smiled. "And now, so do I." He reached out and took John's hand, but turned his attention to Parsons. "Will you teach me?" he asked again. "There's so much I need to know before I can even think of trying to take the throne back from my aunt."

Parsons looked down at the table, his face solemn. Then he nodded. "I will teach you. And we will find others, those who have fled between the worlds and have taken shelter here. We'll build your army, my King."

"I'm not a King yet," Ethriel said. He turned his head. "There's someone there."

John turned in his chair and saw Hopaii leading a girl into the kitchen. She looked curiously at them, and smiled at Avriel.

"Good morning, Mrs. Miller," she said. "Aki says Jeremiah is home?"

"He is, Talula," Avriel said. "We had a long night, so I kept him home from school today. He's probably in the store with his father. You may go find him, if your father says you might. And perhaps you could help him with his history lesson?"

Talula nodded and looked up at Hopaii, who smiled at her. She disappeared from the kitchen like a bird taking flight, and Hopaii came to the table and sat down.

"I'm told you have instructions for me," John said. "But first, I want to know what you did."

Hopaii laughed. "I told you. I called in some favors. You remember when my father died, don't you?"

"That bad winter, yes," John said, nodding.

"I have been Hopaii since I was younger than my Talula. I have served Ohoyo Osh Chishba a long time." He touched his chest, over his heart. "She knows me well. I went out and called her. I asked her if she would speak to Nanapesa and see if word could be passed on to someone who could help. I thought that perhaps it would be one of Ethriel's own folk who answered. I wasn't expecting who I got." He frowned slightly. "He isn't a white man, like they teach."

John burst out laughing. "You've known me for how long? You know how I look. Did you honestly think he would be different?"

Hopaii shrugged. "They make it seem that way. But it wouldn't be the first time that white men lied to us. He's a nice boy, your Joshua. Wish his followers were more like him."

"I agree with you," John said. "What are our instructions?"

"You're to go south. I'll go with you to the Red River. That's as far as I can take you. He said you know the name of the place you need to go—"

"Bandera?" John asked. Hopaii nodded.

"That's right. There are others of Ethriel's folk there. Others who'll help him prepare. Other allies for you both." He paused, frowning. "Don't go back to the dugout. Stay here tonight. Tomorrow, you leave and you go south and west. Don't cross the river. There's a place that will look like a good stopping point, on the far side. But no matter what, do not stop there. It's not safe."

"Wraithtown," Avriel murmured. "It's... yes, not safe is a good way to describe it."

"I've been there," Parsons said abruptly. "I won't go back if I can help it. The mayor there... Wraith. He's... unpredictable. We'll pass it by."

Hopaii nodded. "You'll find allies in Bandera," he repeated. "And, more important, she can't reach you there. Not unless she goes overland. And Wraith won't allow that. He's jealous of his power. He won't let her pass."

"You mean my aunt," Ethriel said. "Why can't she just go around? She can walk between the worlds—"

"There's something in the ground there," Parsons answered. "Something in the stones. There are no portals to our world in

Bandera, for all that the land has magic in it the likes of which I've never felt before. When the time comes for you to go back, you'll have to come back here."

John nodded. He leaned back in his chair and closed his eyes. "There are things I'll need at the dugout. The wagon. Supplies. Tools."

"Tell me, and I'll go," Parsons said. "I saw the wagon in the barn. I'll load it and drive it back."

John smiled. "Thank you." He frowned, thinking. The trip would be long, and over unfamiliar ground. "Before we leave, we'll need good maps. We'll need clothes for both of us. Food that will keep. Weapons, and more ammunition." He looked over at Hopaii. "He wants us to leave tomorrow? Hopaii, I don't think we can. Just getting the ammunition for the Henry will take weeks!"

"He says you leave tomorrow," Hopaii insisted. "Mrs. Miller, mind if I leave my girl here with you? I'll go help Parsons load up the wagon."

"I appreciate that," Parsons said. "John, might I borrow your horse?"

"Of course," John said. "I'll make a list for you of what I'll want you to bring especially."

John spent the rest of the day in a flurry of planning. He wrote up a list that explained exactly where in the dugout everything was, and what he wanted from the barn. Then he sat down with Avriel and went over the mercantile's inventory, picking things out for the journey and making more lists. What they had on hand. What would need to be ordered from Fort Gibson, or further afield. John studied the lists and scowled, trying to keep his temper. Ethriel sat opposite them at the table, his fists stacked one atop the other and his chin resting on them, watching.

"Clothes," John said. "And boots for Ethriel. I'm not sure how much we can sew before tomorrow—"

"We have some ready-to-wear," Avriel said. "I'll fetch what we have, and we can alter it to fit." She stood up and turned toward the kitchen door, only to stop. "Nathaniel! Is it midday already?"

"No, I've got to go back out," Nathaniel said. "I came to see how everyone was."

"I'm about to start pulling my hair out, to be honest," John admitted.

"No," Ethriel murmured, "I like your hair."

"Figuratively, Ethriel."

"I like your figurative hair, too."

John bit his lip and looked at Ethriel, who grinned at him. Then he looked at Nathaniel. "There's no way for me to properly supply us to leave tomorrow. It cannot be done. Not from your stores. Not without sending to Fort Gibson, or to Little Rock. It will take weeks to properly provision us. I don't see how we can leave tomorrow."

"We'll do what we can," Nathaniel said. "Now, is that the plan? Leave tomorrow? And go where?"

"Hopaii says we're to go to Bandera," John answered. "And find Ethriel's people there. Start building an army. Parsons is coming with us, to help teach Ethriel."

Nathaniel nodded slowly. "Right. Abby?"

"Oh. Now?"

"Can you think of a better time?" Nathaniel asked. He sighed. "We'll follow you. It might take us a month or so until we leave, but we'll meet you in Bandera."

"What?" John gasped. "Why?"

"Jeremiah," Nathaniel answered. "He's coming into his magic, and he needs someplace safer than Skullyville to do it. And he needs a more advanced teacher than Annie Connor, and she's the first to say it. So we'll follow you. I've been expecting it, so I've laid the groundwork. Some gossip, here and there, about wanting to head out west. There's a young fellow, a gambler who travels the river. He's been looking to buy the mercantile. The next time he's in town, I'll see what he's offering."

"Nathaniel, bring what we have in ready-to-wear into the house?" Avriel said. "I'm going to have to play seamstress. And, I presume, laundress when Papa and Hopaii come back?"

"I'm not going to ask you to do my laundry, Avriel," John said. "And I can help you sew."

AVRIEL RAISED HER HEAD and laid down the shirt she was sewing. "That sounds like Papa."

John nodded, not looking up from teaching Ethriel to sew a hem. He heard Parsons call his name. Then the man came into the parlor. "John, you want to see this," he said.

John blinked. "What is it? What's wrong?"

"Nothing is wrong," Parsons said. "Just... come and see."

John set the trousers he was working on aside and got up. He followed Parsons out of the parlor and to the back of the house. Outside, and into the yard next to the stable. There, he stopped. Barak was harnessed to a covered wagon.

"That's not my wagon," he said.

Hopaii came over and nodded. "That's what was in your barn, so I would guess it is."

"But..." John looked at the wagon. "I didn't *have* a covered wagon."

"Go look inside," Parsons said.

John looked at him, then walked around to the back of the wagon, climbing up to look in. Boxes and barrels, and all of them neatly packed and labeled. His case was packed with new, clean clothes. There was another case, and he opened it to see more clothes. Would these fit Ethriel?

"It was like this when we got there," Parsons said. "Come look under the seat."

John jumped down and came around to the front of the wagon. There was a metal box underneath the seat, and when he opened it, he found at least a dozen boxes of .44 caliber cartridges. He stared at them for a moment, then leaned on the wagon and laughed.

"John, where did this all come from?" Parsons asked.

"Joshua," John wheezed around his laughter. He looked up. "You know, the loaves and fishes were impressive enough. This... this is just showing off!" A breeze kissed his face, and he heard a distant echo of familiar laughter. He grinned. "Thank you."

THEY WOKE BEFORE DAWN, and were ready before the birds started to sing. John checked the harness, the wheels, walking a wide circle around the wagon before stopping next to Barak's head. He reached up to scratch the horse's forehead, then turned toward Nathaniel and Avriel, who stood in the doorway. Their goodbyes had already been said in the kitchen, but they'd insisted on seeing them off.

"We're ready," he said. "We'll see you again in Bandera."

"Be careful," Nathaniel said. He walked over to John and held up a pouch. "Take this. It's one of Julia's tokens. It might help."

John took the pouch and felt his fingers tingle. "What is this?" he asked, tucking it into his shirt pocket.

"I don't know," Nathaniel answered. "She wouldn't tell me. Be careful, John."

"You, too," John said. "Keep your heads down, both of you. If she comes looking—"

"She won't find us," Avriel said. "We'll follow you soon enough." She smiled, then turned back into the kitchen.

Nathaniel hesitated, then held his hand out. "Be careful," he repeated.

John took his hand, and wasn't surprised when Nathaniel pulled him in and hugged him. The kiss did surprise him, and he smiled as Nathaniel pulled back.

"For old time's sake," Nathaniel murmured. "See you in a few months."

John nodded. He climbed up into the wide seat of the wagon and unwrapped the reins from the brake. He looked back into the wagon, and Ethriel smiled at him from inside. Parsons said that the first spell they'd work on would be the one that made him look human, but until he mastered it, they had decided that Ethriel would stay under cover, at least until they were out of town. Parsons had already ridden out, and was waiting in the street with Hopaii.

"Right. We're off," John said. He snapped the reins, and the wagon started to roll.

As they left Skullyville, the birds began to sing the sunrise.

John Zebedee and the Monstrous Town

CHAPTER ONE
Partings

JOHN HAD NEVER SEEN the Red River before.

It was rare to come across something that he'd never seen before. But then, he'd never been this far west either. Everything was new and different and interesting, and he was having trouble keeping from smiling at the wonder of it all. He was in love with someone who would live as long as he would. He wasn't alone anymore, and now things were new and different. For the first time in a very long time, he was happy. For the first time in a very long time, immortality was the blessing it had been meant to be.

"You are in a very good mood," Ethriel said. John looked at the elf sitting next to him on the wagon seat, and gave in to temptation and the fact that there was no one to see them as he leaned over to steal a kiss.

"I have every reason to be in a very good mood," he answered as he straightened. He snapped the reins and watched as Barak's ears twitched back toward him. Even the horse was amusing him today. He laughed and looked around for either of the men riding alongside the wagon. "How much further?"

"Here." The speaker looked to be older than John, although he'd been a boy when they'd first met. Hopaii was the spiritual leader of the Choctaw people who lived closest to Fort Coffee, and he was one of the few people who knew John's secret. Who knew that John was immortal. "This is where I should leave you."

"Here?" John repeated. He drew back on the reins and the wagon slowed to a stop. "What's special about here?"

Hopaii smiled. "From here I can make it back to shelter before dark," he answered. "I'm going back to the ruins of Fort Towson. Then home."

"You can camp with us tonight." The other rider rode up next to Hopaii. He was another elf, one that was much older than

Ethriel. He had let his human disguise fall away, but John had a hard time thinking of Sir Parciviel as anything but Ben Parsons. "One last night with us before you ride back?"

Hopaii shook his head. "No, it's time for me to go back. I'm far from my own ground. This is where I leave you. Now, listen closely. Before sunset, you will reach Garrett's ferry. He'll offer to carry you across. Do not cross the Red River. Not yet. Stay on the north bank."

John nodded. "All right. For how long?"

"Two days," Hopaii answered. "Late tomorrow, you should reach the place where two rivers come together. The Blue River will come from the north. The Red River comes from the west—"

"Will the water be purple?" Ethriel whispered, and John had to fight to keep from laughing.

Hopaii did smile, but only for a moment. "Stay on the north bank of the Red River for another day, until you reach another ferry. The man who owns it is named Rowlett. Cross the Red River there and go south. You'll come to a town there. I can't remember the name, but that will be a safe place to resupply and to rest. Bandera is south of that. Four days, maybe five, and the path between them is straight as the crow flies."

"Why not cross at the first ford?" Ethriel asked. "Why wait?"

"Wraith," Hopaii answered. "The river is the border of his ground, and the edge of his power. He can't reach you on the north side."

"By all means, we should stay far away from Jacob Wraith," Parsons muttered. He shuddered visibly. "I've been in his town once. I won't go back there again. Not willingly. He wants my head on a platter. Or a pike."

John looked in shock at Parsons. "Why? What happened?"

Parsons shook his head and didn't answer, instead looking up at the sky. "We're past midday," he said. "At least have a bite to eat before you leave?"

Hopaii shook his head. "No. Best if I leave now. If I stay too long, I'll attract his attention, and Wraith... well, it's been a long time. I'm not as young as I once was. Better for me to move on."

"Who is this Wraith?" John asked. "Is he one of..." he paused, trying to remember the word. "Ishkitini?"

Hopaii laughed. "No, he's not. Not Ishkitini. He's not of my folk at all, I know that. I'm honestly not sure what he is, except for old. Old dark power there. A lot of anger, a lot of hate." He paused. "Wraith is dark. Dark and cold, and powerful. And unpredictable. He might be tempted to try his hand against the Hattak Falaya, just for sheer spite. Or boredom. You stay on this side of the river, John.
"

John nodded. He wound the reins around the brake and swung down from the wagon, walking over to Hopaii's horse. "Then this will be the last time I see you for a long time, old friend."

Hopaii's serious expression softened. "Perhaps the last time you see me. I'm not getting any younger. Perhaps the next time you come this way, it will be my Talula who bears the responsibilities of Hopaii and rides out to meet the Hattak Falaya."

"The next time we come this way, it will hopefully be with an army," Parsons said. "Heading for the mounds and the portal."

Hopaii nodded. He swung slowly down from his horse and offered John his hand. John took it, and tugged Hopaii into a tight embrace.

"Take care of yourself, old man," he whispered.

"Who are you calling old?" Hopaii asked with a laugh. He stepped back, his hands on John's shoulders. "Be well, John. Take care of them." He looked past John. "And you take care of him, Ethriel."

"I'll do my best," Ethriel said. He jumped down from the wagon and came to join them, and offered his hand to Hopaii. "I owe you so much, Hopaii. I don't know how to repay any of it."

"You take care of this one," Hopaii answered, nodding toward John as he clasped Ethriel's hand. "He's a trouble magnet."

"I am not!" John protested. Hopaii looked at him, then smiled at Ethriel.

"Take care of him," he repeated. "And yourself. And good luck." He let Ethriel go, and turned to Parsons. "Watch yourself, Parsons. He'll find you if you're not careful."

"Which is why I intend to be exceedingly careful," Parsons replied, his voice grave. "Look in on Avriel for me when you get back, will you? And send my love?"

"I will." Hopaii mounted his horse and resettled himself, then turned his horse back the way they'd come. "Remember. Do not cross at Garrett's Ferry," he called over his shoulder as he rode off.

"We won't!" John called back. He watched Hopaii ride away, then turned back to the wagon. "Let's go. We'll see if we can get past the ferry before we stop for the night."

They stayed only long enough to eat something before starting out again. John drove, with Ethriel sitting next to him. Parsons rode alongside the wagon.

"So what did you do?" John asked. "Why does he want you dead?" He nodded toward the river. "That one. I won't speak his name."

"You know better, hm?" Parsons said. "If you know that much, then you know we shouldn't be discussing this at all. It will attract his attention." He glanced to the south. "When we reach Bandera," he said. "I'll tell you everything. But not here. Not where he might hear us."

"Hopaii said that his power didn't reach across the river," Ethriel said. He leaned forward and looked across John toward the water. "Is the water supposed to be that color?"

"There's a lot of clay in this area," Parsons answered. "It turns the river red after a hard rain. For it to be that red? There must have been a great deal of very heavy rain, quite recently." He glanced toward the river. "I don't want to be disrespectful, but I'm not entirely comfortable with Hopaii's beliefs. I don't trust what lies on the far side of the river, and I'm not going to swear that the river will keep us safe."

John nodded. "Then let's see how fast we can make it to where we really will be safe."

THEY PASSED THE FERRY as the sun sank before them. The ground here was flat prairie, and a person could see for miles in all directions. Which meant that the ferry operator saw them as they passed. John saw someone waving, and waved back without stopping. A few minutes later, Parsons called out, "There's someone coming out to meet us."

John nodded, turning to Ethriel. "Time to be Ethan."

Ethriel nodded. His form shimmered, and a heartbeat later, John was sitting next to a young human, with brilliant green eyes that looked completely normal. He had been practicing this spell under Parsons' tutelage since the night they'd left Skullyville. He still couldn't hold the illusion of being human for very long, but he was getting better at it. John had suggested Ethan as his human name, and planned to tell people who asked that he was Parsons' nephew. Parsons was once again in his human form as well.

"Hello!" someone shouted. "Hold a moment!"

John drew the wagon to a stop, and turned to see the rider coming closer. "We're not crossing," he called back. "Thank you all the same."

"I can offer you a good price," the rider said as he drew his horse in next to the wagon. "I'm Garrett. The ferry is mine. And if you're thinking of heading further west and crossing with Rowlett, I'd think again. There's been flooding west, because of all the storms we've been having the past month. His ferry sank in the last storm."

John blinked and looked at Parsons. "That complicates things," he said. "We were heading for that ferry. We'd been directed there."

Garrett nodded. "Thought you might be heading for him, when you didn't even slow down to ask my prices." He shook his head. "Rowlett is a good man. Runs a good ferry. I normally wouldn't try to steal his custom, but he can't carry you across. Not for weeks. Not until he gets the new ferry built. We have a deal, see. I'm stopping anyone I see going further west, offering them a fair price, especially if they were planning to cross with Rowlett. He gets a percentage of those crossing fees."

John frowned. "And if we kept on?" he asked. "How far past Rowlett's ferry is the next one?"

"That would be Colbert's ferry," Garrett answered. "And another two days, with a good road. But like I said, there's flooding west. It'll be hard going."

John grumbled and looked back into the wagon. They had enough supplies to make it, but just barely. He looked back at Parsons, who shook his head.

"We'll keep on," John said. "But thank you for the warning."

Garrett looked worried. "Are you sure?" He looked back toward the ferry crossing. "If you're sure... how are you set for supplies? I have some trade goods. Dried meat, dried fish."

"Do you happen to have any bread?" Parsons asked.

"Got some waybread," Garrett answered. "Nothing fresh."

"I think we're set for supplies," John answered. "I do appreciate the warning. Thank you."

"You're welcome. Be careful. And if you're looking to camp, there's a good spot upriver about a mile. There's a single cottonwood tree. You can't miss it."

John smiled. "Thank you again."

Garrett nodded and rode back the way he'd come, and John snapped the reins. The wagon started moving, and Parsons rode up alongside.

"That was... convenient," he said.

John nodded. "It was far too convenient. I don't like coincidences."

Parsons laughed out loud. "I would have thought you'd be all over the miracles," he said. "I mean, technically, you are one."

"Coincidences are not miracles," John replied.

"What's the difference?" Ethriel asked. He had, John saw, let the human illusion fall away.

"A miracle comes from God directly," John answered. "Joshua saving you from the elfshot, that was a miracle. And giving you English and Aramaic. Coincidences... they just happen, and never in a good way."

"I can think of one that happened in a good way," Parsons said. "Me being on the *Cavalier* at the right time to meet you."

John considered that as he saw the cottonwood tree in the distance. "There's our campsite," he said. "And all right. I'll give you that one. Coincidences can sometimes happen in a good way."

"John?" Ethriel said, leaning forward and resting his elbows on his knees. "How are miracles different from magic? Elven magic comes from our gods."

John glanced at Ethriel. "I don't know. I only have two bits of magic to my name, so I'm not the one to ask. And up until right this moment, I didn't know you had gods."

Ethriel snorted. "Of course we have gods. I don't think we're as close to our gods as you are to yours—"

"That would be impossible, don't you think?" Parsons said in a dry voice.

"Parsons, don't make me be rude at you," John said without turning. "Remember, I was a soldier. Several times."

"And I was a guardsman," Parsons replied. "We could trade off being rude at each other, and see who is more creative."

Ethriel's eyes widened. "Only if I can listen. And take notes."

"This is not part of your studies, my Prince!" Parsons protested. He sounded so scandalized that John burst out laughing.

"We'll discuss theology later," he said when he could breathe again. "Let's make camp."

The work of setting up a camp meant that they often stopped well before dark. The horses were picketed out to graze, and a fire pit was dug and a fire started. Ethriel was starting to get good at cooking, and he would help John with those chores while Parsons fed and watered the horses. Then, after supper, Ethriel would have his lessons while John cleaned up the supper leavings and set up both the tent where Parsons slept, and the bedroll under the wagon that he shared with Ethriel.

Once the camp was ready for the night, John set the boundaries for his barriers — the first night after they'd left Skullyville, John had asked Parsons how they wanted to handle the night watches. Parsons had just looked at him, then taught him how to set his barriers using temporary markers. There were four stones in the back of the wagon, each polished smooth by water, each about the size of John's fist. He set one at the base of the cottonwood tree, then walked thirty paces and set the next stone. He repeated that until the wagon was at the center of a large square, then went to sit by the fire so that he could watch Parsons and Ethriel. Daily lessons happened in a certain order — weapons training came first, then magic. Usually, by the time John was done with his chores, the weapons training was nearly finished. Tonight, there seemed to be some difficulty.

"John," Parsons called. "Come help me. I'm not explaining this properly."

"What are you doing?" John asked as he got back to his feet. "It's been a long time since I last used a sword. I may not be much use to you."

"I thought we'd be working with knives tonight," Parsons answered. "And I'm not as fast as I once was, nor is it a weapon I was ever very proficient with. It's not a knight's weapon. It's more suited to back alleys than honorable combat." He looked down at the knife in his hand. "But it's also a smaller weapon, more easily concealed, and something that I think Ethriel should know, just in case."

John snorted. "You're trying to teach him to brawl, and you don't know how," he said. "It's a good idea, but I think these lessons are going to be mine to teach. You teach him sword, and all the honorable things that a king needs to know. I'll teach him to fight dirty." He held his hand out for the knife.

"Don't hurt him," Parson warned, passing the blade to John.

"I have no intentions of hurting him," John answered. "After everything we've gone through? You really think I would be so careless?" He weighed the knife, then held his hand out to Ethriel. "Give me yours." Ethriel looked puzzled, but handed John his knife. John took them and went to the fire, sorting through the smaller pieces of wood until he found two branches that were roughly the same length as the knives. He brought one back to Ethriel. "We start with these."

Ethriel looked at the branch as if it were a snake. "I'm not a child, John," he said. "I know how to hold a knife. You saw me, at the dugout. I blooded Buach."

"Oh, I remember. And I remember how quickly the guards took you down. You know how to use a knife, but I doubt you've ever fought the way I'm going to teach you to fight," John answered. "And I'd really rather not be gutted by accident. I'll recover, but I don't want to waste time if we don't have to. We start with these."

Ethriel scowled and took the branch, holding it with clear distaste. John rolled his eyes. Then he rushed the elf, sweeping the branch across his belly in a movement that would have gutted him if it had been a real blade. Ethriel yelped, stumbled backwards, and ended up flat on his back, with John's branch pressed across his throat.

"Now," John said. "Do you understand why we're using branches?"

"I wasn't ready!" Ethriel protested. "Let me up!"

"Oh, I'm sure an assassin will give you a moment to get ready to fight," John said. He shifted off of Ethriel and sat back on his heels. "The point of this kind of fighting is to protect yourself, to incapacitate your attacker, and to either stay alive until help comes, or get out with your skin reasonably intact. There's no honor involved. There are no rules." He paused, then stood up. "No, there's one rule. You stay alive, no matter what you have to do." He held his hand out to help Ethriel up; Ethriel grabbed his wrist, and John saw the devil in his eyes a heartbeat before he went flying. He landed hard, but it wasn't the impact that knocked the air out of him — it was the elf landing in his chest. A branch pressed hard against his throat.

"Like that?" Ethriel asked, grinning.

John just laughed.

CHAPTER TWO
Coincidences

John worked with Ethriel until the gloaming settled over them in deep purple shadows, making it too dark to see. Ethriel was a quick study, and once he understood that John expected him to do anything he possibly could to stay alive, and that there was no dishonor in doing so, he threw himself into learning to brawl with the same complete enthusiasm that he showed for everything else he did. John had to work hard to keep from getting hurt, and to keep from hurting Ethriel by accident. Despite that, he was certain they'd both be covered in bruises by morning.

"Let's walk a bit," he suggested. "Down to the river. Otherwise, you'll ache."

"I'm so glad you didn't stay stiffen up," Parsons muttered, loud enough that both John and Ethriel heard him clearly. Ethriel turned bright red.

"Parciviel!" John snapped, shocked enough to use the elf's real name. "Was that necessary?" For the first time, he noticed the bottles on the ground next to Parsons' foot. "Where did those come from?"

Parsons looked down. "Oh, I tucked a few bottles away in case we needed them, For medicinal purposes."

"And you needed it now?" John asked. "For medicinal purposes?" He walked over and picked the bottle up, alarmed at how light it was. The other was completely empty. "When did you start this?"

"Ah..." Parsons frowned slightly. "One of you were on your back."

"You... you are tight as a drum," John breathed.

Parsons scowled and pointed at him. "I am not! Whatever that means."

"It means you're drunk."

"I am not!" Parsons protested. "At least, I'm not that drunk. I can still lay down without holding on!"

"Wallpapered. You are completely wallpapered. Ethriel?" John said without turning. "Go and fetch a bucket of water. Use the larger bucket."

"Why?" Ethriel asked. John looked back at him, but Ethriel was already heading toward the wagon. He trotted off toward the river with an empty bucket, came back several minutes later, carefully carrying the full bucket that he set down next to John. "Why did you want this?"

John handed Ethriel the bottle. "Hold that for me, will you?" He picked up the bucket in both hands, took a step, and dumped the entire thing over Parsons' head. The older elf yelped and staggered to his feet.

"What was that for?" Parsons demanded.

"How dare you?" John snapped. "You are supposed to be protecting your King, Sir Parcivie_! Right now, I'm not sure you know which end of the sword is which! Is this how you fulfill your oath?" He dropped the bucket, went and took the bottle from Ethriel, and threw it as hard as he could, hearing the distant smash as the glass shattered. "If you were under my command, I'd see you in the buck and gag," he continued. "Now, go to bed, and in the morning, I want every bottle you hid in my wagon poured out. Is that understood?"

Parsons gaped at him, blinking owlishly. Then he straightened, as much as he was able. "I... yes." He closed his eyes and shook his head. "I apologize."

"In the morning, Parciviel," Ethriel said. "When you're sober, and I can trust that you mean it."

Parsons bowed deeply, almost toppling over. Then he staggered toward the tent, not even stopping to take off his wet clothes before crawling inside. John closed his eyes and let out a long breath.

"I'm sorry," he said.

"You don't have anything to be sorry about," Ethriel answered. "You're right. He swore to act as my protector, and he's... what did you say? Tight?"

"Tight as a drum. Or wallpapered. They both mean the same. They mean drunk." John picked up the empty bucket and started toward the wagon, hearing Ethriel falling in next to him. "I never saw him put them in the wagon. I don't even know when he did it!"

"If he hid them with magic, you wouldn't have seen them," Ethriel pointed out. "I might
be able to find them. Do you want me to look?"

"No," John answered. "No, I want you to supervise him tomorrow. Loudly." He glanced over at the tent; he could already hear Parsons snoring. "I don't envy him the head he'll have in the morning."

"What's a buck and gag?" Ethriel took the bucket from John and carried it back to the wagon. He put it inside, then came back. "I'm sorry we didn't get our walk."

John sighed. "So am I. I wanted some private time with you, love."

"I know. But Sir Parciviel is unconscious, so we might as well be private." Ethriel smiled. "Go set the barrier. I'll unroll the bedroll. Then you can tell me about what a buck and gag is."

John nodded. He paused long enough to kiss Ethriel, then went to the cottonwood tree and touched the first of the stones. It warmed under his fingers as the spell woke, and the tingle of magic followed John as he walked the thirty paces to the next stone and woke that one. By the time he'd finished pacing the square and returned to the cottonwood tree, his skin was buzzing with energy, and the spells felt as eager as a new recruit in a brothel. He knelt and touched the first stone once again, and felt the boundary snap up around the camp. He sat back on his heels and nodded in satisfaction. Then he got up and headed for the wagon, seeing the bedroll already unrolled on the ground beneath the wagon box. As he walked, he saw lightning dance across the sky, followed by a distant rumble of thunder.

"Looks like we'll be wet tonight," he said as he stripped his shirt off. "We need to make sure we're closed up tight."

"I wish there was enough room that we could sleep inside the wagon," Ethriel said as he took his own shirt off. He folded it and put it into the wagon. "Or that we had another tent. Are you going to strip completely?"

John looked up at the sky and shook his head. "Not entirely. If the storm gets too bad, we might need to move. I don't know if this area floods."

Ethriel nodded. "Then we should pack up as much as we can, just in case."

They worked quickly, picking up things that had been taken out of the wagon when they'd made camp, and packing up the box that served as their kitchen on the road.

"Should I take down the tripod?" Ethriel asked.

"Leave it," John answered as he lifted the box into the back of the wagon. "It's still too hot to take down. It'll cool once the rain douses the embers. I'll want to move the picket line closer to the wagon. Come help me with that?"

Between the two of them, it was short work to move the horses. Ethriel crooned softly to them while John ran the picket line from the cottonwood tree to the rear of the wagon.

"Ethriel, do they understand it when you sing to them?" John asked. "Barak seems to."

Ethriel looked thoughtful, then shook his head. "Horses don't really understand," he answered. "They're like very young children. They'll understand tone, but not necessarily meaning. I can...

influence them, but if you're asking me to tell them something, they won't understand what I mean."

John snorted. "It was a thought. I was hoping you could tell them that the storm will just be a lot of noise, and that they're not to run away."

Ethriel reached up and scratched the blaze on Barak's face. "He won't run. He likes you. And Windrider won't leave Parciviel." He looked over at the tent, then back at John. "What's a buck and gag?"

"Oh, I forgot you asked about that." John looked at the tent. "Let's go to bed, and I'll explain." He sat down and took off his boots, setting them just inside the wagon wheel. He took the Henry from its place under the driver's seat and slid it underneath the wagon. Then he crawled under and onto the bedroll. Ethriel followed him, and they arranged themselves in what had come to be their usual position — John on his back, with Ethriel on his left, his head pillowed on John's shoulder.

"The buck and gag," John said. "It's... unpleasant. You know there was a war recently?"

"You've mentioned it. Not much."

"You don't need to know much, love. The buck and gag was punishment in the army, for drunkenness on duty. I only ever saw it carried out once. Once was enough." He frowned, trying to think how to explain it. "The soldier who'd been drunk was brought to the middle of camp. He was bound hand and foot, and gagged. They sat him on the ground, and brought his knees up, between his arms. If I could sit up under here, I'd show you. They ran a rod under his knees, and over his arms—"

"There's a *name* for that?" Ethriel gasped. He sounded horrified, and when he pushed himself up on his elbow, there was just enough light that John could see the look on his face. "And... and you've *done* that to someone?"

"Not me," John answered. "I wasn't in command. And when I did have a command, I still never used it. I threatened to, and that was enough for my men. Ethriel, what..." He stopped, feeling the elf shaking. "Ethriel... was that done to you?"

Ethriel nodded, slowly lowering back down to resume his place. But this time, he clung to John for comfort. "It hurts," he said softly. "You can't move, and you can't get away, and it *hurts*."

"Oh, Ethriel," John murmured. He ran his hand down the length of Ethriel's back. "I'm sorry. I had no idea he tortured you. And I want you to understand. I'll threaten, but I would never have done that. I'm just very angry. He's supposed to help me protect you. He can't do that drunk."

"You must be very angry, if you're even threatening to do something so horrible," Ethriel said, his voice very quiet. "The night that Buach did that to me... it's part of why I started trying to escape. Because I realized that he wasn't going to stop hurting me. That he was going to kill me, even if I gave him what he wanted."

John nodded, still running his hand up and down Ethriel's spine. "Ethriel—" he asked slowly. "Did he... hurt you?"

"I just said..." Ethriel paused. Then, to John's shock, he laughed. "Oh. You mean... oh. John, you needn't be..." he paused. "John, did your Joshua give me a nonsense word?"

"What? What word?"

"Squeamish?" Ethriel raised his head again. "That's not a real word, is it?"

"It is," John answered. "It means uncomfortable. Or nervous. And yes, I was a bit squeamish about asking that question. It's not an easy one to ask, especially not to ask you."

Ethriel smiled. He stretched up and kissed John lightly on the lips. "Buach didn't force me," he answered.

A knot that had started tightening in John's gut loosened, but not entirely. "He told me that you'd been in his bed," he said slowly.

"He didn't force me," Ethriel repeated. He yawned and lowered his head again, tracing idle designs with his fingertips on John's chest. "He told me he wasn't going to, because he wanted me to willingly come back to his bed—"

"Back?"

Ethriel sighed. "Yes. Back. He was my first lover. And we parted. Amicably, I thought. But he wanted more. And he told me he wasn't going to force me because he wanted me back in his bed willingly. It was when I said no too many times that he started hurting me."

"I had no idea—"

"Because I didn't tell you," Ethriel interrupted. "I wasn't going to tell you. I don't want to tell you anymore. I don't want to even think about it."

John took a deep breath. "I understand that," he said. "I know exactly what you mean."

Ethriel's fingers stopped moving. "I don't understand," he said. "How?"

John stared up at the bottom of the wagon, now just barely visible. "You have your nightmares, love. I have mine. Remember, I was a man grown when I stopped aging. I've seen..." He stopped. "There are things I don't want to think about. There are things I can't think about, because I've forgotten them. But the body remembers, and the body reacts. And... there are things that have happened recently that I can't forget." He closed his eyes. "The reason I came back to Arkansas, back to the dugout, was because I was running from those memories."

"You're shaking," Ethriel said. "John—"

"I want you to know I understand," John said. "And I won't push you to tell me. Just... know that I do understand."

Next to him, Ethriel shifted, and when John opened his eyes, the elf was leaning over him, their noses almost touching. "One day," he said. "We'll both be able to talk about it without screaming."

John nodded. "One day."

Ethriel shifted again, until he was laying on top of John, bracing his weight on his forearms. His weight was a comforting anchor, and John wrapped his arms around him and held tight, closing his eyes as Ethriel kissed him.

"Parciviel is asleep," Ethriel whispered. "We could—"

"There's not enough room under here," John whispered back. "And we can't leave the boundary for more privacy."

"He won't notice," Ethriel grumbled. "And I'm not sure either of us will sleep."

"I know he's there," John answered. "And frustration will also keep the both of us awake."

Ethriel grumbled. "Too late." He splayed his hands over John's collarbone and rested his chin on them, shivering as thunder rumbled overhead. "It's going to be a loud night."

"Then we should try to sleep now, before it gets bad." John ran his hands up and down Ethriel's back, then raised his head and kissed Ethriel quickly. "Shift over, love."

THOUGHTS OF CAMP SUMTER kept John awake long after Ethriel fell asleep. He lay in the dark, listening to the rumble of thunder growing ever closer, and finally fell asleep as the first raindrops started plopping on the ground around the wagon. Only to wake with a jerk and a curse when something exploded — he rolled, grabbing the Henry, hearing Ethriel yelp something in his own language. His skin felt like it was tingling, and he realized why as he got out into the rain and could see the camp.

Lightning danced across the plains in deadly splendor, and had come too close to the camp — the cottonwood tree was ablaze.

"Ethriel, the horses!" He ran for the picket. Ethriel beat him there, grabbing Barak's halter and dragging him to the far side of the wagon, while John went for Parson's Windrider. They brought the frightened horses to the far side of the wagon, and John shouted, "Give me Barak, and find something to blindfold them!"

Ethriel brought Barak closer. He took the Henry from John, and once John had Barak's halter, ran for the wagon. He was back a moment later carrying cloth in each hand. He threw one over his shoulder, shaking the other out and then twisting what John realized was his shirt into a blindfold. He blindfolded Windrider, then repeated it with John's shirt on Barak.

"Now what?" Ethriel shouted, shaking wet hair out of his face and taking Windrider's halter.

"We need to keep them calm," John called back. "If they run, we'll never find them." He looked up at the burning tree. "My barrier won't stop that if it falls on the wagon."

"Then we need to move the wagon," Ethriel answered. "Can you harness Barak? I'll get the bedroll and our boots out from underneath." He looked at Windrider. "Wait. Can you take Windrider? I'll get things out, then I can hold both horses while you harness Barak."

John nodded and took Windrider, and Ethriel ran to crawl underneath the wagon. As he did, John looked up again at the cottonwood. This... this wasn't right. Lightning-struck trees didn't burn like that. They either split or they burst. John had seen it happen. But this tree had gone up like an oil-soaked torch. Why? The wood hadn't been dry or dead, and the driving rain had soaked through John's clothes before they'd gotten the horses to the far side of the wagon. Surely that would put the fire out?

"Ethriel," he called as Ethriel came back. "Is this a natural storm, or a magic one?"

Ethriel dragged his wet hair out of his face. "I... I don't know," he stammered. "A storm started by magic doesn't feel any different. No more than you can tell if a fire is started by a flint or a match once it's burning. Why?"

John shook his head. "Not important. Can you hold Windrider and Barak while I get the harness?"

Harnessing Barak took twice as long as it should have, even with Ethriel doing his best to calm the frightened horse. The wet leather didn't seem to want to go where John needed it to be, and his hands didn't seem to want to listen. Finally, he snugged down the last strap and Ethriel coaxed Barak to the far side of camp, then took Windrider while John rigged up a picket rope between the back of the wagon and a shovel that he jammed into the wet ground. It wasn't optimal, but it was the best he could do in the rain and dark. They unhitched Barak, put him and Windrider on the picket, and removed the blindfolds. Wet shirts went into the wagon, and John and Ethriel both sagged against the leeward side of the wagon. John closed his eyes and groaned.

"I don't think we're moving tomorrow." He had to raise his voice to be heard over the wind. "I don't think we're sleeping the rest of the night. Not in this."

"John?" Ethriel shouted. "Parciviel hasn't come out of the tent. How can he sleep through this?"

John snorted. "As drunk as he was? He'd sleep through a twenty-one-gun salute. Let's go wake him. If we're going to be soaked, so is he." He pushed off the wagon and started toward the tent, staggering slightly as the winds picked up, roaring like an oncoming train. Both his ears popped, making him wince. The roaring grew louder, and he realized what he was hearing wasn't only the wind. He turned, grabbed Ethriel's hand, and pulled the elf back toward the wagon.

"John, what is it?" Ethriel shouted. John didn't answer, dragging Ethriel back underneath the wagon. He pushed the elf flat and covered him with his own body.

"Tornado!" he shouted, his voice barely audible even to himself. He felt Ethriel tense underneath him, then try to move.

"Parciviel!"

"Stay down!" John shouted. The scream of the storm was even louder, and he could feel it in his ears, behind his eyes. He buried his face in Ethriel's hair and dug his fingers into the ground, hearing the horses screaming...

Then it was over, and rain was pelting against John's back. He raised his head, looked around, and saw the wagon next to them, tipped onto its side.

"Let me up!"

John shifted to sit next to Ethriel, letting the elf get up. Ethriel gaped at the wagon for a moment, then scrambled to his feet. "The horses!"

John staggered to his feet and followed Ethriel, coming around the upturned wagon to find both horses at the end of the makeshift picket line. Ethriel was already crooning to them in Elven. He glanced at John. "I've got them," he said, and gestured; a glowing ball of light appeared in front of John. "Go see if Parciviel..." He paused. "If he's still there."

John nodded and walked across the camp, following the light. The cottonwood tree was almost gone, only a splintered stump taller than John marked where it had been. The stump was still smoldering despite the rain. The tent had fallen in, and there was rain gathering in the canvas folds. John went closer, reaching down and grabbing the canvas, hauling it back to reveal Parsons.

Snoring.

John stared at him for a moment, then started laughing. "You lucky, drunken sot," he exclaimed, and Parsons snorted and woke.

"What...?" he stammered. "John, what are you...?" He rolled, and his eyes widened. "What happened?"

CHAPTER THREE
Contingencies

When the rains stopped, Ethriel conjured several more floating lights, and held them in place while Parsons and John offloaded the wagon. Thankfully, there wasn't as much breakage as John had feared — some glass, including the four other bottles of whiskey that Parsons had hidden. Somehow, the casks of flour and cornmeal and grain had survived, and none of the bags of seeds or beans or rice had torn. Now crates that had spilled were repacked and stacked with barrels, and things that had gotten soaked were spread to dry. By the time dawn started painting the eastern horizon in pinks and purples, John knew that they weren't going to be moving any time soon. He sat on the ground next to the largest pile of supplies and looked at the upturned wagon. He needed to check it for damage next, then think of a way to right it without damaging the axles or the wheels. He scrubbed a hand over his face, trying to think of what he needed to do next. His mind felt as if he was walking through a fog.

"John, I'm going to start a fire, and make something for us to eat," Ethriel said. "Would you help me with the kitchen box?"

"Coffee?" John asked, looking up. Ethriel smiled and nodded. He looked as tired as John felt.

"I'll make coffee," Ethriel said. "Just help me with the box?"

John nodded and slowly got up. He took one side of the box, and Ethriel took the other, and they carried it over to the firepit. As they put the box down, John heard Parsons calling from behind him, "John, I'll just get this righted, and we can start to reload."

"What?" John turned and saw Parsons doing something at the wagon. He saw it shift, and went cold. "Parsons, no!" He started running, but it was too late. The wagon had shifted far enough that gravity took over. He watched as it teetered, as it landed on its wheels... and heard the sound of wood cracking clearly across the camp.

"I DIDN'T THINK I'D break it!"

John growled softly and crawled out from under the wagon, glaring up at Parsons. "Did you think at all?" he demanded. "Both axles are cracked. Both of them!"

"We have a spare—" Parsons started.

"We have one spare. We need two." John got up and looked at the wagon. "We're stuck. We won't make it to the ford where we need to cross. The axles will fail in a mile. Maybe two. We might make it back to Garrett, but there's no guarantee that he'll have an axle to sell." He wiped his greasy hands on his trousers and glared at the wagon. "Is there a way to repair them with magic?"

Parsons scowled. Then he shook his head. "Yes and no," he said. "It can be done. I can't do it."

"I don't know how," Ethriel offered. "Or if I would be able to."

John fought the urge to lean against the wagon, afraid that just adding his weight would be enough to shatter the axles irrevocably. "Then we're stuck. We can't even keep going on horseback. Not and carry the supplies we'll need. I should have insisted on a third horse. That was stupid of me. I should have—"

"John, it's not your fault," Ethriel said. "Come and eat something. Then we'll see what we can do."

John followed Ethriel to the fire, sitting down and taking a bowl and cup from him. He didn't realize how hungry he was until his first bite. That bite made him smile. Rice cooked with pears and cinnamon. He looked at Ethriel, who smiled at him.

"I thought it would help," he said. "But you make it better."

John smiled and sipped his coffee. "This is fine, love. Thank you." He made himself eat slowly, savoring it, and drank his coffee.

Without being asked, Ethriel filled John's cup when it was empty, and added more rice to John's bowl. And when Parsons started to say something, Ethriel snapped something in Elven, making the older elf fall silent. John finished, then waved Ethriel off when he would have refilled the bowl a third time.

"We have two choices," he said, finishing his coffee. "Abandon the majority of the supplies and the wagon, take what we can carry, and ride on. We might be able to buy another horse at the next ferry, when we get there. But resupplying will be hard." He set his cup down. "Or I can leave you both here, and ride back to Garrett's ferry. See if he has an axle to sell. And if he doesn't..."

"You are not crossing the river!" Ethriel blurted. "John—"

"I don't see how we have much of a choice," John replied. "We need another axle. Two, if I can manage it. And the closest town—"

"Is Wraithtown," Parsons finished. "Danu's tits, John, I didn't realize that the blasted thing was so fragile!"

John took a deep breath and shook his head. There was no point in yelling at the older elf again. It wouldn't fix anything. "It's done. There's no changing it. Now, we just need to repair it. And to do that, I'll need to go see about replacing axles." He took a deep breath, let it out. "If we reload the wagon, then things won't get soaked if it rains again. I never checked the tent, but we'll see if we can arrange things so that someone can sleep in the wagon."

"Here's another idea," Parsons said. "You stay here. I'll go back to Garrett. And if they don't have an axle, or if they only have one, I'll come back."

"And then what?" John asked. "You can't go to Wraithtown."

"No, but I can go on to the next ferry upriver," Parsons answered. "And the one beyond it. If necessary, I'll cross and go to that town Hopaii mentioned. In the meantime, you camp here." He sighed. "John, this is my fault. Let me make it right."

John considered the plan, then shook his head. "That would have us camped here for a week, at least. At least four days to the next viable crossing. Then you'd need to come back. I don't like the idea of sitting here for that long." He frowned. "How long would it take to get to... to get there?" He pointed south.

Parsons scowled. "A day, perhaps. If you pushed, you could make it in half a day."

"Then that's where I'll have to go, if Garrett doesn't have what we need." He sighed. "Thank you for offering to go, Parsons. But we can't sit here like lame ducks for a week or more. We'll catch the attention of someone or something we shouldn't."

Parsons' scowl deepened. "So you'll ride into the lion's den—"

"Not if I have a choice," John interrupted. "But at the moment, we don't have a choice." He looked east, back the way they'd come. "Now, if Garrett has a pair of horses, or a horse and a mule, that's another option. Leaving the wagon entirely and going on with just what supplies we need to survive."

"I don't like that idea," Ethriel said. "There's so much you insisted we needed for this."

"And if we get to Bandera with the clothes on our backs, empty bellies and no cartridges in my gun, I'll still count that as a success," John answered. "Because we can come back from having nothing. I'm the only one of us that can come back from being dead." He reached over and took Ethriel's hand, tugged him closer. "I won't be gone long."

"And I can't come with you," Ethriel said. "I know that. I don't like that idea, either."

"I'm not particularly fond of it myself, but we have no choices," John said. He sighed. "Let's reload the wagon and make it so that someone can sleep in there."

Repacking the wagon and reorganizing the load to leave a narrow space where Ethriel could sleep took them until the sun was high. Carefully, they moved the wagon closer to the firepit, and John started to saddle Barak.

"John? You asked me a question last night, and I'm not sure of my answer anymore. I want you to ask Sir Parciviel."

"Which question, love?" John asked.

"About telling if a storm is natural or caused by magic," Ethriel answered. Parsons frowned.

"Do you think last night's storm was caused by magic? Why?"

"I'm not sure," John answered. "It was the tree that made me ask." He nodded toward the scorched remains of the cottonwood. "I've seen lightning struck trees before. They never burned like that. Either the trunk split open, or the tree shattered like glass. I've never seen one go up like a torch before."

Parsons turned and looked at the charred trunk. "I don't know," he answered. "What did Ethriel tell you?"

"That there's no way to tell if the storm was started by magic once it hit us," John answered. "He gave the example of lighting a fire with a flint and steel or a match. You can't tell how it was started once the fire is burning."

"That's a good example," Parsons said, nodded. "A very good one. And exactly right. Once a natural event is triggered by magic, it's a natural event. Only the trigger is magic. And even if the storm was started by magic, it was started miles from here. We'd only know for certain if we were near when it was triggered. There's no way for us to tell."

"John, is it possible that the tree burning is just... that tree?" Ethriel asked. "How many trees of that sort have you seen struck by lightning?"

"I..." John blinked and looked at Ethriel. "I'm not sure cottonwood trees even grow in Europe. And I've never been this far west before."

"So you might never have seen this before. That might be normal for that kind of tree," Ethriel smiled. "You might be worrying yourself sick for no reason."

John smiled. "Perhaps. But being careful isn't the worst trait to have." He cinched the saddle strap, then slid the Henry into the rifle scabbard. "Being careful has kept me from dying unnecessarily more than once. Now, I'm ready. I'll be back as soon as I can be, depending on what I find." He looked around the camp and sighed. "Let me get my coat and hat. Do I even have to say be careful?"

"No, but you will anyway," Parsons answered. He smiled. "John, I wish you'd reconsider and let me go. It's my fault—"

"And we can't lose you to what lies over the river," John answered, putting on his coat. "There are things Ethriel needs to know that I can't teach him. We need you. And right now, I need you to take care of him."

"Or I could come with you, and Parsons can stay here," Ethriel said brightly.

"What?" Parsons gasped. "No! John, tell him!"

John looked at Parsons. "He's a man, Parsons. I'm not going to tell him anything." Then he turned to Ethriel. "I will ask you something, though. Would you be able to hold the disguise spell for however long we'd be gone?"

Ethriel scowled. "No. I'm not that good at it yet." He sighed. "That means I shouldn't go, doesn't it? Someone will see me at just the wrong time, and I don't have the wagon to hide in if I can't maintain the illusion."

"We shouldn't take the risk until you've perfected that spell," John agreed. "Especially if I have to go to Wraithtown. I don't want someone there seeing you and getting notional." He looked at Parsons. "You need to stop thinking of him as a child, Parsons."

Parsons turned pale red. "I... yes, you're right. I do forget. He has so much of Méabh in him, and I remember her as a little girl." He sighed and turned to Ethriel. "I'm sorry."

"There's nothing to apologize for, Parciviel," Ethriel said. "There are times when I forget I've come of age." He ran one hand down the front of his shirt, smoothing out wrinkles. He looked down at his wrist, and the scars that his captivity had left behind, and his entire demeanor changed. His shoulders slumped, and his voice grew quiet, "And times I wish I hadn't."

"Ethriel," John breathed. He shoved Barak's reins at Parsons, and reached out to pull Ethriel into his arms. Ethriel was tense, his muscles rigid, and John held him tight, running his hand up and down Ethriel's spine, over his long braid, murmuring soft endearments and comfort in Aramaic until he felt Ethriel sag against him, until the tears started. "Let it out, love," John murmured. He'd been expecting this. Waiting for it. He'd seen this kind of reaction among young soldiers, when the horrors of what they'd seen and done finally broke them down. Boys forced to become men too quickly, and paying the price.

"I was wondering when this was going to happen," Parsons said softly.

John looked at him and nodded, then turned his attention back to Ethriel, who was clinging to him like a lost child. He let his lover cry, gently drawing him down to the ground, watching as Parsons walked Barak off a distance. He shifted, arranging them so that Ethriel was in his lap, and buried his face in Ethriel's hair.

Ethriel sniffled and shifted, scrubbing his hand over his face. "John," he croaked.

"Do not apologize," John said. "This has been a long time coming, and you needed it."

"I—"

"Do you feel better?" John asked.

Ethriel looked at him, a puzzled expression on his face. "I'm not sure." He frowned. "I think... maybe?"

John nodded. "I thought you might. We've been waiting for this, Parsons and I. The both of us know what happens when a man sees too much to bear. We've both been there."

"You... you were expecting..." Ethriel stammered. "You knew... that... that I wanted to die?"

John took a deep breath and blew it out. "I didn't know that," he admitted. "I didn't know that was how you would react. I know how I reacted. I know how some of the soldiers under my command reacted. And I know what happened to some of the boys in Camp Sumter. The ones who refused food rather than live in that Hell anymore—"

"Tried that," Ethriel murmured.

"That somehow doesn't surprise me," John said. "What I'm saying is that you can only take so much before you try to dull the pain, or try to end it entirely. For me, I turned to alcohol."

"Because you can't end it," Ethriel said softly.

"Because I can't end it," John agreed. "Although I tried."

Ethriel's eyes widened. "You did?"

John nodded. "The beginning of this year, if you want the absolute truth," he answered. He wrapped his arms around Ethriel again. "I can promise you this, Ethriel. Every day makes it a little easier. Every day makes it that much further away. Every day lets the wounds scar over. You've had only a few weeks." He looked up at Parsons. "And now I don't know what to do. I shouldn't leave you. Not when you're this raw."

"No," Ethriel said, and sat up. "No, you have to go. I'll be all right." He grimaced. "Somewhat all right." He looked at John, then dropped his eyes. "I'll still be here when you get back."

"If I thought you wouldn't be, I wouldn't leave," John replied. He leaned forward and kissed Ethriel gently. "Do you remember what you said last night?"

Ethriel frowned slightly, then said, "I said someday we'd be able to talk about it without screaming."

"And you were right. We will. It will get better. I promise you that." John smiled slightly. "We'll make it better. However, unless we decide we're going to make it better right here, you need to let me up. I need to go."

Ethriel smiled, laughing weakly as he got off of John's legs and helped him up. Then he hugged John hard. "Two or three days, you think?" he asked.

"I hope so," John answered. He tipped Ethriel's face up and kissed him, then stood with his forehead against Ethriel's. "I love you. Wait for me."

"I'm not leaving you," Ethriel answered. "I'll be here when you get back."

Parsons came closer, leading Barak over to them. "We'll work on more magic while John is gone," he said. "We'll polish the illusion spell, and I'll teach you some offensive magic. That way, the next time something like this happens—"

"Which it had better not, Parciviel," John growled.

"— You'll be able to go with him," Parsons continued as if John hadn't spoken. He smiled and handed the reins to John. "Good luck," he said. "And be careful."

John nodded as he put on his hat. "You, too. Stay by the wagon and try not to attract attention. If anyone does come past and stops, see if they have an axle that you can trade for. You know which are the trade goods."

"Yes, sir," Parsons said in crisp tones. His grin spoiled the formality, though. "You said something about being in command. What was your rank?"

John blinked. "You really want to know?" he asked. "I was a captain."

"Very well, Captain," Parsons said. "Last night... was an egregious lapse of judgment, and I will accept whatever penalties you decide. I promise you; I will not fail in my duties again." He crossed his right arm over his chest and bowed at the waist. It was an oddly formal gesture that reminded John of Roman soldiers, and he looked at Ethriel.

"Is that how you salute?" he asked.

"How would you do it?"

John laughed and answered with a crisp salute, making Ethriel smile.

"You must have looked magnificent in uniform," Ethriel said. "The green suits you." He looked at the wagon, then back at John. "May I ask a favor before you go?"

"Of course, love."

Ethriel bit his lip. "May I... may I wear your hat while you're gone?" His voice was so quiet, so tentative, that for a moment John wasn't sure if he'd heard properly.

"My hat?" He reached up and touched the brim of his hat, then realized what Ethriel was asking. "Oh, my kepi?" When Ethriel nodded, John hesitated. Then he answered, "Yes, you may. You know where it is. Just promise me you won't wear it if there are people around. I was a Union officer, and we weren't popular in this part of the country. I don't want someone to see it and try to take their anger out on you."

Ethriel's smile was brilliant. "I promise. I'll only wear it when we're alone," he said. "Thank you. I think... I think it might help me feel less alone, while you're gone."

"And I will be back as soon as I possibly can," he promised. He brushed his hands down the front of his shirt, and felt something in his pocket — the token that Nathaniel had given to him. He took it out and handed it to Ethriel. "Keep this, too."

"John!" Ethriel took the pouch. "Shouldn't you take it with you?"

"I want you protected, love," John said. "As much as you can be while I'm away." He kissed Ethriel once more, then he swung up onto Barak's back. He checked the rifle, and looked around. "Right. Be careful. I'll be back as soon as I can be. Maybe tomorrow or the next day."

"Or the day after that," Parsons drawled. "If you keep delaying. Honestly, John, how do you expect him to miss you if you don't go already?"

CHAPTER FOUR
Crossing

John recognized Garrett as he rode up to the ferry. The man was standing with his hand shading his eyes, watching John ride closer.

"I remember you," he said as John reached him. "You were in a wagon yesterday. What happened?"

"We had a mishap," John answered as he dismounted. "The storm last night left us with two cracked axles."

Garrett winced. "Mishap? More like disaster."

John nodded. "I'm hoping not. You said you had trade goods. If you have a pair of axles, I'll pay whatever price you ask."

"Oh, now that's a tempting offer, to be sure," Garrett said. He shook his head. "I wish I could help you. But I haven't even got one."

"A horse, then, or a mule?" John asked. "You'll have your pick of what we leave behind if you can sell me a mount."

"Wish I did. I wish I could help you, but I can't." Garrett shook his head. "I can't think of anything on this side of the river that might help you, either."

"Then I'll need to cross," John said. "What do you charge for passage?"

"Cross?" Garrett looked over his shoulder at the river. "You... you mean to go *there*, don't you? That's not the smartest thing—"

"Unless there's someplace closer, and less... uncanny?" John asked. "Someplace with either a livery or a wainwright? Because from everything I've been warned about, if I have a choice, I'll take it. But to get to the next town and back would take me a week or more."

"To be sure, to be sure," Garrett said, nodding. "And no, there's nothing closer. You came from the east, so you know what's that way. Next big settlement upriver is Bonham. Some small farms out here, but I don't think any of them will have what you need. Most folks... they don't stay long around here. Unless they're a bit uncanny themselves, if you get my meaning. And those that do... well... they stay on the other side of the river. There is a wainwright in Wraithtown, though. They'll have what you need. You just need to get back out again."

John looked at Garrett again. "You don't look uncanny, but I'm learning that I don't know nearly enough about what is and isn't. Do you have trouble with them?"

"Me?" Garrett grinned. "Nah. JW and I, we have an understanding. I run the ferry here, he leaves me alone. Occasionally, he'll come out here to shoot dice and see what I've got to trade. He's... unpredictable, but most of the time, he leaves me alone." He shrugged. "They're nervous neighbors, but so are the Chickasaw, sometimes."

"The tribes don't worry me," John said. "I lived near the Choctaw for quite a long time. You never answered me. How much to cross?"

Garrett shook his head. "I'll take you over for the price of a conversation, and I hope I'll see you again in a day or two."

John blinked. "Mister Garrett—"

"You're walking into the lion's den," Garrett said. "When you come back, I'll charge you to come back over."

"You'll charge me twice the price," John said. Garrett grinned.

"Maybe. Let's get you loaded. It's a long ride."

BOTH THE CROSSING AND the ride to Wraithtown were surprisingly uneventful, although as the town came into view, John couldn't shake the feeling that he was being watched. There was nothing he could see, but he'd learned the hard way that just because he couldn't see something didn't mean it wasn't there.

"I'm no threat," he called. "Just coming to town to visit the wainwright, and possibly your mercantile." The feeling of being watched grew stronger. He looked over his shoulder, but couldn't see anything. He sighed. "I can feel you there," he grumbled. "You're making me itch."

No answer, and he rode on, growing more and more nervous the closer he got to town. Just outside, he dismounted, leading Barak down the wide main street. The windows were dark, doors closed. Where was everyone? John stopped and looked around, trying to remember what day it was. Was it Sunday? He didn't think it was Sunday.

"Looking for something?"

John whirled. There was a tall man in black standing in front of one of the stores, and John would swear he hadn't been there a moment ago. He was so tall and thin he looked as if he had been stretched, and the only part of his face visible underneath the brim of his hat was his wide, toothy grin. That grin didn't reassure John at all.

"Yes, actually," John answered. "Your wainwright, if the shop is open. Mister Garrett at the ferry said I might be able to find wagon axles."

"Garrett sent you? Here?"

John forced a smile. "He did try to warn me off, but I don't have much of a choice. This is the closest place with a wainwright, and I have two cracked axles and only one spare." He looked up the street, and was surprised to see other people. Men and women, moving silently through the streets, going in and out of buildings.

It didn't appear that many of them were bothering with the doors before going in and out.

He turned back to the tall man, wondering if this man was Jacob Wraith. The figure nodded. "Welcome to my town," he said, confirming John's suspicions.

"Thank you. You have an interesting town here," John said. "Very quiet." He looked down the street again. "I don't want to be a bother, or keep you from your work. How might I find the wainwright?"

The grin grew wider. "You don't need to worry about that, John Zebedee. You don't need to worry about anything at all. See, I've been waiting for you."

John went cold. "How do you know my name?" Wraith chuckled, and John took a step back. How could a man's grin get that *wide*? He felt someone behind him, and looked back to see another man looming over him.

No. No, the figure looming — *hovering!* — over him was not a man. A man didn't *look* like that. Didn't look as if they had been dead for weeks. He backed away, realizing that he was between Wraith and this... thing. He stepped to the side, closer to Barak. If he could mount, he could get out of here—

Something jabbed him in the back, and he froze before raising his hands. For one terrifying moment, he was back at Cold Harbor —

"Vagrancy is a crime in my town," Wraith said softly.

John swallowed. "Then it's a good thing that I'm not a vagrant," he answered. "And that I was leaving. If you'd kindly take your gun out of my back? Then I'll just be on my way."

"You'll be on your way, all right. Right to the jail."

"I've done nothing wrong!" John protested. "And I have friends waiting for me. If you don't have a wainwright, I'll go—"

The gun jabbed him harder. "Move."

"My horse—"

"Move!"

The jab was hard enough to push him forward; John dropped Barak's reins, fell forward and rolled. He shuddered as he passed through the specter floating above the ground in front of him, but it didn't seem to bother the thing. He couldn't let it bother him; he rolled up into his feet, started to turn...

He didn't hear the gunshot. Or feel his body hitting the dirt.

JOHN CAME BACK FROM the dead feeling more disjointed than usual. Something had been different about this time. He wasn't sure what it had been. Nor was he sure where he was. He opened his eyes, closed them again, then blinked. Then he realized he was naked from the waist up, and below the waist he was only wearing his drawers.

Where were his clothes?

He sat up slowly, and heard a laugh. "That had to have itched something fierce."

He turned his head to see Wraith sitting in a chair against the other wall, next to a heavy, wooden desk. There were bars between them — John was in a tiny cell, barely big enough for the cot he was lying in. His clothes, he noticed, were folded next to his feet.

"What did?" John asked. He swung his legs over the edge of the cot and winced. "And is there something to eat?"

"I've got a plate for you," Wraith answered. "Get yourself dressed. Now, I've seen a lot of things in my time, but I never did see someone regrow their own head. The hair growing back, that *had* to itch."

John stopped in the process of picking up his shirt. It was, he noticed, freshly washed. "Is that what you did?"

"You couldn't tell?"

John shook his head. "I was dead before I hit the ground." He put on his shirt, reached for his trousers. "How did you know my name, or that I wouldn't stay dead?"

Wraith's grin was still terrifying, even across the room and on the other side of iron bars. "I know a lot about you, Yohanan. Like I said, I've been waiting for you to show up."

John pulled on his trousers, stood up to pull them up. He buttoned the waist and tugged up his braces, then picked up his vest. His coat was gone, as were his hat and his boots.

"Coat isn't dry yet. Boots are out here. Sorry about the hat," Wraith said.

John turned to face him. "You have a plate, you said. And you were waiting for me? How? And why?"

Wraith stood up. He picked a plate covered by a cloth up off the desk, and carried it over to the cell, bending down and pushing it through the plate slot at the bottom of the door. John picked it up and uncovered it, revealing two pieces of cold fried chicken, a large piece of bread, and a chunk of cheese. He sat down on the cot and started to eat, thinking about what had happened. His clothes were clean and dry.

"How long did it take me to come back?" he asked. "And is there something to drink?"

"Whiskey, beer or coffee?"

"Coffee, please," John answered. "It had to have taken a while. My clothes are dry. How long?"

"It's past noon," Wraith answered. There was a stove in the corner, much like the one that had been in John's dugout. He picked up the coffee pot from the top and filled a cup, taking the cup back to the cell and sliding it through the slot. "Took you all night. Gotta says, it was interesting to watch. Ever had that happen before?"

"Dying? Yes. Losing my head? I wasn't sure how that would turn out, so I did my best to avoid it." John set the plate aside, reaching down to pick up the cup as Wraith laughed. He sipped the strong coffee, feeling more himself as his body realized he was alive once more. He finished the chicken, started on the bread and cheese. "So you know who I am. You know what I am. And... you were waiting for me, you said. Why? And how did you know I would come here?"

"Starting with the how I know you? I'm old, boy. Older than old. And when you get to be this old? You know how to find things that don't want to be found. How I knew you were coming? You ain't natural, John Zebedee. And things that ain't natural... they leave a trail like a comet for those who know how to look. So once you were close enough for me to see it, I knew you were there. And how I knew you'd come here?" Wraith leaned against the desk. "Like you said... you didn't have a choice. I wasn't going to let you pass without coming down to say hello. That's not neighborly."

John blinked when he realized what Wraith meant. "The storm. You sent the storm. Did you... I thought your power didn't go past the river?"

"Storms are funny things, John. They're wild things, like horses. And once you spook a horse? They go where they want to go. Now, to the meat of the matter. I've a job that needs doing, and you're the man to do it."

"And I've places to be that aren't here," John replied. "I'm not looking to tarry here. And I'm not looking for work."

"It's a simple thing," Wraith said. "You do this for me, I'll have your wagon mended, and I'll grant you and yours safe passage out of my territory. Even that bastard Parsons, or whatever he's calling himself these days."

John chewed the last of the bread, swallowed it, and chased it down with the last of the coffee. "Now I'm intrigued. He says you want his head on a plate. So you'd be willing to let that go, if I do this? What would you want me to do?"

Wraith chuckled. "You're curious as a cat, aren't you?" he said. "I like cats." He walked over to the bars and held one hand out, palm up. The air over his hand shimmered, and John saw the image of a beautiful girl with dark blue eyes. He closed his hand, then opened it again, and this time showed the image of an older, somber-looking man with the build of a brawler.

"Her name is Rose," Wraith said. "His is Kestrel. Father and daughter. I want them dead."

"What?" John gasped. "No!"

"They defied me," Wraith said, closing his hand. "You're going to kill them for me."

"No," John replied. "No, I am not. I am not killing anyone."

"Like you haven't done it before," Wraith snorted. "Captain Zebedee?"

John scowled. "I really want to know how you know so much about me," he grumbled. "Yes, I was a soldier. Many times over the years. And yes, I have killed people. In battle. I'm no bounty hunter, no hired killer. Nor do I want to be. So no, I will not kill anyone for you."

Wraith's laughter sounded like a rusty gate, swinging in the wind. "Damn," he chortled. "You've lost me a bet. Exact words, too."

"Exact... who were you betting? Who's telling you about me?" John stood up and moved over to the bars. "And what happens now that I've said no?"

Standing as close as he was to Wraith, and as short as he was compared to Wraith, John should have been able to see beneath the brim of Wraith's hat. Should have been able to see his face, his eyes. But there was nothing under there but darkness, and a grin that would have curdled fresh milk.

"Well, now you get to think about what choices you have," Wraith answered. He turned and headed for the door, calling over his shoulder, "I'll be back in the morning to hear your answer."

"In... in the morning?" John sputtered. "Wraith!"

Wraith didn't answer. He didn't turn. He walked out through the door.

Through the closed door.

John stared for a moment, then took a deep breath and let it out, resting his head against the bars. He stood there for a long moment. Then he started to examine the bars.

How had Wraith known so much about him? Who knew John well enough to predict what he'd say?

The possibility was terrifying.

John searched the small cell twice, to no avail. Then, because he was bored, he did it twice more. The bars were solid, which made no sense to him. In a town where people could pass through solid objects, why did you need a jail?

To hold idiots who don't listen to good advice, he finally decided, sitting down on the bed. The shadows grew longer, the corners darker, and John realized that Wraith hadn't left him with anything — no food, no water, no light. There was no blanket on the cot — he'd have a long, hungry, cold night. Hopefully, only one long hungry, cold night. He'd starved to death before, and it was probably his least favorite way to die. If he could be said to have a favorite way. None of them really held any appeal, it was just that some of them were less uncomfortable than others, and quicker.

Starving was neither comfortable nor quick. Definitely not his favorite way to die.

He closed his eyes, wondering if he was going to be able to sleep... and heard something scrape on the floor. He jerked upright, and saw a covered bowl and a cup sitting just inside the plate slot, and a pewter pitcher outside. Where had *they* come from?

He got up and went to see what had been left for him. A bowl of stew, with another chunk of bread soaking up gravy. The cup held water, and the pitcher held more. John sat on the floor and looked around. There was no one that he could see in the room.

"Thank you," he called.

Rusty gate laughter. "*We're civilized here, John,*" Wraith's voice seemed to come from everywhere. "*To a point.*"

"Does that point include a blanket?" John asked. He took a bite of the stew, chewed and swallowed. "You have an excellent cook."

"*Glad you like it,*" Wraith said, sounding amused. "*And before I forget, there's a bucket underneath the cot.*"

"I found it already, but I appreciate the mention," John answered. "I'm still not killing anyone for you."

"*You've still got 'til morning to change your mind.*"

Wraith's voice faded away, and John turned his attention back to the stew. He scraped the bowl, and sopped the last drops of gravy up with a crust. He drained the cup of water, managed to refill it without spilling, and turned back toward the cot.

There was a folded blanket near the head of the cot. John found himself smiling.

"The answer is still no," he said as he picked it up.

"*It ain't morning yet,*" Wraith whispered in his ear.

JOHN DIDN'T EXPECT to sleep. Strange cell, strange bed. Worries about Ethriel and Parsons, and about just how Wraith seemed to know so much about who John was. To his surprise, he did sleep, deeply and without dreaming, only to be jarred awake by the outer door slamming open hard enough to shake the wall. He blinked, not quite awake, and raised his head. Then sat bolt upright.

"Ethriel?" he croaked, scrambling off the bed. He shook his head, trying to wake up. This had to be a nightmare. Ethriel was supposed to be with the wagon, safe with Parsons. Not gagged and handcuffed and *here*.

It wasn't a nightmare. Wraith had Ethriel by the arm, and dragged him into the jail, pushing him down into the chair. He unlocked one of the handcuffs, passed it through a ring set into the wall, and relocked it. Then he untied the gag, patted Ethriel on the cheek, and stepped back, laughing as Ethriel glared pure murder at him.

"Well, now," Wraith said, sounding cheerful. "I'll just leave you two to talk." He smirked at John. "Told you it wasn't morning yet. Now... now you know what else you'll be getting in return for that favor." He left, and the door slammed behind him.

Ethriel was still scowling, tugging against the handcuff. Then he looked at John. "How did I get here?"

"I was going to ask you the same question," John answered. "You were supposed to be safe on the far side of the river."

"The last I remember, I was," Ethriel answered. "I remember going to sleep the night you left. And the next thing I know I was here. I woke up this morning in a bed with that man standing over me." He rattled the handcuff against the ring. "I was already chained. He gagged me and brought me here."

"He didn't hurt you?" John asked.

Ethriel shook his head. "No. I'm fine. I don't know about Parsons, though. Are you all right? What happened?"

John frowned. Parsons? Since when did Ethriel call his teacher Parsons? Usually, when there was a chance they could be overheard, Ethriel referred to the older elf as Uncle Ben. He glanced at the door. "He knows who I am. He knows what I am. And when I got here, he killed me."

"John!" Ethriel sat up straight. "How can he know?"

"I don't know," John answered. "He seems to know a lot — more than I've ever told anyone but you. And he says he'll repair the wagon and let us pass without harm if I do one thing for him." He shook his head. "Two things."

"I don't like the sound of this," Ethriel said softly.

"He wants me to kill two people." John shook his head and leaned his forehead against the bars. "I've killed, Ethriel. You know that. But this isn't the same. And I can't..." He paused, then continued in Aramaic. "I'll get us out of here, love. I'm not sure how, but I will."

"John, you're speaking gibberish."

John looked up. "What?"

"I don't understand you," Ethriel said. "I'm sorry."

John licked his lips and nodded. "I'm sorry," he said slowly. "I was distracted. I said I'll figure something out. I'll get us out here."

Ethriel smiled. "I know you will."

John closed his eyes and rested his forehead against the bars once more, his mind racing.

The elf sitting across from him had called his teacher Parsons, not Parciviel.

And he didn't understand when John spoke Aramaic.

That wasn't Ethriel.

This had officially gone from bad to disaster.

CHAPTER FIVE
Choices

Wraith returned, bringing another covered bowl. He put it on the desk, then leaned against the wall next to Ethriel.

"So, now do you understand?" he asked. "You do this for me, and you get your wagon repaired, you get your friend here, and you get safe passage out of Wraithtown."

"And what happens if I fail?" John asked, not standing up from his seat on the cot. "That Kestrel fellow was a big man. A fighter, from the looks of it. If he rips my head off—"

"John!"

John smiled slightly. "I'm positing, Ethriel."

"I don't like that line of thought. Your head looks better on your neck where it's supposed to be," Ethriel grumbled. "Stop that."

It was so something that Ethriel would say that John had to remind himself that this wasn't his lover. This was someone or something wearing his shape. He looked back at Wraith. "Well? What happens if he kills me, and I wake up to find them gone? For that matter, how do I even find them?"

Wraith nodded. "That's a fair question. I'll supply you with a horse, a weapon, and a map. I know where they are. I just can't reach them myself. And you won't have to get close. You're a sniper. One of the sharpshooters who wore green—"

"How do you even know all this?" John interrupted.

"I know things, John," Wraith said. "So much more than you can even imagine. So that's how I know you can kill them both without them ever seeing you. I've got a nice new rifle for you—"

John held his hand up. "If you want the sharpshooter, then keep your new gun. I'll take my Henry."

"You'll take what I give you," Wraith growled.

"Do you want them dead?" John asked. "If you want a sharpshooter to do the job, don't give me an unfamiliar weapon.

I can hit the targets I sight because my Henry is part of my arm. A new rifle? It'll take me time that neither of us have to be as accurate." He looked down at his hands. "And what about Ethriel?"

"He's my guest," Wraith said. "Prince Ethriel will stay in my house, eat at my table, and be treated with courtesy—"

"Then get these chains off of me!" Ethriel snapped.

John stood up and walked to the bars. "He has a point. You haven't started off all that well if you're talking about courtesy. Handcuffs aren't exactly polite."

Wraith's grin vanished. He reached into his coat pocket and took out the key, then went and unlocked the cuff on Ethriel's wrist. Ethriel rubbed that wrist with his other hand, and his shirt sleeves slipped back far enough that John could see pale skin unmarked by scars.

Definitely not Ethriel.

John wasn't sure if Wraith had realized that he had seen through the lies. He hoped not — the only way he was getting out of this cell was if he played along.

"So," Wraith drawled. "Since we're dickering over guns, that seems to say that you've changed your mind."

"Oh, I haven't," John said. "But I do see that I do what you say, or I stay here." He gestured to the cell, then wrapped his hands around the bars. "If it was just me? Staying here wouldn't be so bad. As I said, you have an excellent cook. But it isn't just me anymore, is it? You hold all the cards."

The grin returned, wide and grotesque. "You're right," he said. "I do hold all the cards. Now, I'll take Prince Ethriel back to the house while you have your breakfast. Then we'll get you on your way." He picked the bowl up and slid it through the slot at the bottom of the cell door. Then he went over to Ethriel's chair. "Your Highness."

Ethriel scowled. Then he looked at John. John nodded, so Ethriel followed Wraith out of the jail. The door closed, and John waited to the count of twenty before slumping onto the bed.

That wasn't Ethriel. He was certain of that. But did Wraith really have Ethriel? Or were he and Parsons still safe on the other side of the river, wondering where John was? John closed his eyes and tried to think. Then he got up and picked up the bowl. Breakfast was some kind of dark porridge, thick and nutty, heavy with cinnamon, honey and cream. Wraith was back before John finished.

"Enjoying it?" Wraith asked, perching on the desk.

"Very much so," John answered. He set the bowl aside and stood up. "I don't think I've ever had that sort of porridge before. Which is unusual. What is it?"

Wraith shook his head. "Not sure, actually. I'll find out for you when you get back. Maybe send you on with a bag or two." He took another key from his coat, and unlocked the cell door. "Leave the bowl. Your boots are under the desk."

John pulled his boots out and sat down to put them on. "Where am I going?"

"East. Shouldn't take you more than two days to reach them. Maybe three if you go slow. Small farm on the far side of Nacogdoches. Near the Sabine."

John looked up. "You're sending me to Louisiana?"

"Not quite," Wraith said. "They're still in Texas. I've got the map, and some supplies for you."

John stood up, stamping his foot to settle the boot. "And my coat?"

"There's a hook around the corner there," Wraith pointed. "And your horse is waiting."

John went and found his coat, then followed Wraith out of the jail. There was a horse hitched outside, and while John recognized the saddle and the empty rifle holster as his own, the horse was an unfamiliar coal-black mare.

"That's not Barak," he said. "Where's my horse?"

"Pulled up lame," Wraith answered. "He's in the livery stable, and the farrier's got a poultice on him. He'll be fine by the time you're back." Wraith walked over and ran his hand down the glossy black neck. "This is Lilith."

John coughed. "You... named the horse... after Adam's first wife?"

Wraith laughed outright. "Shoulda known you'd get the reference. Come meet the lady."

John walked over to the mare, letting her see him. He ran his hand over her neck and smiled. "You're a beauty," he murmured in Aramaic. "He called you a lady. He's right. You are." He kept on talking, letting her hear his voice, occasionally changing from Aramaic to English as he checked her legs, her hooves. There was something odd about her hooves, something that he couldn't quite...

"You done there?" Wraith asked.

"Just a moment," John answered. He finished at her head, laughing as she rubbed her nose against his sleeve. "She's lovely," he said. "Thank you for the loan of her."

"You're welcome. Is there anything you need?"

"My Henry," John answered. "And I'd like to look in on Barak before I leave."

Wraith nodded. "Come on, then. The livery stable is this way." He led John down the street. John looked back over his shoulder. "Don't worry about her. She's mine, and folks here know better than to touch something of mine. Now, she's a runner, so don't take her bridle off. She won't run if you leave it on her."

"Don't... How am I supposed to let her eat, then?" John asked. "Will she still run in a halter?"

Wraith turned to face John. "You take the bridle off, she'll run. Unless you want to walk to Nacogdoches and back, don't take off the bridle." He turned and started walking again.

John shrugged and followed. Wraith said nothing more until they reached the livery stable. An older man stood near the fence, and nodded at them as they approached.

"So you're the one," he said to John, revealing a broad, Scottish burr. "I've heard tales about you, back when I was a lad. The Wandering Jew, they called you."

John stared at him. "Did they now?" he answered. "You all know a great deal more about me than I thought possible. How?"

"Stories, my boy," the old man laughed, and John snorted. *My boy?* Really? The man ignored him, continuing, "Stories and songs. There's truth in them, if you know to look for it. Now, you're here to look in on your brave lad, aren't you?"

"If it's not too much trouble?" John said. "Barak and I have been through some times. What happened?"

"I'll show you," the man said. "And it's no trouble at all." He looked at Wraith. "Jacob, go bedevil someone else. I'm busy."

Wraith laughed. "Be back in a few minutes," he said, and walked off.

As soon as Wraith was out of sight, the old man spat. "And I presume you know that he'll betray you as soon as look at you?" he asked.

John looked around. "That, and I know he can hear when he's not close. So don't risk yourself. Not for me."

"Nah, he can't hurt me," the old man said. Then he paused. "Well, he can, but not so it matters. Call me Tam."

"Tam, it's nice to meet you. I'm John."

"I'd say it was a pleasure, John, but I know it isn't." He turned and led John into the stable. "Now, near as I can figure, your boy — Barak, you said?"

"Barak," John agreed. "It means lightning."

Tam nodded. "For the blaze. I like it." He gestured, and John saw the familiar dark bay stallion. He smiled and walked over.

"Here," Tam held a bag out.

John took it, and opened it to reveal chunks of dried apple. He offered one to Barak, who took it daintily, then rubbed his nose against John's chest.

"He was favoring the rear left foot," Tam said. "I'm thinking that when Wraith shot you, it startled him, and he strained it. It doesn't seem to be too serious. He'll be right as rain by the time you get back."

"I appreciate you looking after him," John said. He offered another piece of apple to Barak, then tried to give the bag back to Tam.

"Keep it," Tam said. "Miss Lilith, she likes them, too. She's a sweet girl, and far too good for Wraith. But he won't give her up or let her go. What he's claimed as his is his." He looked over his shoulder. "You'll do well to remember that."

John nodded. "What else can you tell me? What is this place?"

"A gathering place for the uncanny, or Hell's back garden. Pick one. There are all sorts here, things you wouldn't expect to see under Heaven. Spirits and Fae, and blood-drinkers and skinwalkers." Tam met his eyes and lowered his voice. "There are elves settling here, too," he murmured. "Mountain elves mostly. A few Light elves. Not many of those, though."

"You know the elves?" John asked. "How? And... are there many of them loyal to Siobhan?"

Tam snorted. "I know of you. You probably know me. They tell stories about me, too. Me and my lovely Janet."

Tam...and Janet? It sounded familiar. Then John remembered a verse that Thomas Learmont had sung to him during those long winter nights.

"Tam...Lin," he murmured. "You're Tam Lin. How did you get here?"

Tam shrugged. "When you're touched by the elven-kind, it changes you. When you're claimed by an Elven Queen? It changes you even more. I know the Mountain elves. I know Siobhan." He scowled and shook his head. "Too well, I know that witch. She kept me at her side for a hundred years or more. Cost me my youth, my life, and my love." Then his eyes narrowed. "How do you know Siobhan?"

"If I don't get back to my wagon, she may very well cost me my love," John answered. "Do you know Ethriel?"

Tam's eyes widened. "High Queen Méabh's boy? He's here?"

"You know him?"

Tam shook his head. "I know of him. Siobhan never took me to court, and he'd have just been a boy when Janet stole me free of her."

John nodded and lowered his voice. "It's a long story, but in a nutshell, Siobhan overthrew the High Queen."

Tam swore softly. "That bitch—"

"Ethriel was her son's prisoner until recently."

Tam spat. "Buach. Now that one was a spoiled little bastard."

"And now he's a rotting little bastard."

"He's dead?" Tam looked almost indecently gleeful. "Oh, tell me you did the deed, and I'll be a happy man. He was the Devil's own."

"Buach followed Ethriel when he escaped. Yes, I killed him. Now I'm taking Ethriel to Bandera. There are elves there who might be allies."

"You raising an army?" Tam asked.

"I might be," John answered. "Eventually. But not unless I get back to Ethriel."

"And to do that, you need to do this...whatever it is for Wraith," Tam finished.

"He's sending me after a girl and her father" John said.

"After Rose?" Tam whistled. "He's got a powerful hate for that girl, poor thing."

"Why?"

"She told him no." Tam shook his head. "And she and her father got out of his reach. Your rifle is over here," he said, and started walking away. John slipped Barak another apple, then tucked the bag into his coat pocket and followed Tam into the tack room. The Henry was resting on pegs on the wall; Tam took it down and handed it to John.

"Remember, he'll betray you," Tam said. "Don't trust a damn thing he tells you."

John nodded. "I wasn't planning on it. Thank you, Tam." He checked the Henry to see if it was loaded, then nodded. "When I come back, you're welcome to come with me."

Tam smiled and shook his head. "I thank you, but no. Even if I could leave, there's nothing out there for me anymore." He looked out of the tack room. "I'll take care of your Barak. He'll be ready when you come for him."

"Thank you." John followed Tam out of the tack room, and wasn't surprised to see Wraith waiting just outside the stable. He was holding a rifle, and he held it out as John came closer.

"You'll take this, too," he said.

"I don't need a second rifle," John protested. But he handed the Henry to Tam and took the weapon from Wraith, raising it into firing position. It was a bolt-action rifle, sleek and beautifully made. "This is very pretty, though," he added as he lowered it. "I've never seen one like this."

"It's a newfangled fancy thing," Wraith said. "Italian make. Won it in a card game."

"It's a single shot, though?" John asked.

"You need more than one?" Wraith chuckled. "You aren't as good as I thought."

"My name isn't David," John said. "I can't kill a giant with a single stone, nor two people with a single shot."

Wraith laughed. "Good point. There's ammunition in your saddlebags for both rifles. Bedroll and supplies. And the map." He started walking, leaving John to hurriedly take his rifle and nod his goodbye to Tam before trotting after, triggering a distant memory of running after his brother and their cousins so many years ago.

"East, you said. Near the Sabine River?" John looked around. "May I see Ethriel before I leave?"

Wraith didn't stop walking. "No. You get going. He's fine. He's comfortable. And he'll stay that way until you get back."

They walked down the wooden sidewalk to where the black mare was waiting. John took a piece of apple from his pocket and fed it to her, then scratched her forehead. Her bridle was possibly the fanciest piece of tack that John had ever seen, heavily ornamented in silver. It was pretty, but looked out of place against the plain saddle. He walked around and checked the harness and the saddle girth, then slid the new rifle and his Henry into the holster. They both didn't quite fit – he'd have to be careful with them.

"Right," he said, looking at Wraith. "Look for me in a few days. I'll be coming right back for what's mine."

Wraith nodded. He stepped back as John mounted the mare, waving as John rode away. The temptation to ride out of sight and then head north was strong. But he wasn't going to leave Barak here, for all that he was certain Tam would care for the horse. Barak was his.

"Now, I hope you don't mind," he said aloud, watching as Lilith's ears flicked back toward him. "I talk to my animals. And you're mine, at least for the next few days." He smiled as an idea occurred to him. "Longer, if I can convince Wraith to sell you. You've a lovely gait. I think Ethriel would adore you, and I should have insisted on a mount for him from the start."

Lilith snorted, and it sounded to John's ears like she was laughing. He chuckled along with her, then saw movement. A rider, coming toward him. He pulled the Henry free of the holster, and drew Lilith in. Only to lower the Henry as he stared in disbelief. "Parsons?"

The older elf looked haggard as he rode up to John. "I was hoping I'd find you," he said. "I've been lurking just outside of town ever since Ethriel disappeared. It seemed the mostly likely place for him to have been taken. He is in there, isn't he?"

John fought to keep calm. He knew full well it wasn't Ethriel back in Wraithtown. It followed, then, that this wasn't Parsons. "He's Wraith's guest. And you'll be Wraith's next target if he realizes you're this close. He knows you're with me. He knows far too much about me, too. Where's the wagon?"

"Where we left it, wrapped in concealment spells," Parsons answered. "Where are you going?"

John looked back over his shoulder. "Wraith has me between a rock and a hard place. But if I do this, he'll repair the wagon and grant us safe passage. And for now... well, he has a very good cook. Ethriel is safe."

"At the moment." Parsons shook his head. "I'll come with you."

"No," John said. "I want you here. Close enough to keep an eye on them, and close enough to get Ethriel out if necessary." He turned back to Parsons. "Parsons, promise me you'll get him out if I don't come back."

"You'll come back!" Parsons protested. "You always come back. But... yes, you're right. He's the reason we're out here, after all." He frowned. "I hate to let you go alone—"

"If it goes well, I'll be back in a few days. Keep your head down and look for me then." He scowled. "Do not follow me, Parsons. If anything happens to me, you have to get him out. You swore that to him."

Parsons looked sourly at John, then nodded. "Very well. Be careful."

John smiled. "I intend to. Go hide. I'll see you in a few days." He clucked to Lilith and urged her into a fast walk. When he looked back over his shoulder, Parsons was gone.

"That wasn't him," he muttered. "He never once asked about you. Or Barak." He frowned. "And that wasn't Windrider. Lilith, what in the unspoken name of God is so important about me killing this girl?"

Lilith snorted and didn't answer.

CHAPTER SIX
Discoveries

John stopped to make camp when the shadows grew long. He found a stream, and built a small fire near a young willow tree. Then he took off Lilith's saddle and set it and the saddlebags aside before going through the saddlebags for a brush. He treated the little mare to a good brushing, laughing as she leaned into the strokes.

"You're a wonderful lady," he told her. "And I don't believe that you'll run. You need to graze, and drink, and you can't do that in the bridle." He finished brushing, put the brush back into the saddlebag, then took out a length of rope. A few well-placed knots and he had a crude rope halter. He set it aside and ran his hand down Lilith's left foreleg. "Now, let's see your feet, make sure you didn't pick up any rocks... what in the world?" He stepped back, then walked all the way around the mare. He wasn't seeing things—all four hooves were backwards.

"So... you had an illusion on you, didn't you?" he said. "And that's what was bothering me. I could tell it was there, but I couldn't see through it." He walked back to Lilith and ran his hand down her neck. "It doesn't seem to impact your gait at all, or bother you. You're just different. That's fine. I'm glad some idiot farmer didn't decide you weren't worth your trouble." He reached for the buckles on the bridle, taking it off and replacing it with the halter. He tied the end of the rope off to the tree. "Now, no running off," he said, and went back to the saddlebags. What did he have to eat?

There was a packet of jerky in the saddlebag, and a bundle that contained hardtack biscuits. There was also a large tin mug, a spoon, and a knife. He sighed. "Well," he said to the grazing horse, "At least you'll have a good meal. I haven't eaten hardtack since the war." He took the mug to the stream, filled it with water, and brought it back to the fire, setting it close the flames. Once the water started to boil, he crumbled one of the biscuits into the mug, along with a piece of the jerky. He used the cuff of his shirt to pull the mug away from the heat, letting it simmer while he set up his bedroll and found a few good-sized rocks to set his boundaries. By the time he was done, it was time to move the mug away from the fire and let it sit. He sat down and looked up at the darkening sky.

This was the first time he'd been alone since he'd returned to his dugout and found Ethriel.

He didn't like it. He missed Ethriel, his laughter, his curiosity and his enthusiasm. Ethriel was still frightened of the Henry, but he was learning to shoot. He wasn't having nightmares anymore. John hoped that he wasn't having one tonight.

"I miss him, Lilith," he said, and the mare raised her head and looked at him. "I never thought I'd love someone like this again, and now I have him... and he's not here and I miss him." He looked over at her. "You're lovely company, but you're not a good conversationalist."

She snorted at him, and he laughed. "You're right. I shouldn't go insulting a lady. I apologize." He reached out and picked up the mug and the spoon, and started to eat. Wraith might have an excellent cook, but no one could make hardtack actually taste good. However, it was filling; he ate quickly, then went and refilled the cup. He sipped the cold water as he walked to the first of the rocks.

"We'll be safe tonight, Lilith," he said. "Just don't run off. I can't protect you if you run off." He bent and touched the rock, whispering to it, then walked to the second. He felt the barrier rising behind him as he went from the second to the third, and from the third back to the first one, where he felt the snap as the barrier closed. He looked around, then drained his cup and headed for the bedroll, laying the Henry alongside, and rolling his coat up for a pillow.

He fell asleep thinking of Ethriel.

"I COULD BE JEALOUS."

John heard the words, the woman's voice, but they didn't fully penetrate his slumber. He was dreaming of Ethriel, of having his lover in his arms, in his usual place with his head on John's chest. It was all a dream.

Until someone kissed him.

Suddenly, the weight in his chest, the warmth pressed against his side was real, and he came completely awake, gasping and grabbing for the Henry. Then he stopped — in the dim light of the dying fire, he saw the woman kneeling over him.

The naked woman kneeling over him.

John yelped, rolled, and was on his knees before he realized that she was laughing.

"I didn't think I'd startle you quite so much," she said. He could hear the same broad brogue in her voice that he'd heard in Tam's.

"Who are you?" he demanded. He glanced at her, then looked down. "Where did you come from?"

She laughed again. "I've been here the whole time, John."

He heard her walking toward him, but her steps sounded odd. Odd until she stopped in front of him, revealing not feet and ankles, but fetlocks and reversed hooves. He looked up in shock, then immediately looked down again.

"Lilith?" He looked to the side, and reached for his balled-up coat, which he held out to her. "Put this on, will you?"

"Does my skin bother you?" she asked as she took the coat. "There. I'm covered."

He looked up. The coat was enormous on her, but at least she was decently covered. She was a dainty little thing, but all he could really see in the moonlight was pale skin and long dark hair. "It doesn't bother me, but it's rude to stare at a lady."

She smiled. "John. You're quite the gentleman. You've already had your hands on me, and you've been calling me all sorts of lovely things. You rode me all day, and how many women can say that about a man? Why shouldn't you stare?"

"Because I haven't been properly introduced, and riding a horse is not the same as riding—" He stopped. For the first time in a long time, he could feel himself blushing. "What are you, if I may ask?"

She settled down to sit on the ground in front of him. "Would you know what I meant if I said I was a kelpie?"

John frowned, thinking. He shook his head. "No. But I'm learning that there's a lot I don't know, even as old as I am. What's a kelpie?"

She cocked her head to the side and studied him for a moment, then looked down, rummaging through the coat pocket. She pulled out a chunk of dried apple and popped it into her mouth. "I am a kelpie, and I am a woman when I feel the need," she said. "We come from Scotland, my kin and I. Some of us, we came to this new world to see what was here. And some of us... we fell afoul of what was here. I've been Wraith's slave for a very long time."

John frowned, then looked over to the pile of tack. "The bridle... is that why he told me I shouldn't take it off? It kept you from changing?"

She smiled. "You are the clever one," she said, and ate another piece of apple. "Yes. It trapped me as a horse. I can't even remember when the last time was that I walked on two legs. Or kissed a man." Her smile turned to an impish grin. "I could be that jealous of your Ethriel."

John shifted, sitting tailor fashion on the ground and resting his hands on his knees. "Lilith..." he started. Then he stopped and laughed. "I have no idea how to proceed. I imagine Ethriel would know what to do, but I'm just going to have to trust you."

"You shouldn't, you know. Never trust a kelpie. My kind usually lure people to their deaths," Lilith said. "But you're safe with me. I like you. You're a gentleman, and you treat me nicely." She stretched her arms over her head. "It was so nice to run today. To stretch. Wraith doesn't take me from the stables often." The impish grin returned. "I kick. And I bite. He didn't warn you of that, did he?"

"He didn't. I'll try to not give you a reason to bite me," John answered, and she laughed. "Does Tam know what you are?"

"I think so, but he'd not risk Wraith's anger. Not for a kelpie. Not if he knows anything about us and what we are." She smiled at John. "But you don't know, do you?"

"Are you going to tell me?" John asked. "You said I shouldn't trust your folk, and that you lure people to their deaths. All people?"

She met his eyes. "Some of my kin lure children. I don't like that."

"I'm glad of that," John murmured.

"Some of the males lure maidens to the deep. Some of the females lure men. And some of the females... well, we look for particular men." She smiled and shook her head. "You'd not be on that list."

John considered her words, then nodded. "You hunt the hunters, then."

"Yes. You are the clever one," she repeated. "I like clever. I wasn't, and that is what put me under Wraith's thumb. I wasn't clever, and I was caught. He claimed me, the same way he wanted to claim her. What are you going to do when you find Rose?"

John frowned. He reached over and tossed a handful of kindling onto the embers, letting them build to a small fire. "I have no idea," John answered. "Do you know her?"

Lilith shook her head. "I never saw her myself, so there isn't too much that I know," she answered. "She's got a talent. Some power that Wraith wants as his own. But she refused him, and she and her father escaped him. That's why he wants her dead. If he can't have her, then no one can." She sighed. "She had more care around him than I did. Or more help."

"If I can help it, you're not going back to him," John said. "And I won't ask you to wear the bridle again."

"Will you take it off when we stop?" Lilith asked.

"Of course I will!"

She smiled. "Then I don't mind. It's better for you as a rider, isn't it?"

"The rope harness—"

"Is scratchy and uncomfortable. The bridle is not."

John nodded. "I didn't realize. I apologize."

"How would you know?" she asked. "Do you often get answers when you talk to your Barak?"

He smiled and shook his head. "I'd like it if I did. But no. Then the first chance I get, we'll find you a bridle that won't stop you from changing, and that is comfortable for you to wear. If necessary, I'll have one made to your measure. And a saddle as well. I can't imagine Barak's saddle is comfortable for you. And in the meantime, we'll work out a signal so you can let me know if you want to stop and change."

She smiled, a slow, wide smile that John imagined men would find very seductive. "You are a delight, John Zebedee."

"A tired delight," John added. "Do you think we can get some more sleep?"

"Would you like company?" Lilith asked.

"Company?" John blinked as he realized what she was offering, and felt his face grow warm again. "I... no. Thank you, but no. You're truly beautiful, and I do thank you. But I won't betray my

Ethriel's trust." He looked down at the bedroll. "You are, however, welcome to share the blankets. And since you're currently lacking fur, you can keep my coat."

Her eyes widened in surprise. "You're saying no?" she gasped. "I..."

"Lilith, if it weren't against the law everywhere in this world I can think of, I'd be marrying Ethriel," John said. "I love him. I won't betray his trust in me."

Lilith nodded slowly. "I... I see," she said. "I'm very curious to meet your Ethriel. May I sleep close?"

John smiled and nodded. "You can sleep close. So long as you behave yourself."

She giggled. "I will keep my hands to myself. It's just been a very long time since I was last held."

"Then come here." John held his arms open, and they lay down together. She pillowed her head on his shoulder and draped her arm over his chest, then sighed happily.

"Good night, John."

WHEN JOHN WOKE WITH the dawn, his coat was draped over his chest, and Lilith was a horse again, grazing for her breakfast. The rope harness had been untied, and the rope lay coiled next to his saddlebags. He walked over to her and ran one hand over her withers.

"Good morning," he said. "Did you sleep well?" She raised her head and turned to rub her nose against his chest. He scratched her forehead. "Do you want something other than grass to eat? There's hardtack. It's not something, but it's much." A snort that sounded very close to a laugh, and John laughed with her. "I know. If I had the choice, I'd eat the grass, too. I'm going to put a few pieces of apple in it this morning. Assuming you didn't finish them?"

She snorted again, and John went back to his coat. He took down the barrier and set the mug of water to boil while he cleaned the camp, then made another mug of hardtack gruel, throwing some of the apples in. That made it slightly more palatable, and he ate quickly, wishing for coffee. Then he washed up, packed his supplies away, and put out the fire. Only then did he look up at the sky.

"I've been lax," he said in Aramaic. "I haven't stopped to say good morning to you in days. But I think you understand why. Good morning. I miss you, and I love you. Please keep an eye on Ethriel for me?" He smiled as the breeze ruffled his hair. Once the ashes were cold, he went and picked up the bridle.

"Ready, Lilith?" he asked. "If you need to have this off... ah... stamp twice." She snorted and raised her head, stamped twice, then nodded. John smiled. "Just like that, yes."

She snorted again, coming toward him and letting him put the bridle on. He adjusted the buckles, making sure that it wasn't too tight. "We'll get something without a bit, hm?" he asked, and laughed when Lilith nodded. He picked up the saddle blanket and checked it for burrs, then set it on her back. The saddle next, and he fastened the girth with care, making sure that it was tight but not too tight. He tugged on the saddle, then asked, "Comfortable?"

Lilith nodded again, and John walked around the campsite one last time. The ashes were cold, everything had been picked up and packed away. He checked the saddlebags for balance, then slung them onto the saddle and tied the bedroll in place. The Henry went into the holster with the other rifle, precariously positioned in the too-small-for-two holster.

"Right. Let's see how far we get today," he said as he mounted. Lilith's ears flicked back toward him, and she nickered. Then she started moving, a slow walk toward the east.

THEY REACHED NACOGDOCHES late the next day, and John seriously considered going into town and finding a hotel. A real bed. A bath. A hot meal.

"We could stay the night here," he said. "Go on in the morning. A good meal for both of us."

Lilith shook her head and tugged on the reins, turning away from the town. John laughed.

"All right. That's a no. Fine. Compromise? We might be able to find a mercantile still open, and get something other than hardtack. A bag of oats." He smiled. "More apples, perhaps? We're almost out."

Lilith snorted and stopped. Then she turned toward town and started walking again. John chuckled.

"If there's nothing open, we'll keep going." A thought occurred to him. "Lilith, that illusion that kept me from seeing your hooves. Was that Wraith, or you?"

Lilith stopped again. She stamped twice, so John dismounted. He took the saddle off, then unbuckled the bridle. The moment he took the bit from her mouth, Lilith changed, standing naked before him. John immediately turned to face the other direction.

"Oh, stop that," Lilith chided. "I won't talk to your back."

"If I give you my coat—"

"John!"

John sighed and turned back. "So, was that you, or was that Wraith?"

"That was Wraith. But I can hide myself so I look like naught but a mare." She grimaced. "I just can't when I wear the bridle."

"Which will raise questions, if we go into town with you without a bridle. We'll let it be. I can live on hardtack for another few days, and we're entirely not out of apples yet. I'll save them for you."

"Are you sure, John?"

John nodded. "I'm fine. I'm a long way from starving to death, Lilith. Let's go. We might get there before full dark if we keep going."

She changed back into a horse, and he replaced the saddle and bridle. They started to skirt around the town, and John looked at the buildings, at the windows starting to glow with light.

"We'll stop on the way back," he said. "For supplies."

Lilith snorted and picked up speed.

The shadows were growing darker as the sun kissed the western horizon when John finally saw the distant glow of what had to be farmhouse windows. He drew in Lilith and dismounted, checking the map. Yes, this looked to be the right place.

"I'm going to walk in from here," he said softly. "I want to see, and I don't want them to hear you." She stamped, just once, and he smiled. "It's safer, Lilith," he assured her. "I've done this before." He took the Henry from the holster, then the rifle Wraith had given to him. "Wait here. I shouldn't take long." He started walking, and stopped when he heard Lilith following. "Lilith, wait here."

When he started again, she didn't follow. He walked toward the house, listening and watching, keeping an eye on the growing darkness. If it got too dark, he'd have to wait for morning, and he wasn't looking forward to a cold camp. He started moving faster, until he was loping over the ground. There was a hill, slightly to the south of the farmhouse, and well within his firing range; he headed for it, taking cover behind low bushes so that he could see without being seen.

It looked peaceful. A neat little house. A barn. A fenced corral where a pair of horses grazed. There were chickens scratching and pecking the ground in front of the house. It was everything he hoped for in the home he'd find with Ethriel once they reached Bandera. And as he watched, the farmhouse door opened. A woman came out, and John recognized her from Wraith's illusion. That was Rose. Where was Kestrel?

As if the thought conjured him, the man appeared, coming around the far side of the house, stalking Rose like a tiger. Even at this distance, John could see the grin on his face. He rushed up behind her and grabbed her, sweeping her into the air as she shrieked and laughed, calling him Papa. John remembered scooping Sarai up like that, when she was a little girl. She'd loved it when he did that. She said it felt like flying.

She'd called him Papa, too.

He raised the Henry and sighted — right now, he might just get both of them with one shot. He ran the lever... then ejected the cartridge and lowered the gun.

He couldn't do it.

He couldn't kill them. No matter what Wraith said, or what he promised. From what Lilith said, Rose had just barely escaped a horrible fate.

He'd wait here until dark, then go back to Lilith. Maybe he'd be able to get axles in Nacogdoches. If he could, then they'd go north to the Red River, and back to Ethriel. He had no idea what he could do about Barak. He hated the idea of leaving him behind.

Maybe Lilith would have an idea.

In the meantime... he should warn them. Let them know that Wraith was still hunting them. Confess, and be shriven. And perhaps learn the truth. He stood up and walked down the hill, starting toward the farm.

He never saw the trap that killed him.

CHAPTER SEVEN
Divination

"Well, I'll be—"

A warm chuckle. *"I told you."*

"Child." Fond warning. *"I didn't think he'd actually do it."* A snort. *"I suppose this means that I don't get to keep the guns."*

John came the final distance back to life with a gasp and a jerk, setting himself swaying, which drew a startled yelp from him. He appeared to be in a barn, and was hanging upside-down from his bound ankles, with his wrists tied behind him. His head was pounding, but he wasn't sure if that was from the position, or from having come back from the dead again. And standing in front of him, watching him, were Kestrel and Rose. Kestrel crouched, turning his head slightly.

"Are you really alive?"

John swallowed, tugging against the ropes on his wrists. "At the moment, yes," he answered. "If I stay in this position for long? Then it remains to be seen."

Kestrel laughed. "I like you. It would be a shame if I had to kill you again. What's your name, and what are you doing here?"

"My name is John Zebedee." John closed his eyes. The swinging was making him sea-sick. It was insulting — he was a fisherman's son. He never got sea-sick. "What I'm doing here is a long story," he answered. "But it involves Wraith."

Rose sighed. "We know that," she said.

John opened his eyes to see her coming closer, taking off the gloves she was wearing.

"Rose."

"He can't hurt me," she said to Kestrel. "But you know what I can do to him." She knelt in front of John, then reached out and touched his cheek with one warm hand. There was something about her touch, something comforting. John closed his eyes and sighed. Then her hand was gone, and he opened his eyes again. She smiled, but there was a shadow in her dark blue eyes.

"He's safe, Papa," she said, standing up and putting her gloves back on. "You can cut him down."

"You're sure?"

"Yes. Cut him down before he's sick."

Kestrel brushed past her. "Back up," he called, and John turned, trying to see what was happening. He saw Kestrel pull a large knife from a sheath on his belt.

"No!" he yelped, but it was too late. Kestrel slashed through the rope holding John suspended, and John came crashing down onto the straw-covered floor. For a moment, all he could do was lie there, gasping for breath.

"Are you still alive?" Kestrel asked. John opened his eyes and scowled up at the big man, who grinned. "That's disappointing. I wanted to see if you could do it again!"

"I could, but it's not exactly a comfortable thing," John grumbled. "Or fast. And I presume you want answers?

"Answers would be good." Kestrel nodded. He reached down and slashed the rope binding John's ankles, then sheathed the blade. "So. You said Wraith's involved?"

John squirmed and sat up, folding his legs. There was something very familiar about his accent, but he was having trouble thinking straight. He tugged on the ropes binding his wrists. "I'm assuming I'm not getting my hands untied until I tell the story?"

"You assume correctly," Kestrel agreed. "Talk."

John nodded. "It started a few nights ago. There was a storm... no, I should go further back. What do you know of elves?"

Kestrel glanced at Rose. She nodded. Then they both shimmered. A moment later, John was looking at a pair of elves.

"Quite a bit," Kestrel said. "Now, the question is what do *you* know of elves?"

"Clearly, not nearly as much as you do," John agreed, and started talking. He told them about going back to Skullyville after the war, looking for peace. About finding Ethriel, whose name drew a muffled gasp from Rose. About saving him, only to nearly lose him again. About their journey to Bandera, cut short by the storm and by mischance. Of being taken prisoner by Wraith, and being offered a choice that wasn't really a choice.

"I know that it wasn't Ethriel that Wraith brought to meet me," he said. "And I know that the elf on the road wasn't Parsons. And when I saw you here, when I realized how wrong what I'd been sent to do was, and I couldn't do it." He sighed and shrugged as best he could with his hands still bound. "I was going to warn you, and I was going to leave. Take Lilith and go to Nacogdoches, see if I could find the axles I needed there. I don't know what I'm going to do about getting Barak back." He looked up. "That's the entire story. Do I pass?"

Kestrel looked at Rose, who nodded.

"He's told us the truth. Let him loose. I'll go warm up supper. Mister Zebedee, you'll join us?"

John blinked. "I... thank you. If it won't be any trouble?"

"It's no trouble." She turned and left the barn, while Kestrel drew his knife and walked behind John. The ropes binding his wrists parted, and John stretched and got to his feet.

"Thank you," he said. "I heard what you said about keeping the guns. You can have the bolt-action. I'd like my Henry back. It's been mine for a while, and I'm fond of it."

"You're certain?" Kestrel asked. "That's a very nice rifle. It would fetch you a good price in Nacogdoches if you sold it."

John shook his head. "I don't want it. Wraith gave it to me to kill you both, and would not take no for an answer, even though I told him that I prefer my Henry. I think it's fitting that you keep it, and use it to spite him."

Kestrel chuckled, leading John out of the barn and toward the house. The skies were dark, spangled with stars. "I suppose that's poetic," he said. "I wouldn't have expected Wraith to be a generous... whatever he is."

"Demon?" John suggested. "Is he a demon?"

"I've never met a demon, I don't think. I don't know." Kestrel studied him for a moment. "What do you know from demons?"

John burst out laughing. "Kestrel, if I've learned anything in the past month, it's that I know appallingly little for a man of my years. I've only dealt with demons once before, and that not close up. The ones I saw looked an awful lot like pigs."

Kestrel snorted. "I don't think he's a demon. But I've not dealt with them in any form to know for certain. Now, how are you getting back to Wraithtown? Or anywhere, for that matter? We don't have a spare horse."

"Lilith is probably waiting for me," John answered. "She's... not a normal horse. I'm rather surprised she hasn't tried to get through your fences already."

Kestrel burst out laughing. "Who says she hasn't? Black mare?"

"That's Lilith," John agreed.

"I've seen her. But I haven't been able to go out and try to catch her." Kestrel stopped just outside the house and looked around at the dark landscape. "We've been a bit busy with waiting on you."

"How long—?

"About an hour," Kestrel answered. He looked around again and frowned. "Zebedee, something is bothering me. Wraith gave you the gun to kill us. Even though you already had one. I don't understand why he'd do that."

"It made no sense to me. But I wasn't in a position to refuse," John took a deep breath. "I'll go find Lilith—"

"Come and eat first," Kestrel said. "Then I'll help you."

John turned to face him, and found himself looking at the house. He could see Rose through the window, moving back and forth through what must have been their kitchen. "I shouldn't leave her out there, alone and scared," he said. "I'll—" Movement caught his eye. Not Rose through the window. No, this was something rising up from below the window.

Wraith's rifle!

"No!" John gasped, and bolted into the house. He heard Kestrel behind him, heard Rose's startled voice, but he was focused on the rifle, floating above the table. He saw the bolt shoot back, then forward as if someone had loaded it. There was no time—

He grabbed Rose and pulled her to his chest, putting his back to the rifle. He heard the click of the hammer. Then something hit him, pierced him, burning like fire. He saw Rose's shocked face, heard Kestrel roaring in anger. The burning grew stronger, and he let Rose go and fell backward.

He knew what this was. Had felt it before, not all that long ago. Elfshot.

Wraith had somehow loaded the gun with elfshot. This was stronger than what Buach had done, though. Dying hurt more than the last time. But it was definitely elfshot.

And the pain was already fading. He let out a long breath, took another.

"Mister Zebedee?"

He opened his eyes to find Rose kneeling over him. "I'll be fine in a moment," he said, and knew he was lying. His head was spinning, and he closed his eyes again. "Just..."

"What do you need?"

"Something to eat," John answered. "To tell my body it's still alive. I don't think I've ever died twice in two hours before. That's new. And... I can't say I approve of it. I won't be doing that again, if I can help it."

"I'll get you something," Rose said. "Can you sit up?"

"I can try," John answered. He opened his eyes and slowly sat up. He was alone in the kitchen with Rose. "Where's your father?"

"Dealing with that gun," she said, and came back with a bowl. "Here, and there's more where this came from."

John took the bowl from her and took a bite of warm potatoes, onions and cabbage. "Oh, I haven't had bubble and squeak in ages," he murmured. "Before the war, I think. This is very good."

"Thank you," Rose said, sounding pleased. "It's my father's favorite."

The door opened, and Kestrel came inside. "It's done. Destroyed. I've no idea how he did it, but I'm not taking any chances," he said. He looked at John and grinned. "And you're alive. Again. How do you do that?"

"Even longer story," John answered. "What did you do with the gun?"

"I smashed the barrel, then tossed the entire thing into a bonfire," he answered. "That should destroy all the spells on it. And your mare is in the barn. She's quite smart. I saw her by the fence, and I told her you were here, and safe. She came right to me. Zebedee, how did you end up with a kelpie?"

John smiled and set down his empty bowl. "She's been Wraith's prisoner for years. And she's helping me so I can help her."

Rose laughed. "Papa, bring my wrapper out, and I'll set another place for supper."

Kestrel nodded and walked out of the room, coming back with a blue bundle under one arm that he took with him when he left the house. The door closed, and John slowly got off the floor. He brought his empty bowl to the table and asked, "What can I do to help?"

"You can sit down before you fall down," Rose answered. She put another bowl and fork on the table, then looked at him. "Sit!"

John sat. But only for a moment; the door opened, and Kestrel came back into the kitchen. Behind him, completely dwarfed in Rose's wrapper, was Lilith. John stood up, and was almost immediately knocked off his feet.

"I'm sorry," he told her. He felt her nod. When she stepped back, he really looked at her for the first time.

"You're staring," she murmured.

"I haven't really seen you yet," he answered. "You're that lovely, Lilith. And I'm sorry I frightened you."

"The next time you go off to do something stupid," she said. "Take the bridle off first."

John nodded. Then he asked, "The *next* time I do something stupid?"

"Of course," Lilith said with a sniff. "You're male. You will always be doing something stupid."

"Excuse me?" Kestrel protested. John just shook his head.

"Come and sit, all of you," Rose said. "Lilith? It's nice to meet you."

"I've heard your name," Lilith said, sitting down to face Rose. "I knew of you. You succeeded where I failed. You got away from him. Oh, is that bubble and squeak?"

"You can eat... food?" John asked. "You didn't—"

"Hardtack is not food," Lilith said with a snort. "I'd rather graze. You said you would have preferred to graze yourself."

"True," John agreed. He closed his eyes and took a deep breath.

"Are you feeling all right, Mister Zebedee?"

"You can call me John," he said, opening his eyes. He smiled at Rose. "And yes. Just tired. Thank you."

"Tell us where you found a rifle that shoots elfshot" Rose said.

"Elfshot?" Lilith asked. "What's that?"

"Wraith gave it to me. And I didn't know it fired elfshot. It looked like a normal rifle until it tried to kill you. Lilith, elfshot is a relic from one of the elven wars, I'm told," John answered. "All I really know of it is that it kills. Painfully." He grimaced. "I was told that it's been outlawed."

Kestrel snorted. "Like that ever works."

John nodded. "It didn't work with Greek fire, or gunpowder, or anything that increases a man's ability to kill. Why should the elves be any different?" He took a bite of his supper and considered. "Wraith has elves working for him. Mountain elves. I knew that. Tam told me as much before I left Wraithtown."

"Tam? The farrier?" Rose asked. She smiled. "I remember him from when we were there. He was a good man. He helped us get away."

John ate some more of his potatoes and cabbage before continuing, "Parsons says he thinks that the knowledge of elfshot came from Siobhan. The last time I felt it was when Buach tried to kill me with it."

"Buach is better off dead. And I'm still trying to get my mind around our Prince being alive." Kestrel said. "That's why we fled to this world. Because we thought there was no one left to stand against Siobhan, that the entire royal family was dead. And Mountain elves in Wraithtown? You're certain of that?" When John nodded, he scowled. "So... that means that Siobhan's people are in Wraithtown. She's not going to give that kind of weapon so someone not completely under her control." He snorted and picked up his cup. "I wouldn't."

"More important, that means her people are a day's ride from Ethriel and Parsons, who have no idea there's a threat." John swallowed around a lump in his throat. "Lilith, once you're finished, we'll be leaving."

"Right," Kestrel said, sounding cheerful. "I'll get my bedroll ready."

"What?" John stared at him for a moment. "No! Kestrel, I'm not asking you—"

"You stepped in front of a bullet for my daughter," Kestrel interrupted. "You stepped in front of *elfshot* for my daughter. That's a debt that needs paying."

"You seem to be forgetting that I'm the Judas goat that brought that blasted thing into your house in the first place," John said. "As far as I'm concerned, the debt was mine to pay."

"Technically, I brought it in," Kestrel pointed out. "I'm going."

"And if that was his real plan?" John countered. "To get you to leave her here alone? Undefended?"

"If you go, I'm going, too. I'm not staying behind," Rose said, her voice quiet and firm.

Kestrel growled, and he and Rose started talking in Elven, clearly arguing. Lilith touched John's hand. When he looked at her, she shook her head. "To take her back is to put her in his reach. We can't take them with us," she whispered.

"I know," he whispered back. "We won't. We'll leave as soon as you're done eating."

She nodded. "I'm done."

John pushed his chair back and stood up, offering his hand to Lilith. She took it, standing up.

"What are you doing?" Rose asked.

"Thanking you for a lovely meal," John answered. "We'll be nothing more than a memory in under an hour."

Kestrel turned toward them. "John, I said—"

"No," John interrupted. "You can't come with me. You have to stay here." He gestured to Rose. "You have to stay to protect your daughter, Kestrel. If you insist on paying the debt, then pay it in supplies?" he suggested. "Anything but hardtack."

Kestrel opened his mouth to protest, but stopped when Rose touched his arm.

"Papa, go and help Lilith get ready," she said. "I want to look at John's hands."

Kestrel's brows rose, and he nodded slowly. "If you say so," he said. "Will you put up supplies?"

"When I'm done," she said. "John, sit down. I'll clear the table."

John sat down as Kestrel led Lilith out of the house. Rose cleared the table, then sat down across from John. "Are you right or left-handed?"

"Right."

"Then give me your right hand." She held her hand out, and John put his hand into hers. He looked at his palm and frowned. "Mister Zebedee, how did you manage to misplace your lifeline?"

John coughed. "What?"

She tapped his palm with one finger. "It should be here," she said. Then she held her right hand out, showing him a line on her palm. "It shows how long of a life you'll have."

John chuckled. "My hand isn't big enough," he answered. "I'm immortal. But you've noticed that."

"How old are you?" she asked.

"Over eighteen hundred years old," John answered.

"You're only a little older than I am," she said with a laugh. "And I have one. But if you don't? All right. Just stay there. I need to get something." She stood up and walked away, going through an inner door. She came back a moment later with a small box. She took a seat again, and took a deck of cards out of the box, handing them to John. "Shuffle these."

"Are we playing poker?" he asked, starting to shuffle the cards. "I'm terrible at it."

"Cartomancy," she answered. "Telling the future."

"You can do that?"

She smiled and took the cards from him. "I can do that. I'm a seer, John. That's why Wraith wanted me. One of the reasons. If we'd remained in our own lands, I'd have gone to the deep forests to train my gifts. Do you know about that?" When he nodded, she smiled. "I've learned how humans do it while we were here – palms and cards and looking in bowls of ink or mirrors." She shuffled the cards again, then took the topmost card from the deck. She looked at it and smiled, laying it on the table. "The King of Clubs," she said. "A man of dark complexion. He is upright and true to the bone. This is your card, John Zebedee." She dealt more cards — a column of three to the left of John's card, one above and below his card, and a column of three to the right. She set the rest of the cards aside. "The past," she said, touching the left-most column. "The present, and the future." She touched the center and the right column in turn. Then she turned over the card at the top of the left column. "The Nine of Diamonds. Traveling. You never did settle, did you?"

"When people notice you don't age, things get complicated."

She smiled and turned over the next card down. "The Ten of Spades. Imprisonment." She looked up again.

John swallowed and nodded. "I was a prisoner of war. At Camp Sumter. Do you know about that?"

She nodded, her eyes wide. Then she turned over the last card in the column. "The Two of Diamonds. A secret engagement."

John smiled. "It has to be secret. It's illegal in this world. But if I could marry him, I would. In a heartbeat."

She nodded and turned over the topmost card of the middle column. "Eight of Spades. Danger from imprudence."

John considered it, and nodded. "I wasn't as careful as I should have been. I can agree with this. This is fascinating."

"Thank you," she said, and turned over the base card of the column. "Five of Clubs. Danger from a capricious temper." She met his eyes, and they both spoke as one. "Wraith."

She nodded, and turned over the top card of the last column. "The Eight of Diamonds. A happy marriage."

John smiled. "In your world, men can marry. I can wait."

She turned over the last two cards, and her brow furrowed. She touched the middle card. "The Nine of Spades is a horrible card for your future. It means ruin and death. Which makes no sense with this last card." She touched the final card. "The Ten of Hearts. Health and happiness, and children." She looked up. "Death and ruin, and they all lived happily ever after?"

CHAPTER EIGHT
Return

They set out from the farm when the moon rose, with Kestrel escorting them past the traps. John left him behind at the foot of the hill, and he and Lilith set out for Nacogdoches. He'd get the axles he needed, then they'd head north to the Red River.

"I'm still not sure what to do about Barak," he said aloud. "Maybe... no, if I take you back to town, I'll never get you out again." He yawned. Then he groaned as Lilith stopped walking. "Lilith, I'm fine. I'll sleep when we stop. We have to get to Nacogdoches before dawn, and I'll have to leave you outside of town. So we'll make camp, and I'll leave you there. Without the bridle."

Lilith shook her head and started walking again. John smothered another yawn.

It was, he thought, halfway between midnight and dawn when they finally were close enough to the town for him to walk, but far enough for him to be willing to stop and make camp. He removed Lilith's saddle and bridle, brushed her down, and took off his coat, putting it on the ground next to her. Then he turned his back.

"Will you be making a fire?"

He turned to face the kelpie. "No. Cold camp tonight. And, since I've no place to anchor a barrier, if you want to sleep first, I'll keep watch."

"Go on with you!" she said with a laugh. "And you falling on your nose? I felt it, you know, every time you nodded off. Take your coat back and sleep. I'll watch."

"Lilith—"

She took the coat off and tossed it at him; John caught it before it hit the ground, and looked up to see a mare looking back at him. "Lilith, it's hardly fair to you—"

She snorted and stamped, and he sighed. "All right! I'll lay down. But I may not sleep." She snorted again, and John looked at her in the moonlight. "You are up to something, aren't you?"

She stamped again, and John put his coat back on and lay down, leaning against the saddle. Lilith walked over to him and lowered her head to rub her nose against his shoulder...

And it was morning.

John sat upright, startled by the sun in his eyes. He didn't remember falling asleep. He'd had no intention of falling asleep. How—

"Lilith, did you put me to sleep?" he asked, turning around. Lilith was grazing a few feet away. She didn't raise her head, but there was amusement in every line of her. John had never seen a horse laugh at him before. That was definitely something new. He got up and went over to her, running his hand over her back. "That wasn't fair," he said. "You need to rest, too. You're doing most of the work." She snorted without raising her head. "Fine. Stubborn miss. I'll be off to town. Be careful. If you need to run, don't worry about the saddle or the supplies. I'll be back as soon as I can."

He picked up the Henry and started walking.

THE MORNING IN NACOGDOCHES was well-spent. He found the axles he needed, and a soft head-stall that he hoped Lilith would like. In the mercantile, he bought oats and more dried apples, and a ready-to-wear nightdress that he thought would fit Lilith, and that would probably be more comfortable for her to wear than his coat. And, with the card reading still fresh in his mind, he made one completely impulsive, completely extravagant purchase. He couldn't even remember the last time he'd been either impulsive or extravagant.

Best of all, no one asked him anything, accepting without question his story of broken axles and people waiting for him. No one had even asked about his lack of a horse. He stopped, resettled the pair of axles on his shoulder, considered shifting them, then decided against it and kept walking. He was almost there.

And he was close enough now to see that Lilith wasn't alone. There was a neat little covered wagon drawn up right where John was certain that he'd left the kelpie and her tack, and he could clearly see a familiar man.

"What are you doing here?" he demanded as he reached the camp. He stood the axles up on their ends and let the bundle dangling from them slide to the ground.

Kestrel grinned. "Nice to see you, too."

"You didn't answer," John said. "You shouldn't be here! Not the both of you!" He looked over at the wagon, where Rose and Lilith were sitting. Lilith, he noticed, was once more wearing Rose's wrapper. It was the first time he'd seen her in her human form in daylight — the lamp in Rose's kitchen hadn't told him nearly how beautiful she was.

"I went looking for more answers after you left," Rose said. "We need to be here. So you can put the axles in the wagon, and we'll start north."

"You... need to be here?" John repeated. "What did the cards say?"

"I used a bowl of ink this time. It's more precise," she answered. "I saw all of us, near a burned-out tree. I recognized Ethriel. He hasn't changed much since the last time I saw him. And I didn't realize that Parsons was Sir Parciviel. I remember him, too."

"How do know my Ethriel?" John asked. He looked from Rose to Kestrel. "You knew his name, but this is more. You know *him*. What haven't you told me?"

Kestrel smiled. "Our full names, to start. I'm Kestriel. Sir Kestriel, Knight of the Silver Thorn. I served under Sir Parciviel, but we were away from court when the attacks came and the court fell. My daughter is Roshara. Her mother was noble-born, a cousin of the royal line."

"We lived in the Palace, and Ethriel and I shared tutors as children," Rose added. "I knew him well." She bit her lip. "I should tell you. There were jokes, then. Of marriage contracts. But that was a long time ago."

John swallowed. He never expected that Ethriel might have had another old lover. Or that she'd be a lovely girl. "You must have seen the cottonwood tree that was lightning struck in the storm. That's where we camped." He took a deep breath. "Rose, I don't like you being here. It puts you too close to him."

She smiled. "I'll be fine." She looked at Kestrel. "We need to go straight north from here." She looked at Lilith, then back at John. "You can both sleep, if you want. There's enough room."

Kestrel reached out and took the axles from John, carrying them toward the wagon. John scooped up the bundle so he could follow.

"I bought something for you, Lilith," he said as he came up next to the wagon. This close, he could see that she was tired. She also looked puzzled.

"You bought a gift for me?"

John leaned the bundle on the rim of the wheel and untied it. He took out the headstall first. "I promised you something that wouldn't trap you as a horse. I thought this might work." He passed it to her, and she smiled.

"We can try it later," she said.

"I also got this," he added, taking the folded nightdress from the bundle. "I thought it would be more comfortable than wearing my coat. I hope it fits you."

She took the nightdress and shook it out, and her eyes widened. "You... bought this for me?" she whispered. Her face turned pink, and she bit her lip as she hugged the garment to her. She turned and whispered something to Rose, who nodded. Then she turned and slipped into the back of the wagon, her hooves making heavy thumping sounds as they hit the floor.

"You certainly know how to woo a woman, don't you?" Kestrel said softly.

John blinked. "I'm not wooing anyone!"

"You're doing a horrible job of not wooing, then." Kestrel snickered. "Once she's done changing, you get in the back. We already loaded your tack. We were just waiting for you."

"I don't have a choice in this, do I?" John asked.

Kestrel smiled broadly. "No."

John sighed and shook his head, then laughed. "Fine. I'm just not used to having people go out of their way to help me."

Kestrel nodded. "I understand that. I wasn't used to it either." He nodded toward the wagon. "Then Rose's mother taught me." He clapped John on the shoulder. "She should be done. Go get in."

John walked around the back of the wagon and scratched his nails on the canvas. "Are you dressed?" he called.

"I am," Lilith called back. "You can come in."

He loosened the canvas, put the bundle and the Henry into the back, then climbed up and into the wagon. The back of the wagon was mostly empty — his saddle with the bedroll and the saddlebags, some baskets and boxes that he assumed held supplies for the road. And Lilith. The nightdress was a pale-yellow cotton lawn, and ornamented with white lace. It covered her from neck to wrists to hooves, and the thin cloth hid absolutely nothing.

"It's lovely, John," she said. "Thank you."

He cinched the wagon cover closed, then knelt next to the saddle, picking up the bedroll. He rolled it out on the wagon floor.

"You're very welcome, Lilith," he said. "Now, you're tired. Lay down and rest."

She blushed. "Will you lay with me?"

John swallowed. "Lilith—"

"To sleep. Just to sleep," she added quickly. Too quickly, the words tripping over themselves like foals taking their first steps. "I remember what you told me."

John took his coat off and balled it up, then lay down on the bedroll. Lilith knelt beside him and as she did, the wagon lurched; John caught her before she fell.

"We're leaving!" Kestrel called from the front of the wagon.

"We noticed!" John called back, hearing Kestrel laugh in response.

John closed his eyes, feeling Lilith settle next to him. Against him, pillowing her head on his shoulder, the way she had the first night they'd camped, and every night since. He felt her relax and soften into sleep. He tried to sleep, but it wouldn't come. Instead, the worries rose.

Was he leading Lilith on? Was Kestrel right? What would Ethriel say?

And what would Ethriel say, when John returned to camp accompanied by a young woman who might have a prior claim on his heart?

He lay awake thinking about it. Fretting over it, staring at the canvas until sleep finally claimed him.

HE WOKE WHEN THE WAGON rolled to stop, but couldn't move because of the woman draped over his chest. So he closed his eyes again and listened. Running water. They couldn't possibly have made it to the Red River yet, could they?

He heard Rose's soft voice from the front of the wagon. "I think they're still asleep."

"I'm not," John said softly. "But I can't move."

A soft, warm chuckle. "We're stopping to rest the horses and eat. See if you can wake Lilith."

The wagon rocked — Rose must have gotten down from the bench. John yawned, then ran his hand down Lilith's arm.

"Lilith, wake up," he said. "You need to eat." She hummed softly and cuddled closer, rubbing her cheek against his chest. He swallowed and shook her arm. "Lilith, wake up."

This time, she jerked slightly, and raised her head. She looked confused, but only for a moment. "Oh," she murmured. "I... where are we?"

"I'm not sure, but Rose said that it was time to eat and to rest the horses."

She nodded and sat up, sighing happily and stretching. "I slept beautifully," she said. "You're a lovely pillow, John." She looked at him. "Did you sleep?"

"Eventually," John admitted. "Too many things to think about."

"Worry about, you mean," she corrected. "You worry too much."

"Lilith, the man I love is out there, alone and in danger." John sat up. "Of course I worry. I can come back from the dead. He can't."

She frowned. "He can't?" she repeated. "Will he grow old, then, and die?"

John shivered and closed his eyes. "Don't say that," he murmured. "That... not for a very long time, Lilith. He's young for his people."

"How old is he?"

John smiled. "My age," he answered. "My real age. Eighteen hundred years old."

Lilith's jaw dropped. "You're that old?" she gasped. Then she giggled. "You're older than I am!"

"Not surprised," John said. "Now, let me go first, and I'll help you out."

He loosened the canvas and climbed out, jumping down to the ground. He turned, and reached up, catching Lilith at the waist and lifting her down. She giggled as he set her on her hooves.

"Lilith, will you help me?" Rose said, coming around the wagon. "I'm going to make something for us to eat."

Kestrel followed Rose around the wagon. He was carrying a rifle. "John, come hunting with me."

John arched a brow. "And leave the women alone?"

Kestrel looked around. "We're still outside his reach. It'll be safe enough."

John looked around, then nodded. "Let me get my gun." He went to the wagon and reached inside, taking out the Henry. He ran the lever, and picked up the cartridge that dropped to the ground, tucking it into his pocket. "All right. Lead the way."

Kestrel grinned. He went over to Rose and kissed her. "We'll be back soon," he said. "Keep the pistol with you, and take your gloves off."

"I will. Worrier." Rose laughed and led Lilith around the wagon, and Kestrel started walking.

John hurried to catch up with him. "May I ask you a question?"

Kestrel shrugged. "Might not answer."

"You were away from court?"

Kestrel nodded. "My wife was dying," he answered. "I took her home for the last time. We were nearing the end of the mourning period when the attacks came."

"Oh," John breathed. "I'm sorry."

"There is no way you could have known that, John," Kestrel said. "Now, tell me about yourself."

John nodded. "John Zebedee isn't really my name. Yohanan ben Zavdi is my real name. I am eighteen hundred and eighty-nine years old, and when people in this world tell stories about me, then call me John the Beloved Disciple. Tam called me the Wandering Jew."

Kestrel whistled. "I've heard some of those stories. You have a lot of history," he said. "You were one of the followers in the stories of the son of their God?"

"Yes. Followed. Loved." John smiled. "There's a reason I'm still here."

"I remember hearing that story. He told you to wait. That's why you come back?"

"I can't die. He told me to wait, and I'm waiting." John saw movement, and raised the Henry, running the lever and firing.

Kestrel turned. "What was it?"

"Bird. Possibly a pheasant," John answered. He started off toward it. "Do you have a knife? We can dress it here."

"Can't be a pheasant. We don't have them around here. You're a good shot," Kestrel said as he followed. "Where did it fall?"

John pointed. "There, I think."

Kestrel nodded and walked over, bending and picking up the large bird. It definitely wasn't a pheasant – it was boxy, with white and black barred plumage.

"What is it?" John asked. "And is it edible?"

"Prairie chicken," Kestrel answered, going to one knee. "Good eating. I'll take care of it, then we'll go back."

John nodded and turned to look around, watching for more movement. If he hadn't been able to see the wagon in the distance, he'd have sworn that he and Kestrel might have well been alone in the world. "Kestrel? May I ask you another question?"

"What?"

John looked down at where Kestrel was working. "I... this is awkward, but I've no one else I can ask," he said. "I don't have a great deal of experience with women."

Kestrel looked up. "How old did you say you were?"

"Age has nothing to do with it," John said. "And I didn't say *that*. I've loved women, laid with them. But it's never been quite the same as what I've felt with men. Does that make sense?" He paused. Frowned. "I've loved women. I've been married, multiple times. But it's never been the same. I loved them, but I haven't been in love with them. Really, I've only ever been in love with two men."

Kestrel looked startled. "You're not joking?"

"I'm not. So when you said I was wooing Lilith... am I?" John laughed, feeling oddly nervous. "When I loved Joshua, he also loved Maryam."

Kestrel nodded. "All right."

"He married Maryam. And I loved them both. I lived with them both. Well, we all did, really. But I shared their bed. And when Joshua died, I was father to his daughter."

Kestrel's jaw dropped. "He had a daughter? That's not in the Bible!" He frowned. "Or is it? I've read it. I was curious. But I might not know it as well as some."

"It isn't in there." John laughed. "Yes, he did. Her name was Sarai. They'd say Sarah now. Not many speak of her these days, but most of France is descended from her by now. But there's my problem. Maryam wasn't mine. Joshua was. I took care of her because she was important to him. I loved her, but I was never in love with her. She knew that. She accepted that. Lilith...I don't know what she wants. But I'm certain it's more than I'm willing to give. I mean... she's offered herself to me. And I told her no. I intend to steal her from Wraith—"

"He'll come after you."

"We'll be out of his reach in Bandera, I'm told." John shrugged. "Then, I was told he couldn't reach over the Red River. So I'm not sure—"

"No, Bandera is safe. There are other Light elves there." Kestrel wiped his knife on grass, then sheathed it and stood up. "I'm done. Let's head back. So, you want advice about what to do with her?"

"Yes, please." John fell in next to Kestrel.

"Tell her what you just told me. Tell her that your heart belongs to someone else. Before she gets all her hopes pinned on you." He shook his head. "It might be nothing, truly. She's fixing on you because you're being nice to her. You may be the first person to be nice to her in a long time. If you do accept her offer, it will be taking advantage of that. So... be nice, and keep saying no.

John nodded. "Thank you. I'll do that. And thank you for listening."

"You learn a lot when you listen," Kestrel said. "And Rose says you can be trusted."

"She's a seer, she said. Among other things."

"She's powerful," Kestrel said. "And just coming into that power. That was why Wraith wanted her. He wants her power and her potential. She needs teaching. So if you don't mind, we'll join you on the road to Bandera."

John caught his breath. "But... your house—"

"It's just a place, and one that we haven't been for long. It's not even ours – we were tenants. The owner lives in Nacogdoches. It was a place to rest while I decided where we were going. I hadn't yet made up my mind." He nodded toward the wagon. "She needs more. And if I'd known that our Prince lived, I'd have moved us on sooner. I thought him dead."

John nodded. "There's something else you should know. Parsons told me the prophecy. About the Shining King—"

"And the Undying One?" Kestrel smiled. "I'd made that connection, John. It will be my honor to serve my future King and his consort."

CHAPTER NINE
Deceptions

They crossed the Red River and started west the next day, traveling slowly. John tried not to fret. He could travel faster alone, he was certain of it. But he was held to the pace of the wagon, and the pace set by Kestrel, who refused to push either his horses or his daughter any harder than he had to. So it was four days before they passed Garrett's ferry.

"We're not far," John said. He scanned the horizon, and pointed. "There. See the tree? That's the cottonwood that burned."

Kestrel nodded. "I see it. All right. Go on and warn them you're about to have company. Then we'll get your wagon repaired and decide what we're doing next."

John nodded. "Come on, Lilith. I want you to meet Ethriel."

The kelpie tossed her head and moved into a canter. John laughed, feeling better than he had in days. It was almost over. He'd be back with his Ethriel, and they could figure out what to do about getting Barak back. And...

And there was no wagon by the burned-out cottonwood tree.

"Lilith—"

He didn't have to say anything. She surged into a gallop, and he leaned over her neck and started to pray. They passed the cottonwood, and she circled the site before coming to a stop. John dismounted, and walked toward where the wagon had been. He could still see the ruts where the wheels had been, where they'd sunk into the wet ground when Parsons had pushed the wagon over. And he could see faint traces of the wheels, heading back the way they'd come.

Kestrel stopped the wagon near the tree and jumped down, helping Rose down to the ground as he looked around. "Where are they?"

John shook his head. "I don't know. I don't know how they could have gone anywhere on two broken axles." He started walking around, studying the ground. About halfway between where the wagon had been and Kestrel, he stopped and crouched. Then he looked up. "There was another wagon," he said, pointing to the ruts in the ground. "Someone else was here."

Kestrel came over to join him. He studied the tracks in the ground, then looked around. "Back to the ford?"

John tipped his head back to look up at Kestrel. "If nothing else, Garrett may have answers."

"John."

John stood up, seeing Rose coming toward him. She had something in her gloved hands.

His kepi.

For a moment, he couldn't breathe, couldn't think. Ethriel had wanted to wear it. He'd promised to wear it only when they were alone.

"It... it's mine," he croaked. "It's the last piece of my uniform. I... I saved it, and Ethriel asked if he could wear it while I was gone. He wouldn't leave it."

Kestrel reached out and put his hands on John's shoulders, turning John so that he was facing him. "We'll find him," Kestrel said, his voice firm. "We will find him."

Rose joined them, and held the hat out to John. "There's something in this. Something I can't see."

"That *you* can't see?" John took the hat, and almost dropped it. The wool felt strange, different under his fingers. Warm, where it shouldn't have been. He frowned, turned it over, and a light flared from inside the hat. He blinked, then gaped as a ghostly image of Ethriel appeared.

"*John,*" he said. "*I'm leaving this here for you to find. I know the man here who claims to be you isn't. It's a good illusion, but he doesn't speak Aramaic. And he doesn't know how to kiss. At all."* He looked over his shoulder, then back. *"I don't have much time. They came last night, with another wagon, and people to help. They repaired our wagon, and they got Parciviel drunk. He's passed out, and they're taking us across the river."* He looked back again. *"They're looking for me."* He looked back. *"I know you're coming back. I know you'll find this. Now you have to find me."*

The illusion faded, and John took a deep breath.

"Doesn't know how to kiss, hm?" Kestrel asked. He sounded amused.

John looked at him. "I'm not kissing you to prove I know how, Kestrel."

Kestrel burst out laughing. Rose just smiled. John felt something loosen in his chest. He wasn't facing this alone. But...

"I can't ask you to come with me," he said. "I can't put you in danger." He looked down at the kepi, then put it on. "Thank you for your help. Wait here. Be safe."

Kestrel looked at Rose. "You saw us all here, didn't you?"

Rose nodded. "With Ethriel, and Sir Parciviel." She frowned slightly, then closed her eyes. "No, we have to go. If we stay here, it won't happen."

Kestrel nodded and looked back at John. "We're going with you."

GARRETT WAS WAITING for them as they rode up to the ford, and he openly stared at John.

"Where the hell did you come from?" he demanded. Then he noticed Rose, and blushed. "Ah... I apologize, Miss."

"We need to cross, Mister Garrett," John said. He dismounted and led Lilith forward, then forced a smile. "You're doing very good business on me, aren't you? How many times is it now?"

"This'll be four. And three times in three days is a lot, I have to say." Garrett laughed. "Any more, and I'll have to start charging you rent."

John forced a laugh. "I think this might be the last time."

"Believe it when I don't see you," Garrett said. "Come on."

"I paid you for the crossings, didn't I?" John asked as they boarded the ferry. He tethered Lilith to the railing and rested his hand on her withers.

"You forgot that, too?" Garrett laughed. "You paid me double what I asked, and added a nice bonus for Rowlett. I appreciate that, and I know he will, too."

John nodded. "Good. I took a knock on the head in the war, and sometimes I forget things. Thank you for reminding me." He left Lilith and walked over to the wagon. Kestrel got down from the seat and stood next to him.

"Sounds like they came this way," Kestrel said.

"Yes," John agreed. "Nice to know that the fake me is generous." He glanced over his shoulder at the other bank. "I have an idea that will get me into town. He warned me several times that if I took Lilith's bridle off, she'd run. So I think he'll believe me if I tell him that he was right."

Rose nodded. "He would. He loves being right."

"Then I'll leave you and Lilith out of harm's way, and walk in," John continued. "If I don't come back, you'll be able to get out."

Kestrel scowled. "I don't like this plan. But I don't have a better one." He looked up. "We'll be on the other side soon. We stop when?"

"Before sunset, and I'll leave at dawn." He looked over at Lilith. "And I'm probably going to spend a good part of the evening arguing with my horse."

On the far bank of the river, Garrett wished them well, and John mounted Lilith once more. He rode with the Henry across his legs, feeling uneasy. It took him a moment to realize why.

He was riding into enemy territory.

"John, if you don't relax, you're going to burst into flames," Rose chided gently. "We're still too far for him to sneak up on us." She frowned slightly. "And his spirits can't make it this far."

"Who?" John asked.

"His spies. They're some kind of ghost—"

"Oh," John nodded. "I met one of them. Actually, I passed through one of them, which I would very much like to never do again."

"They can appear a long way from Wraithtown, but not this far."

"So someone actually was watching me when I rode into town," John asked.

She nodded. "They watch for people with power, and lure them into the town. It's how we ended up there." She frowned. "It may have been how they got you, as well. The entire town is a trap, and one we barely escaped."

"How did you escape?" John asked. "In case I need to do the same."

"I don't think you could do what I did," Rose said. She paused. Then she sighed. "Remember how I touched you, in the barn?"

"Yes."

"If there'd been any evil in you, my touch would have been the last thing you knew," Rose said. "I... take it in. Absorb it, the way dry ground absorbs water. Then it turns on the person I touched and kills them. It's... I can't control it." He held up her gloved hands. "It's why I wear these around other people."

"You're a sin-eater?" John gasped. "I thought that was just a myth!"

"Wait, you know something about this?" Kestrel demanded. "How?"

John shook his head. "It's a story, something from the old ways over the sea. I didn't have a lot to do with the Church, back in the old days—"

"What's the old days, to you?" Rose asked.

John chuckled. "Ah... when the years were only three digits?" he offered, making them both laugh. "But there used to be people who were called sin-eaters. There might still be, as far as I know. It's been a long time since I was last in Europe. But they would have a special meal, and in doing that they would ritually consume the sin from people who had died unshriven. Things never ended well for them — their communities eventually turned on them, thinking that anyone who took on that much sin must eventually be corrupted by it." He snorted. "Helped a few of them get away from their former communities."

Kestrel nodded. "Rose?"

"I'm not sure it's the same," she said. "But I don't know. It's as good a name as any for what I do, though."

"I don't know either," John said. "I never witnessed what they were doing." He looked around. "I don't feel anything watching me yet. I could see Wraithtown when I felt that."

Kestrel nodded. He looked around, then said. "John, there's a hole in your plan."

"What did I miss?"

"You'll be coming in from the west side of Wraithtown, not the east."

John blinked. Then he groaned. "You're right."

"So, we go east," Kestrel said, and turned the wagon. John urged Lilith to follow, scanning the surrounding area. There was a copse of trees nearby, and a small stream. It was a pretty sight, but it offered cover for an attacker. It was the sort of place that John would have used during the war to ambush an approaching patrol. So he watched the trees as they grew closer, and kept the Henry ready. And when he saw the figure half-hidden in the trees, he was ready, raising the gun and running the lever... until he saw sunlight on auburn hair.

"Ethriel?" he whispered, and lowered the gun. Kestrel stopped the wagon.

"It's him!" he gasped. "My Prince—"

"It might be a trick," John said. "Wait here." He dismounted and started toward the trees. Halfway there, he stopped and raised his voice, calling in Aramaic, "Is it really you?"

Ethriel moved into view. His clothes were torn, and he was as dirty as he had been the day John had first seen him. There was a bruise across one high cheekbone. "I was going to ask you the same question," he called back.

In Aramaic.

John was moving before the words died away, closing the distance between them. Ethriel barreled into him hard, knocking him backwards. It didn't matter — he was here. Safe, and alive, and in John's arms, clinging to him for dear life.

And babbling like a brook.

"... I pretended to believe them, until Parciviel woke up. I told him that they were fake, that it wasn't you, that you'd never have encouraged him to get drunk. We tried to escape, but there were too many for him to fight. He made sure I got away. They couldn't find me — I concealed myself and I hid, and I waited. I knew you'd come. I knew it." He paused to breathe. "I don't know if he's alive. Or where they went." He took another breath. "I killed one, I think. You said stay alive until help came. You said that was the rule."

"And help is here," John murmured. "I'm here." He buried his face in Ethriel's hair. "You're safe now." Behind him, he heard hooves, and felt Ethriel tense. "It's all right. They're friends."

"John, that's truly him?" Kestrel called.

John turned, keeping his arm around Ethriel. Ethriel went still, but only for a moment.

"Sir Kestriel?" he gasped. Then... *"Roshara?"*

Rose smiled. "Ethriel, I can't tell you how good it is to see you."

Kestrel jumped down from the wagon and went to one knee, "My Prince," he said. Then he looked up. "My King."

"Not yet, I'm not," Ethriel said. "Please, stand up." He looked at John. "Where did you find them?"

"A long story, love. Now, the fourth member of the party is Lilith, who'll say hello later."

Ethriel nodded, then he must have really looked at Lilith, because he gasped, "Where did you find a kelpie? And where's Barak?"

"It's part of the long story," John said. "I'll tell you later. Right now, let's have you in the wagon, and we'll keep going."

"Going? Going where?" Ethriel asked. "Where are we going?"

"East," Kestrel answered. "Now, hop up. There's room on the bench, and we can talk."

"And there's waybread in reach, so you can eat something," Rose added. "You look like you're going to fall over."

"I haven't eaten much in the past day or two," Ethriel said. "Yes, please." He climbed up on the bench, sitting on Rose's other side. She turned, reaching into the wagon, and took out a bundle that she handed to Ethriel.

"Eat. And we'll tell you as we go."

BY THE TIME THEY STOPPED for the night, Ethriel knew as much as they did, and he was sharing what had happened since John left them.

"— they arrived just after midday three days ago. The fake John said that he'd found help, and that once the axles were repaired, we needed to cross the river because of the flooding to the west. He said we weren't going to be able to make it to the ferry." He put down the bundle that Rose had asked him to carry, and sat down on the ground next to where Kestrel was building a fire. "I didn't suspect anything at first. He was a very good impostor."

Kestrel looked up and grinned. "Until you kissed him?"

Ethriel looked startled. Then he turned red. "I... oh. The message...you... you heard that?" He turned toward John. "I..."

"Ethriel—"

"You told me I had to be careful." Ethriel looked down at his hands, clasped in his lap. "That it was different here, and we couldn't be open around others. That it was illegal here, and if we were caught—"

"No," Kestrel said. He reached across and rested one big hand on Ethriel's knee. "No, I was only teasing you. You're safe. Safe with us."

Ethriel looked up through his lashes. "I... I still need to be careful."

"John, you've scared the piss out of him." Kestrel turned back to the fire.

"As I pointed out to Lilith, if I die, I'll come back. If Ethriel—" He stopped, then shook his head. "In Arkansas, the penalty is hanging. I'm not sure what it is in Oklahoma or Texas. I don't want us to find out." He dropped down to sit next to Ethriel and reached out to take his hand. "You're cold, love."

Ethriel gave him a smile as weak as watery gruel. "I'm fine."

"You're not," John said. "You've had a horrible few days." He took his coat off and draped it around Ethriel's shoulders, then put his arm around Ethriel. "And I'm sorry."

Ethriel frowned. "You didn't have much of a choice. You had to go—"

"Not what I meant," John said. "Ethriel, Kestrel is right. I frightened you. I made you afraid of us. That's not fair to you. You shouldn't have to be frightened."

"John," Kestrel said, drawing out the name. "Was it ever not illegal in this world? For two men to be lovers?"

John nodded. "Several times. It wasn't even condemned by the church until... let me think..."

"Were the years still three digits?" Rose asked from behind him.

"They might have just turned to four. It's been a long time," John said. He looked over his shoulder and smiled. "Lilith. Come sit and meet Ethriel."

Ethriel twisted in place. "Oh!" he gasped. "I've never met a kelpie before!"

"I've never before met an elven prince," Lilith answered. "So we're on the same ground. John has told me quite a bit about you. It's very nice to finally meet you." She sat on Ethriel's other side and looked at Kestrel. "Do you need help with that?"

"The wood is wet," Kestrel grumbled. "It won't catch."

Ethriel whistled, and the wood started to smoke. Kestrel straightened, then laughed as flames started crackling through the kindling.

"Very good," he said.

"You couldn't do that?" John asked.

"I was a guardsman for a reason," Kestrel said. "I have about as much magic as a rock. I can hide, and I can change my appearance and that's about it. Rose gets her gifts from her mother. Rose, what's for supper?"

"If you'll get the kettle and tripod, we can have stew. Ethriel brought everything else out for me." She came over to the fire and leaned down to kiss Kestrel on the cheek. Then she turned to face John, Ethriel and Lilith. She cocked her head to the side. "Ethriel, what do you have in your pocket?"

Ethriel looked down. "What?"

"You have something in your shirt pocket. It's glowing."

John looked at Ethriel's chest, then up at Rose. "To your eyes. I don't see it."

"Nor do I," Ethriel said. He took a small pouch from his pocket — the token that Nathaniel had given them. "This? Is glowing?"

She held her hand out. "May I?"

Ethriel didn't hesitate. He handed the pouch to Rose without even looking at John first. She took it, and turned it over in her hands.

"I recognize this," she murmured. "Papa, what was the name of the magic city where we hid?"

"New Orleans," Kestrel answered.

"Yes. This is that sort of magic." She looked up. "Where did you get it?"

"A friend," John answered. "Nathaniel Miller's first wife was from someplace in Louisiana. She made it, and they would send them with the slaves they helped escape to Mexico. He gave it to me when we left Skullyville. He said it would keep us safe. I left it with Ethriel when I went to Wraithtown."

Rose nodded. Then she handed the pouch to John. "Take it with you when you go tomorrow. You're going to need it."

CHAPTER TEN
Infiltration

John rose before dawn, and wasn't surprised to find Kestrel waiting for him by a small fire. He didn't go to the fire immediately, walking away for a moment so that he could say good morning to Joshua, knowing that Kestrel would probably think he was answering nature's call. Then he went back to the wagon and joined Kestrel at the fire.

"You're really doing this alone?" Kestrel asked. He offered John a cup. "I could go with you."

"He wants you dead, too," John answered. He sipped the coffee and sighed. "This is good. Thank you. No, I have to go alone."

"I'll take you, at least part of the way."

John looked up to see Lilith had come up behind him. "I didn't realize you were awake."

"You woke me when you moved," Lilith said. "I'll take you—"

"No. I'll walk. If you get too close, he'll know you're there," John said. He drank the rest of his coffee. "Kestrel, once I'm gone, head back to the ferry. I'll meet you there."

Kestrel stared at him for a moment. "You want us to leave? No!"

"I want you all as far out of range as you can be," John said. "You have your daughter to think of. And... Kestrel, I'm asking you to protect him, too. I'm trusting you with my heart." He looked back over his shoulder, and saw Ethriel standing next to the wagon. He smiled and held his hand out; Ethriel came to sit next to him, pressing against John's side. Lilith sat down on John's other side, not touching, but close enough that he could feel her warmth.

"You're leaving me again," Ethriel said. "I want to come with you. I know I can't, though. I don't know enough. I can't fight the way you can. I don't know enough magic."

"You'll be safe with Kestrel and Rose," John said, putting his arm around Ethriel. He closed his eyes and took a deep breath. "I'll be back with you as soon as I can be. Hopefully with Parsons."

"Do you think he's still alive?" Ethriel asked.

"I hope so," John answered. He took a deep breath and looked up at the sky. "I should get walking."

"You haven't eaten." Kestrel looked over at the fire, and the kettle that John hadn't noticed. "It'll be ready in a few minutes. You'll eat before you leave."

John smiled. "You didn't have to get up early to feed me."

Kestrel chuckled. "No, I had to get up early to feed her." He nodded, and John turned to see Rose had come out of the wagon and was walking toward them. She passed them and went straight to Kestrel, leaning down to kiss his cheek. When she straightened, he handed her a cup of coffee. She sat down next to him, sipped it, and sighed.

"Porridge will be ready in a few minutes," Kestrel said. "And John will be leaving us once he's eaten."

Rose nodded. "Remember to take the token."

John touched his shirt pocket. "I have it right here. Do you know what I'll need it for?"

She shook her head. "No. Just that you'll need it."

"You said it will be a few minutes before the food is ready," Ethriel said abruptly. He turned toward John. "Come walk with me. We won't go far. Just... walk with me."

John nodded. He stood up and held his hand out to Ethriel. "We won't go far," he repeated, and looked around. There was a small stand of trees nearby, and he pointed. "There. We'll be back."

"Don't make me come looking for you," Kestrel grumbled. He grinned when John made a rude gesture at him.

As they walked toward the trees, Ethriel took John's hand. Ethriel's hand was cold, and it was shaking. John waited until they were under the shelter of the trees, then put his back to one and pulled Ethriel into his arms. Into a kiss that he'd been dreaming about for days. He closed his eyes and ignored the burl on the tree that was digging into his back. It didn't matter. Nothing else mattered.

Ethriel sighed and broke the kiss, resting his head on John's shoulder. "I wish I could come with you."

"If you did, the lie would fall apart," John said. He rubbed his cheek against Ethriel's hair. "You need to stay here, where it's safe." He paused. "Safer."

"I don't want to be safe. I want to be with you," Ethriel said softly. "John… the past few days… I haven't felt this… this frightened and alone since I saw my parents killed. Only this time, I wasn't a prisoner. I could fight back." He straightened. "I did fight back."

John nodded. "And you got away from them. You did wonderfully, Ethriel. And you're not alone. I won't leave you alone."

Ethriel met his eyes. "Is that a promise?"

John nodded again. "That's a promise and a vow. I will not leave you alone. And I will always come for you."

Ethriel grinned. "I'd like that, but we don't have time."

John blinked for a minute, then burst out laughing. "Ethriel! That's obscene!"

Ethriel snorted. "It is not!" he protested. "We both still have our clothes on." His grin returned. "You should see your face," he laughed. Then he looked up. "I can see your face. It's getting light. We should go and eat. You have to go save Parciviel."

John took Ethriel's hand and led him out of the trees and back toward the fire. "Once I'm gone, you're going back to the ferry. I will meet you there."

Ethriel nodded. "All right. John… tell me about Lilith."

"You know that she's a kelpie," John answered. "She was captured by… by the one in that town, and she's been his prisoner for years. I promised her that I'd help her get out." He licked his lips. "She's offered herself to me. Several times. I told her no."

"That's what I was wondering," Ethriel said. "She seemed very... comfortable with you last night. Why did you say no?"

"Because I wouldn't do something like that without talking to you first," John answered. "Because you are first in my heart—"

"Second," Ethriel said. "Joshua is first."

John nodded. "Fair. However, he's not here. And not likely to be. You are here, and you are mine, and I won't risk hurting you when I can simply be patient. And I won't risk hurting a sweet girl by taking advantage of her being lovelorn for me because I saved her." He stopped and turned Ethriel to face him. "I love you, and I won't betray your trust in me if I'm away from you." He paused. "Roshara told me that there was talk of you marrying her."

Ethriel laughed. "That was ages and ages ago! We were children!" He shook his head. "She's a friend. I care for her as a friend. I love you." He smiled. "And I won't betray your trust in me, either." He stepped into John's arms. "I love you," he whispered. "Be careful when you go."

LILITH PUT HER HOOF down, and insisted on carrying John at least part of the way, pointing out that he needed to be far enough east that he would not be coming at Wraithtown from the northeast when he arrived. She also pointed out that she could carry two, and that Ethriel could come with them. John knew he should object, but leaving Ethriel was harder the second time. Which was how he ended up riding double, with Ethriel pressed against his back.

"I think this is far enough, Lilith," he called for the third time. After the first two times, John had realized that Lilith had her own opinions of where she was going to leave him. She ignored his protests, and ignored him tugging at the makeshift reins they'd attached to her headstall.

"Will she listen this time?" Ethriel asked.

"Good question," John answered. "Lilith, if we go any further east, I won't make it back to Wraithtown before dark."

She stopped, and Ethriel slid down to the ground. John dismounted, taking the Henry from the scabbard and putting it on the ground. Then he took his coat off and tossed it onto the ground.

"Lilith, run over that a few times, will you?"

She snorted and shook her head, and he laughed. "No, I mean it. I want it to look as though you trampled it. Because that's what I'm going to tell him. That you killed me and ran off."

To his shock, she snapped at him, and sidled away. He held up both hands. "Do I get to explain?" he asked. "And do you want to change back while I do, so you can argue with me in words?"

She snorted, then came closer, letting him take off the saddle and headstall. A heartbeat later, he was faced with a naked, furious woman.

"I would never murder you!" she snapped.

"I know!" John answered. "But he'll believe it." He paused, looked at Ethriel, then back at Lilith. "Unless... do you think he wouldn't?"

She scowled. Then she grumbled, "He would believe it. I tried often enough with him."

"Then please, add some color to the lie?"

He never actually saw her change. One moment, there was a woman standing before him. The next, there was a black mare. She picked her way over to the coat, pawed at it with one backwards hoof, then started stomping on it like she was trying to kill a snake.

"She's not going to leave you a coat," Ethriel said. Then he coughed. "Have her do your shirt, too. If your shirt has no holes, he'll see through the lie."

John nodded and took down his braces. He took the token from his shirt pocket and handed it to Ethriel, then tugged his shirt over his head.

"Lilith, the shirt, too!" he called, and tossed the shirt toward her. She shied away from it, then attacked it as soon as it hit the ground. Then she changed forms again.

"Is that enough?" she asked. John went over and picked up the shirt. There was a long tear in the front, and the sleeves were tattered.

"This is fine," he said. "Just... damn. I didn't think this through." He went to the saddle and took a clasp-knife from the saddlebag, unfolding it.

"John!" Ethriel gasped as John sliced open his arm

"There's no blood," John explained as he smeared his blood into the shirt around the holes. "It'll heal by the time I get there. But if there's no blood on the shirt or the coat—"

"I know. I just don't like it when you hurt yourself," Ethriel muttered, gnawing on his thumbnail.

John smiled at him, then anointed the torn coat with more blood. The cut was already closing when he pulled the shirt back on, tucking it in and pulling up his braces. Then he put on his coat and took the token back from Ethriel, tucking it into his trouser pocket. Then he went to the saddlebag and took out a box of cartridges, putting it into his coat pocket.

"Time for you both to go back," he said. "Lilith—"

"Never you worry about him," she said.

"I'll worry about the both of you, thank you," John said, and she laughed.

Ethriel smiled. "Kiss for luck?" he asked.

John nodded and went to him, taking Ethriel in his arms. "All the luck, love. I'll need it."

By the time Ethriel pulled away, John wasn't sure there was any luck left anywhere else in the world. He had all of it, he was certain.

"John?" Lilith said. She sounded almost shy, and he turned to her and saw the flush in her cheeks.

"Lilith?" As he said her name, he realized what she wanted. "Oh? Is there luck from you, too?"

"If you'll have it?" she said.

He held his hand out, and for the first time in a very long time, he was kissing a naked woman. Somehow, it no longer felt as improper as it had a week before. He held her close and kissed her gently, then made a *mmph* of surprise as she wound her fingers in his hair and took control of the kiss. He heard Ethriel's amused laughter. Then Lilith started giggling, laughing against John's lips. She stepped back, and changed back into a horse.

Ethriel didn't say much as he helped John saddle Lilith. Once she was ready, Ethriel stood for a moment, his hand resting on Lilith's neck.

"If you're not at the ferry by sunset tomorrow," he said. "I'm coming after you."

John swallowed, wanting to say no. Then he realized that he couldn't. Ethriel needed to learn to be a king. And he needed to learn to be a man.

"If I'm not at the ferry by sunset tomorrow," he said. "Then you'll have to find me."

Ethriel stood a little taller as he nodded. He mounted, and John watched as Lilith carried Ethriel off into the west, back to the relative safety of Kestrel and Rose's wagon. Once they were out of sight, he took a deep breath, then set off walking, heading south. Eventually, he too would head west. Toward Wraithtown.

THE SETTING SUN TURNED the buildings of Wraithtown into standing stones of black onyx, flecked with occasional flashes of light that could either be window-glass or mica. The entire thing looked spectral, and entirely appropriate. John stopped, wishing for something to eat that wasn't dried apples. He was hungry, thirsty, and more tired than he'd been since the war. He closed his eyes, took a deep breath, and started walking again.

And immediately felt eyes on the back of his neck. He turned and saw nothing.

"Oh," he murmured. "It's the watchdog. Go tell your master I'm coming, and I'm hungry."

He could have sworn he felt a wave of confusion. Then the feeling of being watched eased. It didn't go away entirely, though. Only one of them must have gone.

But he wasn't supposed to know there were two, and he'd only seen the one. So he kept walking.

When John entered Wraithtown an hour later, the shadows were long and black, and Jacob Wraith stepped out of one to greet him.

"They dead?"

"Yes," John answered.

Wraith nodded. "And where's my horse?" He paused, then laughed. "You look like you were trampled by her."

"That's because I was," John answered. "You warned me not to take her bridle off. You didn't warn me that she was going to try to kill me."

"Might have slipped my mind," Wraith answered. "Did you? Take her bridle off?"

John snorted. "If you're going to question me, perhaps I could make the acquaintance of your cook first? It's been a long walk, and I'm hungry."

Wraith nodded. "This way." He turned and walked away, leaving John to follow. Their destination turned out to be a large house near the center of town. John recognized the jail as they passed.

"How's Ethriel?" he called.

"Fine," Wraith answered. "He's overseeing Tam harnessing your wagon. I assumed you weren't going to want to spend the night. You're welcome to, if you change your mind."

"Thank you for the offer, but we've lost enough time to this adventure," John answered. He followed Wraith up the steps to the front porch, where Wraith pointed at one of a pair of rocking chairs.

"Have a seat. It's a nice night. We'll sit out here."

John sank into one of the chairs and laid the Henry down on the ground next to his feet. When he looked up, Wraith was gone. He hadn't heard the door open. Perhaps Wraith had walked through it again. Which led to the question of could he walk through a door while carrying a bowl or a plate? John shifted in his chair to watch, and grinned when the door opened a few minutes later. Wraith came out, carrying a tray.

"Something amusing, Zebedee?" he asked. He carried the tray over and set it on a small table between the two chairs. On the tray was a plate of sliced meat, roasted potatoes, and a large slab of buttered bread. There was a cup and a pitcher, as well. "There you go," Wraith said. "Water in the pitcher. And don't wait on me. I've eaten. What was funny?"

John turned his chair to face the table and started cutting his meat. "Just wondering. I've seen you pass through solid objects twice now. I was wondering if you could do it while holding something like a plate." He shrugged. "Curious, I suppose."

"Speaking of solid objects," Wraith said. "What happened to my gun?"

"The rifle?" John asked. "It was gone when I woke up."

"You still have yours," Wraith pointed out.

"I found it on the ground when I followed the tracks," John answered. "It must have fallen out of the holster. There wasn't really enough room for the both of them in it. I juggled them the entire way there." He looked up. "Where did you find a rifle that fires elfshot?"

Wraith started rocking. "Won it in a game of cards. They're dead?"

"Yes," John answered. He didn't say more, working on clearing his plate. Thinking fast. He was certain that he knew what the next question would be.

He was right. Wraith waited until the plate was empty, and until John had finished the last crust of bread, then laced his fingers together and said, "Tell me. I want to know how that bitch died. I want to hear that she died in agony."

John picked up his cup and took a sip, then leaned back in his chair. "Once I realized that the gun you gave me fired elfshot, I put another two bullets into them from the Henry."

Wraith growled, sounding like an angry dog. "I wanted her to suffer."

"And I wanted to get back to what's mine," John replied. "She's dead. Does it matter how?" He put the cup down. "I owe you, for your horse. I am sorry about that. She didn't come back to her stable?"

Wraith laughed. "Nah. But I'll find her. If you're done, I'll show you where Ethriel is."

"Is Parsons with him?" John asked. "Is he here somewhere? You have Ethriel and the wagon. Where's Parsons?" He bent and picked up the Henry, then stood up. Wraith stood at the top of the steps and didn't answer.

"Wraith, where's Parsons?" John asked.

"He's here," Wraith answered.

"You said if I did this, you'd repair my wagon and give us leave to go. All of us. Even Parsons. So where is he?"

Wraith snorted. "Come with me." He drifted down the stairs, and John hurried after him. Wraith led him to the jail, and passed through the door without opening it. John followed, but opened the door first.

There was a single lantern lit against the growing darkness, and John could see a figure on the bed in the cell where he'd once been a prisoner. He didn't have to go close to see that it was Parsons.

"Your prince is waiting for you," Wraith said. "This one is staying. He has a debt to pay."

"That's not what you promised me," John said. He turned to face Wraith. "You said he would be free to go if I did as you asked."

"I'm changing the terms," Wraith said. He chuckled. "Call it payment for the horse."

"I'll pay you for the horse. I'm taking my friend." As John spoke, he became aware of a pulsing warmth against his leg. He reached into his pocket, felt the token, and palmed it.

"I don't want your money, and he stays. He owes me a life."

There was movement in the cell, and Parsons sat up. His face was battered and bruised, and one eye was swollen shut.

"John?" he croaked. "Is it really you?"

"I'd say yes, but I doubt you'd believe me," John answered. And too late realized his mistake.

Wraith stepped closer. "Now why would you say something like that?" he drawled. Then he laughed. "You're lying to me."

"You've been lying to me the entire time." John glared at him. "I wonder, what is Siobhan paying you to do her bidding?"

"I don't do anyone's bidding, Zavdi. And who the fuck is Siobhan?" Wraith demanded. He came closer, and John threw the token into Wraith's face. The little pouch burst open, and powder sprayed everywhere.

Wraith screamed as if he'd been impaled. Then he vanished.

CHAPTER ELEVEN
Escape

John wanted to stare, but there was no time. He moved, grabbing the keys off the hook on the wall, and running to the cell. He unlocked the door and threw it wide, "Come on!" he snapped. "We have no time. Can you run?"

"Do I have a choice?" Parsons limped after John, and broke into a shambling run as soon as they hit the street. John led the way down the side street toward the stable, watching for Wraith, for elves, for ghosts. He saw no one until they reached the stable. Their wagon was in the stable yard, with Barak already in harness... and Ethriel was standing next to the wagon.

John took it all in — Ethriel was clean, his clothes unfamiliar but intact. His face was unbruised. He turned and smiled at John.

"You're back!"

The smile vanished as John raised the Henry, ran the lever, and fired. The impostor fell backwards, dead before he hit the ground.

"John!" Parsons screamed. "What have you done?"

"It's not him!" John snapped. "Get to the wagon."

"But—"

John reached out and grabbed Parsons by the scruff of the neck, dragging him toward the wagon. They passed the body, which was now that of an older elf with dark hair. John ignored the corpse and shouted, "Tam!"

The farrier appeared in the stable door. He looked at them, then smiled.

"What do you need, Zebedee?"

"Parsons' horse," John answered. He turned to Parsons. "Can you ride?"

"Not enough time to saddle the beast," Tam interrupted. "Get in the wagon. I'll get the tack in the back and tether the horse to the tailboard."

John nodded and pushed Parsons toward the wagon.

"Where's Ethriel?" the elf demanded.

"Safe." John climbed up into the driver's seat and unwound the reins. He felt the wagon jolt, and looked back to see Parsons in the back. There was a second jolt as Tam tossed Windrider's saddle in. A moment later, Tam slapped the side of the wagon.

"Go!"

"Come with us!" John called.

Tam looked startled. Then he shook his head. "Can't. I leave, I turn to dust. Don't worry about me, John. Go!"

John snapped the reins, and the wagon lurched forward into the night. They cleared Wraithtown without seeing any signs of Jacob Wraith or his ghosts, but John wasn't sure how lucky they'd be.

"Where's Ethriel?" Parsons asked. He'd moved to the front of the wagon, right behind John.

"Safe," John repeated. "And with friends." He glanced back. "Keep watch out the back. I don't know what I did, but he's going to be as mad as a kicked hornet's nest."

"What did you throw at him?" Parsons asked as he moved to the back of the wagon. He raised his voice. "It's clear behind us."

"Keep watching. There are Mountain elves in Wraithtown," John called over his shoulder. "And I threw the token that Nathaniel gave me." He snapped the reins again, urging Barak into a faster pace, worried that he was pushing his horse too hard. And it would be dark soon — at this speed, he was risking Barak breaking a leg.

"There were no elves here when I was here last. That's new," Parsons said, loud enough that his voice carried. "At least, there hadn't been when I was here last. He'd never seen an elf before, he told me."

"Doesn't matter if it's new or old. We need to make the ferry and get across before they catch us." He peered into the gloom. "Which means driving all night."

"In the dark?" Parsons sounded horrified. A moment later, he called, "John, there are riders behind us."

"Damn," John breathed. "Come up here. I need you to drive."

He heard rustling behind him, and shifted over on the bench to let Parsons climb out. The elf groaned and cursed softly as he made his way over the seatback and settled next to John. John handed him the reins, and climbed into the back of the wagon, picking up the Henry and heading to the tailboard. He rested the barrel of the Henry on the wood and squinted into the darkness. Yes, there were horsemen behind them. He couldn't tell if they were ghosts, humans or elves, but they were definitely in pursuit. As John looked, he heard the distant *wheet* of gunfire. Training took over, and he returned fire. He aimed for the horses — he doubted that ghosts needed horses, but humans and elves definitely did.

After the third horse fell, the chase peeled off, and John took a deep breath. He wiped his face, feeling grit on his fingers. Curious, he stood up and murmured his light spell to the tiny lantern that hung from one of the ribs. In the dim light, he saw white powder on his fingers.

"What is it?"

"I have something on my hands," John called. "Not gunpowder. I think it might be whatever was in the token." He doused the light and closed his eyes to let them readjust to the darkness. When he re-opened them and looked out the back of the wagon, there was no one following them. "Parsons, slow a bit. Let Barak rest."

Parsons drew back on the reins, bringing Barak down to a fast walk. John moved forward and climbed over the seatback. Parsons took the reins into one hand and held out his other.

"Let me see your hand," he said. "Whatever was in that token is something we may need more of." John held his hand out, and Parsons took him by the wrist. He sniffed John's fingers. Then, to John's complete shock, he licked them; John yelped and pulled back. Parsons just laughed. "Take the reins. I'll go prepare the weapons."

"Prepare the what?" John asked, taking the reins. Parsons laughed and clambered back into the wagon, and John heard him moving around, and the sound of things being opened. "Parsons, what are you doing? What was on my hand?"

"Salt!" Parsons called. John heard cloth tearing, and Parsons came back and handed him a small bundle. "If something appears, throw that at it. Just like you did to Wraith. I'll make more."

John took the bundle of salt and held it in one hand as he blinked. Now that they were away, the length of his day and the long walk were catching up with him.

"Parsons, once we're far enough away to stop, I'm going to need you to drive," he called. Movement, out of the corner of his eye, and he turned to see a familiar ghost keeping pace with the wagon. He threw the bundle, which burst on contact. The ghost vanished. "I'll need more of those!"

"Coming!" Parsons climbed back into the seat next to him, carrying a large bundle that proved to be full of smaller bundles. "Why do you need me to drive?"

"Because I'm exhausted," John answered. "Today started before dawn, and I walked the last ten miles into Wraithtown."

"You walked?"

"I had to make him believe that the horse he gave me killed me," John answered. "I'll tell you later. First, I want you to tell me — ghost!"

Parsons turned and threw another bundle at the ghost that had just appeared on his right. It wailed and vanished. Parsons peered around the edge of the wagon, then turned back to John. "What did you want me to tell you?"

"Why you didn't tell me you had a problem with the bottle," John answered. He glanced at Parsons, then looked ahead. "I thought you getting drunk that first night was just by chance. I didn't like it, but I didn't think anything of it. But then Ethriel said they got past your guard by getting you drunk again. That's more than chance. Parsons, why didn't you tell me? And... honestly, you carried a flask on the *Cavalier*. You had a drink with me when we waited at Nathaniel's house. Why, when you know what will happen?"

"I didn't think you'd understand," Parsons said softly. "I know what you told me. That you had your own battle with it. But—" He paused. "John, I didn't want Ethriel to know the truth."

"Truth about what?" John asked. "Parsons, what is it?"

"Did you wonder, John, why I was in your world? Why I wasn't fighting against Siobhan in our world? There are still rebels there, trying to stand against her. I should be with them." He sighed, looked back. "It's quiet. We may be far enough."

"I doubt it," John said. "And no, I never thought about it. I don't know enough about your people to think it strange." He frowned. "Is it strange? I mean, you said you were here because your seers said Ethriel would be found here."

"That message came to me when Avriel was a small child. Perhaps forty of your years ago?" He paused again, clearly gathering his thoughts. "We were living... north and west of here, a long way. One of our seers found me there and told me. She said it would be my way to redemption. Find the missing Prince, see him safely to his mother's throne." He snorted. "At that point, I hadn't had a drink since... well, since it all started. I thought I was done with... you know how you feel as if you need it?"

John nodded. "I remember. And I remember I'm stronger than the need."

"You may be," Parsons said. "But I wasn't. The flask... it was illusion. There was never anything in it but water. The drink we had at Nathaniel's was the first drink I'd had in...well, since the night the Palace fell. It... it woke the beast. Do you understand?"

"Yes," John answered, then fell silent. He let the silence stretch out for nearly half a mile. "You said redemption," he said. He looked at Parsons. "Redemption for what?"

Parsons closed his eyes. "Stop the wagon, will you? We should be safe enough. And we should let Barak rest."

John slowly drew the wagon to a stop, climbing down to go and check on Barak. When he looked up, Parsons was walking away from the wagon, back the way they'd come.

"Parsons!" John shouted, and ran after him. He caught the older elf by the back of the shirt and turned him. "What are you doing?"

"Tell Ethriel I died," Parsons said softly. "I don't want him to know the truth about me."

"The truth about what?" John grabbed Parsons' shirt in both hands. "You're not going anywhere until you tell me. What did you do?" When Parsons didn't answer, John shook him. "Tell me, or I swear by all that's holy you'll find yourself trussed like a prize calf."

"I'm the reason his parents are dead!" The anguish in Parsons' voice drove John back a step. "I was the guard captain on duty that night. I was drunk. Drunk on duty." He turned, dragging his hand through his thin hair. He shook his head. "I was dead drunk when the Palace was overrun. When my Queen died. It was my fault. I could have stopped them. I could have stopped all of it. And I didn't. I failed. That... that's what Ethriel cannot know. So... let me go back. I don't care if he kills me. Just take Ethriel to safety."

"You're not going back," John snapped. "You're not running from your mistakes. We need you. Ethriel needs you."

"You don't need me," Parsons said, shaking his head. "You don't. The elves in Bandera can teach him better than I can, and you can keep him safe." He looked back at the wagon. "Take Windrider. You'll need a second horse. I can walk back."

He was turning back toward Wraithtown when John hit him, a solid punch to the jaw that knocked Parsons over backwards.

JOHN HEARD MOVEMENT from behind him in the wagon, and snapped the reins, clucking to Barak.

"Just a little further, Barak," he called. "We'll stop soon."

A moment later, he heard a groan. Then a curse.

"John!" Parsons shouted. "John, damn your eyes! Untie me!"

"No," John called over his shoulder. "We're not stopping yet. So you just have to stay there."

He heard more movement, more cursing. John looked back into the wagon, but really couldn't see anything. He yawned, and pinched himself. Then he blinked. Smoke? Was he smelling smoke?

"John." Movement behind him, and Parsons climbed over the back of the seat and settled next to John. John looked over his shoulder.

"What did you do?" he asked. "Burn the ropes? I thought I smelled smoke."

"Burned myself twice doing it," Parsons grumbled.

"And... are you going to hit me back?" John asked. "Because we'll be stopping soon, and I'll just ask you to wait until we do. We can't afford to stop yet."

"No," Parsons answered. "No, I'm not going to hit you." He took a breath, then added, "I thought about it. But if I did, you'd probably break both my arms. I'm not a brawler, remember?" He took another deep breath. "But you're right. I have to live with my mistakes. I can't run from them anymore. And I can't hide from them in the bottle. Not anymore." He looked over his shoulder. "Has it been quiet?"

"No ghosts, no riders," John answered. "The pouches are by your feet. We're coming up on a stream, and on the far side, I want to change horses."

"Then you can rest," Parsons added. "I'll drive."

John looked at him. "And no tricks?" he asked. "No trying to run off?"

"I promise." Parsons looked up at the sky. "It's coming on to midnight, isn't it?"

"I think so." John looked up. Then he yawned. "We'll be to the ferry by dawn at this pace. The stream we're coming to is about halfway."

"Then that's a good place to change horses, and for you to go stretch out and rest."

They crossed the stream, and John brought the wagon to a stop. He and Parsons unharnessed Barak, letting him drink and graze while they harnessed Windrider in his place. They tethered Barak to the back of the wagon, then Parsons climbed up into the seat while John stretched out in the back.

The last thing John remembered was Parsons, singing softly to his horse. The gentle melody combined with the swaying of the wagon to lull John into a deep, dreamless sleep...

Only to be startled awake by a weight on his chest, a hand pressed over his mouth and nose, cutting off his voice and his air. He struggled, seeing a dark form over him, and a wide, toothy grin. Parsons! Where was Parsons?

"You've made one hell of a mistake, John Zebedee," Wraith growled. "You've made me mad, and you've stolen something of mine. Now?" The grin grew impossibly wider, and John felt sharp nails piercing his skin. "Now, just you remember this. I will be the last thing that you ever see. Remember that, John Zebedee."

"John!"

It was Parsons' voice, and it broke through the seeming reality of John's nightmare; he gasped and sat up straight. "Parsons?" he wheezed, twisting and getting to his knees. It was light out, and Parsons looked over his shoulder at him.

"It's time to wake up," he called, sounding excruciatingly cheerful. "We're here."

"Here," John repeated, blinking and trying to wake up entirely. "Parsons... what happened? Where's Wraith?"

"What?" Parsons looked back again. "Miles behind us, and hopefully staying there. Why?"

John blinked again, rubbing his hand over his face. "I... no, it must have been a nightmare. We're here?" He shifted, moving to kneel behind the seat. He could see past Parsons, could see the Red River shining in the early morning sunlight.

He could see the other wagon.

And Ethriel, smiling brighter than the sunrise, waving them home.

CHAPTER TWELVE
Onwards

Garrett whooped with laughter when he saw John.

"I told you!" he wheezed. "I told you that it wasn't the last time. Now, two wagons?" He grinned. "Not offering a discount."

"I wasn't asking for one," John answered. He led his wagon onto the ferry. "And I promise, this will be the very last time. The next time we cross the Red River will be... whichever the one was after Rowlett."

Garrett nodded. Then he looked south. "You run afoul of... him?"

John grimaced. "You could say that."

"Then I'll get you across as fast as I can." Garrett left him, and John leaned against the wagon. The nightmare had left him shaken, feeling not quite awake, not quite with both feet on the ground.

"John?" Ethriel came to lean against the wagon, his arm pressing against John's. He was wearing his human form, as were the rest of the elves. "You don't look well."

"I'm tired, Ethan," John said. "I slept a little, but I had a nightmare—" He shook his head. "It's nothing."

"It's something." John looked up to see Roshara coming to stand on Ethriel's other side. "You're unbalanced. Badly. What happened?"

John shook his head again. "It was nothing," he protested. When he looked, both Ethriel and Roshara were looking at him, the same reproving glare. He chuckled. "Oh, I'm going to get this from both of you now?"

Ethriel looked at Roshara. When he looked back at John, he was smiling. "I think so. So?"

John nodded. He told them of the dream, of feeling Wraith's weight on his chest, the hand over his mouth. When he said that,

Ethriel's eyes widened. He reached out and took John by the chin, turning his head.

"Rose?" he said. "Am I seeing things?"

"No," Roshara answered. "There are cuts. And there's bruising"

"What?" John touched his cheek, feeling tender spots and what must have been dried blood. "It wasn't a dream? But... Parsons never heard anything. He would have done something if he'd heard." He looked over to where Parsons was talking to Kestrel. The bruises on Parsons' face had already started turning purple, and he looked frightful. "He would have done something."

"Who would have?" Parsons called.

"You." John gestured for him to come closer.

"What would I have done?" Parsons asked. He frowned. "John, did you have those scratches before?"

John looked around to see if Garrett was in earshot. Then he pitched his voice low. "I told you I had a nightmare about Wraith. But it was real enough for Wraith to give me these." He gestured to his face, then repeated what had happened. "You know him better than I. Can he put himself into a person's dreams?"

Roshara frowned. Then she nodded. "I've heard of it. It is possible. I didn't know that he could." She looked at Kestrel. "Papa?"

"That was your mother's area of expertise, my dear. Not mine." Kestrel shook his head. "Regardless, you've made yourself a powerful enemy, John."

John snorted. "I've made others. I tend to outlive them by quite a lot. Wraith doesn't worry me. He has a range, and I know it now. I can stay out of it." He frowned. "No, the fact that he has elves working for him worries me. But he didn't seem to know who Siobhan is."

"John, we both know that Nathaniel and Avriel have been sending elves to this part of the world for years," Parsons said.

"I don't think we should be surprised that some have thrown in their lot with Wraith. I may have been the first elf to walk into Wraithtown, but clearly, I wasn't the last."

John nodded. Then he looked at Parsons. "You never told me why he wanted your head on a spike."

"Oh," Parsons murmured. He looked off down the river for a moment. "The last time I was here was... perhaps sixty of your years ago. And he wants me dead because I beat him at cards."

"You beat him at cards?" Ethriel repeated. "That's all?"

"That can't be all. He said you owe him a life," John added.

"Well, you see, that's what we were playing for," Parsons said. "A young woman, far from her own people. She was a raid captive, and I won her at cards." He smiled. "She didn't speak a word of any language I knew. But we learned to understand each other. Her name was Chumani. I took her back to her people." He gestured. "North of here. And west."

John realized what Parsons was saying. "She was Avriel's mother?"

Parsons nodded. "That's why he wants me dead. He wanted her for himself, and he doesn't forgive." He looked back at John. "He'll never forget that you bested him, John. And he's one you won't outlive."

John smiled and put his arm around Ethriel's shoulders. "Watch me."

THEY STOPPED NEAR THE cottonwood tree to eat, to rearrange the baggage in the wagons, and to allow Lilith to change and properly meet Parsons. John brushed down Barak, then Windrider, then took his coat off and studied the tears.

"Can you fix it?" Ethriel asked.

"It'll take some time, but yes," John answered. "Would you pull out a fresh shirt for me, love? I want one that's all of a piece, and not all over blood."

Ethriel nodded and went to the wagon, going through the cases until he found a fresh shirt. He brought it back, and John stepped out of sight, tossing down his braces and tugging the ruined shirt over his head. He dropped it and put on the fresh shirt, tucking it in and buttoning his trousers again. He pulled his braces back up, then checked his pockets... and touched a pouch that he'd forgotten about. He pulled it out and smiled.

"What have you got there?" Ethriel asked. John scooped the ruined shirt up and dropped it into the wagon, then took Ethriel's hand and led him toward the others.

"I bought something for you, love," he said. "I saw it, and I didn't even think twice. I knew it was right." He looked down at the pouch, then met Ethriel's eyes. "I frightened you—"

"Which time?" Ethriel asked. John smiled.

"I frightened you about what would happen if we were discovered. If someone found out we were lovers." He took a deep breath and licked his lips. "Ethriel, I don't want you afraid to love me. And I'm not afraid to love you." He shook the contents of the pouch out into his hand, and went to one knee, holding up the simple gold ring. "I don't know when I'll ever be able to follow through on this, but will you marry me?"

A WOMAN APPEARING OUT of nowhere wasn't surprising. In Wraithtown, it was a regular occurrence. But this woman wasn't one of Wraith's people. She wasn't one of the elves that had settled here. He didn't know who she was, and that interested him. She entered his office and crossed to his desk as if she owned the town.

Very interesting, indeed.

"My people tell me that you've had dealings with an enemy of mine," she said. "I think that perhaps that makes you an ally?"

Wraith studied her for a moment. "Could be. Depends on who your enemy is?"

"He goes by the name of John Zebedee—"

Wraith snorted. "Oh. That one. Yeah, he'll get his. Eventually. I'm patient. He'll come back this way."

She smiled. "Could I convince you to be less patient? And do something about him sooner?"

Wraith sat up and gestured to a chair that hadn't been there a moment before. She nodded and sat down.

"Seems you haven't introduced yourself, Ma'am," Wraith said. "I'm thinking I know your name, but I'd like to hear it from you."

She smiled. "My name is Siobhan. John Zebedee murdered my son. I want him to pay."

Wraith laughed. "Well then, maybe we do have something to discuss."

John Zebedee Meets the Witch-Queen of the Elvenlands

CHAPTER ONE

Growth

JOHN HAD LIVED IN MANY houses over the years. Old houses and new ones. Of the new ones, there had been ones that he'd built with his own two hands, and ones that he'd paid someone else to build for him. He'd never noticed the difference in the smell or the feel of them before, with the exception of a tiny dugout in Arkansas. All the others had just been houses. This place, the house that they'd only been in a week? This was more than just a house. This was *home*.

He sighed and shifted, tugging the blanket higher as he settled into the still-unfamiliar mattress. Everything in the house was new. Mostly because they hadn't really owned anything to move to the new house. They'd spent part of their first year in Bandera in hired rooms in town, making careful excursions out to the surrounding areas in search of the elves that were living in the area. Finally, they'd found the elven enclave — a small, hidden town called Lightning Tree. Their governor, a woman named Amanial, was skeptical of them at first, but had clearly been unwilling to ban her future King from the town. They'd started spending time there, making connections and building alliances. Taking lessons. Making friends. Laying the groundwork of Ethriel's army.

It had been on one such visit that they'd found this piece of land – an abandoned land grant. It was several miles outside Bandera, along the Medina, and it was perfect. The land would support a farm, or they could raise cattle or horses. It was on the river, so John could fish if he wanted. It was close to Lightning Tree, but not so close as to alarm the elves or cause them to withdraw. And there was a colony of kelpies living in that part of the Medina, including several who knew Lilith and were overjoyed that she'd returned to them.

When they'd returned to town, John had visited the courthouse, asking about how to find if a piece of land was still owned, or if he could claim it as a homestead. He'd been directed to the land office, and the wheels had started turning. He spent a week in San Antonio, filling out forms, paying for the claim, and making arrangements for a surveyor. It had taken several months, but once the survey was completed and the papers filed, they'd moved out to the land. The rules said that they needed to reside on the land for five years, and improve it.

And they had. They'd rebuilt the existing house first, even though it was barely more than a shack. Building a new barn had been more important, and fencing a corral. Preparing the land to grow crops that would feed the horses they intended to raise here. It had been hard, backbreaking work, but they'd done it. They'd had help — the Millers had arrived near the end of the first year, and Nathaniel had turned from shopkeeper to rancher.

It had taken them almost the entire five years to get to this point. The farm was producing well, to the point that Nathaniel thought they might need to hire help for the upcoming harvest. Their herd was still small, but the word of the quality of their horses was spreading — just yesterday, they'd sold a mare and foal to someone who'd come all the way from San Antonio looking specifically for breeding stock from the Midsummer Night ranch. The temporary shacks that they'd lived in were now things of the past. The Millers' house, started second, had been completed first. By necessity — Avriel was expecting her first child with Nathaniel, and when Nathaniel told John, John had insisted that they focus all of their effort on making sure that she had a proper roof over her head. Once the Miller house was complete, they'd turned that same attention to the Zebedee house. This house.

And best of all, they'd finally fulfilled all the requirements and had been able to file for the land patent. That had been granted a month ago, and the papers had arrived the same day as the window-glass for John and Ethriel's house.

Finally, finally they were settled in, on land that was finally theirs, and John could finally notice the little things. Little things like the differences in the scent of a new house that was really a home. The house had the new house smells he was familiar with — new wood and plaster dust, of beeswax and varnish and paint. But there was something more. Lying in the bed in their new bedroom, curled around his beloved Ethriel, he could breathe it in, bask in it. And realize what the difference really was – a new home smelled like hope.

He closed his eyes and buried his face in Ethriel's hair. He really should get up — he had work to do. They all did. But staying in bed was so tempting. Then he heard noise from the kitchen directly below, and voices speaking in low tones. No doubt because Roshara and her father were trying not to wake John and Ethriel. Having them share the house was temporary, only until the final house was finished, something John hoped would be done before winter. He wasn't sure why Kestriel and Roshara hadn't gone to stay in Lightning Tree with the other elves. Kestriel had explained it as having something to do with Elven politics, with the fact that Kestriel was higher in rank than the Governor of Lightning Tree, and therefore a rival to her power.

John had his doubts. He suspected that it might also have less to do with Kestriel's rank, and more to do with his daughter. There was no avoiding the fact that when Ethriel finally took the throne and began his rule with John by his side, he would still need an heir. He'd need a second consort, and Kestriel was clearly trying to have Roshara be the first choice. And Roshara didn't seem to have any objections.

Ethriel didn't seem to notice the way Roshara looked at him, but John did. And he found that he didn't mind. He had come to care deeply for Roshara. Not in the same way that he loved Ethriel, but it was close to how he'd loved Maryam. He'd shared the man he loved before, and Ethriel had enough love in him for more than one person. They'd make it work.

Once Ethriel finally realized what was right in front of him.

"Ethan," he murmured, and kissed Ethriel's bare shoulder. Ethriel's human name had become something of an affectionate nickname over the years, although John was certain that he was the only one to use it. "Time to wake up."

"I've been awake," Ethriel said. "Just laying here listening to the house." He twisted in John's arms and rolled onto his back. "And waiting to smell coffee. John, there's no coffee in my kingdom. How do we fix that?"

John laughed. "It's a plant. Perhaps we can grow it there?" He propped his head up on one hand. "Or we can send messengers through the portals to buy it in Skullyville."

Ethriel smiled. "I don't think that will work after a while. Who knows if Skullyville will still be there once the throne is secure?"

John snorted and sat up. "What do you think they'll do, move the town?" he asked. "I sincerely hope there will never be another war that razes a town. Not here." He stretched and sighed, then sniffed. "I smell coffee. It's time to get up."

Ethriel nodded and rolled out of bed. John followed, and they took turns washing up at the basin before dressing. John made the bed while Ethriel braided his hair, then they both headed out into the hall and down the stairs. The house had four rooms — two upstairs, and two down, off a central hall that allowed for breezes to blow through in the heat of summer. Upstairs were the bedrooms, while downstairs were the sitting room and the kitchen. Both had wide windows to let in light and air, and as they entered the kitchen, John saw Kestriel outside, sitting on the porch that ran the width of the back of the house and looked down to the Medina.

There was a matching porch on the front of the house, overlooking the stable yard and the Miller's house.

"Good morning," Roshara said. She was dressed to work, and hadn't yet put on the illusion that made her look human, or the gloves that she wore when she left the ranch. "I started breakfast."

"You didn't have to, but thank you," John said. "I thought it was my day to cook."

"We'd have starved to death waiting," Kestriel called through the open window. "You're late."

"Not very," Ethriel protested. "John, I'm going to go turn out the horses. Do you want to help me, or help Rose?"

John looked out the back window and saw movement. "Looks like Jeremiah is out already. I'll be there in a moment."

Ethriel smiled and leaned across the table to kiss John, then left the kitchen. A moment later, John saw him trotting across the yard toward the stable, falling in next to Jeremiah, who now stood taller than Ethriel. John turned back to Roshara. "Rose, might I have a word for a moment?"

She looked curiously at him. "Of course," she answered. Then she blinked. "Oh, you wanted to talk in private?" She turned and raised her voice. "Father, go help with the horses."

"Already gone," Kestriel called back. John waited until his footsteps faded to nothing before turning back to Roshara.

"I was wondering," John said. "Why did you decide to stay here and not go to Lightning Tree? You wouldn't have to hide who you are there."

"We wouldn't," Roshara agreed. "I wouldn't have to be human Rose there. I know. And I know what Papa told you. That's only part of it."

"About him having higher rank than Amanial?"

She nodded. "If we settled there, she'd be under pressure to yield to him. Which he doesn't want. So that's partially why we won't stay there. The other reason is that Ethriel is here. You're here. This is where I want to be, and I told him that."

John arched a brow. "I'd already guessed that it might have something to do with Ethriel, but I'm here, too? Is that important?"

"Of course," she smiled. "John, I'm not sure what you're asking. Or why. Do you think I'm trying to put myself between you and Ethriel? Because I'm not. I wouldn't."

John shook his head. "No. I know that. I was asking because I've started to think that we're united in how we feel about him, and I wanted to be sure of how you feel. Now, if we could get him to see you—"

"Oh, you've noticed him not noticing me?" Rose asked with a laugh. "He still sees me as his childhood friend. And honestly, when we first got here? That's how I saw him. He was Ethi."

"Ethi?" John repeated. "Is that what you called him?"

"That's what we all called him, when he was a child," Roshara said with a nod. "Elven names can be long and complex. Diminutives are common, especially among family and close friends. To our families, I was Rose, he was Ethi. So don't worry about calling me Rose. I've always been Rose. You're following one of our traditions when you call him Ethan."

"I didn't realize you've heard me," John said. "I thought I was keeping it as a private thing."

She smiled. "I've heard you a few times," she admitted. "But I don't think anyone else has. If they have, they won't use it. Remind me to tell you about pillow names."

"Later. Now, I've never heard anyone call him Ethi. And he never said anything about it to me," John said. He leaned against the table. "So when did it change? When did you stop seeing Ethi?"

She didn't answer at first. She turned to the stove, moving the coffeepot to the back to stay warm. She put a frying pan in place. "Fried eggs or scrambled?"

"However you decide to make them," John answered.

She turned back to him, looked at the bowl of eggs on the table, then nodded. "Scrambled. I haven't collected eggs yet this morning. There's not enough to make fried for everyone. And I don't call him Ethi because he asked me not to. He says he doesn't like it anymore. He won't tell me exactly why. I think it reminds him too much of what he's lost. And to answer your question, it was when you were in San Antonio."

"Which time?"

"The last trip. There was a storm here while you were gone, one that came out of nowhere in the middle of the day," Rose said. "Remember? We told you about it. It took down the corral fence."

"I remember," John said. "How you didn't lose all the horses I don't know."

"Ethriel is the reason we didn't lose all the horses," Rosa said. "He was out there, in the height of the storm, with Jeremiah and Nathaniel and my father, herding the horses back into the stables. He was in command, John, in ways that I never thought he could be. And when he came back inside, drenched to the skin? He was laughing. That was when I saw him. The first time I didn't see Ethi. I saw Ethriel." She smiled.

"And you liked what you saw?"

She smiled, turning pink. "Very much so."

John nodded and laughed. "Well, we're in agreement, then."

She looked down at the bowl of eggs, then peered up at John through her lashes. "You're... taking this far better than I'd expected."

"I'm not a jealous man, Rose. To be honest, this wouldn't be the first time I shared the man I loved with the woman he loved." John considered, then decided he wanted to know. "I do have another question. You said that part of your reason was I was here. Rose, what did you mean?"

Her cheeks turned even more pink. "I like what I see when I look at you, too."

"I didn't realize you were looking at me that way," John said. "Rose, I just this morning decided that when Ethriel realized what he had in you, that I'd have no objections at all."

"I won't put myself between you, John," she said quickly. "I won't."

"And that's not what I'm saying. You're not putting yourself between us." He smiled, standing up. He reached for her hand, kissed her knuckles, then turned her hand and kissed her palm. "We're putting Ethriel between us, so we can both love him equally."

Her smile was luminous. "You really don't mind?"

"I really don't," John said. "He'll need a consort who can give him an heir. I can do a great many things, but not that." Rose giggled, and he smiled at her. "Rose, if the woman he chooses to stand on his other side is someone who loves him as much as I do? I can't object to that. And if it's someone I care about as well—"

"Not love? Because I do love you."

John paused. "I... yes. But it's different. I'm not sure if it's in me to love a woman the way I love a man," he answered. "I do love you, Rose. Enough that I know I can be comfortable sharing him with you." He paused, then asked, "It's been a long time since humans allowed a union to be more than a single man and a woman. In this country, anyway. They might still in other places in the world, but I'm not sure. Is this something that even exists, among your folk? Can Ethriel have two consorts? Or... a husband and a consort? How would it work?"

"I'd have to ask my father." She frowned. "Which, if you don't mind, I'd rather not ask my father. Not... not yet."

John chuckled. "I can ask Parsons. Unless you'd rather I didn't? If I ask him—"

"He'll tell my father," Rose finished. "I... think not. We'll find out another way. I can ask in Lightning Tree."

John nodded and straightened up. "I should go help them." He let Rose's hand go. She smiled. Then she made a shooing motion.

"Go. I'll call you all in to eat."

JOHN STOPPED TO SAY good morning to Joshua, as he still did every morning, then he headed across the yard, whistling. It was still early-morning cool, although he could tell that it wouldn't last. Maybe he would take Ethriel down to the river for the heat of the afternoon. He waved to Avriel, who was sitting in a rocking chair on the porch, and detoured on his path to the stable.

"Good morning," he called as he approached. She smiled, resting her hand on her very pregnant belly.

"Good morning, John," she answered.

"How are you feeling today?" he asked, resting one hand on one of the porch support pillars.

She tipped her head to the side. "Better, I think. I slept well."

"Good," John said. He studied her for a moment. She looked tired, and she'd lost a great deal of weight over the course of her pregnancy. "Have you eaten?"

"I'm going to try," she answered. "This little one doesn't seem to like food, though."

"Did the midwife say anything?"

Avriel shook her head. "There's not much she can do," she said. "Especially since she's never had a half-elf mother before. She's not entirely certain what to expect with me."

John sighed. "I wish there was more she could do. I don't like seeing you uncomfortable."

Avriel smiled. "I appreciate that, John."

"As do I." Sir Parciviel — who John never could think of as anything but Parsons — came out of the house to stand behind his daughter. "Avriel, there's porridge, if you think you can keep it down."

"I will certainly try."

"Don't get up," Parsons said. "I'll bring it here. And some of that tea." He turned to John. "Good morning."

"Good morning," John said. "Is there any help you need?"

"I think I have everything under control," Parsons answered. "Jeremiah got things started and ate his own breakfast before he went out to the stable." He looked up. "What do you think kept Nathaniel?"

"I'm not sure," John answered. "I was surprised that he didn't come back yesterday, to be honest. Something must have kept him in Bandera overnight. If he's not back by noon, I'll ride into town and see."

Avriel nodded. "Thank you. Now, you have work to do, John. Go on. If we need help, Papa will call you."

ONCE THE HORSES WERE turned out into the corral, John, Kestriel and Ethriel went back into the house for breakfast. As they ate, John watched through the window as Jeremiah worked one of the two-year-olds they were saddle-breaking. He had the mare saddled, and was working her on a lunge.

"I keep forgetting to ask Jeremiah how his lessons in Lightning Tree are going," he said, refilling his coffee cup. "Ethriel, you take lessons together. How is he faring? And how are you faring? I forgot to ask you, too."

"I can't seem to get the grasp of shields," Ethriel answered. "Mine are good and solid, but I can't seem to regulate how much power I put into them. Which means that if I'm shielded, there's enough residual magic that the shields glow. Terensiel says she'd heard of it before, but I seem to be exceptionally talented at it. I have a future as a lamp if being King doesn't work, I suppose. And as for Jeremiah?" Ethriel glanced out the window as he sipped his own coffee. "Ah... do you know the name Taliesin?"

Across the table, Kestriel snorted. "Really? Our Jeremiah? Taliesin?"

"What's a Taliesin?" John asked.

"Who," Ethriel corrected. "Taliesin was a human mage and bard from someplace called Wales. He learned from the elves...." He paused and licked his lips, then laughed. "I was so small. I barely remember him. Just... I remember his voice. He had a beautiful voice. And he was an incredibly powerful mage." He looked at the window again. "After our last lesson, I overheard our teacher calling Jeremiah Taliesin's Heir."

Kestriel nodded. "Taliesin Ben Beirdd made quite the name for himself among our folk, then went back to the humans and did the same. I think there are still stories told about him."

"He was supposed to be incredibly beautiful in more than just his voice, wasn't he?" Roshara asked. "The stories said so. I don't remember him at all."

"Ah, when he was with us, you were still barely out of the nursery, child," Kestriel said, his voice fond. "Still clinging to your mother's skirts."

John chuckled. "Kestriel, you're going into Lightning Tree today?"

"I'm supposed to, yes," Kestriel answered. "Amanial asked me to stand on their Council, and they're meeting today. I may be there a day or two. Or six." He chuckled. "The problem with being long-lived is that there's no sense of urgency. Diplomacy happens slowly."

John smiled and looked out the window again, then finished his coffee. "Roshara, thank you for making breakfast. That was lovely." He got up. "Ethriel, we have stables to clean, and—" He stopped, turning toward the window. He could hear the rattle of a wagon, coming toward the house at speed. "Is that Nathaniel?"

Ethriel jumped up, and they hurried out onto the porch. It was Nathaniel, who drove the wagon into the yard and drew to a stop. As he jumped down to the ground, John trotted out to meet him.

"Nate!" he called. "We were starting to worry. What kept you?"

Nathaniel turned and pointed back the way he'd come. "He did."

John looked, and saw the other rider coming toward them, a young native who didn't look as if he was from one of the local tribes. He looked tired, and it was clear that he'd been badly treated. He drew his horse in and dismounted, walking closer to John.

"I am seeking the Hattak Falaya. Is that you?"

CHAPTER TWO
Messages

John nodded, answering in slow Choctaw. "You're a long way from home."

The young man smiled and replied in English, "Your Choctaw is as bad as I was warned." He turned and took a parcel out of his saddlebag, and held it out to John. "I am Coahoma, and I was sent to bring you this."

John took the parcel and unwrapped it, revealing papers inside. He unfolded them, read them quickly, then looked up.

"I... I'll need a day or two."

"I will tell them," Coahoma said. He turned back to his horse.

"You're welcome to stay," John said. "To rest. And... are you all right? What happened?"

He grimaced. "People in the town objected to me asking questions. There was a fight—"

"That's why I was late," Nathaniel interjected. "Judge Rodriguez wouldn't let him or the Gatlin boys out of jail until morning. And he wouldn't let me post bond. Said young hotheads needed a lesson. Even though Coahoma didn't start the fight." He shook his head and sighed. "If I came back, I'd never have gotten there this morning before they let him out, and I didn't want there to be more trouble."

John nodded. "Those Gatlin boys are troublemakers. Coahoma, thank you for bringing this. At least have something to eat, before you leave."

Coahoma shook his head. "I am already delayed in returning. I will avoid the town, and go home. I'll let them know you're coming." He swung back up onto his horse and rode away, turning off the dirt road toward the north as he left the yard.

"Coming?" Ethriel said. "John, you're going somewhere? What did that say?"

John tipped the papers toward Ethriel. "It's from Hopaii," he said. "He's asked me to come back to Skullyville." He looked down at the papers. "He's dying."

"What?" Nathaniel gasped. "May I see?" John handed him the papers, and he frowned as he read them. "He wants you to come... and to bring Talula back here with you." He looked up, past John. "Jem?"

John turned to see that Jeremiah had come up behind him. "Papa, what's this about Talula?"

"It's about Hopaii," John answered. "He's dying, and he wants me to come back to Arkansas. When I come back, I'll be bringing Talula with me."

Jeremiah swallowed. Then he nodded. "I see. I... well, I suppose I'm getting married when you get back?"

"You're only nineteen, Jem," Nathaniel said. "You don't need to rush. But having Talula here will be nice." He looked over at his house. "I need to go apologize to my wife. Excuse me." He handed the papers back to John, then turned and walked toward the house. John looked down at the paper again, then sighed.

"Come to the house, love," he said to Ethriel. "I need to plan."

"How long will we be gone, do you think?" Ethriel asked. "I'll need to tell Terensiel."

John turned and sat down on the porch steps. "Ethriel, do you think you can come with me? Can you take the time from your studies?" Ethriel sat down next to him, and John took his hand. "I don't want to leave you. Not for as long as this will take. But can you come with me? Can you leave Lightning Tree for that long?"

Ethriel frowned but didn't answer immediately. John let him think, and was finally answered by a growl.

"No," he answered. "No, I can't. My magical studies have advanced as much as I can at my age, so really, it's just honing the skills. But there are too many other things I'm working on there.

Too many alliances I'm building. If I leave for as long as this might take, it will all fall apart." He shook his head. "John, you'll be gone at least a month."

"I know," John answered. "I know, and I don't like it. But I owe Hopaii so much." He turned to Ethriel. "I owe him your life. I can't not go to him. I can't not honor his last wish."

Ethriel nodded. "I wouldn't ask that of you." He looked past John, toward the road. "I don't like you going alone, though."

"I could go with you," Jeremiah offered. "My studies can wait."

John looked up at him. "I'll want to talk to your father before I say yes or no," he said, and got up. "Which... let's go talk to Nathaniel." He turned around. "Kestriel!"

"You don't need to shout," Kestriel said as he came out of the house. He put down the rifle he was carrying, and smiled. "Wasn't sure if it was trouble or not."

"It isn't, but we need to talk. You and Rose come over to the Millers.'"

Kestriel nodded, looking over his shoulder. Roshara came out of the kitchen, wiping her hands on a towel.

"I heard," she said. "Let's go."

They walked over the Miller house, where Parsons was waiting for them. "Nathaniel told me," he said. "Are you going?"

"I have to," John answered. "I've known him his entire life. I can't not be there for him when he's dying."

"And I can't go," Ethriel added. "I can't risk the alliances I'm building here."

"I can be ready to go in the morning," Nathaniel offered, coming out of the house with Avriel on his arm. John looked up, then shook his head.

"No, Nate. You need to be with your wife," he said. "You need to be here when the baby comes."

"Then I'll get ready—" Parsons started. He stopped and straightened when Ethriel raised his hand. Kestriel did the same, and John realized that he was seeing what Roshara told him that she'd seen.

King Ethriel was speaking.

"I need you here, Sir Parciviel," he said. "There are too many in Lightning Tree who look at me and think I'm too young. They listen to you where they won't listen to me." He turned to Jeremiah. "We need you here, too. As much as I appreciate you offering to go—"

"You what?" Nathaniel gasped. "Jem!"

Ethriel continued as if he hadn't been interrupted, "We need you here on the ranch. We're going to be short-handed, especially since Sir Kestriel will be in Lightning Tree for Council for however long that takes."

Jeremiah scowled. Then he nodded. "You're right. But... Uncle John can't go alone!"

Ethriel nodded. "I know." He frowned. "I don't want you to go alone, John. If anything happened, we'd never know."

"Oh, thank you very much for your confidence," Roshara said. She folded her arms over her chest. "Do you honestly think I won't be watching?"

"Oh, I know you'll be watching," Ethriel said. "But you have to sleep. And if you do see something, we'll be here. Miles and days from where we're needed." He looked at John again, his brow slightly furrowed. Then he looked up. "Sir Parciviel, this is something on which I can call the tithe, isn't it?"

"Call the tithe?" John repeated. "What tithe?"

Parsons nodded slowly. "Yes. Yes, it is."

"What would you say to an escort?" Ethriel turned back to John. "When you go, you'll have a personal guard. Unless you wanted more than one. How many would you want?"

John coughed. "What would I say? Besides 'It's nice to meet you?' I don't know. What's the tithe? You're going to have to explain, love."

Ethriel laughed, and King Ethriel vanished like morning mist. "The tithe is what we call the services and duties owed to the royal family. I can invoke the tithe in Lightning Tree, and you'll have an escort of Elven knights. As many as you like.." He turned to Kestriel. "Would you mind company going in to Lightning Tree?"

"I haven't agreed to this!" John protested.

King Ethriel looked back at him and arched a brow. "I don't remember asking your leave, John. If you're going to be away from me, you'll be going with a guard of my choosing." He turned back to Kestriel. "When do you need to be in Lightning Tree?"

"By midday," Kestriel answered.

Ethriel nodded. "I'll be ready. But we'll have to hurry to get our work done before then. The stables won't clean themselves."

Kestriel stepped back and saluted. "As you will, My King."

Ethriel smiled, nodding once. Kestriel saluted again, nodded to Parsons, then turned and headed back to the house. Roshara smiled at John, then hurried after her father.

"John, you and Ethriel should get to planning," Nathaniel said. "I'll help Jeremiah." He brought Avriel back into the house, then came back out. He and Jeremiah hurried toward the stables. John took a deep breath and refolded the pages of the letter.

"I'll need to make some plans," he said. "I... my head is spinning."

Ethriel held his hand out. "Come inside. There's probably coffee left, and I can help you plan. How will you go? Train?"

"I'll need to look at the map," John answered. They went back into the house, and he turned into the sitting room. His desk was in here, and he went and sat down, staring for a moment at the wooden surface. He reached into the drawer and took out a rolled map, unfurling it across the desk. He'd made liberal use of this map over the years. He'd marked the borders of the land that they'd claimed, and he'd added Lightning Tree, and the kelpies' nest. He'd also added what he believed were the borders of Wraith's power, based on what he remembered — north to the Red River, east to Nacogdoches, and the equivalent south and west. Having that marked out showed that neither the railroads nor the mail coach were safe options for travel – both passed within Wraith's reach. Knowing that meant that John was hesitant to travel anywhere east of San Antonio without first going north of the Red River.

Ethriel pulled a chair over and sat down next to him. They sat in silence for a moment, until Ethriel reached out and pointed to San Antonio.

"Will you go by train?" Ethriel asked again. "You'll have to go to San Antonio, but it will be faster than going by horse or by wagon. The train will take you there, won't it?"

"It will, but it will also take me through Wraith's territory," John said, running his finger over the railroad line. "So will the mail coach. I don't trust him not to try his mettle against the mail coach. Or an entire train, for that matter. Better if I go north and cross at the ferry."

"The reverse of the way we came," Ethriel said, nodding. "Minus all the crossings at Garrett's ferry."

John snorted. "Definitely minus all those crossings." He took a deep breath. "I'll be gone a month, possibly two. There will be a baby by the time I get back." He looked at Ethriel. "Ethan, I don't want to leave you."

"I know," Ethriel said. "I don't want you to go. But you're right. You have to. We owe him too much to not be there. I hope you make it in time." He leaned back in his chair. "I just don't like the idea of you being gone for so long. And not just because I'll miss you, or because I don't know what to do here."

"I'm not worried about the ranch, Ethan. I know you'll be able to handle things here, with the farm and the horses. Jeremiah can handle breaking the yearlings — he's good at it. And Nathaniel can handle sales." He smiled. "And I've heard how you can take control if necessary."

"You have?" Ethriel asked, arching a brow at him. "Where... oh. What did Rose say? And about what?"

John grinned. "She said you took command during the storm. That she saw you as King for the first time."

"I'm having to learn how to act like my mother," Ethriel said. "Because in Lightning Tree, some of the elders won't listen to me if I don't. And some won't listen to me unless it comes from Sir Parciviel. I don't have to act like that here. You all listen to me."

"Because we know you," John said. "I will say that today was the first time you showed me how you'll be as King."

Ethriel cocked his head to the side. "When I told you that you'd be going with a guard. You... you're not angry are you?"

John shook his head. "No. I'm not. I'm intrigued. It's the first time I've seen you take on that mantle fully." He reached out and took Ethriel's hand. "I like it."

Ethriel blushed. "Do you now?"

John nodded. "I do. I can't imagine you doing something like that even a year ago." He squeezed Ethriel's fingers. "You've come a long way from the escaped prisoner I found in my barn five years ago."

Ethriel took a deep breath and nodded. "And I've still got a long way to go. But I can see the way a little more clearly now." He leaned back in his chair. "The core of my army is coming together. When you get back, you'll have to come meet them."

John nodded and turned back to the map. "I'll do that. For now, I need to get ready. I'll need to be on the road tomorrow morning." He traced his route with one finger, then looked at

Ethriel. "I was talking with Roshara this morning," he said. "That's when she told me about how you took control during the storm when I was in San Antonio."

Ethriel shifted in his chair. "I had to," he said, his blush returning. "We couldn't lose the horses. We've worked so hard, and Parciviel and Nathaniel... well, they're good men, but they didn't know what to do. I did. So I did it." He looked down, then back up. "Is that what being a king is?"

John shrugged. "I haven't a clue. I've never been a king." He smiled. "I just seem to have a habit of loving them."

Ethriel chuckled. "I'll try to live up to Joshua's example. Except for the dying part. Can I not do that?"

"I'm all for you not doing that," John agreed. He looked down at the map. "Oh. Back to what I was saying. I talked with Roshara this morning."

"About the storm—"

"About you, love," John said. "Ethriel, you're going to take the throne. I know you are. When you do, you're going to need an heir." He looked up to see Ethriel staring at him, his eyes wide. "You are."

"I know," Ethriel stammered. "I just... I didn't think you'd be thinking of that. I thought I'd have to bring that to you slowly." He licked his lips and looked away. "And you talked to Roshara about this? Why?"

"Because I noticed how she looks at you," John answered. "The look in her eyes, it's the same one I see when I look in a mirror."

Ethriel nodded. "I... I'd noticed. And I noticed her looking at you, too. I just wasn't sure how I felt about it. I mean... I promised you that I wouldn't betray your trust in me."

"I missed how she was looking at me, until she confessed this morning." John reached out and took his hand again. "Ethan, it wouldn't be the first time I've done this – loved a man who also loved a woman. Although it might be the first time I loved her as well. Maryam and I cared for each other, but it wasn't the same as what I feel for Rose. She and I talked. She was afraid that I would think she was trying to step between us, and she loves the both of us too much for that. What I told her is what I'm telling you right now. She's not between us. She's on your other side."

Ethriel ran his thumb over John's knuckles. "So I'm the one in the middle?"

"Be loved and supported by two people at the same time," John answered with a nod. "So... while I'm gone, if you decide to talk to Roshara about this. Or more than talk... just know that I'm aware, and in favor. You're not betraying me, or us. You're closing the circle."

Ethriel nodded slowly. "I... I will have to think about this. Rose... I do care for Rose. I've known her my entire life. I've noticed her looking at me, since the storm. I've noticed her looking at you—"

"She thinks you haven't noticed."

"I had to get very good at keeping my thoughts to myself," Ethriel said. He leaned back in his chair, not letting go of John's hand. "Buach—"

"You don't need to say more," John said. "I understand."

Ethriel nodded. "I'm still trying to get my thoughts around it. They're chasing themselves around like the kittens in the stable when they chase mice, when they trip on their feet and fall all over. The only thought I've managed to catch is that I can't sire an heir. Not until I have the throne. Not until it's safe." He looked at John. "You can protect yourself. We can protect Rose. I won't bring a baby into this. Not yet." He took a deep breath and blew it out, like he was blowing out a candle. Then he smiled. "I wasn't sure how to talk to you about this. Thank you for bringing it up first." He cocked his head to the side. "How do you feel about Rose?"

John smiled. "I care about her. I think we'd be happy together, the three of us." He laughed. "And since I can't give you an heir—"

Ethriel hooted with laughter. "That would be another miracle for you!"

"Not one I'd care to experience, given how horrible Avriel has been feeling," John said.

"For this trip, will you ride, or take the wagon?" Ethriel asked.

"I'm trying to decide, to be honest," John answered. "The wagon would be more comfortable, but it would be slower. Riding will be faster, and I think Barak is up for the trip. Which I think decided it. I want to go fast, to attract as little attention as possible." He paused, then rolled up the map. "All right. You need to go to Lightning Tree. I need to put together my travel kit, get some money from Nathaniel. I'll need to go into Bandera for travel supplies. One guard, please. And make sure that whoever you choose is ready for several days of hard riding and living off the land."

Ethriel nodded. "I'm not leaving yet. Let me help you. Then I need to change. I can't go to Lightning Tree dressed to muck out the stables." He stood up, tugging John out of his chair. "I'll miss you."

"I'll miss you as well," John said. "I know you'll be watching me. I will try to bore you senseless."

Ethriel tipped his head back and smiled. "So long as you don't bore me tonight," he murmured. "I want memories to keep me company for the entire time you're gone."

John blinked, feeling suddenly warm, his trousers suddenly tight. "You're going to say something like that, and then leave?" he whispered.

Ethriel stepped closer, resting his hands on John's waist. "I'm not leaving yet. And I do still need to change clothes." He leaned in and kissed John lightly on the lips. "Which means I have to take these off. Want to help?"

"Go upstairs. Go upstairs right now."

CHAPTER THREE
Preparation

John escorted Ethriel to the stables and helped him saddle his horse, a pretty mare named Cloud. Once Ethriel and Kestriel had ridden off for Lightning Tree, John returned to the house to pack and to plan.

Roshara met him on the porch.

"I heard you before," she said. "I heard you making the case for me."

"I wanted him to know that I had no objections, in case anything happened between you both while I was away," John said. "And since you heard me, I don't have to tell you. If anything happens while I'm away, I'm fine with it. Will you come help me?" She followed him up the stairs to the bedroom, standing in the door as he pulled his old saddlebags out of the closet. He started picking things out, choosing carefully for the trip.

"Are you sure you won't take the wagon?" Roshara asked. "It'll be more comfortable. And you'll be able to carry more."

"You know I just had this same conversation with Ethriel. The wagon will slow us down and make us conspicuous," John answered. "I wish I could take the train, but I'm not willingly putting myself into Wraith's reach."

"Can you take the train if you went north and around his range?" she asked. "Is there a railway on the north bank of the river?"

John looked at her. "I... I'm not sure," he answered. "I'll check the map. If there is, then perhaps that's an option. But I won't count on it." He rolled a clean pair of trousers around a fresh shirt, tucked them into the saddlebag. He added socks and his comb and toothbrush.

"Take a mirror," Roshara said. "I'll be able to see you in the mirror."

John turned to stare. "You will? Will I be able to see you?"

"I don't know," Roshara answered. "We can try it. Do you have a mirror?"

John went to the dresser and picked up a small hand glass, showing it to Roshara. She nodded, coming over and taking it from him. She held it for a moment before giving it back to John. Then she turned, walking across the corridor to the room she shared with her father. A moment later, he heard her call. "Hold the mirror up."

He did, studying the glass. It seemed to shimmer, growing warmer in his hand, but he only saw himself. He frowned, turning to call to Roshara and tell her it didn't work.

"You look so fierce when you frown like that."

John nearly dropped the mirror — Roshara's voice seemed to be coming from the glass! "How did you do that?"

"I can see you. And I can hear you."

"I can only hear you," John said. "Will I be able to hear Ethriel if he's with you when you do this?"

"We'll try it later when he's here. And we'll have to plan when we'll do this. If I try and the glass is in your pocket, it won't work."

John nodded. The glass seemed to shimmer again, then stilled. Then Roshara came back to the door. She smiled, looking very satisfied.

"Rose, that was extraordinary!" John said. He wrapped a handkerchief around the mirror, and tucked it into his saddlebag.

"Be careful with the glass," she said. "If it breaks, it will break the connection, too."

John nodded. "I'll be careful." He looked around the room and sighed. "I don't want to leave. I don't want to leave you all behind."

"We don't want you to go," Roshara said. "But sometimes, what we want and what we have to do are vastly different things."

John nodded. "True. I need to go talk to Nathaniel about money. Will you come with me?"

"I'll see what else Avriel needs," Roshara said, and turned toward the door. John caught her hand before she started walking, and she looked up at him. Her eyes weren't green. Not like the other elves. Rose's cat-like eyes were a dark blue, ringed with black, and she had a way of looking through a man that John suspected the young men in Bandera found disconcerting. When they all went to town, the young ladies all sighed after Ethriel and Jeremiah. The young men may have looked at Roshara, but they never looked more than once.

The more fools them.

"Rose," he said softly. "Take care of him for me."

She smiled at him, reaching up to brush her fingers over his beard. "Of course I will," she said, softly. "And when you get back, then we'll see what we see. But we need to get you ready. You'll need your gun, and ammunition."

John nodded, looking at the pegs on the wall where his Henry rested. Kestriel had set barriers to keep predators away from the horses, so he rarely needed to use it. When was the last time he'd taken it down and fired it? He'd last cleaned it... when? He wasn't even sure.

"I should test it," he said, and bent to take several boxes of cartridges out of the unending supply in the metal box on the floor. He tucked all but one into his saddlebag, then took the Henry down. "Go and tell Avriel and Nathaniel I'm target shooting, will you? I'll meet you there after I'm done."

"Of course," she said, and hurried down the stairs. John followed her, and went out the back door, walking down toward the banks of the Medina. He veered off toward the west, wondering if the kelpies were out in the swimming hole.

They were, and several of the younger ones splashed into the water, vanishing from sight as he approached. A pair of black mares ambled up the bank toward him, and one walked right up to him and rubbed her nose against his shirt.

"It's good to see you, Lilith," he said, scratching her forehead. "Will you change, so we can talk? I have news."

Between one breath and the next, both mares changed, turning into beautiful, naked women, lovely in every way, although their legs ended in reversed hooves. One of the women was young and voluptuous — the appearance of a maiden that would make any man's heart swell and his trousers tighten. The other woman was older, the Queen of the Herd, beautiful and regal. John bowed to her.

"I'm honored, Queen Aileen," he said. "Thank you for changing so we can talk."

"I'm curious to hear this news," Aileen said. "There have been ill omens in the waters, and nothing we can see that would cause them. I'd thought to send Lilith up to speak to your seer. Then you came."

"What news?" Lilith asked. "Is Ethriel all right? Where is he?"

"Ethriel just went into Lightning Tree," John answered. "And I'm going to be going away for a month, possibly two. An old friend sent word to me that he's dying. He asked me to come and be with him, and to escort his daughter here."

"Escort his daughter?" Lilith frowned. "That would be Talula? Jeremiah's intended?"

"He's told you about her?"

She nodded. "He will come down to the water sometimes, to practice his lessons. He's good company." She blushed, and John wondered just what company his honorary nephew had been providing the kelpie. None of his business, he decided. He'd been nineteen once, too, a long time ago.

A very long time ago.

"So I'll be gone for a while," he said. "And no one here can come with me. Ethriel can't risk the alliances he's forming, and Kestriel was asked to sit on the Council. And Nathaniel and Parsons need to be with Avriel."

"Which leaves Jeremiah doing everything else," Lilith said. "That's a great deal of work, John."

"I know, but it can't be helped," John said.

"Are you going alone, then?" Aileen asked. "There's danger in that."

"Especially from... from that one," Lilith added, shivering slightly. Even five years after John had stolen her from Wraith and freed her, she still refused to speak his name.

"Ethriel is arranging for a guard to ride with me... he said it was calling in the tithe that is owed the royal family. And we'll be sure to avoid that one's range." He looked down at the gun in his hands. "I needed to check the Henry. It will be loud, and I didn't want to frighten you unnecessarily."

Aileen inclined her head. "I appreciate the thoughtfulness, John. Lilith, go and warn your sisters there will be noise."

"Your Majesty—"

"I wish to speak to John," Aileen interrupted. "Now go."

Lilith shifted back into a mare and ran off. John watched her go, then bowed again to the queen mare.

"Your Majesty?"

"As I said, there have been ill omens," she said. "Ill omens that we cannot interpret. But perhaps that is because they were not warnings for us. They were warnings for you." She looked at him. "Do not leave, John Zebedee. Remain here. Your friend will understand."

"I can't," John answered. "I owe him too much to ignore this call. Your Majesty, I owe him Ethriel! If it hadn't been for him,

Ethriel would have died five years ago. That debt... how can I repay it if I ignore this?"

Aileen stamped one hoof. "The omens are so unclear. Has your seer seen nothing?"

John shook his head, turning to look back at the house. "She's said nothing. I'll ask her when I go back to the house. But right now, I need to test this rifle."

Aileen shifted back to a mare and turned, walking slowly back to the water. John waited until she had vanished before loading the Henry, then walked down the bank away from the swimming hole. There was a dead tree that he used for target practice when he was teaching Ethriel and Jeremiah to shoot, and he headed for that, stopping at the stump that was his usual marker. He set himself, ran the lever as he raised the rifle, and fired. Bark flew, and he saw a puff of sawdust as the bullet hit the tree trunk. He sniffed.

"You're out of practice, Yohanan," he said to himself. "That was off center. Sloppy. The General would have had your head."

It was easier these days to think back to the war, to his time as a soldier. The old wounds had scarred, but the scars were fading, as all scars did over time. He raised the rifle again, running the lever and firing until the rifle was empty, until spent shells littered the ground, and he once again felt as if the Henry was part of his arm. He took cartridges from his pocket and reloaded, turning to walk back up to the house. As he did, he saw movement, a duck taking to the air. He raised the rifle and fired, and the duck fell.

"That's better," he said aloud, and went to retrieve their supper.

JOHN'S PACKS WERE IN the sitting room, and his coat and hat were waiting. He'd gotten money from Nathaniel, which was in a money belt in the bedroom. Now, he sat with Nathaniel in the office in Nathaniel's house, going over ledgers and breeding records. Roshara had been busy doing something with Avriel, so John planned to talk to her when he was done.

"Mariposa is coming along nicely," Nathaniel said. "We need to decide if we're going to keep her or sell her. We have so many mares. Do we need another broodmare?"

John looked at the papers, at the charts that Nathaniel kept meticulously, tracking the bloodline and breeding of every horse on the ranch. "Nate, we might want to keep her, even though we don't need another mare. Let her be a gift from Jeremiah to Talula, when she gets here."

Nathaniel looked startled. "I... oh. You know, I like that idea. I'll tell Jeremiah."

"Tell me what?" Jeremiah asked. He came into the office, rubbing a towel against his dripping wet hair. He grinned at them. "Washed up under the pump. Don't worry. I'll stay back," he said. "No drips on the charts."

"That we should keep Mariposa, so you can give her to Talula," John said.

"You think Mariposa?" Jeremiah asked. "I was going to ask you about a horse for Talula, but I was thinking Cinnamon. He's shaping up nicely and he's younger than Mari. Talula will be able to bond with him, where she might not have as easy a time with an older horse. And we need another colt. Barak isn't getting younger."

John looked at Nathaniel, who looked amused. "Well?"

Nathaniel went back through his charts, then nodded. "I was thinking Cinnamon to sell. He's a handsome lad, and he'll make a fine hunter. He'll bring in a pretty penny."

"How much are you thinking?" John asked.

"I think we can get two hundred dollars for him, easily," Nathaniel said.

Jeremiah whistled. "You think we can get that much?"

Nathaniel nodded. "Cinnamon has good lines, and excellent breeding, and colts of Barak's line are turning out to be quite the commodity. He'll bring in at least two hundred dollars, possibly more, if we bring him to the right market."

"Which is the right market?" John asked. "Because it doesn't sound like you mean San Antonio."

"No, I was thinking of going further afield," Nathaniel said. "I'm just not sure where. I haven't finished researching. Tulsa, perhaps. But we'll need more than just one hunter to sell if we're making that trip." He frowned and looked at his book. "Let me see.... if we sell Mariposa, and... let me see." He turned pages quickly. "Damask. If we sell Mariposa and Damask, we'll do just as well, if not better than if we sold Cinnamon. And it will help us relieve the surfeit of mares and fillies." He leaned back in his chair. "John, when you get back, I want to talk to you about starting a second breeding line. Bring in a heavier stallion, start breeding for a working horse. A plow horse."

"Don't most people around here use oxen?" John asked. "Oxen are easier to keep and cheaper to feed, aren't they? Given that, would we be able to sell a plow horse? I mean, they're not good for much else. There isn't much call for men in armor these days, and that's the only other use I can think of for a heavier horse."

"What about a different line?" Jeremiah asked. "Not for a heavier horse. A smaller one, one bred for speed. I was reading in the newspaper about horse racing, and it seems to be popular. There's even a breeder's group, from what I understand."

"Chariot racing?" John asked. "Is that still done?"

"Yes, but that's not the kind of racing I meant," Jeremiah answered. "And they call it harness racing now, Uncle John. But this race I read about was back east somewhere, and the sketch showed the horse with a saddle. They rode to race."

"Interesting," Nathaniel said. "We might have to look into this." He pulled a piece of paper closer and wrote a note, then laid his pen down. "There's another reason to bring in another stallion. All the colts are Barak's get. Most of the fillies are, too, so maybe it is a good idea to keep Cinnamon and sell Mariposa. We need to sell off some of the fillies, and we need to bring in fresh blood. If we get careless with breeding... well, that's not good husbandry."

John chuckled. "When did you learn about horse breeding?"

Nathaniel gestured to the bookcases. "I've been learning. I'm still learning. And it seems I have more to learn. Jem, when did you read about this horse race? And what about this group?"

Jeremiah leaned against the wall, tossing his towel over his shoulder. "Let me think. Ah... last month? I think? The race was in the spring, but the papers might still be in the kitchen for kindling, since Mama or Granddad light the stove with magic more often than a match. Should I see if I can find them?"

"Please," Nathaniel said. "And... when do you have lessons again?"

"Tomorrow," Jeremiah answered. "I should have gone today, but I sent a message to Terensiel, asking her leave to stay and help Uncle John. She said I might."

"I appreciate that, Jeremiah," John said. "I'm not sure what other help I need. Except... I need to speak to Roshara. Queen Aileen says that their seers have been seeing bad omens, and she thinks I should stay. I want to see if Roshara has seen anything. She's with your mother."

Jeremiah nodded. "I'll go find her and those papers." He left the office, and John turned back to Nathaniel.

Nathaniel was frowning.

"What's wrong?"

"Just... starting to feel like a hen mothering a duck," Nathaniel answered. "You can't see the way he glows. Julia's magic was never as strong. Jem's power... it's more like elven magic than human. And he's stronger than all the elves here, including Ethriel."

John looked at the door. "Ethriel says that their tutors are comparing Jeremiah to another powerful human mage."

Nathaniel arched a brow. "Please let them not be comparing him to Merlin?"

John shook his head. "Someone named Taliesin," he answered. "Taliesin Ben Beirdd. Welsh, Ethriel said."

"Oh, is that why Jeremiah ordered three volumes of Welsh stories from Boston?" Nathaniel laughed. "I'd wondered. He was never interested in fairy tales as a child." He glanced at the window, then closed his book. "I think we're done here."

John smiled, "And even if we're not done here, we're done here? Why?"

Nathaniel nodded toward the window. "You can't see out. I can. Ethriel is back."

John got up and hurried out of the office, hearing Nathaniel laughing behind him as he went out onto the porch. Ethriel hadn't even dismounted yet, and there was another rider with him, another young elf. The stranger had dark hair, and his complexion was closer to John's olive skin than Ethriel's ivory.

Ethriel smiled when he saw John, and swung down from the saddle. "John!" he called "Come and meet Maniel!"

John came down the porch steps. Ethriel took Cloud's reins and walked over to John, taking his hand. "Come and meet Maniel," he repeated. "He's a high squire, and he'll be sworn to the Silver Thorn at the winter solstice. He's agreed to act as your escort and guard for this journey."

"A high squire?" John asked, letting Ethriel tug him across the yard. "I'm not familiar with the term. It's not one that humans used when we had knights and squires."

Ethriel turned to look at him. "Were you one? A knight?"

John laughed. "No," he answered. "Well, once. I discovered that I don't like most armor. It's heavy and uncomfortable. And hot."

"We'll have to try you with our armor," Maniel offered. He held his hand out. "Tiarna John, it is an honor."

John smiled at the title. The first time he'd been called Tiarna, Ethriel had tried to explain what it meant – something approximating "Lord," but with connotations that indicated a bonded partner or spouse. He still wasn't clear on the exact meaning, but he didn't care. The elves recognized him as Ethriel's partner. That was all that mattered. He clasped Maniel's wrist the way Parsons had taught him. "I'll be honored to have you at my side, Maniel. Thank you."

Maniel bowed over their linked hands, then straightened. His eyes widened, and John looked over his shoulder to see that Jeremiah had come out onto the porch with Roshara.

"Uncle John, you said you wanted to talk to Rose?" Jeremiah called. Then he laughed. "Maniel?"

John nodded. "I do. Jeremiah, will you help with the horses while I do? Then we'll go over the travel plans with Maniel." He turned back to Maniel. "You know my nephew?"

Jeremiah trotted down the stairs and took Cloud's reins from Ethriel. He smiled at Maniel. "Hello, Maniel. Good to see you."

"It is good to see you, as well," Maniel answered. He turned to John. "We shared a weapon-master," he added. "Before I advanced to high squire."

John felt a touch, and turned to see Roshara had joined him, resting one of her gloved hands on his arm.

"Maniel, I don't think you've been properly introduced," Ethriel said. "This is the Lady Roshara, daughter of Sir Kestriel. She is part of my household."

Roshara nodded her head slightly in acknowledgment as Maniel bowed to her.

"My lady," he murmured. "It is a pleasure."

"Squire Maniel," she replied. "You are welcome here."

"Maniel, I seem to remember you were particular about your mount," Jeremiah said. "Follow me, and I'll show you the stable."

Maniel led his horse after Jeremiah, but kept glancing back over his shoulder at them.

"You have an admirer," John murmured to Roshara.

"I don't want him. I've met him before," Roshara answered. "He doesn't seem to remember, but I do. Papa threatened to horsewhip him."

"What?" Ethriel gasped. "What did he do?"

"He was cruel to a stableboy in Lightning Tree," Roshara answered. "It was not long after we first arrived. Perhaps he's changed." She shook her head. "Oh, Avriel invited me to stay with them tonight. So Maniel may have the bedroom."

"Perhaps," John said. "Rose, have you had any visions? Any omens?"

Roshara frowned. "I... no. Why?"

"Because the Herd Queen says that they've had several, and she doesn't think I should go. She'll want to talk with you."

Roshara looked thoughtful. Then she nodded. "I'll walk over to the river. But I've seen nothing. I can look, if you want."

John glanced at Ethriel, then nodded. "Please."

"After supper," Roshara said.

CHAPTER FOUR
Portents

Dinner was a savory stew, thick with hominy, beans and tender pieces of duck. There was warm bread to go with it, and they shared the meal crowded around the table in the Miller house. John and Ethriel sat side by side on a bench, with Roshara on Ethriel's other side. Across from them were Jeremiah, Parsons, and Maniel. Nathaniel sat at the head of the table, and Avriel at the foot.

"Rose, this is wonderful," Nathaniel said. "You've never made this before. What is it?"

"It's called pozole, and Senora Rodriguez gave me the recipe," Roshara answered. "Sometimes, when I go into town, we'll have tea. She's been teaching me to cook the way her mother taught her in Mexico. She wrote this down for me the last time I was there, and I've been wanting to make it."

"When we go to town next, I want to thank her," Ethriel said. "It's delicious. And even Avriel likes it."

"You mean the baby likes it," Avriel corrected. "It is very good, Rose. Thank you."

"Yes, thank you," Ethriel agreed. He tore a piece of bread in half and used part to soak up what broth was left in his bowl. "Is there more?"

"There's plenty in the pot," Roshara answered. "Let me have your bowl."

"I'll get it, Rose," Ethriel said. "Does anyone else want more?" He took Parsons' offered bowl and went to the stove, coming back with the filled bowls and sitting back down.

Maniel looked puzzled. He'd eaten quietly, but it was clear to John that he'd had no idea what he was actually eating. He kept looking around, as if he was expecting someone. Finally, he took one more glance around the room, then blurted, "You have no servants? You... this is the royal household. How can you have no servants?"

Ethriel paused in the act of passing the bread basket across the table to Jeremiah. "The only thing that make this the royal household is that I live here. I'm trying to not call attention to myself, Maniel. Especially since I'm not king yet, and I won't be king for some time. Not until I go back through the portal to the Elvenlands."

"But your station—" Maniel protested.

"Doesn't matter. Not here," Ethriel finished. He handed the bread to Jeremiah, then turned to Maniel. "Maniel, I have no rank in the human world. I have no station here, other than as part-owner of this place." He gestured, taking in the entirety of the ranch outside. "In Lightning Tree, I'm recognized as the King-in-exile, and when I'm there, I tend to behave more like you think I should. But that's because the people of Lightning Tree are our people, and the place is Elven, not human. There, I am the King. Here, among my family, I'm just Ethriel. Or Ethan." He turned and smiled at John. "I've rather grown to like the name Ethan."

John smiled in return, his shoulder brushing against Ethriel's.

Maniel shook his head. "I... I don't understand."

"You were born here, Maniel? Or in the Elvenlands?" Parsons asked.

Maniel looked across at Parsons. "I... I was born in the Elvenlands, Sir Parciviel. But I've been here since I was very small."

Parsons nodded. "I understand. And you know all the stories? The shining palace by the sea? The winter palace of the snows? The music and the flowers, and the never-ending celebrations?"

Maniel smiled. "Those were my bedtime stories," he admitted.

Avriel laughed. "Mine, too," she said, looking fondly at her father.

"Well, then, the both of you should know that there's nothing but story about those stories," Parsons said. "Yes, there was a palace by the sea. And yes, the winter palace was almost always covered in snow. But they were just places. There weren't never-ending celebrations, and there were only flowers in the spring." He frowned slightly. "Life in the Palace wasn't as... I'm not sure of the word. It wasn't perfect."

"Idyllic?" John suggested.

"Yes," Parsons said with a nod. "That's the word. It was never idyllic. And there were times, especially when Méabh had just taken the throne, when she was still mourning her father, still fighting with her counselors over her marriage—"

"I don't know this story," Ethriel said. "What about my father?"

"He was a Mountain lord," Parsons said. "And there were some among Méabh's counselors who were certain that he was going to try and overthrow her. Never mind that he clearly adored her." He snorted. "Never mind that they were all clearly looking at the wrong Mountain elf."

"Parciviel," Ethriel murmured.

Parsons nodded. "Of course. Back to the point. There was a great deal of conflict in the Palace, because the courtiers thought that Méabh should be doing just about anything other than what she needed to do. One thing that Méabh did after your grandfather died was throw herself completely into caring for her people. There was a drought, not long after she became High Queen. And she went out and learned the basics of farming—"

"She never did!" Maniel gasped. "The High Queen?"

"Oh, it was quite the scandal in court. The High Queen with dirt under her nails and in grubby trews because she'd been digging in the fields? Never mind that Eiriell would have done the same thing," Parsons paused. "Had done. He had done the same thing, now that I'm thinking of it. And Méabh was right alongside him.

Her courtiers wanted her to stop, but she told them that one of the things that she learned from her father was that if she didn't understand what her people were doing and how they were suffering, then she didn't know enough to help them properly. And she was right. Once she understood what the farms needed, what the plants needed, then she was able to better plan out the greater magics that alleviated the drought entirely." He rested his hands on the table. "It's one of the reasons the people loved her the way so much. She tried her best to get to know them, to understand them. She learned to farm. She learned midwifery, and if I remember what I was told, she was quite good at it." He paused, then looked across the table. "She'd have been proud of you, Ethriel. I'm certain of that. Especially that you're keeping both feet on the ground and learning anything you can."

Ethriel looked down at his bowl. Then he nodded. "Thank you."

Parsons turned and looked at Maniel. "Here's a bit of wisdom that comes from being a great deal older than you, Maniel. There's no such thing as menial labor. There is only work that needs to be done, and no one is too good to do that work." He chuckled. "So come with me, and I'll instruct you in the fine art of washing dishes."

John started to rise, intending to help clear the table, but stopped when Parsons waved him off. "You have things to finish, I'm sure. We'll take care of things here. Jeremiah, will you clear?"

"John, you wanted to know if I've seen anything," Roshara reminded him. "I haven't, but I can look before you go. We'll have to go back to our house to do it.."

John nodded and stood up, stepping out of the way so that Ethriel could slide off the bench. Nathaniel got up from his chair and walked around the table to help Avriel up.

"I may not see you before you leave," Avriel said. "If you're going to leave as early as I expect you to."

"I don't expect you to wake up to see me off," John said. "You need your sleep."

"Then you'd best come and say goodbye now, because I'm about to fall asleep." Avriel laughed, and hugged John tightly when he came around the table. "Stay safe," she told him. "Tell Hopaii that we love him."

"I will tell him," John said. He hugged Avriel again and stepped back, letting Nathaniel take her arm and lead her from the room.

ROSHARA LEFT THEM IN the kitchen of their house, going upstairs to her room. John lit the lamps and sat down at the table in his usual seat. Ethriel sat down next to him.

"What sort of omens did Aileen say?"

John frowned. "She didn't. Just ill omens that they couldn't interpret, and maybe it was because they were warnings for someone else."

Roshara came back into the kitchen. "Aileen told me the same. And gave me no details." She shook her head. "It was not at all helpful." She set a large bowl in the middle of the table, and took a small bottle out of it. "Ethriel, would you fill this with water, please?" she asked as she took off her gloves.

Ethriel nodded and took the bowl to the cistern, filling it to the brim. He came back and put it on the table, but didn't sit down. He looked around. Then he frowned and raised his hand. The lights brightened – no, it wasn't the lights that were glowing. It was the walls.

"What did you do?" John asked. At the same moment Roshara asked, "Now, why did you do that?"

Ethriel grinned. "What I did? Put a shield around this room. Protecting us from sight, sound, and magical attack. Why? I'm not sure. But Terensiel says that instinct can be a powerful warning."

Roshara nodded. "It can be. I just didn't feel anything myself. All right. Let's see what we can see." She picked up the small bottle and poured the contents into the water; the ink swirled and spread, slowly darkening the water to midnight blackness. John stood up to watch. He'd never seen anything any of the times Roshara had done this, but he always looked. Roshara leaned over the bowl and blew on it, sending out ripples that sparkled and danced. She frowned.

"Mist," she murmured. "The future is... unclear." Her frown deepened. "No, no, the future is blocked. Someone is trying to hide this from me!" She reached out and tapped the surface of the water with one finger. "Show me!"

The water rolled, cresting toward the outer edges of the bowl, and John saw movement in the darkness. Nothing distinct, nothing that he could make out. But for the first time, he looked into the bowl and saw... something.

Then the bowl shattered, spilling inky water all over the table and onto the floor. Roshara staggered back from the table, her eyes wide.

"Someone doesn't want me to see what's going to happen," she said slowly. "And I don't know who."

"Rose!" Jeremiah appeared in the doorway. "What was that?"

"Jeremiah, wait—" Ethriel started to say. Then he stopped, as Jeremiah came the rest of the way into the kitchen. The glow from the walls went out, and Ethriel blinked, his face going white as Jeremiah stopped and looked around.

"I... there was a shield?" he stammered. "Oh, blast it, Ethriel, I'm sorry! I wasn't expecting one, not just for scrying. Are you all right?"

"I think I got enough of it down before you tore it open. I don't think I'll have a headache," Ethriel answered. "Let's get some rags to clean this up."

"I'll do it," Jeremiah said. "And I'm sorry. I rushed in, and I should have looked first." He held one hand out, palm facing down, and John watched as the water vanished from the floor.

"What did you do?" he asked.

Jeremiah smiled. "Sent it to the river, downstream from where we fish. It's the largest body of water nearby."

"And Ethriel's shield?" John asked. "You walked right through it."

Jeremiah blushed. "It's... something mages can do. Especially when they're powerful. They can walk through a weaker mage's shields."

John looked at Ethriel. "Is that how you got into my barn? You never did tell me how you did that."

Ethriel nodded. "And it's why Buach couldn't follow. He wasn't a very strong mage, even though he was older than I was. I'm stronger than he was, but I wasn't trained and he was. And Jeremiah... has Terensiel found anyone yet whose shield you can't walk through?"

Jeremiah looked down and fidgeted slightly. "Not yet, no."

Ethriel smiled. "I didn't think so. I'm making you my head mage. I hope you know that."

Jeremiah laughed. "You keep saying that. Raise that army first. While I'm still alive. Then we'll talk." He leaned against the wall. "I mean, there has to be a reason I've got all this power, right? Maybe it's to help put you on the throne."

Ethriel nodded. "I'll need all the help I can get," he said. "The army I build here is... well, you've seen it, Jem. It's not going to be very big."

Parsons stepped into the kitchen, with Maniel behind him. "What happened here?" Parsons asked. "Why did Jeremiah run over here like that?" He looked at the bowl and coughed. "What happened here?" he repeated, this time with little more heat.

"I haven't answered Jeremiah yet, so I'll answer all of you at once," Roshara answered. "Something is blocking my sight. There was a veil between me and the greater sight, and when I pushed through... well, that's what shattered the bowl."

"Who could block you like that?" Jeremiah asked. "Sight isn't one of my talents, so I don't know much. I didn't think it was possible to do something like that."

Roshara reached out and picked up a piece of the broken bowl. "Someone would have to know me," she said slowly. "Know my power, and know that I'd go looking for this portion of the future."

"Which means that someone knows that John is leaving," Ethriel said. "Wraith?"

Roshara bit her lip. "Possibly," she murmured. Then she frowned. "Probably. I can't think who else would know that much about me, and know that I'm with you."

"He doesn't know you're with me," John said. "If he believed me, then he thinks you're dead."

"But Garrett might very well have told him otherwise," Parsons said. "We don't know what he knows. We do know that he promised that you would pay for eternity for walking into his trap and escaping again. It's only been five years. That's not long enough for him to forget." He snorted. "Five hundred years might not be long enough for him to forget."

"By that time, we'll be through the portal and out of his reach entirely," Ethriel said.

"But we've no idea what going to happen while Uncle John is gone? We don't know what's coming?" Jeremiah asked.

"Do we ever?" John asked in reply. "Jeremiah, none of us can know what's coming. Not for certain. All we know is that eventually, it will end." He smiled ruefully. "Even for me, someday."

"What... what does that mean?" Maniel asked. "Even for you? And... Wraith? That's the ... the power that rules the area to the east of here, isn't it? The spirit? Or.. or whatever he is? I think I've heard the name. We occasionally have elves reach us who've been under his thumb." He shook his head. "You'd not last an eternity with that one. You'd not last a day."

"Maniel, you haven't properly been introduced," Ethriel said. "John is the Undying One."

Maniel scoffed. "Go along with you! That's a story!"

John shook his head and folded his arms over his chest. "How old do you think I am, Maniel?"

Maniel sniffed. "You humans are mayflies. Here today and gone tomorrow. I can't ever tell with you."

"John and I are the same age," Ethriel said. "According to... someone who knows—" He shared a quick smile with John. "We're exactly the same age, and were born at the same moment."

Maniel looked shocked. "That's not possible. Not for a human."

"I'm not your ordinary human," John said. "In a nutshell, I can't die. If you want to know more, I'll tell you about it as we go. It'll pass the time."

Maniel nodded slowly. "Yes. Please. I'd like to hear this. My parents told me about the story—"

"Prophecy," Roshara corrected.

"About the Shining King and the Undying One. And how they would bring peace to all the Elven lands."

"Your parents are Mountain?" Parsons asked. "They're the ones who call the Shining King prophecy a story, and who deny that it was a true seeing."

Maniel nodded again. "I was Mountain born. I barely remember it, though. My parents held their lands near the Spires, but they lost everything in the early days of the war. My father died in battle, and my mother not long after. That's why I'm here with my grandmother." He cocked his head to the side. "Was it a true seeing?"

Parsons nodded. "I was there, Maniel. It was a true seeing. I heard the seers with my own ears."

"My grandmother would spit to hear you say that," Maniel said with a wry grin. The grin widened to one of pure mischief. "If you tell her, can I watch?"

Parsons laughed. "I know a little about your grandmother, and I'm not brave enough, son. Not at all. Now, if you'll excuse me? I'll ride to Bandera with you in the morning. But that means I'm for my bed now."

"Sir Parciviel, wait," Ethriel said. "I want you to witness this." He turned to Maniel. "When the time comes, Maniel, I give you my word that there will be a place for you with me. In my house." He smiled. "Just look after my John while he's away from me."

Maniel saluted, his arm across his chest. "As you wish, my King."

Parsons and Roshara left together; Roshara took the pieces of bowl with her. To bury them, she said, so they wouldn't cause mischief in the house. John wasn't sure just what mischief broken pottery would be able to cause, but he'd learned to defer to the elves with regards to such things. He showed Maniel to the bedroom where he was going to sleep.

"We'll be on the road at dawn," he said. "And we'll stop in Bandera for some supplies. Have you mastered the spell so that you look human?"

Maniel nodded. "I'd not be allowed out of Lightning Tree if I hadn't. The human name they gave me was Manuel."

John nodded. "Close enough that you'll answer to it. That makes sense. All right. I hope you're ready to live rough for the next month." He snorted. "I hope I'm ready. It's been quite a few years since I last did this. I may have gone soft."

Maniel smiled. "Somehow, I doubt that. Good night, Tiarna John."

John laughed. "Once we're on the road, Maniel, don't call me Tiarna. You're welcome to call me Uncle, the way Jeremiah does."

Maniel licked his lower lip, then nodded. "Thank you, Uncle. Good night."

John turned from the closing door to see Ethriel waiting at the top of the stairs. He smiled at John.

"Ready for bed?" he asked.

"I…" John looked at the bedroom door. "Bed? Yes." He reached for Ethriel's hand, leading him toward the door. As they reached it, he leaned close. "Sleep? Not any time soon."

CHAPTER FIVE
Separation

"You're very quiet."

John turned to look at Maniel. They were several hours past Bandera, and John realized that he hadn't said a word since they'd left Parsons behind.

"I'm sorry," John said. "I've been brooding, and that's hardly fair to you."

Maniel smiled slightly. "I understand. You're homesick already, and we've only just left." He chuckled. "In a day's time, you'll be a sodden mess. I'll have to wring you out."

John burst out laughing, watching as Barak's ears swiveled back toward the sound. The stallion didn't balk at the sound — he was used to it. Maniel's gelding danced slightly, but the elf gentled his horse and brought it back to an even pace at Barak's side.

"I was hoping you'd take that for the teasing it was, and not box my ears over it," he admitted. "It was a risk."

"And one that I appreciate," John said. "Maniel, I think a week is the longest I've been away from home in five years."

"The longest you've been away from him, you mean?" Maniel asked.

John nodded. "He is my home. My whole heart. And I can say that to you, but we'll not speak of this where human ears can hear. Humans are... strangely antagonistic where men loving men are concerned."

Maniel blinked. "How so?" he asked. "I don't have a great deal of experience with humans. At least, the ones outside of Bandera. How do they react?"

"It's a crime, and the penalty is hanging," John answered. "At least, I think that's the current penalty in Texas. But I may be mistaken. Regardless, the price is your life. And if they find out that

I can't die... well, I like Bandera. I don't want to have to uproot everyone and everything we've built."

"Hanging?" Maniel gasped. "You mean they'll execute you? For loving someone?"

"For loving the wrong someone," John said with a nod. "Needless to say, Ethriel and I are very careful when we leave the ranch together."

Maniel frowned and fell silent. John let him be alone with his thoughts, looking around as they rode. They were north of Bandera, and heading slightly east — he'd promised Ethriel that he'd go easy until he was once again used to being in the saddle for days at a time. So they were heading for the appropriately-named town of Comfort. The town had been established by Freethinkers, and it showed. Before they'd stopped in Comfort, John had never before been in a town that had no churches. Nor any place where he and Ethriel were recognized and welcomed as what they were – two men in love, and who were as close to married as was possible. He'd come very close to demanding that they settle in Comfort when they'd first passed this way.

"Did I tell you where we were going before I started brooding?" John asked.

"A town, you said. Comfort? Why?"

"Because we're neither of us used to being in the saddle for an entire day, and I promised Ethriel I wouldn't push either of us too hard the first day," John answered. "We'll take our comforts while we can. We'll stop again in a hotel in Bonham, but once we cross the Red River, it'll be a week or more before we see a proper bed again."

Maniel nodded. "This is going to be interesting. I've never been this far from Lightning Tree before." He looked at John. "Are there many elves out here?"

John shook his head. "Until I met Ethriel, I didn't know there were any. Now, I'd met two, but they were disguised. So I didn't really know they were elves until they showed me. And I mean Parsons and Avriel, to be clear." He paused. Frowned. "Wait. There were three. I'd met three. I keep forgetting that Buach was there, too."

"You met Buach?" Maniel asked.

"I did," John answered. "When Ethriel escaped him, he gave chase." He nodded in the general direction of north and east. "The closest portal to your world is near where we're going. It's probably where you came to this world."

"I don't remember. I know we can't create portals in Lightning Tree," Maniel said. "The natural power in the land disrupts the spells."

"So I've been told," John said. "If you want to go out to the mounds before we come back, we can. It's not far."

"I'll think about that," Maniel said. "Tell me about Buach."

"I barely knew him," John admitted. "He was masquerading as a preacher, and I didn't know he was an elf until right before he killed me."

Maniel burst out laughing. "You're teasing me now!"

"No, I'm not," John laughed with him. "I told you. I can be killed. But I don't stay dead. It's part of being the Undying One. Buach actually killed me twice before I killed him."

Silence. For a long several minutes all John could hear was the wind and the horses. Then Maniel looked at him.

"You killed Buach?" he asked. "You... you really killed him?"

"He came damned close to killing Ethriel," John answered. "With elfshot."

"Elfshot?" Maniel's voice was hushed. "That... that's filthy! Surely it wasn't elfshot!"

John nodded. "It was elfshot," he said. "Buach used it on me, and he almost killed Ethriel with it. And when we were coming here, Wraith had a rifle that fired elfshot. That was a surprise." He shook his head. "I've died by elfshot twice. It's not pleasant, Maniel."

"You... you said Ethriel *almost* died from it." Maniel looked pale. "How almost? You don't almost die from elfshot. No one almost dies from it. If you're even grazed by it, you die."

"I have... a very powerful friend," John said slowly. "He saved Ethriel's life."

Maniel whistled. "He must be powerful," he murmured. "Is that who we're going to see?"

"No. No, we're going to see Hopaii. Which is his title. His name is Hiloha. He's a holy man among the Choctaw, and I've known him almost his entire life. He's old now, and dying, and his daughter is pledged to Jeremiah. We'll be there for him when he dies, and we'll bring Talula back with us."

Maniel nodded. "Do you think we'll get there in time?"

"I hope so."

THEY STOPPED IN COMFORT, boarded their horses at the livery stable, then went to the hotel. A woman met them at the door: she looked at John, then looked again.

"I remember you!" she said. "You were here... what, six years now?"

"Five," John corrected. "Forgive me, I don't remember your name?"

"Oh, I don't remember that we were properly introduced," she said. "I'm Marie Ingenhuett. My husband owns the hotel."

John nodded. "Thank you," he said. "I do remember you now. You and your husband treated us well when we were here." He smiled. "I'm ashamed I didn't remember you right off. Now, if you have two rooms, we'd like to rent them for the night."

"Of course, of course." She led them into the building and down a short hallway. "No other guests at the moment, so you can pick your own rooms. It's a dollar a night, and if you want supper, it's fifty cents more."

John nodded. "That's more than fair. What time is supper, Mrs. Ingenhuett?"

"Six o'clock," she answered. John took his pocket-watch from his vest and looked at the time.

"More than enough time to wash up so we can dine properly with a lady," he said. "Manuel, you'll want a clean shirt."

"Yes, Uncle," Maniel said. "I'll take this room, if that's all right?"

"That's fine, young man," Mrs. Ingenhuett said. She smiled as Maniel went into the room, then turned to John. "You were traveling with another lovely young man when you were here last. And a young woman and her father. But I remember your young man and his lovely manners. How is he?"

"Ethan is doing very well, and I'll tell him you asked after him." John smiled. "I'll tell Kestrel and Rose you asked after them as well. I'm having to go to Arkansas for family matters, and Ethan stayed behind on our ranch."

"I see," Mrs. Ingenhuett said, nodding. She looked at the door to the room Maniel had chosen. "Mister Zebedee, I know this is none of my business. If you don't mind my saying so, you're not that young man's uncle. You're not nearly old enough."

"I'm older than I look, but you're right. Manuel calls me Uncle by courtesy, not by blood," John admitted. "He's making the trip with me because Ethan didn't want me to travel alone."

"And you're not—" she paused, as if she was searching for a delicate way to put something distasteful. John immediately realized what she was trying to ask.

"I'm not," he said, keeping his voice low. "One of the things I liked very much about this town was that everyone realized and accepted the truth about Ethan and me. I'm still devoted to him. If I could, I'd marry him in a heartbeat. I'm not going to betray him."

Mrs. Ingenhuett blushed. "I'd worried. He's such a nice man, your Ethan." She nodded. "Now, I'll leave you to wash up. The outhouse is behind the house. Be on time for supper."

AFTER SUPPER, JOHN returned to his room. He closed the door behind him and checked his pocket-watch, then went to his saddlebag, taking out the small, cloth-wrapped mirror. He unwrapped it and sat down on the bed. He looked at his watch again, and as the time ticked over to eight o'clock, the mirror in his hand warmed.

"*John?*" Roshara's voice came from the mirror. John stood up and went to the window, putting more distance between himself and the door.

"I can hear you," he said. "We're in Comfort, at the Ingenhuett Hotel. Mrs. Ingenhuett remembers us."

"*Does she?*" Roshara sounded amused. "*Is she still making that wonderful goulash?*"

John laughed. "It's what we had for dinner. Is Ethriel with you?"

"*I'm here,*" Ethriel said. "*How was the first day?*"

"Maniel says I was brooding," John admitted. "Which, I was. I miss you already. It was quiet. I'm hoping that it stays quiet."

"*I miss you, too,*" Ethriel said. "*We all do. Today... well, everyone was distracted, I think. We all kept looking for you.*"

John closed his eyes. He could still turn back. He could be home by this time tomorrow. In his own home, in his own bed.

But he had promises to keep.

"I'll be home as soon as I can be," he said. He looked at the mirror, saw only his own face. "I wish I could see you."

He heard a laugh. *"Roshara can see you. I can't. And we can't hold this spell for much longer."*

"Oh," John murmured. "Well, hearing you every night will have to hold me over until I see you again." He smiled. "I love you, Ethan. I miss you. And I'll talk to you tomorrow night."

"I love you, too."

"We both do," Roshara added. *"Stay safe."*

The mirror went still and cooled in his hand. He smiled and went to wrap it up again, putting it back into his saddlebag before getting ready for bed. This would be his last night in a bed for a few days, and he had no intentions of wasting a moment of it.

ONCE THEY LEFT COMFORT, the days flowed one into the next. They stopped again in Bonham, and the next day crossed the Red River. As they continued east, John kept a wary eye on the far bank. But nothing happened, and they saw no one until a mile past what remained of a lightning-struck cottonwood tree, when a man hailed them at the ferry. When he saw John, he burst out laughing.

"I remember you!"

John smiled. "I'd have been surprised if you didn't. How are you, Mister Garrett?"

"Can't complain," Garrett answered. "Now, you're not crossing, are you?"

"Oh, no. Not this time or any other. But you'll see us again in a month or so," John answered. "Been called to a friend's deathbed."

Garrett sobered. "That's a shame, that. I wish you an easy trip, and him an easy passing." He looked back at the river. "You could cross here, if you wanted. Been two years or more since I last saw JW. Something happened down that way, and I sure am not brave enough to go find out what."

John nodded. "When we come back, maybe we'll linger a bit. For now, I need to go on."

Garrett nodded. "See you in a month, then." He waved as John and Maniel rode on.

"Friend?" Maniel asked.

"Acquaintance," John answered. "I've never been sure exactly whose side he was on."

Maniel nodded. "I see. How much further?"

"We'll stop in Fort Towson tonight, and then head north. A few more days."

IT WAS COMING ON SUNSET three days later when John started recognizing the area. He smiled. "We're close. But it's late, and we'll have to cross the river. We'll stop for the night, and go on tomorrow."

Maniel looked around. "Stop here?"

"No, I think we'll have a roof over our heads tonight," John said. "It's been a while since I was last there, but we'll go to my old place." He turned Barak, taking the old familiar trails to the dugout. But something looked odd, and he waved Maniel to a stop and dismounted, letting the reins fall as he took the Henry from the saddle holster and walked through the trees until he could see clearly.

The dugout was gone. The roof had caved in, and the door and the windows were broken on the ground. He stood and stared at the wreckage for a moment, then turned. The barn was gone as well, scorched timbers marking where it had once been. He lowered the Henry and sighed, turning to see that Maniel was coming closer, leading both horses.

"It's all right," John called. "Except the shelter I planned for us to sleep in tonight is gone. I wonder what happened here? That couldn't have been natural."

"What was this?" Maniel asked. "Other than a large pile of dirt?"

John smiled. "Now it's a large pile of dirt. Five years ago, this was a dugout. An underground house. I built this... oh, fifty years ago or so? About that. I can't remember any more. But it was the first place Ethriel and I lived," John answered.

Maniel chuckled. "I have a hard time thinking of Ethriel living underground like a rabbit."

John laughed. "Sir Parciviel said the same thing. It wasn't for very long. And it was a very comfortable rabbit hole." He shook his head and looked at the pile of rubble. "We'd better go before it gets too dark. There's no hotel in Skullyville. We'll go on and cross the river, and camp on the far side."

He turned back toward Maniel, and blinked. Maniel and his horse were gone. John walked over to Barak and took the hanging reins, then turned and raised his voice, "Maniel? This isn't the time to play hide and seek."

He heard movement. Far more movement than there should have been for one elf and his horse. He turned, raising the Henry, and saw the elves blinking into visibility. Unfamiliar men in armor, several of them carrying crossbows that were aimed at him.

He was surrounded.

"If I'm trespassing," he said slowly in poorly-accented Elven. "I apologize. This place used to be mine. If you've claimed it, I'll go." He looked around. Still no signs of Maniel. "If you've taken my companion, I'd like him back. We've harmed no one."

One of the elves started to laugh. The others joined in, until one voice cut through the laughter.

"Enough. Take him. And you don't have to be gentle about it. He won't stay dead. Just secure him and bring him to the portal." Maniel appeared out of nowhere, standing behind the ring of armed elves. "Surprised, Uncle?"

John went cold. "You've betrayed us? Why, Maniel? You're a friend. You've a place waiting in the King's household."

Maniel snorted. "As Ethriel is so fond of saying, he's not the king yet. Knowing what he has available to him in Lightning Tree, he won't ever be king. And I already have a place in my Queen's household." He smiled. "You'd be surprised how many in Lightning Tree serve the Queen."

John licked his lips. This wasn't going to end well. At all. But he wasn't going to go down without a fight. And maybe, if he could get in the saddle, he could get away. But first...

He ran the lever as he raised the Henry, aimed and fired, and Maniel fell, his chest a red ruin. John kept firing, even as he heard the snap of crossbows, felt the agony as they hit — his left leg, his side, his shoulder. He stepped back, forcing himself not to fall. He had to move, he had to get mounted. Getting into Barak's saddle was torture, but he did it, and turned the horse toward the south. He needed to get clear, needed to get someplace safe. He kicked Barak into a gallop.

And heard the snap of crossbows.

Barak screamed and pitched forward, and John went flying, He saw the rocks, and tried to twist in mid-air, to protect himself from the impact.

He heard the sickening crunch of his bones breaking as he hit and slid to the ground. Moving was impossible. He couldn't find the Henry. He saw the elves coming to stand over him, taking to each other. He couldn't translate, could barely hear them over the pain. Then one raised his crossbow

WHEN JOHN CAME GASPING back to life, he was in the back of a moving cart, and Maniel's dead body was lying next to him. The sky was dark, and he wasn't sure where he was. But he was fairly certain where he was going. The mounds. They were taking him to the portal.

He needed to get away. He closed his eyes, trying to take stock. He didn't hurt anymore. They must have drawn the quarrels. Good. His wrists were bound in front of him, but that wasn't a hindrance. He had a clasp-knife in his pocket. Once he got away, he'd be able to cut the ropes and free himself. And then...

Well, he'd worry about what came after he got away once he got away. He opened his eyes again, and saw the knife on Maniel's belt. Maybe he didn't need to wait. He reached out and tugged it free, turning it and awkwardly sawing at the ropes around his wrists. They parted easily; he held onto the knife, took a deep breath, and threw himself off the back of the cart. He hit the ground, stumbled, and ran.

He heard the elves shouting behind him, heard horses closing. He didn't slow, didn't dare look.

Something hit him, tangled around his legs, and he fell. He twisted, slashing at the rope around his knees, seeing the horses coming closer. He sawed harder, but the cord wouldn't part.

"Use the chains this time," one of the elves called, clear enough that John could translate. "And hurry. The moon is rising."

One futile struggle later, John was back in the cart, his wrists chained behind him. They tugged off his boots, and his ankles were crossed and bound with the tangling cord that they'd used to bring him down.

"I don't know why she wants you," the same elf said, guiding his horse alongside the cart. "Except that you're not a mayfly, are you?"

"And I speak your tongue," John answered, maneuvering himself into a sitting position.

The elf laughed. "Badly. Your accent is atrocious."

John snorted. "Not much practice," he said. "She wants me because I killed her boy."

"Oh, you're the one?" the elf said. "I understand now. I underestimated you. I won't do that again. You're not escaping us this time. So behave, and perhaps we'll feed you while we wait for the portal. I can hear your belly from here."

John closed his eyes. "Don't bother."

"As you wish."

When John opened his eyes again, the elf was gone, and they were slowing. He turned, and saw torches. A camp. A camp just like the one where Ethriel had been held five years before. They'd saved Ethriel from the portal.

But there was no one to save John.

CHAPTER SIX
Encounters

John wasn't sure how long they traveled. Right before they went through the portal, his captors hooded him like a falcon, a leather thing that covered his eyes and ears but left his mouth free. There was a brief sensation of being doused in cold water, then they'd started moving again. He thought he heard the muffled sounds of a fight, but couldn't tell what was happening, and it didn't seem to delay them at all.

It quickly became impossible to tell how much time had passed. They traveled, they stopped. He ate what was pushed into his mouth, and slept. No one spoke to him. No one asked him any questions at all. He didn't fight them. There didn't seem to be a point — he had no idea how to get through the portal, assuming he could even find it again.

It was at least a few days, though. Maniel was starting to stink.

The cart stopped rolling, and John listened to the muffled sounds around him. It didn't sound like the usual noises. Something was different.

Then rough hands grabbed him, dragging him out of the wagon. His ankles were freed, and he was dragged forward, tripping on what felt like cobblestones. Then the floor evened out. They turned, and turned again, and John heard a raised voice clearly enough that he could translate.

"Clean him up and get him dressed properly. She wants him."

"May I have the hood off?" John asked. "I'm not going anywhere. I don't even know where here is. And my scalp itches."

He heard laughter, then there were hands on his arms. He heard jingling, and the manacles around his wrists were taken off. He moved slowly, stretching and feeling the muscles in his shoulders and chest protesting.

"You will take your clothes off," someone said.

John nodded. "Gladly. You should bury them. Burning them will pollute the entire area." He took off his coat and vest, tossed down his braces, unfastened his trousers. Stripping to the skin in front of strangers normally would have given him pause, but the promise of a bath, of clean clothes? He already knew firsthand that a prisoner was allowed no dignity, and therefore should feel no shame. He could salvage his dignity when he was a free man.

Cool hands took his right arm. "You're human, they told me," a man said, speaking English with an accent that John could almost place. "Do you speak English?"

"Yes," John answered.

"This way," he said. "There are steps. Five steps down into the water."

John nodded and let the man lead him, stepping down into water hot enough to sting his skin. He realized the floor had been warm under his feet, and remembered Roman baths with steam-heated floors and hot pools to soak in. This, however, appeared to be a hot pool to scrub in — John smelled fragrant soap, and something rough started scraping against his skin.

"I can do it," he said. He held out his hand, and was given a rough sponge. He went to work with enthusiasm. The first bath he'd had after Sumter had felt like this, like he'd needed to scrape his skin off to ever be clean again.

"Dunk yourself," the man said. "All the way. No, wait..." John felt water swirling around him, then tugging against the back of his head. "Close your eyes."

He did, and felt the hood being pulled off. Immediately, he ducked under the water completely, and came up scratching his head hard enough that he was sure he'd raise welts, and possibly draw blood. He heard laughter, and opened his eyes.

The man in the bath with him was as human as he was. He looked young, and he was smiling. And there was a silver collar around his neck.

"Better?" he asked.

"Not quite," John answered. "Thank you." He looked around and whistled at the sight of the large, ornately decorated bathing room. "Did they learn this from the Romans, or the other way around?"

The man laughed. "Before my time. Long before my time. The water will cycle in a moment. Come over here." He led John to the edge of the pool, where there was a seat just beneath the water. They sat, and John watched the dirty water swirl out of the pool. "I'm Wat, by the by. If you'd like another scrub, be my guest."

"Thank you," John said. "I'm John. Now, where's the soap?"

He picked up the sponge and waded back out into the deep water, scrubbing again. He worked soap into his hair, then dunked underwater again and ran his fingers through it, feeling strands tugging and tangling in his fingers.

"I have a comb," Wat called as he surfaced. "And I can trim your beard and hair. We have to make you presentable."

John nodded. He looked down at himself. "I think I'm clean."

"Then come out, and we'll get you ready. The guards will come back for you soon." He splashed out of the water, and John followed him, taking the towel that Wat handed to him. By the time he was dry, Wat was waiting with a linen wrapper. John put it on, and followed Wat into the next room. He sat where he was bid, in front of a mirror as tall as he was, and closed his eyes as Wat attempted to make him presentable.

"What's going to happen?" he asked softly.

"Don't know," Wat answered. "Been a few years since she last had a prisoner presented to her. Two, maybe three."

John opened his eyes. "Years... human years or elven years?"

"Elven years," Wat answered. "I've been here six years, I think?"

"When were you born? And where?"

"Born in London in the year of our Lord 1156. I was seventeen when I got taken and brought here. Not sure how old I am anymore. Or how long it's been there. Years, I expect. I doubt my family are still alive. Your clothes, they don't look anything like what I know. What year is it now? When they took you?"

"1875."

Wat whistled. "That long? Well..." He stepped back from the chair. "You're done."

John nodded, turning his head to see how Wat had trimmed his beard. "You're a good barber," he said. "Thank you, Wat."

"Now, let's get you dressed." Wat gestured, and John followed him into a third room. There, he was given clothes of the sort he remembered from his time in Italy, right before he'd made the choice to leave Europe entirely. Linen braies, and a silken shirt so fine that John was curious to see if he could read newsprint through it. Hosen of fine velvet, and a heavy, quilted doublet that he was certain was silk. Soft shoes and a jeweled belt completed the outfit, and John stood in front of another tall mirror and turned, looking at himself from different angles.

What would Ethriel think, to see him like this?

What would it be like to see Ethriel dressed like this? He smiled. Or to undress him when he was dressed like this?

Wat cleared his throat. "The guards are here, John," he said.

John nodded and turned. Then he groaned. One of the guards was carrying manacles. "I don't suppose you'd take my word that I'll come in peace?" he asked. The guard stepped forward, and John nodded. "I understand." He held his wrists out, and was surprised that they chained him with his arms in front of him. Then they led him out without a word.

The halls of the Palace were just as ornate as the bathing chamber, and John remembered Parsons talking about the shining Palace by the sea. Was this that Palace? Or was this the other one, the winter palace in the snow? Was it winter here? He kept looking around, and one of the guards laughed.

"You have never seen anything like this, have you?"

"I've seen similar," John answered. "But not recently, and I don't remember them being quite this fine."

"You're lying," the other guard said. "Humans have never had anything so fine."

"I'm not lying," John replied. "The Doge's Palace in Venice. The Alhambra in Spain. There are probably others, but I haven't seen them myself." He paused to look at a mosaic. "There was tilework like this in Rome. It's gone now, destroyed over time."

The guards shared a look, then one of them nodded. "Come along."

John continued walking, and passed through an open set of double doors into a large hall. No... it was the throne room. The fine tilework and draperies were marred by grotesque statues along both long walls, figures of men and women that seemed to be cowering from something. The room was empty, except for a woman sitting on the throne.

Siobhan, sitting in what should have been Ethriel's throne.

She stood up and came down from the dais, waving one hand. "Leave us." The guards saluted, leaving the room and closing the double doors. Once the doors were closed, Siobhan came closer. She was painfully beautiful, her eyes as crystalline green as Ethriel's and her skin as pale and flawless as alabaster. She stopped out of arm's reach of John, and he bowed. When he straightened, she smiled.

"You're the Undying One, I'm told. And the one who killed my son."

"He tried to kill me first," John replied. "He didn't know it wouldn't work."

She sniffed. "And I understand that my nephew has taken you to his side as his consort?" She walked a large circle around John, smiling again as she came back to stand in front of him. "He has excellent taste in humans."

John blinked. "This... you went to a great deal of trouble to get me here. How did you know about me, and why did you want me?" He paused, realizing something. "The man who brought the message. He wasn't Choctaw, was he? He was one of yours? But we would have seen... Nathaniel would have seen he was an elf!"

"Your pet human with the Sight? Buach told me about him. He may be able to see through Elven glamours, but there are other beings who can hide their shapes, and who were willing to assist me when I sought information on my son's killer," Siobhan answered. "And what I found intrigued me. I wanted to know more. I knew from my son and from that fool Wraith what bait would bring you, and what measures I would need to take to fool you. So I sent for you. And here you are." She stepped closer. "And now, seeing you, I've decided that I want to know you."

"Know... me?" John repeated. She was too close. He could have killed her in a heartbeat, even with his hands bound. What was she... oh. She wanted to *know* him. "I didn't realize that particular turn of phrase was known in your tongue," he said. "It would have made language lessons more interesting."

She laughed. "You're very clever," she said. "And comely. And you'll not burn out in a day, like other humans." She reached out and rested her hand on his chest. "Join me. Swear to me. Be mine."

John took a deep breath. Then he met her eyes and shook his head. "No. I am true to my King."

"You're human. You have no king here."

"I'm the Undying One," John replied. "I'm true to the Shining King, my King, my Ethriel." He nodded toward the throne. "You're keeping his chair warm for him. But he's coming. And he'll come for me."

The smile faded from her face. "You've lost me a wager, you know."

John blinked. "Should I apologize?"

"It doesn't matter," she said. "I should have realized you'd be stubborn. But you're male, and human, and I thought I could turn you. I thought you would agree. He thought not, but it was still amusing to try." Her smile returned, but this time, there was a cruel edge to it. "You say Ethriel will come for you? We're counting on it." Her nails dug into his chest. "I can't wait to see his face when he finds you."

"STILL NOTHING?" ETHRIEL asked. He looked at the mantle clock. Five minutes past eight. It had been nearly two weeks since Roshara's scrying spell had last found John's mirror, and Ethriel was well past worry.

"Nothing," she said, laying aside her own glass. "The mirror must have broken. I'm sorry, Ethi."

Ethriel bit his lip, trying not to snap at her. She had started slipping and calling him Ethi again recently. Because, he suspected, she was as worried as he was. So he didn't snap. He went to the window and looked out at the river in the distance.

"It's been a month," he said. "Over a month. They'll be back soon." He forced a smile. "Tomorrow, maybe."

She joined him at the window, sliding one arm around his back. Ethriel put his arm around her shoulders, trying to take comfort from her closeness.

"Maybe tonight," she suggested. "I can't imagine him stopping if he was close. He'd come straight home to you."

Ethriel smiled slightly and turned to look at her. She met his eyes and blushed slightly. "He would!"

"He'd come home to us," Ethriel said. He hugged Roshara more tightly to his side. Then he sighed and let her go. "I should go see what help Jeremiah needs."

"And I promised I'd help Avriel with Johanna," Roshara said. She grinned. "What do you think John will say when he comes home to find he has a namesake?"

Ethriel laughed. "Oh, I think he'll be as besotted as everyone else on the ranch. She's a darling." He turned, and heard Jeremiah's voice, calling his name. He froze.

"Rose—"

"Go see!" Roshara pushed him gently. "Go on!"

He ran out of the sitting room and out onto the porch. Jeremiah was coming up the stairs, but it wasn't excitement Ethriel was hearing.

It was fear.

"What is it? What's wrong?" Ethriel demanded.

Jeremiah pointed, and Ethriel saw the old man that Nathaniel was helping down from his horse.

"Hopaii?" he breathed. "He's here?" He ran down the stairs and across the yard, hearing Jeremiah and Roshara behind him. He stopped and turned. "Rose, get your father. This... I think this is going to be very bad."

Roshara nodded and hiked up her skirts, running back to the house. Ethriel continued on. He could see the look on Nathaniel's face now, the poker face that he used when he was dealing with traders.

"Hopaii," Ethriel said. "What are you doing here?"

Hopaii turned. He looked puzzled. "There was an ill wind in our lands, an ill wind that carried the scent of the Hattak Falaya. Where is John?"

Ethriel went cold to his core. "John went to Skullyville a month ago. We had a message, a letter carried by one of your people. It said you were dying, Hopaii. And that you wanted John to come to you."

Hopaii took a deep breath, let it out slowly. "I'd wondered why. Why everything said for me to get on my horse and come away from my people and my place."

"Hopaii," Jeremiah asked from behind Ethriel. "Where's Talula? John was supposed to bring her back with him. But if you're here, where is she?"

"She is in our lands," Hopaii answered. "She has taken the mantle of Hopaii for our people." He looked down, then back at Jeremiah. "She asked me to tell you that she was sorry. But she has married another."

"She..." Jeremiah stammered. He stopped, swallowed, then nodded. "I hope that she's happy. I hope she knows I wish her well." He looked past Hopaii. "Papa, let me take the horse to the stables. You should take Hopaii inside. It's damp out here."

"Wait," Hopaii said. "You said John went to Skullyville? He was coming to me? I promise you, I did not see him. Nor did I meet him on the road."

"We stopped being able to reach him nearly two weeks ago," Ethriel said. He heard footsteps behind him, and turned to see Roshara and Kestriel. "Hopaii, allow me to introduce Sir Kestriel and his daughter, Lady Roshara."

"Hopaii?" Kestriel said. "The holy man that John was going to see? I thought he was dying?"

"Who was the one who came to you?" Hopaii asked.

"His name was Coahoma," Nathaniel answered. "Hopaii, come inside."

"Not yet. This needs to be spoken in the open," Hopaii said. "I do not know anyone by that name. There is no one in my tribe named Coahoma. And you say he came to you with a letter?"

"And John went. I sent him with an escort, a man of my own people," Ethriel answered. He turned to Roshara. "Do you think you can scry?"

"When I tried the night we lost contact, I couldn't see him. Someone is still blocking my sight where John is concerned. The only reason I could reach him by the mirror was because I paired them," Roshara said. "We can try again, though. I think we need to try again."

"Can I help, Rose?" Jeremiah asked. "Maybe... maybe I can punch through? Open whatever is between us and him? I know you said no the last time I asked—"

"I don't think we have a choice," Roshara interrupted. "Not anymore. Yes." She looked at Ethriel. "We'll need more room than the kitchen."

"Here," Jeremiah said. "I'll start preparing. Papa... go inside to Mama. I'll come tell you what we find."

Nathaniel nodded slowly. "I'll take care of Hopaii's horse first. Then I'll send Parsons out," he said. "Maybe he can help."

Jeremiah nodded. "All right. Rose, go get what you need."

Kestriel followed Roshara into the house, and a few minutes later they both reappeared. Roshara was carrying a pitcher and the wide flat bowl that Jeremiah had given to her to replace the one that had shattered. Kestriel was dragging a table, and Ethriel ran over to help him. They carried the table to the center of the yard, then Ethriel took the pitcher from Roshara and went to the pump. When he came back, Jeremiah was scratching runes into the dirt, making a circle that surrounded the table.

"Stay inside the line," he said without looking up. Ethriel carefully stepped over the line and handed the pitcher to Roshara. She filled the bowl and set the pitcher underneath the table, then took a small bottle out of her apron pocket.

"I'm ready whenever you are, Jem," she said. Jeremiah scrawled one last figure in the dust, then looked up.

"Once I set this, no one goes in or out of the circle until I clear it. Understood?"

Ethriel nodded. "What should I do?"

Roshara frowned slightly, then asked, "May I borrow your ring? Leave it on the chain."

Ethriel reached under his shirt and pulled out the gold ring that John had given to him. He pulled the chain over his head, looked at the plain band for a moment, then kissed it. He handed it to Roshara, who smiled slightly.

"I'll be very careful with it, Ethriel," she murmured.

"Just find him."

Jeremiah stood up and dusted off his knees. "All right. Ah... Granddad, you and Sir Kestriel need to stay outside the circle."

"Jem, we both know how protection circles work," Parsons said. "We've both known since before you were born."

Jeremiah grinned. "Right." He closed his eyes and held his hand out, his fingers wide. The runes in the dust started to glow, the light snapping together into an unbroken circle. As the connection formed, Roshara poured the contents of the little bottle into the water. Once the water was darkened, she let the ring dangle from her fingers. It swayed gently at the end of the chain like a pendulum, touching the surface of the water and sending out tiny ripples.

"Show me," she commanded. The ring began to move, swinging in circles and setting the water in motion. Roshara's eyes narrowed, and she shook her head. "Jem—"

He reached out and rested his hand on hers; the circles grew smaller, tighter, and the wave created were higher. Jeremiah growled, low in his throat.

"Get out of the way," he snarled, and made a gesture with his other hand, as if he was pushing someone.

The chain snapped. The ring fell into the water with a plop, and an image rose.

John.

He was standing in a clearing, one that Ethriel recognized.

"That's right outside the dugout," he said. "Where we lived, near Skullyville."

"*It's all right,*" the phantom John called. "*Except the shelter I planned for us to sleep in tonight is gone. I wonder what happened here? That couldn't have been natural.*"

They heard Maniel's voice, "*What was this? Other than a large pile of dirt?*"

John turned and smiled. "*Now it's a large pile of dirt. Five years ago, this was a dugout. An underground house. I built this... oh, fifty years ago or so? About that. I can't remember any more. But it was the first place Ethriel and I lived.*"

Laughter. "*I have a hard time thinking of Ethriel living underground like a rabbit.*"

John laughed. "*Sir Parciviel said the same thing. It wasn't for very long. And it was a very comfortable rabbit hole.*" He turned to look at something they couldn't see. "*We'd better go before it gets too dark. There's no hotel in Skullyville. We'll go on and cross the river, and camp on the far side.*" Then he turned back, and a startled look passed over his face. He walked toward them, reached for something, then turned and raised his voice. "Maniel? *This isn't the time to play hide and seek.*" Then he turned, raised the Henry, and spoke in Elven, "*If I'm trespassing, I apologize. This place used to be* mine. *If you've claimed it, I'll go. If you've taken my companion, I'd like him back. We've harmed no one."*

Laughter, cut off my Maniel's voice, *"Enough. Take him. And you don't have to be gentle about it. He won't stay dead. Just secure him and bring him to the portal."* A pause. *"Surprised, Uncle?"*

John looked stunned and hurt. *"You've betrayed us? Why, Maniel? You're a friend. You've a place waiting in the King's household."*

Maniel snorted. *"As Ethriel is so fond of saying, he's not the king yet. Knowing what he has available to him in Lightning Tree, he won't ever be king. And I already have a place in my Queen's household."* He smiled. *"You'd be surprised how many in Lightning Tree serve the Queen."*

CHAPTER SEVEN
Action

The vision faded. Roshara rested both hands on the table, closing her eyes.

Ethriel swore softly. "It was a trap."

"I got a taste of the magic that was blocking you," Jeremiah said. "I'll know it again."

"Was it Wraith?" Ethriel asked. "Can you tell?"

Jeremiah shook his head. "No. But the sense of place about it...it wasn't from the direction he'd be coming from. Well, it was, but it was further away."

"It wasn't Wraith. I know him. This was a woman. I could tell," Roshara said. "I think it was Siobhan. If it was, that means she knows I'm here, with you."

"Jem, open the circle," Parsons said.

Jeremiah made a slashing gesture, and the runes faded to darkness. He scrubbed his foot over the markings, erasing them. "Rose, you need to go sit."

"I'm fine," she answered. She straightened and swayed, and Ethriel caught her before she could fall. He picked her up and carried her to the porch, settling her in one of the rocking chairs.

"What do you need?" he asked.

"Something to drink or something to eat?" Jeremiah asked from behind Ethriel.

"Both," Roshara answered.

"I'll get it." Jeremiah went into the house, and Ethriel turned to look at Parsons and Kestriel.

"She has John," he said. The words were awful, cutting his mouth like razors. He fought the rising panic, pushing it back and locking it away. He couldn't fall apart. Not now. "She has my John." He closed his eyes and rubbed his hand over his face. "There are traitors in Lightning Tree. That's how she knew. She knows everything because she has people right under our noses. And I trusted one of them." He opened his eyes. "I thought I'd have more time."

Parsons frowned. "More time...oh, no. Ethriel, you're not ready!"

"I need to be ready, Sir Parciviel," Ethriel said. "I need to be ready to take back what's mine, and claim what should always have been mine. And I need to be ready now." He stood up. "Will you stand?"

"Ethriel—"

Ethriel glared Parsons into silence, then growled, "Will you stand, Sir Parciviel?"

Parsons straightened. Then he saluted and bowed. "I will stand, my King."

"I will stand," Kestriel echoed, bowing as well.

Ethriel nodded. Then he snorted. "I have an army of two."

"Three," Jeremiah said as he came out of the house. He handed a plate to Roshara. "I'm coming."

"You most certainly are not!" Parsons blurted. "Your father will never allow it!"

"You can ask him," Ethriel said. He nodded to where Nathaniel and Hopaii were coming out of the other house. They walked across the yard and stood in front of the porch.

"What did you see?" Nathaniel asked.

"It was a trap," Ethriel answered. "They lured him back, and they took him. He's probably through the portal now. Siobhan has him." He looked at Parsons and Kestriel. "And I'm going to get him back." He licked his lips. "Nathaniel, you have the paperwork to take full ownership of the ranch. I know you do."

"I do, but—"

"Nathaniel, I am going after him," Ethriel said. "And when I go through that portal, I will either take my throne, or I will die. Either way... I won't be back. Which means—"

"That John won't be back either," Nathaniel murmured. "I... damn it, Ethriel. It wasn't supposed to be like this! We were supposed to build this together, and you'd go off and get killed after I was dust!"

Ethriel arched a brow. "You have that little faith in me?" he asked, trying not to show the hurt.

"That's not what I meant," Nathaniel protested. Then he sighed. "All right, it is what I meant. You're not ready, Ethriel."

"I have no choice but to be ready," Ethriel answered. "And it's worse than we thought. Siobhan has her own people in Lightning Tree. That's how she knew about Roshara and how to keep her from seeing."

Nathaniel gaped for a moment. "That... how can you know who to trust? Ethriel, your own army might rise up against you the minute you get through the portal."

"I'll know," Roshara said. "I'll be able to tell." She held up one bare hand. "All I have to do is touch them."

"Oh, Rose," Ethriel breathed. "I can't ask you to do that."

"For you? For John?" she answered. "I'd destroy the entire damned town!"

Ethriel reached out and took her hand, kissed her palm. "I love you, too," he murmured. She blushed. Ethriel let her hand go and straightened. "We need to go to Lightning Tree. We can trust Amanial—"

"I've shaken hands with her," Roshara interjected. "Without my gloves."

"And we can trust Terensiel," Ethriel continued. "They'll help us weed through the rest."

"Papa," Jeremiah said. "I'm going with Ethriel when he leaves."

"What?" Nathaniel gasped. "No. No, you're not old enough." He shook his head. "No. I forbid it."

"Papa!" Jeremiah gasped. "I have to! I have to go. Why else do I have all this power? This is what I'm supposed to do with my life!"

"And you're not old enough—"

"How old is old enough?" Ethriel interrupted. "How old would he have to be?"

"He's not of legal age for another eighteen months," Nathaniel answered.

"Seventeen," Jeremiah grumbled.

Ethriel ignored him. He closed his eyes and tried to think. "I... I can't wait that long," he said slowly. "John can't wait that long. I have to go, and I have to go now." He opened his eyes and looked at Jeremiah. "I'm sorry. But your father is right."

"But Uncle John needs my help, too," Jeremiah said softly. "I can't just stay, knowing that he's in trouble and I could do something."

"Jem, that's exactly what you're going to do," Ethriel said. "I'm sorry."

Jeremiah nodded. He turned and walked away, going into the house. A moment later, Ethriel heard the back door slam.

"He's going down to the river," Nathaniel said. "He's probably gone down to the kelpies. If he doesn't come back in an hour, I'll go look for him."

"Ethriel, when are we going to Lightning Tree?" Kestriel asked. "Parse and I need to arm ourselves."

Ethriel walked down the steps and back to the table. He tipped the bowl, letting the water spill into the dust, and caught his ring before it fell. He looked at it for a moment, then slipped it onto his finger and looked up at the others.

"Now."

THERE WERE BARRIERS set around Lightning Tree — ones that caused confusion and misdirection and muddled the memory. If a human rode out this way, they'd find themselves five miles to the west, and with no memory of how they'd gotten there. In truth, Ethriel and John had fallen afoul of those spells four times before they found the right approach to enter the town. Now, between one breath and the next, they passed from the human world and into the Elven town.

To Ethriel's surprise, the governor was waiting for them, looking as if she'd been roused from her bed.

"Jeremiah sent a bird to Terensiel," Amanial said. "He said that you were coming, that it was urgent, and that you'd explain."

"Siobhan has people in this town," Ethriel said. "Maniel was one of them. He's betrayed us, and now Siobhan has John."

Amanial's jaw dropped. "Traitors? In my town? And... Maniel? But... no, I've known him since he first came here!"

"He betrayed my John," Ethriel repeated. "We saw it in the scrying bowl. Amanial, I have no time left. My army must move, and it must move as soon as we are able."

She went white. "That..."

"If you're going to say it's not possible," Ethriel said slowly. "I'm telling you to make it possible. And I want every person who lives in this town to come before me tonight. They will swear to me." He looked at Roshara, who had brought her horse up besides his. He arched a brow; she nodded, and he turned back to Amanial. "And to my Lady Roshara, who stands by my right side as my consort, as my John stands on my left."

"I... had not known you had taken a second consort," Amanial stammered. "Your Majesty—"

"We were waiting for John to return to share the news with everyone," Roshara said. She smiled sweetly, and reached out to touch Ethriel's arm with one gloved hand. He smiled back at her, feeling oddly warm. It was the same oddly warm feeling he had when he smiled at John.

He turned back to Amanial. "I'll be waiting in the meeting hall," he said. "In an hour's time."

She bowed from the waist, saluting. "The Residence will be ready for you while you wait," she said as she straightened. "If I may?"

Ethriel nodded, and she turned her horse and rode off.

"A second consort?" Kestriel demanded. "And just when were you going to speak to me about this? Not that I have any objections—"

"Somehow, I didn't think you would," Ethriel answered, and saw Sir Kestriel blush slightly. "And I was going to talk to you when we actually made the final decision. Which wasn't going to be until we all of us had a chance to sit down and talk about it. There wasn't time before John left." He looked at Roshara. "Remind me never to play poker with you."

She laughed. "John should never play poker with either of us. You carried that lie off beautifully."

Ethriel smiled. "Not so much a lie as premature, I think," he said. "Sir Kestriel, John and I discussed this before he left. And we were truly waiting for him to return before we went any further with it. But now—"

"Now it gives Roshara an excuse to touch every single person in this town," Parsons said. "That was very clever. But what happens after the first one dies?"

Roshara shrugged. "We tell them exactly what happened. That I am a sin-eater, and that they were traitors to my lord, and that any other traitor will share the same fate. And if they refuse to swear... well, that's an answer, too."

"Sin-eater?" Parsons repeated. "What is that supposed to mean?" He didn't wait for an answer. "At first, I thought you were just a seer, but I pieced together the rest from conversations. I didn't know how to ask, though. It didn't seem polite. But after all this time, I have to ask — why didn't you ever come out and tell me that you were a diviner?"

Roshara twisted in her saddle. "A what? What's a diviner?"

"You don't know?" Parsons asked.

"I've never heard the term before," Roshara said. "Is it a kind of a seer?"

"Oh, of course you don't know," Parsons murmured. "You wouldn't know. Not if you came to your power here. Diviners are so rare. The last one that I know of died... well, I was young. Long before you were born, Kes."

"Are you going to tell us?" Kestriel asked.

"Once we get to the Residence," Parsons answered. "Let's get out of the night." He looked around. "And out of the open."

They rode on into town, and toward a pretty, two-story house near the center of town, and next to the large, central meeting hall. This was the Residence, a place kept solely for the use of the Elven King. Ethriel had been told there was a Residence in every Elven community, a place prepared in the hope of his return. Ethriel and John had stayed in the Lightning Tree Residence a few times over the years; it was comfortable, but Ethriel much preferred being out on the ranch, even though their first house there had been a shack with a leaky roof. A servant came running to take their horses, holding Roshara's horse as Ethriel lifted her down from the sidesaddle. He led her into the house, where a fire was already lit in the fireplace in the front room, and a kettle hung over the flames. Ethriel looked around and realized something.

"What?" Roshara asked. "You suddenly look so sad. What's wrong?"

"I just... we're not going back to the house," he said. "Well... we'll stop there, to get anything we want to bring with us. But that's not home anymore, is it?"

Roshara sighed. "We've barely had a chance to live in that house. I like it there."

Ethriel nodded. "We were happy there." He held his hand out to Roshara and led her to the couch. They sat down together, and he looked down at their hands. At the ring on his finger. "Things aren't ever going to be simple again."

Roshara leaned into his arm. "Was it ever truly simple?" she asked. "You've been working on the ranch for five years. And you've been building toward this for five years. You've been making these connections. You've been building to this moment since we came here. It's just come sooner than we thought. Things have never been simple. Not since we were children, Ethi." She paused. "Oh. I forgot. You asked me—"

Ethriel shook his head. "Right now, Rose? It's the least of my worries."

"I shouldn't be adding anything to your worries. I'll try to remember to call you Ethriel." She looked toward the door. "Papa and Parciviel must have gone to help with the horses. Come with me." She stood up and tugged on his hand.

"What?" Ethriel stood up, letting Roshara pull him toward the door. "Where are we going?"

"Upstairs," she answered, and led him toward the stairs. "We have an hour. I'm putting you to bed."

"Rose—"

"Someone needs to take care of you, and I'm the consort that's here to do it." She turned and looked at him. "Until John comes back to us, taking care of you is my responsibility. Not that I mind." She smiled and squeezed his hand. "I like taking care of you." She tugged his hand again, leading him up the stairs.

The bedroom at the top of the stairs was larger than the one he shared with John at the house, but someone had decided that a room fit for royalty needed to be decorated on every possible surface, and in every possible way. John said it was ornate, and that he'd seen worse, but Ethriel wasn't sure how it could possibly have been any worse. The Palace where he'd grown up was ornate. This was cluttered, and edged close to being messy, which made the room very uncomfortable.

"I'm always afraid I'm going to break something in here," he admitted as they stepped inside and Roshara closed the door. "That I'll move wrong and knock over a table and everything will shatter. There are too many things in here."

"They're your things," Roshara said. "Would it make you feel better if you did break them? No one would ever say anything."

"Rose!" Ethriel gasped. "No! Someone picked these out for me. They thought I'd like them. Someone thought having them would make me happy." He looked around. "I can't just break them. It would hurt someone. Besides, we're never here long enough for it to really bother me." He moved over to sit on the bed. "The bed is comfortable, at least."

"Is it?" Roshara asked. She came over and joined him on the bed. "Oh, it is." She bounced a little, then laughed. "I should let you rest. I'll go make some tea and find out where my father went." She smiled. "He's probably giddy."

"What, that you'll be my consort?" Ethriel shook his head. He looked down at his hand. "John asked me to marry him."

Roshara nodded. "I was there. It was lovely."

Ethriel looked at her, his throat feeling tight. "Can I have a husband and a consort, Rose?" he asked. Then he swallowed. "What do I do if he doesn't come back?"

"Ethriel, we're going to get him back," Roshara replied in a firm voice. "We're going to steal him back from her. She can't kill him. We will get him back."

Ethriel met her eyes. "He's supposed to be with me," he whispered. "He's the Undying One." He swallowed. "But maybe I'm not the right one. Maybe I'm not the Shining King."

"Ethriel!"

He shrugged and looked away. "I never had my coming-of-age ceremony. I know what the seers told my mother." He snorted. "Everyone knows what the seers told my mother. But I don't know what they'd have told me. Maybe I'm not the one. Maybe I'm just... wrong."

"You are not!" Roshara protested. "You're not!" She reached up and grabbed his chin, turning him to face her. "You are the Shining King. I know it. And since I'm a seer, there's your answer."

Ethriel stared at her, then started to laugh. It triggered the avalanche of emotions that he'd been holding back by force of will, and left him sobbing in Roshara's arms. She held him tightly, rocking him like a child until he could breathe again. He sat up slowly, rubbing his hand over his face. She reached out and rubbed her thumb over his cheek, wiping away tears. Then she leaned in close and kissed him.

The avalanche turned into a firestorm; he pulled her into his arms and returned her kiss with interest, forgetting his worries and fears as his mind went blank. Somehow, by the time he could think again, they were tangled on the bed. He was on his back, his shirt unbuttoned, with Roshara over him. His hand was underneath her skirts, and when he stopped moving, she moaned against his mouth. He broke the kiss and closed his eyes.

"Rose, we need to stop," he whispered. "Rose—"

"We don't," she answered, and nipped his lip. "We don't have to stop. John gave his permission. I heard him."

"Not what I mean," Ethriel swallowed and tipped his head back, staring at the shadowed ceiling, feeling her fingers on his skin. "Rose, please stop. Listen to me. Because if we start again, I'm not going to stop, and you'll be staying here."

"What?" Roshara gasped. "I... why?"

Ethriel shifted, waiting until she'd done the same. Then he sat up and reached for her hands, holding them tightly. "I've known how I feel about you for years. I was dizzy in love with you when we were growing up together, and everyone knew it. I thought I'd grown out of it. I mean, I told John that I'd grown out of it after we found you again. He was worried I might favor you over him."

"That's silly," Roshara murmured.

"I know. But sometimes John worries overly much." Ethriel took a deep breath. "I'm fairly certain that the main reason your father decided to stay on the ranch was because he hoped that having us together would rekindle that spark. Which... it did. I remembered how much of a part of me you were, and I saw how much I wanted you to be a part of us now. And I've known how you feel about me. I noticed how you were looking at me. And I know how you feel about John. I just..."

"You didn't say anything. Not a word! I couldn't tell!"

Ethriel smiled. "I learned to keep my thoughts out of my face. Learned it the hard way, Rose. I can keep secrets. It saved my life. But this... Rose, I told this to John. Now I'm telling you. I know we can protect you. I'm not sure we can protect a baby."

Her face paled. "I... did hear you tell him that. Ethriel, there are ways—"

"And if we wait, then we don't have to worry about those ways failing," Ethriel interrupted. "Rose, we're leaving. We're leaving within the next few days, as soon as I can muster my army. If we do this now, you won't know for certain until I'm a month on the road. I'm not taking you with me if there's even a hint of a chance that you might be pregnant. I can't take that risk." He licked his lips. "I can't lose you, too."

Roshara nodded slowly. "I understand. And given the choice of riding with you or waiting here and not knowing if I'll ever see you again? That's hardly a choice." She looked down at their hands. "I'm not staying behind. So... not yet?"

He nodded. "Not yet." He paused, then said, "Take your gloves off?"

She looked quizzically at him, but tugged off her gloves. He took her hands and raised them to his lips, kissing her fingers. She slipped one hand from his and cupped his cheek.

"You need to rest. You're already in a state."

Ethriel nodded. "I'll lay down. I doubt I'll sleep, but I'll lay down."

She smiled and slowly moved off the bed. Ethriel watched as she brushed down her skirts and tried to tidy her hair. "I'm rumpled. But it can't be helped. I'll tidy up, and we'll be ready for them in an hour." She looked back at him as she pulled her gloves back on. "Lay down. I'll have tea waiting when you come down."

He stretched out on the bed. "You could stay with me."

"I thought we'd just determined that was a bad idea?"

"Just to sleep?"

She laughed. "I don't have the willpower to avoid that temptation. And I don't want to stay behind." She came back to the bed and leaned over to kiss him on the lips. "Rest. I'll be right downstairs."

CHAPTER EIGHT
Muster

When Ethriel came back down to the sitting room, Parciviel and Kestriel were sitting and talking in low voices. Parciviel started to rise, stopping when Ethriel waved him back.

"It's just us," Ethriel said. "I'm not going to stand on ceremony. How much time have I got before I have to go be King?"

Parciviel smiled. "About ten minutes. Did you have enough of a rest?"

"Probably not, no," Ethriel answered. He heard a footstep behind him, and turned to see Roshara. She smiled, and moved around him to a tea service on the table. She poured a cup, then brought it to him.

"Sit and drink," she said. "Sir Parciviel, you said you wanted to wait for Ethriel to explain about diviners."

Parciviel nodded. "Just so I didn't have to repeat myself, yes." He waited until Ethriel was sitting before he continued. "Now, you know about seers. The information that you all seem to be missing is that there is another type of seer. A diviner is a seer with the ability to see into a man's heart. The High Kings of old would keep them close, so that they always knew who was true among those closest to them. Several of them married their diviners, so the ability is in your line, Ethriel. And it came to be that they were rare to find outside court." He frowned. "The last one was... oh, your great-grandmother, Ethriel. On your mother's side."

Ethriel frowned, sipping his tea and trying to remember the lineage his mother had taught to him. "Was that Galania? Or Varansis?"

"Lady Galania," Parciviel said. "She died when your grandfather was still young, long before he married Lady Xanthe." He sniffed. "I always suspected there was more to her death than age, and I know Eiriell did as well. But there was never any proof.

Regardless, after she died, Eiriell went in search of a diviner to serve in his court, and there were none to be found. None anywhere."

"And diviners could kill?" Roshara asked. "That would make them formidable weapons to have."

"I remember Lady Galania uncovering assassins in the court, but I don't recall her ever killing them," Parciviel said. "I wonder if it's something to do with you not having the proper training."

Roshara looked at her father. "I've never heard of diviners before."

Kestriel shook his head. "Nor have I. But I wasn't raised in court circles. I came up through the ranks." He rubbed his forehead. "I always said that your mother married beneath her, Rose."

"Mother loved you," Roshara said. "She said you were the best thing that ever happened to her."

"No, that was you," Kestriel replied. "Her line must be where you get this from. She had the royal blood — Ambari's grandmother was Galania's sister." He looked thoughtful. "You didn't start showing this until long after Ambari died. She'd have known what it was, I'm sure. But... we were here when you started seeing."

Roshara nodded. "And the first time I killed someone was in Wraithtown. Long after we got here."

"I'm sure there will be records in the Palace, or with the seers in the forest," Parciviel said. "You'll get the training you lack."

"Rose, where did you train?" Ethriel asked. "You're very good as a seer, but if you were here—"

"In New Orleans," Roshara answered. "There is so much magic there, so many gifted humans. It was easy to hide from Wraith there, and easy to find someone to teach me the tools that human seers use." She looked at the mantel clock. "It's time."

Ethriel drained his tea and stood up. He looked down at his rumpled, dusty clothes. "I look like a child, playing king of the mountain," he grumbled.

"You look like a King who's not afraid to get his hands dirty," Parciviel said. "Truly, you're looking more like Eiriell these days."

Ethriel smiled. "Right. Let's go see if I can act like him." He turned and held his hand out to Roshara, palm down. She smiled, took off her gloves, then rested her bare hand on top of his.

THE MEETING HALL WAS full of elves, many of them looking cross and confused. There was a steady buzz of low conversation that fell still when Ethriel appeared, making his way down the center aisle of the room to the dais at the front, trying to decide what he was going to say. His mind was racing, and terror was teasing at the edges. How could he do this?

How could he not? There was no other way to rescue John.

He took the stairs up to the dais, leaving Roshara on the step below as he took the last step and turned to face his people. He drew himself up, rubbed his thumb over the ring on his finger. Then he moved to the single chair that sat on the dais, an ornate thing that John said might have come from an old church. It was meant to signify the royal presence, and Amanial said no one ever sat in that chair.

Ethriel sat down. He rested his hands on the arms, and looked out over the room. Then he spoke:

"There are traitors in this town," he said, his voice carrying to every corner of the room. "And one of them has lured our consort John into a trap. Siobhan has taken him through the portal." He looked from side to side, scanning the faces, seeing the shock written clear on so many. Was it because he'd told them that there were traitors, or because he'd used the royal 'we' for the first time in their hearing? "We thought we would have more time, that there would be a better time to rise against the murderess who holds our throne. But she has forced our hand." He paused. "It is our will that our army rise. We shall march immediately, and take back what is ours." He looked to Roshara and held his hand out; she came the rest of the way up onto the dais and stood next to him. "But before our army marches, we will have assurance of the loyalty of our people. So tonight, the people of Lightning Tree shall swear allegiance to us, and to our second consort, the Lady Diviner Roshara."

Amanial moved forward, coming from the back of the room to the front. As she approached the dais, Ethriel rose, leading Roshara to the bottom of the steps. There, Amanial went to one knee in front of Ethriel, clasping her hands and holding them up. Ethriel wrapped his hands around hers, and let his power flow, speaking the opening words of the binding aloud as their combined hands started to glow. The binding was a simple spell, one that his mother had taught to him long before he had the power to even cast it. It was, she had told him, a mark of the seal between a liege lord and their vassal.

"I, Ethriel, rightly born High King, do bind our faithful Amanial to our service," he announced. "We swear that our power shall be raised only to protect and provide, and that if we should betray that oath, that all hands shall be raised against us."

"I, Amanial, daughter of Clestori, governor of Lightning Tree, do swear and bind myself to my King Ethriel. Let all know that I am loyal to his will, and that I shall rise to protect him and his own," Amanial finished. She looked up at Roshara, and mouthed the word. "Diviner?"

Roshara nodded slightly, and as Ethriel released Amanial's hands, she reached out to catch them. She smiled, and released them. "Our Amanial is true, my King," she announced.

Ethriel nodded and looked out over the crowded room.

"Amanial," he said. "How best shall we do this? We don't want our people to wait all night. It's late, and people want to be abed."

Amanial's lips twitched. "I suggest you ask who will be unwilling to swear to you, my King," she said. "Who among us is unwilling to lay their heart open to a Diviner?"

Ethriel nodded. "A fair question," he said. "Who among you refuses to swear to us?" he asked. "Who among you has sworn to my traitoress aunt? Who among you will refuse to let my lady see into your hearts?" He held up one hand as muttering started. "We are not going to ask you to reveal yourselves to us," he added. "We will turn to face the wall. If you will not swear, you will leave. And by the day after tomorrow, you will leave Lightning Tree, and you will never return."

A hand raised, near the rear of the hall. A woman stood up. "And go where?" she asked. "Where will they go?"

Ethriel stepped down and walked down the aisle, noticing that Parciviel was pacing him along one wall, his hand on his sword. He didn't look, but he imagined that Kestriel was behind him, along the other wall. When he reached the woman, he could see that she was his age.

"Will you swear to me?" he asked gently. She bit her lip.

"My father swore to her," she said. "To Siobhan. He served in her army. He followed her to the Palace, and when we were sent here, he said that she would be good to us, that if we stayed true to her, she'd reward us."

Ethriel nodded. "When did he tell you that?"

"When she first sent us here," she answered. "Father said we were supposed to serve her here. I've been here... I'm not sure...."

"She's been here some fifty years," Amanial called.

"Ah," Ethriel breathed. "And... has she? Been good to you, I mean. Has she rewarded you? Does she even know your name?" He thought for a moment. "Your name is Elshevin, isn't it?"

She blushed. "Yes... my King." She blushed harder. "And no. I don't think she does. She doesn't know me. She doesn't know that my father died before we even got to Bandera. Or that my mother died that first winter here." She frowned. "I... my father swore to her. I didn't."

Ethriel nodded. "Elshevin, who do you want to serve?" He stopped her before she could answer. "I'm not asking who your father served. Who do you want to serve?"

She met his eyes. Then she smiled. "You. Will you take my oath, my King?"

He held his hand out to her. "Gladly." He led her from her place and back to the dais, and repeated the ritual; Elshevin started crying as she gave her oath, and sobbed harder when Ethriel drew her to her feet and embraced her. Then Roshara embraced her, and brought her back to her chair. When she returned to Ethriel's side, he looked out at the room.

"We will turn our back now," he said. "If you do not wish to swear your allegiance to us, if you are loyal to Siobhan, leave. You will have until sunset the day after tomorrow to leave Lightning Tree." He turned, looking at the wall behind the dais. A hand slipped into his, and he looked sideways to see Roshara next to him.

"That was nicely done," she whispered, her voice just barely audible over the buzz of conversation behind them.

He smiled. "Thank you." He squeezed her fingers. "How long should I give them?" he asked.

"My King?" Amanial called. "You might want to turn back."

Ethriel turned, and saw that the room looked the same. He looked at Amanial, and she smiled. "No one left."

Ethriel paused for a moment. Then he took a deep breath. "Then we should get on with this," he said with a laugh. "It's late, and there are children who should be in bed."

It was well past midnight by the time the last oath had been taken, and Ethriel sank to sit on the dais steps, leaning back on his elbows and taking a deep breath.

"They all swore to me," he said. Then he grimaced. "My throat hurts."

"Come back next door," Roshara said. "We'll have something to drink, and we'll get some sleep."

Ethriel nodded. "We'll need to go back to the ranch. I want John's map. And we need to say a proper goodbye to Nathaniel and Avriel and Jem, and see if Hopaii wants to come back to Arkansas with us." He looked around and saw Parciviel sitting at the end of the first row of seats. "Sir Parciviel, are you going to stay with your family? You've earned it, I think."

Parciviel looked up. "Oh, I haven't. I'll be coming with you, my King. If you'll have me."

"If?" Ethriel snorted. "Of course I'll have you. I just wasn't sure you wanted to go. It'll be a long road, with no promise of any sort of happy ending." He sat up, resting his arms on his knees. "Parciviel, stay here. Enjoy your family. I'll send word when it's over. Or..." he shrugged. "Or I won't."

"No," Parciviel stood up and walked over to the steps. "I owe you a debt, Ethriel. I'm not even close to having paid what I owe you. I'm going with you."

Ethriel blinked. "What debt?" he asked. "What are you talking about?"

Parciviel swallowed. Then he shook his head. "It's mine to pay. Let's leave it at that," he said. He took a deep breath, then bowed. "My King. I'll go and put the kettle on." He turned and left.

Ethriel watched him go, then looked at Kestriel and Roshara. "Do either of you know what that was about?" he asked.

Kestriel frowned slightly. Then he shook his head. "Nothing I can say with any certainty, my King," he answered. "It's his choice. Let him make it."

Ethriel sighed and stood up. "All right. Maybe one day he'll tell me what's weighing on him. For now, I'm tired. It'll be a very busy few days, and I need to sleep."

AN EMPTY, UNFAMILIAR bed meant that Ethriel was awake before dawn, so he started the fire in the stove and put the coffee on. He was cracking eggs into a bowl when he heard a knock on the door.

"Come in," he called, then looked over his shoulder. "Good morning, Amanial. Have you eaten?"

"Not as yet," she answered, coming into the kitchen. "Have you slept?"

"Badly," Ethriel admitted. He mixed the eggs, then dropped a knob of butter into a pan. The kitchen filled with the scent of melting butter, and he poured the eggs in and started scrambling them. "Rose will be cross with me. It bothers her that I'll cook if she isn't up before I am. It's turned into a game, honestly."

"It's odd that you know how," Amanial said. "I wouldn't have expected it. May I help with anything?"

"Cut the bread?" Ethriel asked. "And John taught me to cook." He looked down at the eggs, reached for a spoon and stirred them. "I'm not as good at it as he is, but he's had a lot more experience."

"Ethriel, what happened?" Amanial asked. "The idea of Maniel betraying him... I've known that young man almost his entire life!"

"Roshara scried, and Jeremiah cleared the way for her. We watched what happened," Ethriel turned the eggs, then took a cloth and wrapped the handle of the pan, pouring the cooked eggs into a bowl. He set the pan down and took the eggs to the table, then went back for the coffee pot. "Maniel told John that there were people here who served Siobhan, and that he had a place in her court." He sat down, folding his hands on the table. "And yet, everyone swore to me last night. And to Roshara. They could lie to me, certainly. But not to her."

"A diviner," Amanial murmured. "I didn't know there were any left."

"No one did," Ethriel said. "Now, was everyone in Lightning Tree at the meeting last night?"

Amanial frowned slightly, and Ethriel let her think as he poured coffee and spooned eggs onto her plate.

"No," she finally answered. "No, I can think of an even half-dozen who were not and who should have been. And I want to say there were a dozen or so young men who call themselves the King's Guard, who were out overnight. But I'd lay a wager that every one of them would swear to you."

"The King's Guard?" Ethriel repeated. "I have one of those?"

"They're not quite old enough to be part of your army, but they're preparing for when they are," Amanial answered. "Most of them are a year or two shy of their majority."

Ethriel sighed. "Which means we'll have the same problem with them that we're having with Jeremiah. They're old enough to want to go, but not old enough to actually do it."

"What about Jeremiah?"

"He's nineteen. That's not an adult by human rules," Ethriel answered. "He's seventeen months from his majority. And his father says he's not old enough to go with me."

Amanial's eyes widened. "But—"

"I know. He's Taliesin come again. I need him. But he's not old enough, and I can't wait seventeen months for him to be old enough." Ethriel shook his head. "She's forced my hand, Amanial. There's nothing else I can do but march. Now, who wasn't at the meeting?" Ethriel asked. He sipped his coffee and closed his eyes. "I will miss coffee. I don't know if it will grow in our lands."

Amanial chuckled. "I never acquired a taste for it," she admitted.

"You cooked?"

Ethriel turned and smiled at Roshara. "That means I win this round, doesn't it?"

"Yes, but did you sleep?" Roshara asked. She came over and leaned down to kiss his cheek, then stole his coffee cup and sipped it. "You let it brew too long."

"I like it like this." Ethriel took the cup back. "And I did sleep. But not well. I don't think I'll sleep well until I have John back. Now, Amanial tells me that there were people missing last night."

"Then I know what we're doing this morning." Roshara sat down and held a plate out. "My king?"

CHAPTER NINE
Meeting

Parciviel and Kestriel joined them in the kitchen, and they ate and discussed what they would be doing. Parciviel volunteered to meet with the men and women who would form the heart of Ethriel's army, while Kestriel accompanied Ethriel and Roshara out to meet the people who had been absent the night before. They left the Residence on foot, with Amanial leading.

"Who are we meeting first?" Ethriel asked.

"The blacksmith and his apprentice. They're closest," Amanial answered. "And they might have very good reasons for not being at the meeting. Fioriel is a very gifted healer."

"Is that the smith or the apprentice?" Roshara asked. "I don't think I've met either."

Amanial smiled. "Fioriel is the smith. Renziel is the apprentice, and he is also a healer. He looks to be as talented, but he's only just come into his power." She turned down a side street, and Ethriel started hearing the rhythmic clang of a hammer against metal. The blacksmith shop was set away from the other buildings, and had a large fenced corral around it. Amanial led them around the empty corral to a large window.

"Fioriel!" she called. "A moment!"

"I don't have a moment," a man growled from inside. "It'll have to wait."

Ethriel stepped closer to the window, looking inside to see the forge, and the largest elf he'd ever seen, squinting fiercely at the glowing horseshoe he was holding in a pair of long metal tongs.

"What's wrong with it?" Ethriel asked.

Fioriel scowled. "It's not setting right," he answered. "I'll have to fit it hot." He turned and shoved the shoe back into the forge, then looked over his shoulder at them. He blinked, and sputtered. "Amanial, you could have told me that the King needed me!"

"I don't need you to interrupt your work," Ethriel answered. "In truth, I would enjoy seeing you do it. I've always been fascinated by the blacksmith's art. I used to watch the smiths in the Palace when I was small. And the human smith in Bandera is used to me asking a million questions when we bring the horses in."

"Which is something I've been meaning to ask you, Sire. You're not bringing them to me why?" Fioriel asked.

"Because then we'd have to explain who we had do the work, since Eduardo is the only human smith this side of San Antonio," Ethriel answered. "John and I talked about it, and decided we didn't want to risk too many questions."

Fioriel nodded. "Thought that might be it. It would be a difficult question to answer, especially since you're selling them. I've seen your horses, my King, the ones you've sold to our folks. You've a nice line there."

Ethriel smiled. "Thank you. Now, I should have my Cloud reshod. I'll bring her to you."

"You weren't at the meeting last night, Fioriel," Amanial said.

"There was a meeting?" Fioriel asked. He frowned. "Amanial, the boy and I were out at Wyonra's last night, all night. Her oldest fell off his horse and broke his leg in two places." He shook his head. "He shouldn't have been on that beast. It's too much horse for a boy of only sixty, but that's none of mine to say. You know how she dotes on that boy."

Amanial nodded. "He was in good hands, then."

"Thank you. What was the meeting?" Fioriel frowned, looked at Ethriel. Then his eyes widened. "That mare of yours doesn't need reshoeing. I've seen her. Her shoes are good, and the human smith does good work. You don't need new unless you're planning a long trip. Which means you're marching. You're going to take back the throne, aren't you?"

"You're a good guesser," Ethriel said. "Yes. Siobhan has taken John—"

"She's what?" Fioriel gasped. "How?"

"Lured him away with a fake letter, and a call to attend an old friend on his deathbed," Roshara answered. "And she blocked my sight, so we were none the wiser until that dying friend arrived at the ranch."

"Fioriel," Amanial said slowly. "Maniel turned on him. Turned on us. And claims that there are others in Lightning Tree who serve Siobhan."

Fioriel spat. "Not in this forge, there aren't," he said. "My King, I'll swear to you in cold iron, if you'll have that oath." He turned and shouted, "Renziel! Boy, where are you?" He frowned. "Where is that boy? I sent him out to bring in the horse that needs shoeing. Should have been here by now."

Ethriel looked over his shoulder. "There wasn't a horse in your corral. It was empty when we passed it."

Fioriel turned and looked at him, then looked back at his forge. "Well," he murmured. "Amanial, I'll be a minute. Just let me put things to rights here." He looked around again. "You'll be needing a new smith."

The words took a moment to make sense to Ethriel, and he was stunned when they did.

"You're coming with me?" he blurted. "Fioriel, I can't ask you to uproot—"

"You're not asking," Fioriel interrupted. "I'm volunteering. Truly told? I remember you as a boy, though it seems you don't remember me. The smith you were watching as a boy in the Palace was my father. My mother got me out of there when he fell trying to stop Siobhan and her men. I promised her that I'd see him avenged. So I'm coming. You'll need a smith on the road, in any case. And a healer. I'm both." He turned and waved at the flames in the forge; they died immediately, giving off a billow of iron-scented smoke. He walked out of the forge, and a moment later came around the building with a large sledge slung over his shoulder. "Let's go find that boy of mine. I've got some words for him."

Ethriel took a deep breath, trying to collect his thoughts. "Amanial, who else wasn't there last night?"

"Let me guess," Fioriel said. "Besides me and Renziel, the missing ones were Glethin, Amartin, Fantiel, and Avorn."

Amanial blinked. "Yes. How did you know?"

"Because that's the group that's always around that troublemaker Maniel," Fioriel answered. "Tirgana's boys. And if you'd have asked me before you sent him, Amanial, I'd have told you Maniel was a troublemaker, for all that he's noble born and a high squire."

Kestriel snorted. "I'd have told you the same," he muttered. "I have told you the same. He was nice enough to someone of his own rank, but woe to the servant who caught his ire. I warned you about that, Amanial."

"You did. And I spoke to his guardian about that incident. If she hadn't assured me that he'd matured somewhat, I'd never have sent him...." Amanial stopped, turned to stare at Fioriel. "Oh, you don't think Lady Tirgana—"

"I'm thinking just that," Fioriel said with a nod. "Let's go. We'll need horses. I'll meet you at the Residence."

Ten minutes later, they were riding toward the edge of town.

"Tirgana has a big house out near the barrier's edge," Amanial said as they rode. "She's Maniel's grandmother, and unofficial godmother to all of the ones Fioriel named. They all live with her. She's Mountain blood, of the old noble line—"

"Which means she's probably related to me. Have I met her?" Ethriel asked. "I don't think I've met her. I don't know her name. But my father was of the Mountain noble line."

"You never met her because she never comes to town," Fioriel said, bringing his big gelding up next to Cloud. "I can't think of the last time I saw her."

"And as to how you're related, I'm not sure," Amanial answered. "Kestriel, do you know?"

"I haven't any idea," Kestriel answered. "The royal line is a tangled web that never made any sense to me."

"I'm not sure it matters," Ethriel said. "I never met any of his family. My father told me once that he'd been cast out by his clan for agreeing to marry my mother."

"He was? That's terrible!" Roshara gasped. "And so unfair!"

Ethriel nodded. "Father didn't talk about them. At all. I asked him once if he had brothers and sisters. When I did, he said that marrying my mother brought him a better family than the one he left behind. But he was very sad when he said it." He frowned. "Amanial, Siobhan is of the old Mountain line. Her mother was pure Mountain blood. Is she related to Tirgana, too?"

"That's a very good question," Amanial said. "One to which I don't have an answer."

"We'll see what we see when we get there," Kestriel said. "Amanial, how much further?"

"Not far," Amanial called.

The road curved around a hill, and as they came around, Ethriel saw the house.

"That's bigger than our house," he said to Roshara. She nodded.

"Lady Tirgana was one of the first of our people in Lightning Tree," Amanial said. "It's said that she founded the town, and was the first governor."

Ethriel nodded. "And she wasn't at the meeting last night, either, was she?"

"No," Amanial confirmed. "But she never comes to town anymore. I can't say that I've seen her..." She frowned. "I don't actually remember when I last saw her. Fioriel?"

"Not even when I did work out here," Fioriel said. "I always dealt with Maniel." He drew his horse to a slow walk. "I'm not liking this, Amanial."

"Neither am I," she agreed. "Go around the back. Conceal yourself. I'll take Ethriel to the front of the house." She looked at him. "We're here to visit your distant kinswoman, whom you've only just learned about?"

"Odd, how I never knew I had relatives in town," Ethriel agreed. "But yes. I think she may be related to my father, and I asked for an introduction, since I have no kin in this world. Now, I'll follow your lead, Amanial."

Fioriel left them, and Amanial led Ethriel, Roshara and Kestriel into the front courtyard. They dismounted as the front door opened, and a young man came out.

"Governor," he said, a surprised look on his face. "To what do we owe the honor?"

"Good morning, Amartin. I'm here to visit Lady Tirgana," Amanial announced. "I was visiting with King Ethriel this morning, and it turns out that he had no idea he had a possible kinswoman in town. He asked to be presented to her."

Amartin's face went white. "Kinswoman?"

"Through my father, I think," Ethriel said, helping Roshara down from her horse. "Which was a surprise to me. As far as I knew, I had no living kin. I'm eager to make her acquaintance."

"I... I see," Amartin stammered. He looked back over his shoulder, then nodded. "Lady Tirgana is still abed. We'll tell her you called—"

"I'd be happy to wait on her," Ethriel said. He smiled, suddenly feeling oddly excited. "It would be an honor, in truth. I've never known any of my father's family."

Amartin nodded again, and looked back inside. There was some heated whispering, and Ethriel clearly heard Amartin hissing, "I can't just leave them outside! It's rude!"

More whispering, and Amartin turned back and smiled. "Why don't you come in?" he said. "And I'll see if she's taking callers today." He stepped backward into the house, holding the door open for them.

Amanial turned and bowed. "After you?" she said. Then she whispered, "And be wary."

Ethriel nodded and offered his arm to Roshara. She met his eyes and smiled at him, then let him lead her into the house. There were three other men just inside, and Ethriel stopped and stepped to the side to let Amanial and Kestriel enter.

"My King," Amartin said. "My brother Glethin, our cousin Fantiel, and our friend Avorn. He's..." He stopped. "What are you to Lady Tirgana again? I always forget."

"Her nephew's stepson," Avorn answered. He gestured. "Please, come in. The sitting room is this way." He led them into a room that was only slightly less ornate than the bedroom at the Residence. Ethriel led Roshara to a chair and let her sit, then turned to the others.

"Governor Amanial says that Lady Tirgana doesn't come to town very often," he said. "I hope she's in good health?"

Avorn nodded. "She's quite old, but she's in very good health," he said. "I'll go see if she's taking callers today. She doesn't always." He bowed slightly and left the room, and Amartin moved to stand in the doorway. He looked over his shoulder, then back at them. Then, he blushed, and suddenly seemed much younger.

"I apologize. Usually, it's Maniel who plays host when there are callers," he said. "Since he's her blood-kin and we're all... well... adopted. Sort of. So if we're all a little awkward, that's why. We're not sure how it's done."

Ethriel grinned. "You're doing better than I would," he said. "This is...I wouldn't even know where to start. When we have guests, John usually is the host." He looked at Roshara, who smiled at him. "He says I get shy around new people."

"You do," Roshara said, reaching up to take his hand. "It's very sweet, actually."

Amartin looked surprised and amused, all at once. "Truly? But... you were born in the Palace. You—"

"And when things were at peace, I was a child. When there were important visitors, I rarely got to do more than bow and be shown off as the Heir before I was sent off to the nursery or my tutors.." He shrugged. "And when I was old enough..." He paused, then decided to be blunt. "Well, I was just old enough to start learning real court behavior when my parents were murdered and I became Buach's slave."

Amartin went pale. "What?"

Ethriel glanced at Amanial, who shook her head, looking perplexed. "You didn't know?" Ethriel asked, and pushed up his shirt sleeve. He held his left wrist out, showing the worst of the scars left over from the manacles that Buach had locked onto him that horrific first night. The manacles that John had broken when he'd freed him. "I thought everyone knew. Amartin, where did you think I was all this time?"

"I... I never thought about it. Not really. I mean... I didn't know," Amartin murmured. He stepped closer, took Ethriel's hand and looked closely at the scars. "I had no idea." He let Ethriel go. "Glethin? Did you know? Fantiel?"

Glethin shook his head. "Fan?"

"Lady Tirgana never said anything," Fantiel said. "Maniel never said anything either. When she taught us of why we were exiled from the Elvenlands, she never told us about you, except to say you'd disappeared..." He turned and went to the door. "Avorn?"

"Don't shout!" Avorn said as he came to the door. "Lady Tirgana is asleep. So I'll have to ask you to come again another day. And maybe later in the day."

"Avorn, did you know?" Amartin asked. "That when the Palace fell, that Ethriel didn't just disappear? That he was a captive?" He looked at Ethriel. "A slave? Buach's slave?"

Avorn sniffed. "What? No! You met Buach—"

"You did?" Ethriel gasped. "When?"

"Look at his wrists, Avorn!" Fantiel hissed. "Look at the scars!"

Avorn rolled his eyes, and turned toward Ethriel, who held out his bare left arm again. Avorn blinked, and he grabbed Ethriel's hand and pulled him closer, leaning in to better look at the scars.

"This... what is this?" he demanded.

"Buach kept me in chains for a year. For one of our years," Ethriel said, trying to keep his voice level. It didn't work, and Avorn looked up sharply.

"One of our years," he repeated. "How...how did you escape?"

"I had help," Ethriel answered. "Someone who got me through the portal and away. And got me to John. You knew Buach?"

Avorn nodded. "He was a guest here, quite a few times. Lady Tirgana is his mother's aunt. My stepfather was Siobhan's half-brother."

Ethriel looked at Amanial. "You never once told me that he'd been here."

"I had no idea that he was!" Amanial sputtered. "It's not been since I became governor!"

Avorn snorted. "It's been three times since you became Governor," he corrected. "But he never came through the barrier in the usual place. Because he didn't come from the portal to the east. He came from the south—"

"There's a portal south of here? Where?"

Avorn shook his head. "I don't know. I just know it's south, and far enough that the magic actually works. When Buach came, he'd send a bird, and we'd meet him in the box canyon." He looked back down at Ethriel's wrist, then let him go. "I knew him... but now I think I never knew him. Will he come after you again?" He blinked. "You said I *knew* Buach. I... is Buach dead?"

"Buach is dead," Ethriel answered. "He came after me from the portal in Arkansas. And.. you haven't met my John, have you?"

Avorn shook his head. "We've heard stories about him," he said. "But no. Lady Tirgana... ah... she suggested we not socialize with him. Since we're all dependent on her, we listened. And we didn't ask questions. It was always better to not ask questions." He glanced at the others, who all shifted and looked at each other.

Finally, Amartin cleared his throat. "Maniel didn't like questions either," he said slowly. "So, why should we know John?"

"He's the Undying One," Ethriel said. "Buach killed him. Twice. The second time with elfshot. He tried to kill me with elfshot, too. John killed him."

Avorn dropped Ethriel's hand and went to the fireplace, spitting into it. "No," he said. His voice was shaking worse than Ethriel's had. "My father, my real father, he was killed with elfshot. There's no saving a man from that."

"John died from it twice. Once in front of me," Roshara said. "He saved me from it, took the shot that would have killed me."

Avorn turned, his face pale as milk. "And you?"

"John has a very powerful friend," Ethriel said. "Powerful enough to defeat elfshot."

Avorn looked at her. Then at Ethriel. "You're not lying. I... I can tell. My grandmother was a seer, and I've got that much sight. I can tell when a man lies." He swallowed. "Lady Tirgana told us you vanished. I.. I never thought to ask Buach. Why would I? I could tell that Lady Tirgana told us the truth."

"It's true enough. He did vanish. And she never said she knew where he was, did she?" Kestriel said.

"Avorn?" Fantiel asked. "Were we taught the truth? Or were we lied to?" He looked at Ethriel. "He's telling the truth, isn't he?"

Avorn nodded slowly. "They can't both be telling the truth," he whispered. "Lady Tirgana, she told us that Siobhan was older than Méabh—"

"That is true," Ethriel said. "My aunt is older than my mother was."

"Then the throne should have been hers? Truly?" Glethin asked. "If she was oldest—"

"It's pretty commonly known that there's no possible way that Siobhan and Méabh shared the same father," Kestriel said. "Xanthe was gone from court for a long time after Eiriell put her aside and married the Lady Aoife. At least a full year, of our years. But Siobhan and Méabh aren't that far apart in age. Anyone who can count knows that they can't share a sire, for all that Eiriell welcomed the girl."

Ethriel went to rest his hand on Roshara's shoulder. "Avorn, there's something else you should know. And Sir Kestriel will vouch for this, I think." He looked at the knight. "The only ones using elfshot when Siobhan took the Palace were her people. My parents, their men... they didn't have those spells."

Kestriel nodded. "I remember talking to John about this, when he saved my daughter from it," he said. "And I checked it with Parciviel. Elfshot was outlawed, in my grandfather's time. After the Battle of Twin Mountains, Parciviel says, when so many died from it. It was thought that the knowledge was lost. Until Siobhan's forces used it against Méabh. Now, the only people who hold the knowledge are those who are close to Siobhan. She was never the sort to trust that kind of weapon to someone not entirely in her control."

Avorn stared at them for a moment. "My father died from elfshot. I remember hearing him screaming as he died." He looked at the others. "I..."

"Avorn!" a woman shouted from somewhere outside the sitting room.

Avorn flinched. "She's awake!" he gasped. Then he turned to Ethriel. "You should go. You should go now."

CHAPTER TEN
Alliances

Ethriel stepped forward, standing in front of Roshara. "What's wrong?"

Avorn shook his head. "No time. Go. Get out of here. Fan, take them out through the kitchen. I'll go see to her."

"Don't tell her—"

"Do I look like an idiot?" Avorn snapped. "Go." He looked at Ethriel, then sketched a fast bow. "May we come to you tonight? It might be late. Will you be at the Residence?"

Ethriel nodded. "Of course. Be careful, all of you," he said. "Fantiel, which way?"

Fantiel went to a door on the side wall and opened it. "This way. It goes right into the kitchen, and I'll take you out the back and around."

Ethriel took Roshara's hand and nodded to Kestriel, who went before them as they followed Fantiel down the short hall. Fantiel paused for a moment and looked through another doorway, then nodded.

"No one here," he said. "Good." He led them out into the kitchen and to another door. He opened it and stepped out, looking around again. "Come," he said, keeping his voice low. "If we go around this side of the house, we'll get to where your horses are tethered. Lead them out, so you don't make noise. We don't want her looking out."

"Why are you so afraid of her?" Kestriel asked.

Fantiel shook his head. "No time to explain. Just go." He bit his lip and looked around. "Thought I heard... never mind. Let's go." He started walking, only to stop short as another man stepped out from around the side of the house. He was almost as big as Fioriel, and Ethriel guessed that this was the smith's apprentice.

"Renziel!" Fantiel said with a nervous laugh. "I was wondering where you were."

"What's this, then?" Renziel asked. He shifted, and hefted a large, solid-looking walking stick onto his shoulder, the same way that Fioriel had hefted his sledge. He looked at them, and his eyes lingered just a bit too long on Roshara; Ethriel stepped in front of her, and Renziel laughed. "What's he doing here?"

"I'm just showing them around the place," Fantiel said, laughing. "Lady Tirgana is still asleep, so I'm showing them around before they leave, and they'll come back another time to visit."

"I'm quite eager to meet my kinswoman," Ethriel added. "But I hardly want to disturb her. And I can't imagine us having a conversation underneath her window will be good for her sleep." He started forward, only to freeze when Renziel swung the stick down and blocked the way. Ethriel eyed the stick – a heavy, knob-headed thing that looked more like a cudgel than a cane. He saw light glinting off the knob, and realized that it was weighted. A fighting stick.

"Nice bata," Kestriel murmured. "Loaded with lead?"

Renziel smirked at him. "Think you could take me, old man?" He stepped forward, only to stop when a woman's voice rang out.

"Well, what have we here?"

Ethriel turned back toward the door. He smiled and bowed to the old woman standing in the doorway, the measured bow of a courtier meeting a respected elder. "Lady Tirgana," he said. "I apologize for disturbing your rest. It's hardly the way I wanted to meet a kinswoman."

"Kinswoman?" Tirgana repeated.

"So I understand," Ethriel said as he straightened. "I believe that my father Cathail was your kin, though I'm not certain of how close."

"I claim no kinship to that one," Tirgana said with a sniff. "He was cast out of my clan, and I deny any claims he may have made to shared blood."

Ethriel blinked. "Then I'm mistaken," he said slowly. "And I will trouble you no further." He bowed again and turned, only to find that the way was blocked by Renziel.

"Lady Tirgana?" he called. "What do you want me to do with them?"

Kestriel growled and stepped forward, his hand on his sword.

"Sir Kestriel, hold," Ethriel said softly. He stepped forward, letting Roshara's hand fall. He looked Renziel up and down, then sniffed. "Is this the best you can do?" he asked softly, and heard Fantiel hiss in warning as Renziel's face turned red. It was a warning Ethriel didn't need — John had taught him well. The moment Renziel moved, so did he, striking hard and fast, driving the heel of his hand into Renziel's nose. The apprentice smith stumbled backwards, howling as blood poured down his face, then snarled and rushed at Ethriel again, dropping his bata. Ethriel was ready, sidestepping and driving the hard heel of his riding boot into the side of Renziel's knee before darting back and grabbing the fighting stick. When Renziel rushed at him again, Ethriel swung the bata; the big man fell with a heavy thud, and didn't move. Ethriel stood straight, and pointed the bloody knob of the stick at Lady Tirgana.

"Now heed me, woman," he snapped. "Lightning Tree is under royal rule now. My rule. There is no place for the traitoress here, and no place for those loyal to her. By courtesy of the blood we share, I will allow you to leave—"

"Will you now?" Tirgana purred. She stepped out of the kitchen and into the yard, and as she came out into the light, she flicked her fingers at him. Ethriel saw the glittering darts a heartbeat before someone hit him, knocking him to the ground. As he hit, he heard Lady Tirgana scream.

"Avorn!"

Ethriel struggled out from underneath the heavy body, feeling hands on his arm. He looked up to see Fioriel, who had put aside his sledge and was kneeling to turn Avorn over. He held his hand over the young man's brow, frowned slightly, then shook his head.

"Elfshot," Ethriel breathed. He stood up and glared at Tirgana, who was standing at the point of Kestriel's sword. She was crying, shaking, and Ethriel couldn't tell if it was from sorrow or rage. "You hate me so much that you've murdered your own nephew," he said.

"I wouldn't have hurt him!" Tirgana wailed. "He was supposed to be true—"

"He was." Ethriel turned and saw Amartin and Glethin in the door. "In the end, he was true to me. Come out. Both of you. You're leaving with me."

Amartin and Glethin both slipped out of the house, hugging the wall. Glethin kept glancing back at Tirgana as they made their way around to where Fantiel was standing, and continued on to where Fioriel knelt with Avorn.

"She's murdered him," Amartin whispered. "She..." He looked up. "She used to tell us that if we didn't mind her, we'd be sorry. But I never..." He shuddered, and Glethin put his arm around his shoulders.

"You should say your goodbyes," Ethriel said. "Then... Amanial, take them around to the front?"

Roshara looked at her father and Tirgana, and arched a brow. Ethriel nodded, so she stepped back and let the three move to one by one kneel next to Avorn, leaned down to whisper to him. Fantiel kissed him gently on the forehead. Then Amanial gathered them up and took them around the building.

"My King?" Avorn whispered, his voice quiet and full of pain. "My King?"

Ethriel knelt and took Avorn's cold hand. "I'm here," he said.

"I'm sorry," Avorn whimpered.

"You have nothing to be sorry for," Ethriel said, reaching out and brushing Avorn's hair back. "My faithful Avorn," he murmured. "I, Ethriel, rightly born High King, do bind our faithful Avorn to our service," he said softly, calling the binding. "We swear that our power shall be raised only to protect and provide, and that if we should betray that oath, that all hands shall be raised against us."

Avorn smiled softly. "I, Avorn, son of Malfrin, do swear and bind myself to my King Ethriel. Let all know.. let all know... that I am loyal..." Avorn coughed, and blood stained his lips. He grimaced, then moaned, "It hurts."

"You are loyal," Ethriel repeated. "And true to us unto death." He looked up at Fioriel. "Give him mercy," he said softly, the words tasting bitter in his mouth. If only... He looked up. "No. No, wait. There's a chance... we have to get him to Hopaii."

"Where's that?" Fioriel asked.

"That's not a where. It's a who. He might be able to get to John's... friend. The one who saved me. But we have to hurry. Do you know where my ranch is?" When Fioriel nodded, Ethriel continued. "Get Sir Parciviel. Tell him that he needs to get Hopaii to do... whatever it was that he did when it was me. He needs to get to Joshua."

Fioriel nodded. "Joshua. I understand." He nodded. "Well, I don't, but I don't have time to understand. That Fantiel, he's going to want to come."

"Take him," Ethriel said. "And when you get to Parciviel, tell him we need guards out here immediately. And Terensiel. Now hurry." He stood, getting out of the way as Fioriel picked Avorn up and carried him away. Once they were around the house, he turned his attention to Tirgana. She was staring at him.

"My King," Kestriel said. "If she moves, if she so much as sneezes, I'm killing her. I'm not risking your life."

"Did you say there's a chance?" Tirgana whispered. "That he might live? How?"

"My John has a very powerful friend," Ethriel repeated. "Buach used elfshot on me, and Joshua saved me. If we can reach him, he may be able to do the same for Avorn."

"But John—" she stammered. Then she stopped, her face turning red.

For a moment, all Ethriel knew was rage. "You knew," he breathed. "You knew he was going into a trap." He closed his eyes for a moment, trying to think past his anger. He could strike her down, and no one would say a word... a soft touch on his arm reminded him that Roshara was still with him. He opened his eyes and looked at her.

"I know," she whispered. "I know. But we need to know who came to her, how this was planned. And the location of the portal to the south, and who holds it."

Ethriel nodded. "Would you be able to get that information from her?" he asked softly.

She frowned and shook her head. "I don't have that kind of control. If I touch her, I'll kill her, and we'll learn nothing. I'll admit I'm sorely tempted, though. But we need the information." She looked up. "But she also knows the spells for elfshot. She's not safe."

Ethriel swallowed. Then he turned back to face Kestriel and Tirgana. "Sir Kestriel, attend," he said.

"My King?"

"Tirgana, for your crimes against us, our consort, and our kin, we declare your lands and titles forfeit," Ethriel said. "By our charity, you shall be allowed to remain in this house, alone, under seal and under guard for the remainder of your days." He looked around and pointed. "That house there. What is it?"

"The groundskeeper's house." Ethriel turned to see Amartin coming up behind him. "Glee and I drew straws. He's going with Fan. I'm attending my King."

"Thank you," Ethriel said. "Does anyone live there now?"

"No," Amartin answered. "It's been empty for years."

"Sir Kestriel, escort Tirgana to the groundskeeper's house. She gets her house back once it's been searched and cleared. And then she gets sealed inside." Ethriel turned to look at Amartin. "If any of you have anything inside, you'll want to pack."

Amartin nodded, but didn't say anything until Kestriel had taken Tirgana away. "I'll take care of packing our things. I'm not sure where we're going to go, though. We've got no other kin in Lightning Tree. Or anywhere else, for that matter. And no one else wanted us. That's how we ended up here." He paused. "Do you want to see her personal papers? I know the spells to unlock her writing desk." He grinned. "She used us as secretaries. Secretaries and servants. I know enough about scrubbing pots and shoveling shit to make my mother weep. But between the three... the four of us, we know... well, maybe not all the secrets. But some."

Ethriel smiled slightly. "Thank you. And thank you, for staying." He shook his head. "There's no shame in shoveling shit. Or scrubbing pots. I've done both."

Amartin looked at him with wide eyes. "You? You've shoveled shit?"

Ethriel grinned. "I have shoveled shit, scrubbed pots, swung a hammer—"

"Badly," Roshara added softly. Amartin burst out laughing.

"Fine, I'm a horrible carpenter," Ethriel said. "But I can cook." He smiled. "Sir Parciviel says there's no such thing as menial labor.

There's just work that needs to be done. And he says my mother learned to farm, so I'm following in her footsteps."

"The High Queen," Amartin said. "Learned to farm. Really." He shook his head, laughing. Then he took a deep breath. "My King—"

"You can call me Ethriel."

Amartin looked at him. "Ethriel," he said. "How are you going to seal the house? She's old, her power is fairly strong. She might be stronger than Terensiel, just because she's older."

"I thought I'd ask Jeremiah Miller to do it, actually," Ethriel answered. "Have you met him?"

"Terensiel's human protege?" Amartin asked. "Yes. I like him. And he's... oh..." His eyes widened. "Ethriel, if he seals the house, it's not going to be unsealed, ever. By any other mage. She'll starve to death."

"Not if we make it a one-way seal, so things can be passed to her," Ethriel said. "Or personalized it, so that it only keeps her in." He frowned. "I'll talk to Jem about it before I leave."

"Before... you leave?" Amartin frowned. "Where are you going?"

"To get my John back," Ethriel answered. "And take my throne."

Amartin went very still. "Get John back. I think you left this part out. What's the whole story?"

"John was lured away, lured into a trap," Ethriel said. "And Maniel led him there. He's been taken through the portal, and I'm going after him."

"I see," Amartin breathed. "And you're not taking the very powerful mage with you why?"

"Because he's not old enough," Roshara answered. "He's not of age."

"Oh. Like the boys who run around calling themselves the King's Guard," Amartin said. He nodded, then looked at the house again. "When are we searching?"

"When the guards get here," Ethriel answered. He reached for Roshara's hand. "Do you want to take the first look, love?"

"Unless there's a seer I don't know about in Lightning Tree, I'm the only one who'll see any traps," Roshara said. "Unless... Amartin, are there traps?"

"Nasty ones," Amartin answered. "They won't kill a man. She didn't want us dead, but she did want us out of her private areas. So the traps are enough to be a misery for a month or more. The worst ones are in her bedroom and on her writing desk. I know the counterspells for those, though. The writing desk, I mean. The ones in the bedroom, I don't know. I wasn't allowed in there."

Ethriel nodded, looking across at the groundskeeper's house, and at Sir Kestriel. "That's strange."

"What is?" Roshara asked.

"Tirgana. She can throw elfshot, but she hasn't tried to kill Sir Kestriel."

"Ethriel!" Roshara gasped. "That's my father!"

"I know, love," Ethriel said. "I'm going to go and check." He left them, jogging across the yard toward the house. "Has she tried anything?"

"Not a thing," Kestriel answered. "I think she may be mourning the boy." He nodded toward the house. "Thought I heard her crying."

"She has only herself to blame for his death," Ethriel said. "If he dies." He went to the door and rested his hand on the wood, sealing it shut, then letting the power flow outward, seeking windows and doors and sealing them as well. He added mirroring spells to the insides, then stepped back.

"That won't stop her for long," Kestriel said.

"I know. But it will hopefully hold until Terensiel gets here." He looked back at the big house. "Once that house is cleared, it'll be her prison. And I'll have Jeremiah seal it so that it stays sealed."

Kestriel whistled. "And so she'll never be seen or heard from ever again."

"Exactly." Ethriel folded his arms over his chest. "And she'll have to live with the knowledge that she killed her own kinsman."

"Even if he doesn't die?" Kestriel asked. "Ethriel, is it possible? This friend, this Joshua? Can Hopaii get to him in time? Where is he?"

"It's... complicated," Ethriel answered. "And it's not entirely mine to tell. When we get John back, you can ask him about Joshua."

Kestriel turned to look at Amartin and Roshara. "They turned fairly quickly," he murmured.

Ethriel nodded. He waited, and Kestriel sighed.

"A man who'll turn that fast may turn back just as fast," he said. "Watch them."

"If Avorn lives, I think they'll be the truest courtiers a King has ever had."

"And if he doesn't..." Kestriel's voice trailed off.

"I'll watch them."

TERENSIEL ARRIVED WITH a dozen guards. Two of them took charge of Renziel, who had started to whimper and moan on the ground. While they took the apprentice smith away, Ethriel explained to Terensiel what had happened.

"Is that why Parciviel rode off like he was being chased?" Terensiel asked. She shook her head. "Ethriel, I'm not sure what you told them, but there's no cure for elfshot—"

"I'm still breathing," Ethriel said. "There's a cure for elfshot. But there's only one person I know who can do it, and I don't know if we can reach him."

"Who?" Terensiel demanded. "Who knows this magic?"

"He's a friend of John, and I don't know if it's something he can teach to us," Ethriel answered. "Can we do one thing at a time? We need to clear that house. There are things that need to be packed and brought into town, and then Tirgana needs to be sealed inside." He nodded toward the groundskeeper's house. "And that needs a better seal, while you work. Like I said, she can cast elfshot."

Terensiel nodded. "I'll take care of everything. Do you want to go back to town, to see to the wounded man?"

"I thought I'd help Amartin, actually," Ethriel answered. "And help with clearing the house. There is information that Tirgana has that I need."

Terensiel frowned. "I want to sweep the house first. There could be traps. Lady Roshara has already offered to help, but I don't want to put her at risk—"

"Mage Terensiel?" Amartin interrupted. "There are traps, and I know where most of them are. How can I help?"

Terensiel smiled at him. "Come with me, lad. Show me." She turned and bowed to Ethriel,. "My King, I know you want to help, but I think you'll be more help by taking your lady back to town. I'll bring Amartin to the Residence when we're done here. Or would you prefer I bring him to Midsummer?"

Ethriel frowned. Then he let out a long breath. "Midsummer. I should be there. And there are things we need there. We'll come back to the Residence later."

"Very good, Sire. I'll send a bird to Jeremiah when we're on our way." She turned and led Amartin into the house. Amartin looked over his shoulder at Ethriel, who nodded at him.

"I think we've been dismissed," Roshara murmured.

"We'll let them work," Ethriel said. "Let's collect your father and go back. I should be there when whatever happens happens."

CHAPTER ELEVEN
Faring

Nathaniel met them on the road between Lightning Tree and the ranch. Ethriel slowed Cloud from the fast trot to a walk as he drew up next to Nathaniel.

"I was hoping I'd meet you," Nathaniel said. "Ethriel, what is going on? Who are those boys?"

"It's a long story, but please tell me that Hopaii can do something?" Ethriel said. "Nathaniel, he stepped in front of elfshot for me."

Nathaniel sighed. Then he shook his head. "Hopaii can't do anything," he said softly. "He understood what Parsons was asking. We all did. But he says he's too far from his own ground. He's trying, but... he can't do what he did to save you."

Ethriel closed his eyes and swore softly. Not softly enough — Nathaniel gasped and turned pink.

"Ethriel! Where did you learn *that*?"

"It doesn't matter," Ethriel said. "Let's go. I should be there." He tapped his heels against Cloud's flanks, urging her forward, easing her back into a trot, then giving the mare her head and letting her run.

Glethin was sitting on the porch steps when Ethriel rode up. He looked up, then went back to studying the dirt with a fierce intensity. Ethriel dismounted, tying Cloud's reins to the porch railing.

"Glethin?" he said, going to kneel in front of him. "How is he?"

"They said they can't get to the man who could save him," Glethin answered. "Jeremiah and Fioriel are up with him. The holy man... he's with them, too." He looked over his shoulder. "And Fan. I... I didn't realize they were that close. They kept it hidden. Lady Tirgana wouldn't have approved. She wanted to marry us all off to Siobhan's maids, for alliances." He looked down again. "I went to her when I wanted to start courting. She told me I was too good for any girl in Lightning Tree, and she forbade me from even speaking to Asynia again." He looked around. "She's married now. Asynia, I mean. I wished her well, and.. where's my brother?"

"With Terensiel. He's taken charge of packing your things. I think he'll bring them to the Residence."

Glethin nodded. He took a deep breath and let it out through his nose. "The waiting is going to drive me mad," he said, and stood up. "What can I do to help? What can I do? I need to do something."

"How are you with horses?" Ethriel asked. He turned as the others rode into the yard. "We'll need to get the horses taken care of. Where are yours?"

"We turned them out into the corral," Glethin said. He looked around. "I can take care of horses. Just show me where everything is."

Ethriel took Cloud's reins, and led Glethin to the stables. As they reached the door, Nathaniel caught up with them.

"I'll help, Ethriel," he said. "And... Glethin, wasn't it? Come on, lad. Let's get to work."

Glethin smiled slightly, and Ethriel walked back to the house. Avriel and Parciviel were standing with Roshara and Kestriel. Avriel was cradling little Johanna in her arms.

"Ethriel," Parciviel said. "Did Nathaniel tell you?"

"That Hopaii can't reach Joshua?" Ethriel asked. "Yes. What are they doing?"

"I'm not sure," Avriel answered. "Jeremiah said he wanted to see if he could help Fioriel. I didn't know there was a healer in town."

"He won't be, for long," Ethriel said. "He's already said he's coming with me when the army moves." He looked up at the house. "I need to start putting together supplies. I want John's map."

"Just make a list, and we'll make sure it's ready," Avriel said. She shifted the baby, then laughed as Parciviel took her.

"I'll take her," he said. "Let me spend time with my granddaughter, and you go and rest."

"Rest, he says," Avriel laughed. "I'll be helping Ethriel—" Her voice died away as she turned toward the house. Ethriel looked, and saw Fantiel on the porch. He swallowed and walked over to the bottom of the steps.

"Fantiel?"

"They sent me out," Fantiel said. He stepped down, then sank to sit on the top step. "They... Jeremiah said there was one more thing they could try. But that I should come out." He looked around. "The person you said could save him... he isn't coming. The holy man, he said he couldn't reach him. I... how was he going to do it?"

"His own magic," Ethriel answered. "But his magic is stronger where his people are. And we're a long way from there."

Fantiel nodded. "I've heard of that. Power localized to a place. I've read about that. I..." He stopped and dragged his fingers through his hair. "I don't know what to do."

Ethriel sat down next to him and held his hand out. "I know," he said. "We're here."

Fantiel stared at his hand for a moment, then took it. "You're nothing like she told us," he whispered. "I wish we hadn't listened to her. I wish we'd run away. He wanted to. Avorn. He wanted us to run, so we could be together. I told him no. I should have listened to him." He shook his head. "I shouldn't have been so afraid." He looked around. "Where's Glee?"

"He asked for something to do," Ethriel answered. "He's in the stable with Nathaniel."

Fantiel nodded. "Maybe I'll go help them. I like Nathaniel." He looked around again. "Maybe Nathaniel will let us stay here. We can't go back to Lightning Tree. And... you don't want us, do you? We were hers."

"You were lied to," Ethriel said. "And if you want to come with me, I'll have you. If you want to stay here, you're welcome to, and I'm sure Nathaniel will appreciate the help. For now, you don't have to decide anything."

Fantiel nodded. "I'll go help with the horses. I like horses." He turned, a clearly-forced smile on his face. "Thank you."

Ethriel squeezed his hand, then let him go, watching as Fantiel lurched toward the stable. Roshara took his place on the steps.

"He's dying," she whispered. "That poor boy. I don't think he'll last long after Avorn dies."

Ethriel sighed. "I know," he said. "And I'm not sure what to do about him." He rubbed his forehead. "John would know."

Roshara leaned against his arm, then jumped as they heard boots behind them. They both turned, seeing Fioriel on the stairs inside the house. He saw them, and came to the door, holding it open. But he didn't come outside. He turned, looking back. Ethriel looked at Roshara, then stood up on the porch, looking inside.

Jeremiah came down the stairs first, going slowly and walking backwards, clearly helping someone down the stairs. Ethriel stepped into the doorway and stared.

Standing on the stairs, pale and weak-looking, was Avorn.

"Jeremiah," Ethriel breathed. "What did you *do*?"

Jeremiah turned and looked at him. Then he smiled. "Go get Fantiel, will you?"

Ethriel nodded. Then he ran out the door and jumped down the stairs. "Fantiel!" he shouted. "Fantiel, we need you now!"

Fantiel ran out of the barn, Glethin behind him. "What?" Fantiel shouted. "What is it? What—" He stopped short, and Glethin ran into him. They both stumbled, catching on to each other to keep from falling.

"Danu's tits!" Glethin gasped, his voice carrying clearly. Fantiel shook off his hands and staggered forward.

"Avi?" he moaned. "Is it... you're alive?"

Ethriel looked back at the house, to see that Jeremiah had helped Avorn down the porch steps to the ground. Fioriel and Hopaii were both on the porch, and both of them were looking on in wonder. He turned back to Fantiel, who was walking toward Avorn, one slow step at a time, staring.

"You're supposed to be dying," Fantiel gasped. "I thought I'd lost you."

Avorn shook off Jeremiah's hand and stepped forward. "Not leaving you," he croaked in a weak voice. "You're here. I'm staying."

Fantiel sobbed and threw himself into Avorn's arms, nearly knocking him over. They stood, laughing and crying all at once, and Ethriel went to stand with Jeremiah.

"What did you do?" he repeated. Jeremiah smiled, looking oddly satisfied.

"Took a gamble," he answered. "I figured it couldn't hurt. And it worked." He held his hands out, his right hand cupped over his left, like he was holding an invisible ball. A sphere appeared, a shimmering thing that encased something that glittered. "You all call them darts," Jeremiah said. "Darts are small arrows, right? So... I pulled it out the way you'd pull out an arrow."

"You... you pulled out... *elfshot*?" Ethriel repeated.

Jeremiah nodded. "I need to send a bird to Terensiel. She needs to come here so I can show her what I did." He nodded toward Avorn. "He's weak as a kitten right now. But he'll live. Fioriel says he'll be fine in a few days." He opened his hands, and the ball vanished.

"Where did you put it?" Roshara asked.

"It's safe," Jeremiah answered. "It's... well, it's hard to explain. But it's safe. And once I show Terensiel what I did and how I contained it, I'll destroy it." He cocked his head to the side. "I'll need to talk to my father again," he said. "I can't stay behind. Not now. Not when I'm the only mage who can beat elfshot." He looked around. "No time like the present," he added, and started toward the barn.

ETHRIEL SAT DOWN AT John's desk in the sitting room, rested his elbows on the blotter, and covered his face with his hands. It had been a long rest of the day, and by the time it ended, it was too late to send anyone back to Lightning Tree. Avriel and Nathaniel had found room in their house for Hopaii, Kestriel, Roshara, Fioriel and Terensiel, while Ethriel had given his room to Avorn and Fantiel, putting Amartin and Glethin into the other bedroom. He glanced at the couch, where he was going to sleep. But even as tired as he was, he knew he wouldn't be able to settle. He reached over and turned up the lamp, unrolled John's map, and started trying to figure out how he was going to move an elven army across Texas without being noticed by humans.

"My King?"

Ethriel jumped, turning in his chair. "Amartin?" he laughed. "What are you doing awake?"

"I couldn't sleep. And I could ask you the same question." Amartin came into the sitting room. "I looked in on Fan and Avi. They're both completely unconscious."

"I'm glad someone is getting some sleep," Ethriel said. "You should, too."

"And we're back to the beginning," Amartin replied with a grin. "Where did you learn to fight like that?"

"What, the brawling?" Ethriel smiled. "John taught me. He said he wanted to be sure I could defend myself and get away from an attacker, or keep myself alive until help came. He was a soldier in their most recent war."

Amartin nodded. "I heard about it, but Tirgana didn't like us to pay too much attention to human affairs. I don't know more than that it happened." He looked at the map. "What are you doing?"

"Trying to plan," Ethriel said. "Come pull up a chair. Maybe some fresh eyes will help." He waited until Amartin was sitting down before pointing. "The portal we want is here. And we're here. We need to get from here to there without being seen."

"What about the other portal?" Amartin asked. "The one Buach used?"

"Amaniel says that she's not sure where it is, who holds it, or where it comes out. I know the Arkansas portal comes out in the foothills of the Twin Mountains." He took a deep breath. "I just don't know if the other side of the portal is under guard. Or if this side of the portal is under guard." He paused, then looked at Amartin. "I don't know anything, really. And I have to plan."

Amartin shifted closer. "How big is the army?" he asked.

"Not nearly as big as I'd like," Ethriel answered. "I have a solid core, but it's only fifty—"

Amartin looked up. "Your something-something-great grandfather won the Battle of Spires with twelve men." He studied the map. "Where's the best place to cross the river? I don't know the terrain."

"That's another thing," Ethriel said. "There are three ferries that I know of. There's the one here, directly north, but we have to pass through or around Bonham."

"Which increases our risk of being seen," Amartin said, nodding. "And... a ferry? We'll definitely be seen!"

"Which is why I think we need to cross here," Ethriel reached out and tapped the map. "I've met Garrett. That's the man who owns this ferry. He is used to the uncanny, and he won't ask questions if we pay him well for the crossing. But to get there, we have to cross through Wraith's territory, and that's begging for trouble."

"Wraith," Amartin repeated. "That one, I've heard of. We all have. He's like the boggart you threaten small children with here. Be good, or Wraith will come steal you away. He's real?"

"Real, and dangerous, and his power extends for miles outside his town." Ethriel traced the lines on the map that marked Wraith's territory. "He attacked John when he was nearly to the ferry, left him with bruises and cuts."

"Avoiding that would be the best plan," Amartin said.

Ethriel nodded. Then he steepled his fingers and sighed. "I agree. I just don't see any way to do it."

Amartin leaned forward, trailing one finger over the map. "Do you have a herald yet?" he asked without looking up.

"Not yet, no," Ethriel answered.

Amartin looked up. "You do now. I'm volunteering. I'll go ahead of the army, and I'll negotiate passage."

"Amartin!" Ethriel gasped. "I can't ask that of you. Wraith is dangerous—"

"You didn't ask. I volunteered," Amartin smiled. "Can he throw elfshot?"

"He had a rifle that fired it."

Amartin looked startled. "Did he really? A human weapon that fired elfshot? That's impressively horrible." He laughed. "If he can't throw elfshot himself, then he's nowhere near as dangerous as Tirgana. But I'll take Glee if that will make you feel better." He stood up and looked at the map. "Plan the most direct route between here and that ferry. Glee and I will make it happen." He rested one hand on Ethriel's shoulder. "And get some sleep." He bowed slightly, then left, and Ethriel heard him going back up the stairs. He leaned back in his chair and looked at the map, then nodded. The most direct route would shave days off their journey. It would make getting to John that much faster.

He just needed to convince Parciviel.

"I'M SORRY," SIR PARCIVIEL said. "I understand why we're not using the portal to the south. I agree with that reasoning. But did you just say we'll be passing near Wraithtown? On purpose?"

Ethriel took a deep breath as he turned away from the stove, then sat down at the table with the others. He picked up his coffee and took a sip. "The most direct route between here and Garrett's ferry passes a few miles from Wraithtown. So yes, we'll be passing Wraithtown." He picked up the bowl of scrambled eggs and served himself. "Someone pass the bacon?"

"We're not going north?" Kestriel asked. "Through... oh."

"Exactly," Ethriel said. "If it was a half-dozen of us? We could go through Bonham. Or around Bonham. This is an army. We need to move, move fast, and not be noticed. We need to go where the humans aren't."

Kestriel nodded. "And... yes, I can see your point. But dealing with Wraith... you know he wants us dead." The sweep of his arm took in Parciviel and himself, and Ethriel knew it included Roshara, who hadn't yet joined them.

"Maybe... you both can take Lady Roshara and go north?" Avorn suggested. He was still pale, but seemed stronger than he'd been the night before. "Take the safer route? Fan and I could go with you. I'm not going to be good for much for a while, but I'm not staying behind." He looked at Fantiel, who smiled and reached over to take his hand. Avorn smiled back, then continued. "We could meet the army when it crosses the river?"

Ethriel frowned. "I'm not sure I like the idea of splitting the group," he said. "I don't like the idea of sending the people most important to me off alone. Not when Siobhan has to know I'm coming."

"And there's another reason to go the shorter route," Amartin said. "It's the more dangerous one. Siobhan won't expect us to take the more dangerous route."

"There are Mountain elves in Wraithtown, though. Or at least, there were," Parciviel said. "We don't have enough information about what's there now."

"I think we have to take a chance," Ethriel said. "We need to be on the road as soon as we can, and we need to get to the portal as soon as we can." He finished his coffee, and started on his eggs, looking up at the sound of footsteps outside on the porch. A moment later, Nathaniel, Jeremiah and Roshara came in. Roshara smiled.

"Ethriel, did you cook again?" she asked. She came around the table and leaned down to kiss him. "And bacon? You never cook bacon."

"Because John doesn't eat bacon," Ethriel said. "And I didn't cook the bacon. Glethin did."

"I like bacon," Glethin added. He reached over and picked up the plate, taking some bacon and offering the rest to Roshara. "Have you eaten?"

"With the Millers," Roshara answered. "Thank you."

"Ethriel," Nathaniel said. "I need to ask you a question." He glanced at Jeremiah. "Jeremiah says that it's absolutely vital that he go with you. That since he's the only mage who can defeat elfshot, that he's key to your winning your throne back and saving John. Do you agree?"

Ethriel swallowed and sat up, resting his hands on the table top. He didn't even have to think about his answer. "Yes," he answered.

"If necessary, I think I might be able to do what needs to be done. But there are no truly strong mages who will be riding out with me when I leave. Terensiel won't leave Lightning Tree, and I can't ask her to. She's all that stands between Lightning Tree and the human world. The fact that Fioriel is willing to come still astounds me. But there's nothing he can do against elfshot, and I know I don't have any mages strong enough to face the ones who follow my aunt." He took a deep breath. "Yes, I need Jeremiah if I'm to save John. And honestly, if I save him, and bring him back here? I'll count that as a success. I don't need the throne. I need John. And to get him back? I need Jem."

Nathaniel nodded slowly. He lowered his head for a moment. Then he turned to Jeremiah. "You promise me something," he said. "You're going to come back."

"Nathaniel!" Parciviel gasped. "You... you're sending him?"

"After last night?" Nathaniel replied. "I don't see any way I can keep him here." He glanced at Jeremiah. "Not when he's determined to do this. He'd probably run away and follow you if I forbade him."

"I wouldn't," Jeremiah protested. "Papa, if you said no, I would listen."

"And if I said no, I'd have to face the fact that saying no may have damned my dearest friend to Hell, and cost people I care about their lives in the bargain." Nathaniel shook his head. "I can't do that. You're old enough to know your own mind, no matter that the law says. So you may go, with my blessing. Just promise me that you'll come back to us."

CHAPTER TWELVE
Closure

Over the next few days, Ethriel spent a good portion of his waking hours in the saddle, traveling between Lightning Tree, the ranch, and Bandera. He finalized paperwork with Nathaniel, transferring his portion of the ownership of Midsummer Night ranch into Nathaniel's name. He laid the groundwork for the story that they would tell to explain his and John's absence – everyone already knew that John had gone east. They told Senora Rodriguez that a messenger had arrived, and that John had taken ill, and needed Ethan to join him. The dear lady made sympathetic noises, and there was no doubt in Ethriel's mind that the entire town would know he was leaving before sunset.

The next day, he met with his army, arranged for supplies and transportation, and assigned Kestriel as his quartermaster, with Fantiel and Glethin to help. He formally passed judgement on Lady Tirgana, and Jeremiah carried out the sentence. Then Jeremiah turned to trying to teach Terensiel what he'd done to defeat elfshot and save Avorn's life while Ethriel started to go through the papers that had been taken from Tirgana's house.

That took him an entire day, working with Avorn and Amartin — Tirgana had apparently saved every letter that Siobhan had ever written to her, as well as an enormous stack of letters from someone named Farathir. Ethriel set those aside, focusing first on the letters from Siobhan. By the time they were done, Ethriel knew exactly what his aunt had promised Tirgana, and had an idea of what Tirgana had promised in return. There was even a long letter containing Siobhan's detailed instructions on just how to lure John to Arkansas. There were things in that letter that Ethriel wasn't sure how either of them knew, details about John's relationship with Hopaii, about the dugout in Skullyville. About the promises made between Nathaniel Miller and Hopaii for their children.

"It was Siobhan who arranged it?" Amanial said when Ethriel showed the letters to her. "How did she know so much about John? About the marriage promise? Or that he'd drop everything and go if he was called?"

Ethriel shook his head and laid the pages down. "I don't know. Neither does Nathaniel. He thinks it might have come from when Buach posed as a religious leader when he was in Skullyville. He would have learned about Talula then, and the marriage promise. But some of this is current, and I don't know who could have given her that information." He looked at Amanial. "You have no idea what Hattak Falaya even means, do you?"

"I don't even know what language it is."

Ethriel smiled. "It's Choctaw. And no, I don't know how to speak it. But John does." He laughed and shook his head. "Badly. He speaks it badly."

"His Elven must not be much better," Amanial muttered, and Ethriel chuckled.

"He is trying," he said. "He's trying." He paused, his heart suddenly in his throat. He closed his eyes, and felt Amanial's hand on his arm.

"I was wondering when you'd crack," she said softly.

Ethriel drew in a shaking breath. "Already did," he admitted. "The first night, before the meeting. And every night since then. If I was sleeping, I'd say I've been crying myself to sleep. But it's mostly just crying."

"Ethriel—"

"I'm getting him back, Amanial," Ethriel said. He stacked the papers, gathering them up and tapping the sides on the table to make sure the pages were neat. Then he put them down and touched them with one finger.

They burst into flames.

Amanial jumped up, staring at Ethriel in shock. He looked up at her and smiled.

"And I'm not letting anything stop me," he added. "Don't worry about your table. It's shielded." He picked up the other pile of letters. "Who is Farathir? Do you know?"

"If it's the one I'm thinking of, he leads the Mountain elves." Amanial paused. "He's one of the last males of the old Mountain line, now that Buach is dead. Maniel is the only other one."

"He's not. Because I'm alive. Amanial, he calls Tirgana 'sister.' And there's this..." He turned pages, then read aloud, "*Sister, it would have been better for all of us if you'd drowned the bastard at birth.*" He looked up. "Amanial, could they be talking about my father? That would mean Tirgana is his mother. My grandmother."

"I don't know." Amanial shook her head. "I think the only person who can answer that is Tirgana."

"Then I'll have to ask her," Ethriel said. "Now, you've spoken to Sir Kestriel? When will the army be ready to march?"

Amanial was silent for a moment, then cleared her throat. "I saw him right before I came to meet you. The army will be ready to march tomorrow. We're just finishing the provisioning."

Ethriel nodded and stood up, glancing at the fire burning merrily on the table. "Then I'm going back to the ranch. I've some things to pack, and I need to say my goodbyes there. I'll go collect the others, and we'll be back. We'll be staying in the Residence tonight, Amanial."

She bowed. "Yes, my King."

TIRGANA'S FORMER WARDS dubbed themselves "Ethriel's Boys," and they were on their way to fulfilling Ethriel's theory that they'd become his truest courtiers. The four of them were never far from his side, throwing themselves fully into helping his plans.

They surrounded him on the ride back to the ranch, talking back and forth about the plans for the journey. Ethriel listened to the conversation that flowed around him, but only with half an ear. He was trying to plan, trying to think of contingencies. Trying not to think about what might be happening on the other side of the portal. Buach had learned his lessons on how to hurt people somewhere, and Ethriel knew full well how brutal he'd been....

"What are we supposed to call you?" Avorn's vice broke through his reverie.

"I'm sorry?" Ethriel turned to look at Avorn, who was riding on his left.

"Well, we have Fan, Glee, Mar, and I'm Avi, because Avorn is hard to break into a diminutive. What do we call you?" Avorn grinned. "If you use the usual patterns, it would be Eth or Ethi. Is that what you want to be called?"

"No," Ethriel answered. "I was called Ethi, once. I don't like it anymore, and I don't use it. The only person who dares is Roshara, and only because she's known me since we were both in our fifties, and she only does it when she forgets that I asked her not to." He shook his head. "I'd appreciate it if you didn't."

"Can we come up with a new one?" Amartin asked. "See if you like it?"

"Why?" Ethriel asked. "I mean... I have a name."

"A diminutive is something for the people who are close to you," Fantiel answered. "I mean, you call Roshara Rose, and you call Jeremiah Jem. We've heard Sir Kestriel and Sir Parciviel call each other Kes and Parse. You're the only one who doesn't have one. And... it gives the wrong message. Not using one will tell our people that you don't let anyone close. Why don't you like Ethi?"

"Because Buach called me Ethi when he was torturing me," Ethriel snapped. "Is that reason enough not to want to use it?"

"Danu's tits," Avorn breathed.

"Right. Avi, stop it," Glethin said. "Stop pushing, right now." He rode up on Ethriel's other side. "Ethriel, you didn't have to tell us that. And I'm sorry. None of us knew—"

"No one knows that," Ethriel said. "I... haven't even told John that. He never knew the name, or how our people shorten names, so it didn't seem like something he needed to know."

Glethin nodded. "Still, I'm sorry we pushed. It's just... you've taken us in, all of us. You didn't have to do that. Especially not after what Tirgana did.. Now... well, we'll follow you anywhere. I think you know that?"

Ethriel nodded. "I know."

"Good. And if you decide we're safe? And close enough? And you're ready? Let us know." Glethin looked around at the others. "In the meantime... well, you're welcome to use ours. We decided it."

"Decided... what?" Ethriel asked.

Avorn laughed. "We decided that you're ours now, Ethriel."

"Your what?" Ethriel asked. "I mean... really. What am I? Because I have John and Roshara, and you've got your hands full with Fan."

Fantiel burst out laughing, and Avorn grinned at him. "Not arguing," he said. Then he turned back to Ethriel. "You're our friend, Ethriel. Our brother, if you'll have us. When you're ready to let us close, you tell us."

Ethriel looked at him. Then he looked down at his hands.

"Ethan," he said softly. "John calls me Ethan. It started when we were on the road, when I had to wear my human illusion. Then it... it became something that he called me. His name for me. And...you can call me that."

For several breaths, the only sound was the steady rhythm of the horses' hooves. Then Avorn cleared his throat. "Ethriel... if that's John's name for you, then we shouldn't use it. Not his private name. That's..." He blew out a short breath. "How do I explain this?"

"Ethriel, you weren't of age when everything happened, were you?" Amartin said. "You didn't get the talk from your father the night you came of age?"

Ethriel looked around. "I have no idea what you all are talking about. What talk?"

Avorn snorted. "Right. We can do this now, or we can ask Parciviel to do it. But... well... it's part of becoming a man."

Ethriel chuckled. "All right. Tell me. Because Parciviel will turn red and stammer. And Kestriel will tease. So... please? What am I missing?"

"Well, we don't have to cover what happens when two people love each other very much," Fantiel said. "You know that part. But... when you're paired, there are private names. Pillow names. Things you only ever are called by your lover. Have you heard me call Avorn Ori? That's why. If your consort calls you Ethan, and no one else does? That's your pillow name."

Ethriel blinked. "Oh," he breathed. "Oh, that answers something I'd almost forgotten about." He smiled. "My father's diminutive was Cat. But my mother called him Hail. She told me I wasn't allowed to call him anything but Papa. And that he'd explain why she called him something different when I was older." He took a deep breath and nodded. "Thank you. I didn't know that." He looked around. "What else am I missing?"

"A lot. We're going to have some interesting nights on the road," Glethin answered, and the others laughed.

Ethriel grinned. "While we're at it, we'll have to think of something else for you to call me. Just not Ethi, and not Ethan."

They rode into the yard, and Ethriel dismounted and looked around as the others led their horses to the corral. Everything looked the same, but somehow, the ranch didn't feel like home anymore. It was just another place. He'd miss it here when he was gone, but he knew in his bones that he didn't belong here anymore.

"Ethriel, what needs to be done?" Avorn asked as he came back. "Let me take Cloud to the corral."

Ethriel handed Avorn his reins. "There's a second wagon in the barn," he answered. "Near the back. We'll want that and we'll need to set up the ribs and the cover. And there are some things in the house that I haven't moved to the Residence. Then... well, the last thing is to say goodbye." He looked around. "I'm going in to pack. Bring the wagon out, and I'll help you with the ribs and cover when I'm done." Avorn nodded and waved the others toward the barn, and Ethriel headed into the house.

At the top of the stairs, he stopped and looked at the closed bedroom door before letting himself in and looking around. He had barely had a week with John in this room, in this bed, and he hadn't slept here at all since they'd learned the truth. Ever since, he'd either been on the couch in the sitting room, or at the Residence. He didn't have many things left here, but what he did have, he wasn't leaving behind. He'd have to go down to the sitting room to get his portable writing desk and the map, but he'd start with the bedroom. He started taking things from drawers and laying them on the bed. His good clothes. The boots that John had given to him last winter. He pulled John's case from under the bed, and packed things away, then turned to the chest at the foot of the bed. There was only one thing inside that he wanted — he reached in and took out a paper-wrapped bundle. He sat down and carefully unwrapped it, revealing the rifle-green wool kepi inside.

"What's that?" Ethriel looked up to see Fantiel in the doorway. "I got sent out before I hurt myself," he said. "I'm as bad a carpenter as you are, apparently."

"That's not hard," Ethriel said with a smile. "And this is John's kepi. The last part of his uniform from when he was a soldier in the last human war."

"The last one?" Fantiel frowned and came closer. "But it's green. I thought they all wore blue or gray?"

"I know, but John wore green. He said his company was special, but you'd have to ask him. I can't remember why." Ethriel put the kepi on, then stood up and pointed to the metal box on the floor. "That needs to come with us. It's heavy."

Fantiel went over and tried to lift the box, then looked at Ethriel. "You weren't joking," he said, and stood up. He held his hand out, and the box rose off the ground to float. "What's in this?"

"Ammunition for John's rifle. He'll want it, once we find him."

"Do you think he'll still have it?" Fantiel asked.

Ethriel picked up the case and left, leading the way down the stairs and out of the house.

He the case down on the porch. "Leave the box here. We'll load the wagon once the cover is on. And I don't know. But I'd rather have the ammunition and no rifle than a rifle and no ammunition."

"Can you use one?" Fantiel asked. "A human weapon?"

Ethriel nodded. "John taught me. They're terrifying at first. They're so loud!" He laughed. "But you get used to your ears ringing. He said I was a good shot. Rose shoots, too. Maybe she'll show you?"

Fantiel looked thoughtful, then nodded. "We should learn. It might be useful when we go through the portal. Weapons that Siobhan can't counter—"

"She's used human weapons," Ethriel corrected. "She changed a rifle to fire elfshot."

"She what?" Fantiel's voice spiraled up. "That... that's obscene!"

Ethriel nodded. "It is. And you can ask Kestriel or Roshara about it — they both saw it. I wasn't there. John told me." He took a deep breath. "Let's go fix the wagon."

They started down the steps and headed toward the wagon, where Ethriel could see Jeremiah had joined the others, and was helping bend the ribs into position. He nodded as Ethriel came close.

"If we're doing this, I assume this is it?" he asked. "We're leaving?"

"We'll spend the night at the Residence," Ethriel answered. "And we'll march first thing tomorrow. Are you ready?"

Jeremiah didn't answer at first, holding one of the ribs in place as Glethin slotted the other end into its bracket. "That's got it, Jem."

"Thank you," Jeremiah said. He wiped his hands off on his trousers, then nodded. "I'm ready. And a little nervous, truth be told."

"Nervous is understandable," Ethriel said. "I'm terrified."

"That's understandable, too," Amartin said. "I think we're all scared. This is... this is big." He looked around. "This is bigger than big. This is huge." He took a deep breath. "I need to stop before I piss myself. Who's here that we need to say goodbye to? Just Nathaniel and Avriel and Hopaii?"

"I should go down to the river and say goodbye to the kelpies," Ethriel said. "Jem, come with me?" he asked. "And... will the rest of you come?"

"The kelpies aren't sure what to do with us," Glethin said. "I don't want to make them uncomfortable. It was nice meeting them, but we're not close to them the way you are."

"He's right. You go. What can we do while you're gone?" Avorn asked.

"The case and the box on the porch both need to go into the wagon," Ethriel said. "The box fits under the seat. There are some other things in the house, but I'll get them when I come back." He looked around. "The day isn't getting any longer. Let's go."

He and Jeremiah walked around the house and down toward the river.

"Jem, have you been down here since we came and told them that we were leaving and that you were coming with us?" he asked.

"No," Jeremiah answered. "I've been too busy. Lily came up to the house once or twice, Mama said, but I was in Lightning Tree."

Ethriel looked at him. "I thought you and she were through?"

"We are," Jeremiah said with a sigh. "But you know her. She cares about all of us, and she worries. She thought I might have left without saying goodbye." He waved. "They've seen us."

Ethriel turned to see a familiar black mare ambling toward them. She changed from mare to woman as she reached them, a lovely woman clad only in water droplets and her long hair, and with reversed hooves instead of feet.

"I was wondering if you'd gone," Lilith said. "And not stopped to say goodbye." She frowned. "Is this goodbye?"

Ethriel nodded. "We're leaving tomorrow. We'll march at dawn. You may see us pass—"

"Or I may come with you myself," she added, and looked at Jeremiah. "I've thought about this, and my Queen has said I may go. So I will come with you, Jem, since you're going." She paused, "Unless you want to leave me behind?"

"Lily, we left each other behind a year ago," Jeremiah said. "It was sweet while it lasted, but you and I both know it wasn't going to be forever. It couldn't be." He frowned. "I was promised to someone else, and you're immortal. Even though Talula isn't coming now, you're still immortal. There's no forever for us, and I won't hurt you like that."

She smiled. "There could be forever. If I come with you. In the Elven lands, you won't age."

Jeremiah looked shocked. "I won't?" He looked at Ethriel. "I won't?"

"You won't," Ethriel said. "Until you come back here. Then the time that passed while you were with us will all settle at once. You'll turn to dust."

Jeremiah frowned slightly. "I didn't think that part of the stories was true," he murmured. "I... Lily, is that what you want? You really want to come with me?"

"I want to go with you." She paused, then smiled. "So, does the High King's mage need a mount?"

Ethriel smiled at the stunned look on Jeremiah's face. "I'll let you two discuss this," he said, and started back to the house.

He wasn't sure either of them heard him leave.

ETHRIEL HELPED WITH putting the cover onto the wagon, then helped load. He had an idea of using the wagon as a mobile office — he'd been told that he'd have a tent, but the wagon seemed to make more sense to him. So he brought his bedroll in here, and he'd taken a small, sturdy table and a chair from the house. He was arranging them so that nothing would fall over and break while they were in transit when he heard someone calling his name. It sounded like Avorn.

"What is it, Avi?" he called back. Avorn appeared at the back of the wagon, grinning.

"First, thank you for calling me Avi," he said. "Second, you want to see this."

"See what?" Ethriel asked. Avorn laughed and disappeared. "Avi! See what?" Ethriel went to the back of the wagon and jumped down to the ground, hearing voices off to his left. He came around the wagon and stopped next to Avorn. "Oh."

Roshara had joined Amartin, Glethin and Fantiel. He'd seen her dressed to travel before, but not like this — instead of her usual plain skirts, she was dressed identically to the men, wearing trousers and boots, and a hip-length coat. Her long hair had been braided into a single plait down her back. She saw him and smiled, and for a moment, he forgot how to breathe.

Avorn laughed again. "Told you."

CHAPTER THIRTEEN
Parley

"Are you sure?" Ethriel asked, watching as Nathaniel harnessed a lovely, dappled mare to the wagon. "I thought you were going to sell Damask."

Nathaniel nodded, buckling the last strap. "You're leaving me this entire place. I can make sure you have proper horses to take you away, at the very least. And you have the money?"

"Locked in my writing box, yes," Ethriel said. He looked around and shook his head. "We should go. It's getting late."

"You could stay and have supper," Nathaniel said. "One last meal with the family?"

Ethriel smiled. "Nate, really, we have to go." He held his hand out. "Thank you. I'll send word, if I can."

"When you can, and you'd better," Nathaniel said with a watery-sounding laugh. "I know where that portal is. If you don't send word, I'll come find a way through!" He took Ethriel's hand, then pulled him into a tight embrace. "Take care of yourself, Ethriel," he whispered. "And find him."

"I'll find him," Ethriel answered. "And I'll send word, as soon as I can." Nathaniel let him go, and he stepped back. "I'll send Parciviel or Jeremiah. So you know who to look for. If it's anyone else, don't believe them." He paused. "Unless they call me Ethan, and refer to John as Yohanan."

Nathaniel nodded. "Use the names you don't use. I understand." He turned. "Let me get Abby and Hopaii, and we'll see you off."

Ethriel went to stand by Damask's head, crooning to the mare and murmuring nonsense. Cloud was tethered to the rear of the wagon, and her tack was packed. The other horses were ready, except for Lilith, who wanted to say her goodbyes as well. Jeremiah and Lilith came around the wagon, followed by all of the elves.

"Is it time?" Kestriel asked.

"As soon as we say our goodbyes," Ethriel answered. He turned, and saw Nathaniel, Avriel and Hopaii coming out of the house. Nathaniel had baby Johanna cradled in his arm, and stood back as Avriel embraced Ethriel.

"Be careful," she murmured in his ear. He nodded, and hugged her tightly.

"Take care of Nate and Johanna," he said as he let her go.

"We'll be fine," she said. "Let me go say goodbye to my son and my father." She moved past him, and Ethriel turned to Hopaii.

"If you want to ride with us, you're welcome," he said. "If you want to go home?"

Hopaii shook his head slowly. "My place isn't there anymore. My time there is done." He took a deep breath. "My time is nearly done. I am glad I saw you again. I wish I could have seen John once more."

"When I find him, what do you want me to tell him?" Ethriel asked.

Hopaii smiled gently, his weathered face creasing into deep wrinkles. "Tell him that I said thank you. And that I treasure his friendship."

"I know he treasures yours," Ethriel said. "There was never a question about him going to your side when we thought it was you who called for him."

"I wish it had been true, and that he was safe." Hopaii shook his head. "Go and find him, Ethriel. Be well."

Ethriel stepped back, then bowed deeply to Hopaii. "It's been an honor to know you," he said as he straightened. He went over to Nathaniel, looking down at the baby in his arms.

"I wish John had gotten the chance to see his little namesake," Nathaniel said.

"I'll show him," Ethriel said. "And... don't count us lost, Nathaniel. Perhaps we'll come and visit." He looked over his shoulder and took a deep breath. "We need to go."

"What's your plan?"

"Leave in the morning," Ethriel answered. "Avoid Bandera and San Antonio, and stop outside Wraithtown while Amartin and Glethin act as my heralds. Then... we'll see." He looked back again. "It's time. I'll send word as soon as I can."

DAWN WAS JUST A HINT on the horizon as Ethriel left the Residence and rode out to the big house near the barrier. Amartin and Jeremiah went with him.

"Are you sure?" Amartin asked as they rode up to the front of the house.

"This is my last chance. I need to know," Ethriel answered. "And I need to see if she'll tell me. Wait out here, Mar." He dismounted and waited for the others. Jeremiah rested his hand on Ethriel's shoulder, and Ethriel felt his skin tingle.

"A shield?" he asked. "I can shield, Jem."

"This one will stop anything she throws," Jeremiah said. Then he grimaced. "I think. I haven't been able to really test it."

Ethriel snorted. "Hope it works, then." He headed for the door. There was a moment of resistance as the spells that kept Tirgana prisoner awoke, but it passed just as quickly. Ethriel stopped just inside the door, waiting for the others. Then he raised his voice.

"Tirgana!" he called. "I want to talk."

He heard footsteps, and Tirgana appeared at the top of the stairs. "You assume I want to talk to you."

Ethriel looked up at her. "Are you my grandmother? Was Cathail your son?" He didn't wait for an answer. "He never told me anything about his family, you know. Just that he'd been cast out for agreeing to marry my mother. I never knew anything about you." He paused. "I'd have liked to. I would have liked to know you, Tirgana."

"I told you—"

"I know what you told me," Ethriel interrupted. "I frankly don't care what you told me." He looked over his shoulder at Jeremiah, then back up the stairs. "I would have liked to have known you, Grandmother. But you made your choice. You threw him away. And I want you to know that your choice hurt him. He missed you. I don't think he ever stopped loving you."

Tirgana frowned. "I—"

"I'm leaving today. Leaving now," Ethriel continued. "You won't see me again. I'm leaving orders that you be tended to as befits your station, for as long as you live." He turned. "Let's go. We still have a lot to do before we leave."

"Ethriel."

Ethriel stopped and looked back. "Yes?"

"Avorn," she asked, and came down several stairs. "Was he properly burned?"

Ethriel smiled. "We don't burn the living, Grandmother."

Her face went pale, and she staggered and sat down hard on the steps. "He's alive? How?"

Ethriel shook his head and walked out the door, feeling the push of the spells for a moment. Then he and Jeremiah were outside, where he could no longer hear Tirgana's voice. He walked over to where Amartin stood with the horses.

Amartin nodded toward the house. "She's in the window. Looks like she's trying to get your attention."

Ethriel shook his head. "It's too late for that. Let's go."

"SIRE," KESTRIEL SAID. "The heralds are back."

Ethriel looked up from the map he was studying with Roshara. They'd been camped for a day and a half on the shores of a small river at the very western edges of what Ethriel, Parciviel and Kestriel had deemed a possibly safe distance from Wraithtown. Possibly had turned to probably, as nothing had happened — it had been a very quiet camp. He and Roshara were trying to plan out alternative routes if passing Wraithtown proved to be impossible. The best they'd come up with had been "north, as fast as possible."

"We'll come out," Ethriel said. He rolled the map and put it into his writing desk. Then he walked to the rear of the wagon and jumped down to the ground, turning to help Roshara down.

Amartin and Glethin stood outside the wagon, and saluted together. "Sire," Amartin said. "I know we've heard all the stories about the powerful thing that lives out here, but are you completely certain that Jacob Wraith is the same creature?"

Ethriel looked at Roshara, then back at the scouts. "Yes," he said. "Why?"

"Because the town is a ruin," Amartin answered. "And there's only one... thing. One spirit, I think. I can't really tell what it is. What he is. He says his name is Jacob Wraith, but his power is so weak... I don't think he could hurt anyone, or stop us from passing. He's asked to speak to you. But he says you'll have to come to him. He says he can't leave the town. Frankly, I believe him."

"Can't leave?" Roshara repeated. "But... his reach used to spread for miles!"

"Something's changed," Ethriel said. He frowned and looked toward the east. He couldn't see Wraithtown, but he knew it was there. Then he nodded. "I think I'll take this risk," he added. "Roshara, will you come with me?"

"You think I'll let you get close to Wraith alone?" she demanded. "Of course I'm coming with you. But I wish you wouldn't. He's dangerous."

Ethriel shook his head. "Somehow, I don't think so."

They rode out, heading east. Amartin and Glethin led them back to Wraithtown. With them were Jeremiah, Parciviel and Kestriel, and a small troop of guards. Ethriel had asked Lilith to stay behind, putting Jeremiah on Damask. Better not to take too many chances, he'd said, and Lilith agreed. As the town came into sight, Ethriel stayed on guard, but nothing came to meet them, and he realized that he wasn't feeling the sense of being watched that John had described.

"This is very strange," Roshara murmured. "His pet spirits should have come to see us by now."

"So it's not just me," Ethriel said. "John said he could tell he was being watched, long before he reached the town."

Roshara nodded. "I know what he was talking about. Yes, we should have been met long before this. And… look, it looks like there was a fire." She pointed, and Ethriel noticed for the first time that she'd taken off her gloves. "Do you see?"

Ethriel could see, and he saw more as they got closer. Buildings that were no more than burned out hulls, nothing left but blackened timbers stretching up at crazed angles. No one moving in the main street at all.

"This is wrong," Roshara said. "There's no one here."

The heralds led them down the street to the charred remains of what had once been a large house. Sitting on the porch, in a broken rocking chair, was a thin, dark figure, his head bowed to his chest so far that all Ethriel could really see was his hat.

"That's him," Roshara whispered, her voice squeaking slightly. Ethriel reached for her hand, feeling it tremble.

"Wait here," he said, and kissed her fingers. "Wait with your father. I'll speak to him."

He urged his horse forward, past the heralds and closer to the porch. "Jacob Wraith?"

"Nice of you to come," he said. "Appreciate it. Haven't had someone to talk to for a while."

Ethriel looked up and down the street. "This isn't what I expected. What happened here?"

Wraith's laughter sounded like a rusty gate. "I played a bad hand," he answered. "Lost." He waved one hand. "Lost everything." He frowned. "Where's John?"

Ethriel paused, then asked, "Before I answer you, answer this for me. I'm told there were Mountain elves here. What—"

"Mistake on my part," Wraith interrupted. "Shouldn't have messed with your lot when they first showed up. Should have driven them all off. And that last one, that bitch Siobhan—"

"Siobhan did this?" Ethriel looked around. "Were you actually allied to her? We weren't sure if that's where you got the rifle."

Wraith shook his head. "Nah. That came with one of the others your sort, about six months before John passed through. Told John the truth there. Won it in a game of cards. No, Siobhan came here after John got you all away. Said she wanted to work with me. Said that if I helped her, she'd deliver a certain Elven girl to me." He chuckled. "I see you over there, Rosie. We could have been something."

"Nothing I wanted," Roshara called.

"She's mine, now," Ethriel added. "So take your eyes off her." He stopped and cocked his head. "Do you even have eyes? John said he never saw them."

"Trust me, he didn't want to," Wraith answered. "Neither do you. So you got yourself a matched set, hm? Good for you." Wraith shifted in his chair. "Siobhan didn't want a partner. She wanted what she could get out of me...."

"That's how she knew so much," Ethriel breathed. "We'd wondered."

"Could be," Wraith admitted. "Once she got what she wanted about you lot, she wanted me to be her slave. And I don't bend, not for anybody. When she realized I wasn't going to bow to her, she did this." He turned his head. "I'm the last one. And I'm not going to be here much longer. So where is he? Where's John?" He paused. "She got him, didn't she? Shit."

"Siobhan lured him back to Arkansas, and took him captive. He's in my world now, and I'm going after what's mine."

Wraith nodded. "Well, then. Good luck. For what it's worth, I'm sorry. I had a hand in that, and it wasn't how I wanted the game to play out. If I had the power, I'd help you, just to spite her. But... I got nothing left. Once you're gone, well, I won't be here much longer."

"I'm sorry," Ethriel said. "Is there anything you need? Anything we can do?"

"Can't fix this," Wraith said. "Though I appreciate the asking. Your folks, they take family duty seriously, don't they?"

Ethriel nodded. "We do. And if there was ought I could do to make up for her betrayal, I would. Except you can't have Roshara."

Wraith burst out laughing. "Like I could keep her now," he wheezed. "No, there ain't a damn thing you can do for me, little King. But you can do me a favor." He tipped his head back. "When you get to killing the bitch, right before you do the deed, you tell her that Jacob Wraith sends his regards. Will you do that for me?"

Ethriel nodded. "I will. And I wish you an easy passing to whatever awaits you."

Wraith smiled. "Thank you. And when you find John, you tell him I regret not getting to wrangle with him again. That was the most fun I'd had in years." He waved his hand, a dismissive gesture. "You get on now," he said, his voice growing quieter with every word. "You got a long way to go. Remember what I asked."

"I'll remember," Ethriel said. "Go gently, Jacob Wraith." He turned his horse, and rode back to the other elves.

When he looked over his shoulder, the porch was empty.

"YOU'RE VERY QUIET."

Ethriel looked to his right, to see that Parciviel had ridden up next to the wagon.

"Thinking," Ethriel said. "About Wraith. He caused so much grief to you and to Rose and Kestriel. And to John. But I'm feeling sorry for him. He's alone there, waiting to... well, I suppose he's waiting to die." He looked back over his shoulder. "Just wondering if I should have stayed so he wasn't alone at the end."

"He told you to go," Parciviel pointed out. "He didn't want you there."

"I didn't offer," Ethriel said. "I should have."

"You asked if there was anything you could do, Ethriel," Parciviel said. "If he'd wanted you there for the end, he could have asked it. Ethriel, I don't think there was anything more you could do."

"It still feels like I should have done more," Ethriel grumbled. "There's the ferry."

Garrett was standing on the bank, his eyes wide, as Ethriel drew the wagon to a stop and climbed down. "We need to cross, Mister Garrett."

Garrett blinked. "I know you. I remember you. You came through here..." He paused. "You looked different. You looked human. Didn't know you were an elf, then." He looked around. "Lots of elves, huh?" He looked back at Ethriel. "I saw your friend a month ago on the north bank. He said he'd be back this way, but I haven't seen him."

"Because he's been waylaid," Ethriel said. "And we're going after him. How much for us all to cross, Mister Garrett?"

Garrett turned slowly, clearly counting. Then he shook his head. "Lost count," he said. "How many horses, how many wagons, how many men?"

Ethriel turned and raised his voice, "Kestriel? Will you come and arrange things with Mister Garrett?"

Kestriel came around the wagon. "I'm here. And I heard the question. There are sixty of us. Eleven wagons —"

"Lot of trips, then," Garrett interrupted. "Right. This is going to take the rest of the day. Are you going to camp tonight on this side or on the far bank? That will decide what order you go in."

Kestriel looked at Ethriel, who nodded and answered, "The far bank makes sense. I'll defer to you in how we arrange things. Just tell me what the crossing will cost." He stepped back and let Kestriel and Garrett talk, walking around the wagon to where Parciviel was standing with Jeremiah and all four Ethriel's Boys.

"What's happening?" Jeremiah asked. "And have you seen Rose? I saw her horse, but not her."

"They're working out how and when we're going to cross, but we'll be camping for the night on the far side," Ethriel answered. "And I haven't seen Rose yet. I'll look for her once we're done here. Tell Lilith to stay a mare, will you?"

Jeremiah nodded. "We already discussed it. And she's looking, too."

"Ethriel," Kestriel called. "We're ready."

Ethriel turned. "That was faster than I thought."

"Mister Garrett and I are in agreement," Kestriel said. "We can manage in six trips, possibly seven — two wagons and their teams at a time to start, and then the rest of the men, with your wagon as the last wagon to cross. And once there are enough on the far bank, they'll start setting up camp."

Ethriel nodded. "Very good. And the cost?"

"Two hundred dollars," Kestriel answered slowly. "He won't go any lower."

Ethriel nodded. "Nor should he. This is going to be an onerous job. Tell him that if we need to help him, all he has to do is ask. I'll get the money." He turned toward the wagon, and saw Garrett standing near the front wheels.

"I heard you. And yeah, I will need to ask for volunteers. But... you came from the south," he said. "Tell me, did you pass near Wraithtown? I haven't seen JW in a long while."

Ethriel froze, then looked at Kestriel. "I... Mister Garrett, when did you see him last?"

Garrett shook his head. "Been two years now. Maybe more. He used to come out here once in a while. Visit a while, play cards. But not in a long time."

Ethriel nodded. "Mister Garrett, let me get your money. Then we'll talk."

Garrett held up his hand. "What's wrong? Just tell me."

"Wraithtown is gone," Ethriel answered, and watched Garrett turn pale. "They were attacked. I don't know when it happened. But almost everything was burned."

"Attacked?" Garrett repeated. "Burned? But—"

"We saw Jacob Wraith," Ethriel continued. "He says he's the only one left. And that he'll be gone soon, too." He looked back toward the south. "Garrett, if you were close to him at all, go. He told me to leave, told us to go on. But he's dying, and I think he'd want someone there."

Garrett nodded slowly. "I... yeah, I'll do that. But I have to get you all across first. So you go ahead and get the money, and lend me a brace of strong backs so we can get you moving."

"How many is a brace?" Avorn asked. "Because you have five—"

"Four," Fantiel corrected. "You're not up for it yet, Sir I-bloody-near-died-not-even-a-week-gone."

Jeremiah chuckled. "You stay with Ethriel, Avorn. Mister Garrett, how can we help you?" He led the others away. Avorn growled softly.

"So what do I do in the meantime?" he asked.

"Help Kestriel and Parciviel?" Ethriel suggested. "Kestriel needs to arrange who goes first and get them all in order. That's not a small job, but it's also not going to involve you overdoing things and making yourself sick."

Avorn nodded. "Sir Kestriel?" he called. "How can I help you?" He walked away, and Ethriel climbed into the back of the wagon. To his surprise, Roshara was inside, sitting with her back to the side, her knees drawn up, and her arms resting on them. Her head was buried in her arms.

"Rose?" Ethriel said in a low voice. "How long have you been in here? Are you all right?" He moved over to sit next to her. "What is it?"

"I hated him." Her voice was muffled in her arms. "I hated him and I was so afraid of him." She raised her head. "But it didn't start out like that. And now I can't stop thinking of him dying all alone. And how not even he deserves that."

Ethriel put his arm around her shoulders. "I know. I've been thinking the same thing. That I should have stayed so he wouldn't be alone."

Roshara leaned into his side, resting her head on his shoulder. "We went to Wraithtown when we came here. We thought we'd be safe there, because it wasn't a human place." She took a deep breath, reaching out to lace her fingers with Ethriel's. "He was kind to us when we arrived. Welcomed us. Everyone was so different, but it was nice. It was... it was nice there." She took a deep breath and shook her head. "He was so... charming, when we first got there.

And I was so young. I didn't realize what he wanted, never realized that he never did anything where Papa could see. I was his little Rosie for... I don't know. Seventy years? More? Then I came into my gifts. That night, Jacob came to us and said I was his. That I was going to live with him in his big house, and be his woman. I told him no, and he told me that if I didn't change my mind, if I didn't say yes, that my father would pay." She took a deep breath. "He set a guard on us... and I killed him. I didn't mean to. But it let us escape, and Tam helped us get out of Wraithtown and away. We went to New Orleans, and we stayed there until the war. Papa could tell that the war would come to New Orleans, and he didn't want any part of it. So we left, and we tried to keep ahead of the war and away from Wraith." She turned and looked at Ethriel. "I hate him... but he's dying and I just... Ethriel, I'm so confused."

Ethriel nodded. "I understand," he said.

"You understand?" She frowned. "Oh. Because of Buach?"

He nodded. "Because of Buach. Because I loved him once, and he betrayed me." He took a deep breath. "So I understand. And I don't know if you heard, but Mister Garrett will be going south once we're across. He'll be there when Wraith... dies. So he won't be alone." He hugged her to his side. "Now, do you want to be alone?"

She took another deep breath. "I... yes. For a little. And you have things you need to do." She smiled and leaned closer, kissing him. "Thank you."

He let her go and got up, unlocking his writing box and taking out the money. Then he left her in the wagon and went in search of Kestriel and Avorn.

"The first group is crossing," Avorn told him as he reached them. "Ethriel, once we're all across, how far is it to where we're going? How much longer?"

"A few days," Ethriel answered. "Depends on how far and fast we travel with the wagons. At the most, a week."

CHAPTER FOURTEEN
Discover

Five days after they crossed the Red River, Ethriel called the army to a stop. "We're close to where John was attacked," he said. "I want to see what's there. Sir Kestriel, you know the way to the portal from here, don't you?"

Kestriel nodded. "I know it. Been a while since I was last around here. But yes."

"Then take the army on and secure the area," Ethriel ordered. "We'll meet you there."

Kestriel frowned slightly. "Who are you taking with you?"

"Sir Parciviel, my Boys, and Jem and Lilith," Ethriel answered. "And we won't be there very long. I want to see if anything was left behind." He smiled. "We might even catch you before you get to the portal."

Kestriel smiled. "Perhaps. Be careful."

Ethriel nodded. He looked around, and saw Roshara on her horse. "Rose, will you take the wagon?"

"I'd rather come with you," she answered. "There might be something I can see there."

Ethriel glanced at Kestriel, who nodded. "She has a point. I'll get someone to drive the wagon."

"Thank you, Sir Kestriel," Ethriel said. He wound the reins around the brake and jumped down, walking around to where Cloud was tethered. The mare snorted at him, and he smiled. "We can have a run on the way to meet the others," he promised her, and reached into the back of the wagon for her tack.

They crossed Deadman's Slough, and separated at the shattered standing stones that had once anchored John's barriers. Ethriel led his group down the trail toward the dugout. He knew it was a pile of dirt now — what he'd heard from Roshara's vision had warned him of that. But the warning wasn't enough to protect him from actually seeing the shattered windows on the ground. He moaned softly.

"Easy, lad," Parciviel murmured.

"I... I knew," he stammered. "We knew what happened here. I knew it was gone. But..." He swallowed and drew Cloud to a stop, dismounting and walking over to the shattered glass. He crouched, picking up one of the pieces. "We didn't see what it looked like. I knew, but I wasn't ready to see it." He looked up to see that the others had dismounted.

"Where should we start looking?" Fantiel asked. "Or just spread out?"

Ethriel stood up and tossed the glass shard away, turning. "I think they were that way," he said, and pointed across the clearing. He started walking that way, hearing the others behind him. As they walked, he smelled something foul, a stench that grew stronger.

"Is that... what is that?" Avorn asked. "It's awful."

"Sir Parciviel?" Ethriel turned. "That's a body we're smelling, isn't it?

Parciviel nodded slowly. "Go slowly," he said. "The wind is coming from that direction." He started forward, taking the lead, and Ethriel turned to the others

"Spread out," he said. "Fan, you and Avi check the ruins of the barn. Mar, you and Glee go that way. There's a swimming hole. See what you can see." He looked at Roshara and Jeremiah. "Will you come with me, or go with one of them?"

"I'm with you," she said. "The smell is coming from the same direction that we were going."

Jeremiah nodded. "Lily's staying with the horses. She really doesn't like that smell. So I'm with you."

Ethriel nodded, and they started walking again. Something caught his eye, and he stooped and picked up a spent cartridge shell. He looked up. "This is where it happened," he said. "This is from the Henry, and it can't be from when we were here five years ago. It's too new." He stood up and looked around. "There's another one." He walked toward it, and saw the crossbow quarrel embedded in the ground.

"Ethriel," Parciviel called. "You want to see this."

Ethriel turned, seeing Parciviel standing with his back to them. He walked closer, and noticed the smell was getting stronger. He realized what it had to be, and stopped.

"It's Barak, isn't it?" he asked.

"I think so," Parciviel said. "Not much left of him. John must have been trying to get away from them. I can't tell what killed Barak, poor beast."

"Rose, you and Jem wait here." Ethriel walked closer, and saw what remained of the body on the ground, the familiar tack. He swallowed and looked away... and saw metal at the base of a large rock outcropping nearby. "Danu's tits," he breathed.

"Ethriel!" Parciviel gasped. He sounded so shocked that Ethriel laughed.

"You say it!" he protested. He walked over to the rocks, and picked up the Henry.

Parciviel looked at it, and blurted, "Danu's tits!"

Ethriel stared at him for a moment, and they both burst out laughing. Ethriel looked down at the rifle in his hands, then went back to the rocks and looked around. "There's nothing else here, I don't think."

"Does it work?" Ethriel turned to see Avorn and Fantiel had come toward them. Avorn cocked his head to the side. "There's nothing at the barn but burned timbers. That... does it work?"

"The rifle?" Ethriel looked down at it, then ran the lever and ejected the cartridges one by one. He picked them up and reloaded the gun. "We'll find out if it still works once everyone is in one place." He looked back at Barak's body. "Jem? Would you—"

"Of course," Jeremiah said. He pointed, and the body burst into flames. "It'll burn itself out," he said. "And it won't burn anything but the body and the tack." He looked around. "Let's go."

"I want to test this first," Ethriel said. He whistled, and heard an answering whistle. Then another. A moment later, Amartin and Glethin were trotting toward them. Amartin coughed when he saw what Ethriel was holding.

"Is that John's?" he asked.

"Yes, and I need to see if it will still fire," Ethriel said. "Come stand behind me. Cover your ears. It will be loud." He waited until everyone was out of range, then raised the rifle, ran the lever, and squeezed the trigger. The Henry roared, and he saw the bark fly off a distant tree.

"You're right. That was loud," Amartin said as he lowered his hands.

"Loud enough that Kestriel probably heard it," Ethriel said. He looked around. "There's nothing else for us here. Let's go."

ETHRIEL HAD TO BALANCE the rifle across his knees as they rode toward the portal. "I'm going to need a holster on my saddle like the one John had on his," he called to Parciviel.

Parciviel nodded. "We'll see if anyone has one."

"Unlikely," Jeremiah called as he rode up on Ethriel's left. "That's the only firearm in the whole army." He grinned. "Which might be to our advantage. Do we have enough ammunition? Lily and I can ride into town for more. Maybe even find a holster?"

"You just want to see your old friends," Ethriel teased, and Jeremiah grinned.

"Well, seeing Widow Connor might be nice," he admitted.

Ethriel laughed. "No, we don't need anything," he said. "That metal box in the wagon? Is full of ammunition. It's always full of ammunition. Didn't you know that? You met Joshua."

"Only briefly, but I don't think I knew about the box. What did he do?"

Ethriel shook his head. "John said something about loaves and fishes, but I didn't make any sense of it."

"How is it possible that the box never empties?" Roshara asked. She guided her gelding up on Ethriel's other side.

"Both of you back up just a bit, will you?" Ethriel warned. "John warned me that this gun has one flaw — it goes off if it gets jostled. I should have unloaded it." He waited until Jeremiah and Roshara were both out of range. "And the box... John's powerful friend? Isn't a mage. He's a god."

"You have a god on your side?" Avorn gasped. "Really? And... oh, is that who you wanted to save my life? That same powerful friend?"

Ethriel nodded. "That's who saved me. And I never really understood how a Choctaw holy man managed to get a god of an entire other religion to come help. Hopaii explained to John, and John tried to explain to me, but... well, it didn't make much sense. I tried reading their holy book, but that didn't make much sense either. And John isn't in it as much as I thought he'd be."

"Why would your John be in the holy book?" Avorn asked.

Ethriel twisted in his saddle to better see Avorn, keeping one hand on the Henry so it didn't fall. "John was Joshua's lover, a long time ago when Joshua walked the world. That's why John is immortal now. When the human god tells you that you're not going to die, you don't."

"Joshua is one of the human gods," Jeremiah corrected. "There are... well... not all of us are Christian. And working with mages... you come to realize that there isn't just one real religion. There are a lot." He looked, then frowned, raising one hand. "Rider incoming."

Ethriel felt his skin tingle, and realized that Jeremiah had put a tight shield on him. He turned and saw the single rider coming toward them. "One of ours?" he asked. "Can you see?" He frowned. "That's a big horse. That's Fioriel, isn't it?"

The big smith drew closer, and slowed his horse to a walk as he reached them. "Told Kestriel I'd come out looking. We heard a gunshot."

Ethriel groaned. "Sorry. That was me," he said. "I needed to see if John's rifle would fire."

Fioriel looked at the weapon Ethriel carried. "If I might, I'd like to take a closer look at that," he said. "Never seen one close up."

"While we wait for the portal," Ethriel said. "I need to clean it, so you can watch while I do it. Are the others at the mounds?"

"Yes, Sire, and it's the strangest thing." Fioriel urged his horse to a walk, falling in next to Ethriel. Jeremiah gave way, riding behind them. "There's not a sign of anyone there. No guards, no sentries. And the portal is partly blocked. Looks like they tried to seal it behind them when they went through."

Ethriel nodded. "We'll have to tread carefully. She has to know I'm coming."

"Kestriel is already assembling a scouting team to go through and secure the portal on the other side," Fioriel said. "As soon as the moon rises." He looked up. "We've got a wait. It won't be dark for a few hours."

"So we'll wait," Ethriel said. "And we're not going to town, Jem."

"I wasn't going to ask again!" Jeremiah protested. When Ethriel looked at him, he grinned. "Not much, anyway."

THE HOURS SEEMED TO crawl. Ethriel disassembled the Henry while Fioriel and the Boys watched, cleaned the rifle meticulously, then reassembled it and reloaded it with ammunition from the box. He laid it underneath the seat of the wagon, then looked around. The camp was orderly, and men and women — his army — busied themselves with caring for their horses, cleaning or repacking their belongings, and cooking.

"Are we shielded?" he asked.

"For sight and sound," Avorn answered. "Jem took care of it when we got here and shielded the entire camp."

"Can he do that?" Ethriel turned. "Is anyone helping him?"

"He refused when we offered," Avorn said. "Says we'll all need to be ready when we go through the portal."

"And he won't?" Fantiel came up behind his lover and put his arms around him.

"He says he'll be fine," Avorn answered. "I'm not arguing with a human who could turn me into a bug if he put his mind to it."

"Jem wouldn't do that!" Ethriel protested.

"That you know of," Fantiel answered. He tugged on Avorn's belt. "Come walk with me, Ori."

Avorn turned to look over his shoulder. "Just walk?"

"Well—"

"Go on, the both of you." Ethriel shooed them off, smiling as they walked away, no doubt to find a convenient hiding place. He leaned against the wagon and wondered how many other pairs were doing the same.

He heard footsteps, and Roshara came around the wagon. She smiled at him. "Alone?"

"Avi and Fan just went off together," Ethriel answered. He held his hand out, and Roshara came closer, ignoring his hand to press against his side. He chuckled and hugged her to him. "Rose?"

"Hm?"

"What do you want me to call you?" Ethriel turned to face her. "What will your pillow name be?"

"Excuse me?"

"Well, the Boys have been teaching me the things I should have learned from my father."

Her brows rose. "What sort of things?"

"It started with pillow names," Ethriel admitted. "When I told them to call me Ethan, and told them that only John calls me that. They refused and we realized that I never had what they call the talk. So they explained. Said it was my pillow name, and it wasn't right for them to call me that." He grinned. "They still haven't decided on a diminutive for me."

"Not Ethi," she said.

"No," Ethriel agreed. "Not Ethi. I...I should tell you why I don't want to use Ethi anymore." He shook his head. "Later. But I know that Ethan is my pillow name. What do you want me to call you?"

She smiled and moved closer, sliding her arms around his waist, and setting his blood sizzling in his veins. "We haven't shared a pillow yet," she murmured. "You don't get to call me a pillow name until we do."

Ethriel swallowed, wondering where his words had all run off to hide. "You can call me Ethan," he blurted, and she giggled.

"I've stolen your wits," she teased, and kissed him. "That's very flattering. Ethriel, when we finally share a pillow, you can choose my pillow name. But not before. And I won't be calling you Ethan until then." She looked up at him. "Why don't you want to be called Ethi?"

All his ardor vanished like morning mist. He swallowed and closed his eyes. "I... you left court. When you were gone, I... well, I was lonely. You'd always been there. I didn't have anyone else in court my own age. So... I started sharing my time with Buach.

And eventually, I was sharing a pillow with him." He opened his eyes to see Roshara staring at him. "It was entirely of my own will, Rose. I was lonely. And I liked him. Then we had... I don't even remember. But my mother and I left court for a time to go visit the borderlands. When we came back, Buach had another lover. I thought we were done, so I didn't pursue him."

"He was trying to make you jealous, wasn't he?"

"I don't know," Ethriel said. "But I thought he was happier with her, so I let him be happy. Then... then the Palace fell, and Buach claimed me. Said I was his. That I'd always been his. That he expected me back in his bed. And... when I refused...he hurt me..." His voice failed completely, and he rubbed one hand over his face. "He called me Ethi when he was hurting me, Rose."

"Mother Danu," Roshara breathed. "Ethriel, I didn't know!" She hugged him tightly, and he put his arms around her, burying his face in her hair. The feel of her in his arms, the scent of her in his nose, it helped.

"John knows, a little," Ethriel whispered. "I've told him some of it. As much as I can without screaming. It's time you knew, too."

She nodded, her hair tickling his nose and making him want to sneeze. Then she looked up at him again, held his eyes, and ran her hand up to tangle her fingers in his hair, bringing his mouth down to hers. He tightened his arms around her, turning them both so that his back was against the wagon. It wasn't more than five steps to get them both inside the wagon, and his bedroll was there...

"Ethriel!" Glethin came around the back of the wagon, and Ethriel and Roshara both turned to face him. His eyes widened when he saw them. Then his face turned bright red. "I... oh. Uh... I apologize?" I...oh, my... I..." He shifted from one foot to the other. "I... it's not important. I... I don't even remember what it was now." He bit his lip, then stepped back. "So... ah... you just go back to who... what! What you were doing... I... umm..." He snorted. "Excuse me, I'm going to go and drown myself in the river."

He vanished behind the wagon. Ethriel heard a muffled giggle next to him, and looked back at Roshara. There was no hiding the mirth in those blue eyes, nor how infectious it was; the giggles went on until they were both leaning against the wagon, panting for breath.

"Oh... oh..." she gasped. "Oh, poor Glee."

"I should go find him," Ethriel wheezed. He wiped tears from his face and straightened.

"You should. Make sure he doesn't actually throw himself in the river." Roshara shook her head and straightened her coat. "And make sure—"

"Make sure that we both remember that we decided to wait?" Ethriel finished. She smiled.

"Yes. But mostly make sure that Glee doesn't go and kill all the fish. I'm not sure when he bathed last."

Ethriel started laughing again, but managed to stop before he fell over once more. He stepped closer to Roshara, close enough that he could feel her warmth, and cupped her face in his hands. This kiss was less lust and more promise, and left her smiling.

"Go on," she said as he let her go. "Go find him."

CHAPTER FIFTEEN
Crossing

When the moon rose, Ethriel sent the scouting party that Sir Kestriel had ordered through the portal to see what awaited them. Then he waited, pacing in front of the portal and glaring at it every so often.

"You're going to exhaust yourself," Parciviel said. "They'll be back when they're back."

"And if it comes on midnight, and they're not back? Then they probably won't be back." Kestriel added.

"That is neither helpful nor inspiring, Sir Kestriel," Ethriel said. "I don't like the idea that I may have just sent my people to their deaths."

"Sire," an older woman called as she came jogging toward him. "There are riders approaching."

Ethriel blinked. "Riders. From what direction?"

"The way we came," she answered. "A small party. Looks like six people. Five men and a woman, and wearing the clothes of the native people."

"Oh." Ethriel nodded. "If you would find Jeremiah? Tell him that I think we're getting a visit from the current Hopaii."

The woman bowed and hurried off, and Ethriel turned to Parciviel and Kestriel, "Shall we? I'm curious why they came all this way. They could have intercepted us hours ago."

"You think it's Talula?" Parciviel asked, falling in on Ethriel's left. "I hope she has a good explanation as to why she broke my grandson's heart."

Ethriel looked at him. "I honestly don't think she did. I think she set him free. Or haven't you noticed how happy he is with Lily?"

Parciviel sighed. "I have noticed. And I do like Lilith." He paused. "There are Jem and Lily."

Ethriel nodded — he'd already seen Jeremiah and Lilith coming toward him.

"Ethriel, are you sure?" he called. "They shouldn't be on this side of the river. Not this late."

"I'm not sure it's her, and what do you mean?" Ethriel asked. "Will they get into trouble?"

"I don't know," Jeremiah answered. "It wasn't illegal when we left, but it wasn't safe either. When we left, there were starting to be more people in Skullyville who didn't like the Choctaw, and who thought that the only good Indian was a dead one." He looked out into the darkness. "She shouldn't be here."

They walked to the edge of the camp, and watched as the riders came closer. In the moonlight, Ethriel couldn't see them clearly until they stopped. A young woman dismounted and walked towards them.

"Hello, Talula," Jeremiah said. "You look good. But should you be here?"

She smiled. "Hello, Jem. It's good to see you. I have missed you since you left." She looked over her shoulder and gestured, and a young man dismounted and came to join her. "The people in Skullyville won't know that we were here. The same way that they won't know you were here. But I wanted to see you before you left this world." She turned to Ethriel and nodded her head. "I wish you luck, King Ethriel. I remember you."

"I remember you, too. But you were much smaller when I saw you last," Ethriel said, and she laughed.

"Talula, your father refused to come back with us," Jeremiah said. "He was well when we left. And... do you know what happened to John?"

"Not entirely," Talula answered. "I knew the Hattak Falaya was here, but he was here and gone so quickly there was nothing we could do to help him." She shook her head. "We couldn't reach him in time. I am sorry for that."

"Thank you for trying," Ethriel said. "Now, you came all this way, and put yourself at risk. What can we do for you?"

Talula smiled slightly. "There is nothing that we need from you. And not much that we can do to help you. I came because I knew my dear Jeremiah was here, and I wanted to see him one last time. To explain."

Jeremiah shook his head. "Talula, you don't have to explain anything. We were children, and that agreement was between our parents. Not us. I can't imagine it was long after I was gone that you realized what we had wasn't love. It was habit."

She blinked. "Yes. That's exactly what I realized. And what you realized, too?" She let out a breath. "I am... relieved," she said. "When I met Nashoba, I worried what you might think. That you might think I had betrayed you."

Jeremiah looked at the man standing next to Talula. "And this is Nashoba?"

Talula looked up at him, and the answer was clear in her face. "This is my Nashoba."

Jeremiah stepped forward and held his hand out. He said something in Choctaw, and Nashoba looked startled. Then he smiled, and took Jeremiah's hand. Jeremiah looked at Ethriel, said "Excuse us," and led Nashoba away.

"While Jem is busy," Ethriel said. "Talula, may I introduce Lilith?"

Talula turned to face Lilith, and her eyes widened. "You are not people," she said slowly. "Nor are you any spirit I know. What are you?"

Lilith giggled. "I'm a kelpie. My people are from across the sea."

"And are you and Jeremiah—?" Talula looked over at where Jeremiah and Nashoba were talking. "I should not be asking this."

"You and he were close long before I met him," Lilith said. "You may ask me anything you wish." She held her hand out. Talula took it, and a moment later they were off to one side, talking. Ethriel stepped back and turned to walk back to the portal, only to see Avorn running toward him.

"Sire!" Avorn shouted. "The scouts are back! The portal is ours."

Ethriel nodded. "Thank you, Avi. Spread the word. Strike the camp and be ready to move." He turned and shouted, "Jem! It's time!"

Goodbyes were said quickly, and Talula and her escort rode back the way they'd come. Jeremiah was quiet as he helped Ethriel reload his wagon and harness Damask.

"Is she well?" Ethriel asked. "Is she happy?"

Jeremiah nodded. "Both." He looked at Ethriel across Damask's back. "And she's pregnant. I told her I was happy for her. For them. And I am, truly." He frowned. "I need to send a bird to Terensiel. She can tell Hopaii that he'll be a grandfather. Talula said that she didn't know when he left them."

"I'll finish this," Ethriel said. "Go and send the bird."

Jeremiah smiled and walked away, and Ethriel saw Lilith join him before turning his attention back to the harness. He called a light so that he could check his work, then ran his fingers through Damask's mane.

"Are you ready?"

Ethriel turned to see Avorn. "I'm ready," he said. "Everything packed away. Cloud is tethered to the wagon. Damask is in harness. And I'm terrified. So yes, I think everything is in order."

Avorn chuckled. "You're terrified. I'm terrified. Fan's already puked behind a bush. Twice."

"Oh—"

"Fioriel says it's nothing," Avorn hurried to add. "That some people take like that before a battle. Which...we're going into battle, aren't we?"

"Not yet, but possible soon," Ethriel answered. "We hold the portal, but once we leave it, we'll be facing Siobhan's forces."

"There are still rebels in the Twin Mountains, Sir Parciviel says."

Ethriel climbed up into the driver's seat. "So he's told me. And our first task once we're through is to find them and to convince them to follow me. We won't be marching on the Palace until we triple our numbers. At least. Ride with me?"

Avorn shook his head. "Fan is waiting with our horses. I'll ride alongside." He looked around. "Let's go. I think you're coming through halfway through the crossing?"

"That's the plan," Ethriel confirmed. He reached down and picked up the reins. "Go mount up and take your place in the line. And I'll see you on the other side."

Avorn stepped back and saluted, then turned and headed off. Ethriel snapped the reins and drove the wagon toward the portal.

PASSING THROUGH THE portal was like passing through a curtain of ice-cold water. It washed over Ethriel, chilling him to the bone for the space of a breath. Then it was gone, and he was in his own lands for the first time in five human years. Five human years were barely a heartbeat to his own kind, but he hadn't realized how much he'd missed it, not until the scent of the air was in his nose once more.

"This way, Sire," Kestriel called. "Come over here, and we'll wait for the rest of them."

Ethriel guided the wagon to where Kestriel indicated, tied off the brake, and jumped down. He walked back to check on Cloud, reaching into his coat pocket for the bag of dried apple pieces that

John always kept on hand for the horses. He fed a few pieces to Cloud and told her she was wonderful, then went back to Damask and did the same.

"We're going to need to make camp," he said as Kestriel came over to him. "And make plans. We can't camp here. It's too open."

Kestriel nodded. "I was going to ask if you wanted to send out scouts to find a good place to stop for the night."

"Yes," Ethriel answered. "Do that." He looked around. "I'm surprised this area isn't under heavy guard. Or was it?"

"There were no guards, the scouts said," Kestriel answered. "Which strikes me as odd. I'd like to get us away from here as soon as possible. If it's not being held by Siobhan's people, there's a reason." He bowed to Ethriel. "I'll go and arrange things, Sire. And it looks like the next wave is coming through. That would be Rose's group."

Ethriel nodded, and Kestriel hurried away. Ethriel moved back to lean against the wagon, closing his eyes. He wanted to sleep, but he couldn't do that until they were in a safe camp. Not until his people were settled someplace away from the portal. He heard raised voices and straightened, opening his eyes. As he turned, something crackled behind him, and he saw the man rushing toward him a heartbeat before he was bowled over. Training took over — he shielded and lashed out at the attacker, hearing a cry of pain as he rolled up onto his knees and got to his feet. He heard Kestriel shout his name, but didn't turn to look; he scrambled up into the driver's seat and grabbed the Henry. As he ran the lever, he looked at the man who'd attacked him, at his gaunt face and ragged clothes. He had gotten back to his feet, and was staring up at Ethriel like he'd seen something extraordinary.

Ethriel raised the Henry and fired into the air, hearing the shot echoing and reechoing off the rocks. Everyone went still, and he raised his voice and shouted, amplifying his voice with power, "Enough!"

His voice echoed off the rocks just as the gunshot had, and as the echoes died away, there was silence. Ethriel heard someone's harsh voice break the stillness, "It's him."

"It can't be!"

"It is! Look at him! That's Cathail's son, and no mistake!"

"The Shining King!"

Ethriel looked, trying to see who'd said that. There were more ragged people coming closer, men and women both, some of them younger than he was. He could see them all clearly, and realized that his shields were glowing again, bright enough that he'd have been able to read by the light. He bit down on a laugh — the Shining King, indeed!

"I am Ethriel, son of the High Queen Méabh and her consort Cathail," he said. "And I've come back to claim what's mine."

The man who had attacked him stepped forward, then sank to his knees. "My King," he said. "My King, I'm sorry. I didn't know."

"There's no way you could have known," Ethriel said. He smiled. "Now, if I come down, are you going to hit me again?"

"No!" The man bent forward, his forehead hitting the ground. "My King, we've been waiting, hoping that the rumors that you were dead with your parents were false. We've kept true to you and the hopes of your return." He looked up. "Do you know me, Sire?"

Ethriel frowned, looking at the kneeling man. His voice was familiar, and there was something— "Mathiri?" he blurted, realizing who the man actually was. "Master Mathiri?" He put the Henry down and jumped down to the ground. "Stand up!"

"You do remember me!" Mathiri got to his feet. "It's been so long—"

"Not so long that I wouldn't remember my favorite teacher!" Ethriel protested with a laugh. He walked over to the man, hugged him, then stepped back and shook his head. "You used to be ten feet tall," he added.

"Well, I seem to remember you being small for your age," Mathiri answered. "Oh, Ethi—"

"I don't use the diminutive anymore," Ethriel said. "And I haven't decided on a new one. Please—"

"Of course," Mathiri said. He looked confused, but Ethriel wasn't going to explain. "Now, we hold this land, and the bitch who calls herself queen doesn't try us often. But it's still not safe to stay here. We've a safe camp, and not far."

Ethriel nodded and looked around. "Sir Kestriel!"

"I'm here," Kestriel called. "You handled that very well, Sire." He came closer, sheathing his sword. "Mathi, it's been a long time."

"Kes." Mathiri held his hand out, and Kestriel pulled him into a tight, quick embrace. "I'd wondered what happened to you. The last I remember was your wife taking ill and you leaving court."

Kestriel nodded. "I took Ambari home, and she died in peace. We had just finished the year of mourning when we got word of the attack. I took my daughter and ran, and we ended up in the human world." He turned to Ethriel. "Her group just came through the portal. I was about to send her back through—"

"And I was telling you I wasn't going," Roshara added, hurrying to Ethriel's side. She threw her arms around him. "Are you all right?"

"I'm fine," Ethriel answered, holding her close. "I'm sorry that I frightened you."

"This can't possibly be little Rose!" Mathiri gasped. Roshara turned in Ethriel's arms.

"Master Mathiri?" Roshara ran to him and hugged him. "Oh, it's so good to see you! What are you doing here?"

"Unfortunately, knocking my king on his arse," Mathiri admitted. "Who taught you to fight, Ethriel?"

"My first consort," Ethriel answered, and watched Mathiri's face as understanding bloomed.

"The Undying One?" Mathiri asked.

"His name is John, and Siobhan kidnapped him a month ago. They came through this portal." Ethriel licked his lips. "Tell me you stopped them? Tell me that he's with you?"

Mathiri shook his head. "Yes, we saw them. Saw they had a captive. But we couldn't stop them. We tried. Lost quite a few good people, but they were determined to keep their prize. Now I know why." He shook his head, then looked around. "This place won't be safe for much longer. Let me take you to our camp."

Ethriel looked at Kestriel, who nodded. "Leave us with guides," he said. "We've still got three more groups to come through."

Mathiri turned and started barking orders, and six of his followers went to Kestriel and saluted. The rest disappeared back into the trees.

"Where are they going?" Ethriel asked.

"To make sure the way is clear," Mathiri answered. "My King, if you'll come with me?"

"Ride with me, Mathiri," Ethriel offered. "Tell me what you know. Rose, will you come with us? You can ride in the bed."

"About?" Mathiri asked as he climbed up into the wagon.

Ethriel helped Roshara into the back of the wagon, then climbed into the seat next to Mathiri and picked up the reins. As he snapped them, he answered, "About everything."

"WE'VE HAD A HARD TIME of it. But we've adapted. We've struck back. There hasn't been a moment's peace in nearly half a year," Mathiri said, pointing out the trail. "That way. We're almost there."

"And are there enough of you to stand with the force I've brought?" Ethriel asked. "I knew I'd need to spend time raising more of an army. Kestriel told me there were rebels in the mountains here. Are there enough who will follow me?"

Mathiri took a deep breath. "Perhaps. If we bring together the other bands that are in the Twin Mountains? Perhaps. And there will be more, people in the lowlands who wait and hope and suffer. When you make yourself known, they will rise. You'll have your army. They might not be trained, but you'll have it."

Ethriel nodded, taking a deep breath. "Rose, there's a waterskin back there. May I—?"

"Here." She passed it forward, and Ethriel shot a stream of water into his mouth, and more over his face. He shook his head, then passed the waterskin back.

"Ethriel?" Mathiri said. "Are you all right?"

"I'm tired," Ethriel admitted. "But I need to wait for my people to be safe before I can rest. How much further?"

"Ethriel, I can drive," Roshara said. "You can nap—"

Ethriel shook his head. "No, Rose. Thank you. Not until we're settled." He turned to Mathiri. "How much further?

"Not far," Mathiri answered. "There are standing stones around the next bend. Pass between them."

Ethriel nodded. As he drove between the stones, he felt the cold-water sensation of passing through a portal. On the far side, he looked back over his shoulder. "A portal? Where did it take us? Where are we?" He turned back to Mathiri. "And who created that?"

"The portal took us from the Twin Mountains to the far side of the Black Canyon," Mathiri answered. "And if the portal maps were still in the archives, you'd find this one listed among them." He smiled. "A shame that all the portal maps vanished, though.

I'm told that Siobhan was quite upset by the loss. Odd how it happened, really."

Roshara giggled. "You stole them, didn't you?"

"My apprentice did, the scamp." Mathiri chuckled. "Ethriel, I wish we'd been able to do more for you. If I'd had any idea who that prisoner was, we'd have—"

"I doubt there was any more you could have done," Ethriel said. "You already said you took casualties. How many more lives would you have thrown away?"

Mathiri looked at him. "You're very cavalier about his life."

"He's the Undying One," Ethriel pointed out. "She can't kill him. She can hurt him, but she can't kill him." He swallowed and looked forward. "It gives me time I wouldn't otherwise have. But I have to do this right the first time. Because he can't die, but I can. So I won't get a second chance to get to him. I'm just hoping he forgives me that I'm having to make that choice."

CHAPTER SIXTEEN
Negotiation

Ethriel fell asleep on his feet twice waiting for the last group of people from Lightning Tree.

"You should go to bed," Roshara murmured after nudging him awake again.

"Not until everyone is here," Ethriel said. "They'll be here soon." He straightened and took a deep breath. "Listen. It sounds like they're here." He walked toward the sound of the commotion and saw Jeremiah dismounting. Behind him was Sir Parciviel, who looked about as tired as Ethriel felt.

"I am getting too old for this," he declared as he dismounted. "Once this is over, and you're on the throne, I'm retiring."

"Oh, to be sure," Ethriel scoffed. "Pull the other one, while you're at it. Retired and just be a grandfather by the fire? You?"

"My King, is this the last group?"

Ethriel turned to see Mathiri coming toward them. "It's the last group. Master Mathiri, I want you to meet my Head Mage, Jeremiah Miller. And—"

"Parciviel." The chill in Mathiri's voice threatened frostbite. "I'm amazed you have the gall to show your face."

Parciviel went still. "I am atoning, Mathiri."

"There's no way under Danu's sky you can atone for what you did," Mathiri snapped. "And now you've attached yourself to the King's company?" He looked at Ethriel. "Do you even know what he's done?"

"Mathiri—"

"No," Mathiri silenced Parciviel with a sharp wave of one hand. "No, you don't get to talk yourself out of this. My King, do you know what this man has done?"

Ethriel looked at Parciviel, who went pale. "No," he said. "But I will hear it from him. You've told me you were atoning, Sir Parciviel. But you've never told me why."

Parciviel closed his eyes. Then he nodded. "I told John. I asked him not to tell you. I told him... well, I told him that you didn't need to know." He took a deep breath. "I was the Guard Captain on duty the night of the attacks. It's my fault. Everything. All of this. It's my fault." He raised his head and looked at Ethriel. "I was drunk on duty, my King."

"You... you were *what*?" Ethriel stammered. "No. Parciviel..." He looked at Roshara, then turned. "Kestriel!"

"My King?"

"Did you know this?" Ethriel asked. "Did you know that Parciviel was drunk on duty the night of the attacks? I know you weren't there, but did you know any of this?"

Kestriel shook his head. "I didn't know anything for certain. But I suspected. Parciviel's love of the bottle wasn't a secret from anyone except perhaps your parents. I can't imagine he'd have kept his post if your father knew."

Ethriel nodded, closing his eyes. Trying to think through his exhausted haze. He shook his head. "I trusted you," he said softly. "You've been... you've been everything to me since I escaped. You helped save me. You taught me what I needed to know to survive, and you've been the closest I will ever come to having a father again. Why didn't you tell me?"

"I was ashamed," Parciviel answered. "Especially after..."

"After what happened on the way to Bandera," Ethriel finished. "Where you were drunk on duty again."

"On the way back from Wraithtown, I told John. And I told him to tell you I'd died," Parciviel said. "I was that ashamed of myself. Of my weakness. We were out of Wraithtown, out of danger, I thought. I told him I was going back. I didn't care what

Wraith would have done with me. I would have let you think I'd died, so that I didn't ever have to tell you the truth." He snorted. "John knocked me out and threw me into the back of the wagon. Tied me up so I wouldn't run off. He would not let me take the coward's way out."

"And yet you never told me." Ethriel said. "That's still the coward's way. You think you've been atoning, but you've never once admitted to me what you did, or asked my forgiveness." He closed his eyes again. "I'm tired. So we're not doing this now. Mathiri, find someplace for him to sleep. We'll talk more in the morning."

"Sire?"

"In the morning, Mathiri," Ethriel repeated. He turned and looked at Parciviel. "You are not to take the coward's way again, Parciviel. I expect you to be here in the morning."

Parciviel smiled slightly. "Am I that obvious?"

"Granddad!" Jeremiah gasped. "You were not going to run off!"

"I was seriously considering it," Parciviel answered. He saluted. "My King, I serve."

Ethriel nodded in acknowledgment and turned to Roshara. "My lady?" he said, and offered his hand. She looked puzzled, but took it, and he turned to Mathiri. "If you'll show everyone to where they'll be camping? I'll introduce you properly to Jeremiah in the morning."

Mathiri bowed. "Of course, my King," he said. "Go get some sleep."

Ethriel turned and led Roshara off to the wagon.

"There's a bed for you," Roshara murmured. "Mathiri was insistent you take his."

"And I was insistent right back that I wasn't putting him out of his own bed. My bedroll in the wagon is fine," Ethriel replied. He stopped and turned to her. "Stay with me?" he asked. "I don't want to be alone right now."

She nodded. "Of course."

THE LIGHT FILTERING through the canvas cover of the wagon was enough to wake Ethriel, but he didn't move. He couldn't move — Roshara was still asleep, curled up next to him with her head on his shoulder. He turned his head to breathe in the scent of her hair, closing his eyes again. The idea of going back to sleep was tempting, but he needed to get up. He needed to plan.

He needed to decide what to do about Parciviel.

Someone scratched at the canvas, and Ethriel raised his head to see Avorn looking in at him.

"We heard," Avorn whispered. "Jeremiah told us this morning. What do you need?" He smiled. "Other than for me to leave?"

Ethriel smiled, waving his hand, and Avorn laughed and moved away from the wagon. Ethriel smiled and ran his fingers over Roshara's cheek, down the length of her neck.

"Rose?" he whispered. "Time to wake up."

"No, it isn't," she answered. "You need to rest."

"How long have you been awake?" Ethriel laughed. "My Ara."

She raised her head. "Ara?"

"We shared a pillow—"

"You were the pillow," she corrected. "Ara." She smiled. "I like it." She stretched up and kissed him. "My Ethan. We need to get John back. We're not complete without him."

Ethriel nodded. "Then you have to let me up. I need to start planning." She shifted, and he sat up. "What do I do about Parciviel?"

"I don't know," Roshara answered. "I'm not sure what would be appropriate. You may want to talk to my father."

"Maybe." Ethriel nodded. "I know that I don't want to talk to Mathiri. Not about this. He's too angry."

"And you're not angry?"

Ethriel shook his head. "I'm more hurt than angry. But I don't have time to dwell on it. I have to do something and keep moving." He shook his head, raked his fingers through his hair, and grimaced. "Think they have a bathhouse here?"

"I'll find out while you do what you need to do."

Ethriel leaned over and kissed her again, then got up and climbed out of the wagon. Avorn was waiting nearby, and came over to join him.

"This is a big place," he said. "Bigger than Lightning Tree by a good bit. We're going to have a big army."

Ethriel nodded. "Show me around. And we can talk."

They walked around the encampment, picking up the rest of the Boys as they went. They all knew, just as Avorn had said.

"I'm not sure what to do with him," Ethriel said.

"I know what to do with you," Fantiel said. "You haven't eaten. Let's get you some food, and we'll find an answer." He pointed. "That's the communal kitchen. Then... I might have an idea." He led the way to the kitchen, and Ethriel felt everyone staring at him as he picked up a bowl of porridge and another of stewed fruit. He carried it to a table in the corner, where he stirred the latter into the former.

"I could wish for coffee," he murmured as he swallowed his first bite. "Now, what's this idea, Fan?" He looked around. "In English. I don't want this to be the talk of the camp."

Fantiel took a seat and folded his hands on the tabletop. "He's disgraced himself," he said in English. "He's not fit to wear the Silver Thorn anymore. Strip him of his rank and his titles."

"I'm not even sure he has titles, but stripping him of his knighthood?" Ethriel considered. "That's a start. What else?"

"Isn't that enough?" Avorn asked. "He's a Knight-Commander. That's a huge part of who he is and has been for... more years than any of us have been alive, I think. Stripping him of that will be like stripping him naked in the middle of Lightning Tree. And he has served you well the past five years."

Ethriel nodded. "He has. Except for not telling me the truth. All right. Let me finish, and we'll go find him. And we'll get started on our plans."

On the way out of the kitchen, Jeremiah and Lilith found them. "There you are! Rose said she wasn't sure where you'd gone."

"I needed to eat," Ethriel said. "And now I need to deal with your grandfather."

"You're not going to kill him, are you?" Jeremiah asked in a low voice.

"Of course not!" Ethriel stared at his friend. "That never even occurred to me! How could I? What I said last night was true. He's like a second father to me!"

Jeremiah nodded. "Which is what I told him. But he's convinced you're going to order him executed for regicide."

"Could he be any more melodramatic?" Glethin muttered, just loud enough for them all to hear. Jeremiah grinned.

"I don't think so, since he's already told me what he wants done for his funeral. No... wait. He hasn't composed a funeral dirge yet. So maybe. Can we go put him out of his misery? Or us out of our misery before he decides to sing?"

Mathiri met them at the wagon. "My King," he said. "I've had the hall prepared, and Sir Kestriel has brought Parciviel there."

"There's a hall?" Ethriel looked around. "I haven't seen a hall. Did I miss it?"

"It's not actually a hall," Mathiri admitted. "It's a large field that we use for gatherings. It's this way."

The field was full of people, all of whom turned to stare as Ethriel passed through them to what Mathiri indicated was the front of the hall. There was no dais, nothing to raise him up high enough to see over heads, and he wondered how he was going to be heard over the chattering voices. Then Mathiri raised his own voice.

"Attend to your King!"

The chatter fell silent, until all Ethriel could hear was the wind and the muffled sound of a child crying somewhere in the distance. He looked around again, then cleared his throat.

"I am Ethriel, son of the High Queen Méabh and her consort Cathail," he announced. "I have returned to claim my kingdom and my first consort, who was taken from me by the traitor Siobhan." He looked from side to side, studying the faces. "I'm told you are my army, and that you are loyal to me and to mine?" A resounding roar of approval, and Ethriel fought to keep from shying away from the noise. He waited for them to fall silent again, then continued, "There are matters to be settled before we march. Where is Parciviel?"

"Here!" Kestriel's voice rang out, and he escorted Parciviel around the crowd to stand in front of Ethriel. Without being bid, Parciviel knelt, and Ethriel had to fight the urge to roll his eyes.

"Parciviel," he said. "Tell the company why you've been brought before me."

Parciviel looked up at him, his eyes wide. "I..." He licked his lips. "I failed in my sworn duty to my Queen. I was in command of the guard on the night of the attacks, and I was drunk on duty," he said, his voice flat. "I betrayed my oath to my Queen, and I failed her."

"And you upheld your final promise to her. You told me that you swore you would find me. Is that true?"

"I... yes, Sire."

"You fulfilled that vow," Ethriel said. "You have taught me and acted as my mentor and protector ever since I escaped from Buach and fled to the human world. Without you, I would not be alive here today." He looked at Parciviel. "Do you deny this?"

"I... no," Parciviel said. "I... I must atone for my failings."

"And so you shall," Ethriel said. "We now pronounce our judgment. Sir Parciviel, Knight-Commander of the Silver Thorn, you are now stripped of your rank and any titles you may have held. You will continue to serve us to atone for your failings, but you will continue only as Parciviel." He looked around. "Is there anyone who objects to this judgment?" he asked, and looked at Mathiri.

Mathiri blanched. "No, Sire," he stammered. "I do not object."

"Good," Ethriel said. He looked around again. "How soon can we begin to move against Siobhan? What will be the best course of action to take?"

IT WAS THREE DAYS BEFORE they left the Canyon and started the journey to the Palace. Three days of preparation and planning.

Three days of arguments.

"I want to come with you!" Roshara protested, following him as he walked through the camp, heading from one meeting to another.

"I need to know you're safe," Ethriel explained. It was the third or fourth time — he'd lost track. "This place is hidden and defended. I need you to hold this for me so we have a safe bolt hole if everything goes wrong. I've already appointed you Governor of Black Canyon."

"Without telling me! Or asking me!" she snapped. "Ethan, I want to come with you!"

"No." He stopped and faced her. "Ara," he said, his voice low. "I can't lose you, too. I can't give Siobhan another hostage to use against me, especially not one that she can kill. You're staying here." He kissed her. "Ara, please. I need to know you're safe."

"Then you're taking me to bed," she said in a low voice. "If I'm staying behind, that's the price."

He blinked. "Ara, are you sure?"

"I'm sure," she said. "If you don't come back, I'll have your heir, and we'll keep fighting."

He smiled, stepped in and kissed her. "Then I suppose we'll be putting Mathiri out of his bed tonight."

THE NEXT MORNING, THEY left the Canyon and started marching overland toward the Palace. Ethriel refused the use of the portal, telling Mathiri and Kestriel that he wanted his people to see him. And everywhere they went, people did come to see the Shining King at the head of his army. Word spread, and every night there were more people in the van than they had when they started marching. Non-combatants were sent back to the camp at the Black Canyon, and new recruits were sworn to the service of the King at the evening courts. By the time they reached the lowlands, the army was large enough that Ethriel started to believe that they could do this.

And by the time they reached the lowlands, there was a force waiting for them, one that they handled easily.

They kept marching, and their numbers kept growing. And the forces facing them grew smaller, more desperate.

Easier to defeat.

They were within sight of the Palace spires when they saw a single rider on the road ahead of them. He carried a white banner.

Ethriel called a halt and summoned Amartin. "You're still my herald?" he asked.

"If you'll still have me," Amartin answered. "Am I meeting with him?"

"He's carrying the white banner of a herald. I should send mine to meet him. So... go and see what he wants. We'll make camp."

Amartin was back by the time the camp was made. "She wants to meet you under Danu's truce. Tomorrow at dawn. There's a field about a mile up the road. We'll meet there."

Ethriel nodded. "Ride out and take a look at the field. Take Jeremiah and be back by sunset."

The next morning, they rode out just before dawn. Ethriel dismounted and left Cloud at the edge of the field. There was a tent at the far side of the field, and a table set up in the center.

"That wasn't there last night," Jeremiah said. He rested his hand on Ethriel's shoulder, and Ethriel felt his skin tingling.

"Shields?"

"Shields," Jeremiah confirmed. "My strongest ones." He smiled. "The ones that will stop elfshot. Because I don't trust her at all."

"Neither do I," Ethriel said. He took a deep breath. "Shall we?"

As they approached the table, Ethriel saw the tent flaps open, and his aunt walked out, flanked by two guards. He'd known that he was going to see her here, had prepared himself for that.

He was not prepared to see her wearing his mother's crown.

"Three?"

"Three? Three what?" Ethriel asked, turning to Amartin.

"No, that's you. You're Three. It was all we could think of that wasn't close to Ethi, and wasn't going to be confused with someone else." Amartin grinned. "If you agree to it?"

Ethriel laughed, feeling some of the tension draining away. "Now? We're doing this now?"

"If I didn't do it now, you'd shatter," Amartin said in a low voice. "You looked like someone hit you. So I did it now, instead of at supper, which was when we were going to tell you." He looked over at the three people walking to the table. "What is it?"

"She's wearing my mother's crown," Ethriel answered.

"Ah. Well, it'll be yours soon enough. Then you'll need to have it cleaned." Amartin rested his hand on Ethriel's arm. "Now, you need to be King. So... let's go tell that bitch that she needs to hand it over, hm?"

Ethriel took a deep breath, let it out, then reached over and hugged Amartin. "Thank you, Mar." He drew himself up, looked over to the table where his aunt now sat, and started walking. He heard the others behind him — Jeremiah on his right, Amartin on his left. Behind them were Avorn and Fantiel, while Glethin waited with the horses. Somewhere behind them, Sir Kestriel had a troop of soldiers concealed in the trees, in case of treachery.

In truth, Ethriel was expecting some sort of treachery. He fully expected there to be an army concealed behind that tent.

He reached the table and nodded his head the precise degree due to an older relative. "Aunt."

Siobhan sniffed. "I thought you had manners, boy," she said. "That's not how you greet a Queen."

"I haven't seen a Queen today," Ethriel answered, and sat down. "Now, shall we begin?"

"With your surrender?" Siobhan asked.

"No, I thought we'd begin with yours," Ethriel answered. "You cannot stand against me. Your forces are failing, and they are falling. The throne is mine by right of blood, and you know it. Everyone knows it." He smiled, feeling oddly calm. "My mother loved you, and out of respect for her, I am willing to be generous. You always loved the Summer Palace. I remember that. I'm offering it to you, along with a full complement of servants. Stand down and let this be ended."

"And if I refuse?" She smiled, and held up a hand. "I have a counter offer," she added. "Rule with me."

Ethriel coughed. "What?"

"I have no heirs, thanks to your human. He's killed both of them."

"Both?" Ethriel frowned, thinking. Who would the other heir have been? "Oh. Is Maniel dead?"

Siobhan nodded. "I have no heirs," she repeated. "Rule with me, as my consort—"

"No. I have two consorts," Ethriel interrupted. "I'm not looking for a third. And there is nothing you can offer me that will change that. You will stand down and accept imprisonment in the Summer Palace, or I will see you executed as the traitor you are."

"Two?" Siobhan laughed. "You've replaced John already? And he was so certain you'd come for him." She smiled. "There is one thing I can offer you, Ethriel. Accept my offer, and rule with me, and I'll give you your John back."

"For how long? Ethriel asked. "How long before you poison my cup, or have me strangled? I told you, Siobhan. I will not yield to you. And you have no choice but to yield to me. Your options are imprisonment, or death."

Siobhan sniffed. "Stubborn little fool," she murmured. Then she flicked her fingers at him. Ethriel saw the glittering darts a moment before they hit his chest; they flared, then vanished. Siobhan's eyes widened.

"What have you done?" she gasped. "What did you do?"

"May I present my head mage?" Ethriel said with a slow smile. "Jeremiah Miller, Heir to Taliesin. The human mage who has defeated elfshot." He stood up and raised his voice, amplifying it with magic, "Your mistress has violated the sanctity of Danu's truce and violated the law by the use of elfshot. Who among you will still stand with the traitor?"

Movement near the tent, and a man walked forward, breaking the spells hiding Siobhan's army from sight. Then another came forward. A third. More, and they stalked across the field; one of them glared at Siobhan for a moment, then looked at Ethriel.

"My mother was a seer. She'd have drowned me at birth if she'd seen that I was serving someone who violated Danu's truce," he said. He dropped his sword on the ground. "I surrender."

"How dare you!" Siobhan spat, and waved her arm wide. Darts flew from her fingertips, and Jeremiah cursed and threw one hand out. The darts all flared bright, then vanished before they hit any of their targets. For a moment, there was silence.

Then a wild howl rose, as Siobhan's forces rushed onto the field.

CHAPTER SEVENTEEN
Obfuscation

It had been years since Ethriel had last seen the Palace.

This wasn't how he expected to return. It had been weeks since the day that Siobhan had violated Danu's truce, and the days since had been one skirmish after another. Each one a little easier to win. Each one bringing more and more soldiers who refused to serve the traitor who violated the sacred peace, and who turned on her own forces with outlawed magic.

Each one bringing them to this — a siege against the Palace. Siobhan was inside.

John was inside.

Ethriel looked over the ridge at the place he'd once called home, then ducked his head and crawled back down to where Jeremiah and Avorn were waiting for him.

"She's barricaded herself in there," he said, rolling onto his back. "Guards all around the walls. Not many, but it never took many to hold it when it was sealed. We could lay siege to it for years and not do any good."

Jeremiah nodded. He looked up the ridge, to where they could see the spires on the towers. "Unless we got them to let us in," he murmured.

Ethriel looked at him. "What are you thinking?"

Jeremiah grinned. "I have an idea. Let's go back to the camp."

They crept back down the hill to where the horses waited, mounted, and rode off. The camp wasn't far from the Palace, but it was hidden from Siobhan's patrols by the same sort of barrier that kept Lightning Tree hidden from the human world. Jeremiah had tried to explain how he was keeping the elven guards from seeing his magic, but all he'd managed to do was reinforce how much more advanced a mage he was than Ethriel.

They passed through the barrier and dismounted. Ethriel looked around.

"There are more people here. The scouts must have brought more in since we left," he said. "We're going to have to send more non-combatants back to Roshara."

Jeremiah nodded. "First, let's find the rest of the Boys."

"What are you thinking?" Ethriel asked. They started walking, leading the horses to the picket line. A pair of younger elves came running.

"Sire, I'll take your horse," the older girl said. "Minx can take the other, and we'll come back for Lady Lilith's tack. Good morning, Lady Lilith."

Ethriel smiled and handed her Cloud's reins, watching as they took the horses off. Jeremiah stripped off Lilith's saddle and the bitless bridle she wore, and pulled a light robe from out of the saddlebag. He held it open, and she changed shape and let him help her dress.

"Now, what are you up to?" Ethriel asked.

"I'm wondering if anyone in your realm has ever heard of the Trojan Horse," Jeremiah answered. "I know the books were around the ranch, because I had to read them in school. And I know Uncle John knew them, because he told me he'd read them in Latin. Did you ever read them?"

Ethriel frowned. "Which books?"

"**The Iliad, The Aeneid** and **The Odyssey**." Jeremiah shook his head. "You'd know what I was talking about if you'd read them. It's a way to trick someone into letting you through their defenses. The Greeks used a giant wooden horse to get into the walls of Troy. We're going to use magic. But I need to see..." He looked around. "There they are!" He waved, and Glethin, Amartin and Fantiel joined them.

"All of you, stand next to each other," Jeremiah said. He watched intently as Ethriel lined up with the Boys, then nodded. "Avorn, you and Fan are out. You're both too tall."

"Too tall for what?" Avorn asked. He and Fantiel moved over to stand with Jeremiah. "Oh, we're both taller than Ethriel? Is that it?"

Jeremiah nodded. "Amartin, I think you'll do. Glee, come over here." As Glethin moved out of the way, Jeremiah held up one hand. Ethriel felt his skin tingle, and when he looked to the side, he saw...

Himself?

"Jem, why is Mar me?" he asked slowly. "And... who am I?"

"Right now? You're just in disguise. And Mar is you because if this goes pear-shaped, I don't want you to be the one they have."

"The one who has?" Amartin asked. "What are you doing, Jem?"

"Is that what I sound like?" Ethriel stared at Amartin. "Jem, this is too strange, Make it stop, then explain."

Jeremiah laughed and Ethriel's skin stopped tingling. When he looked at Amartin, he looked like himself again.

"So, here's the plan," Jeremiah said.

"OPEN THE GATES! I HAVE the false king!"

Ethriel was sweating, and his skin was tingling from the shields and illusions Jeremiah had laid on him. He glanced to his right, to where Fantiel stood.

"You ready?" Fantiel whispered.

Ethriel nodded and turned to face forward. In front of him, Amartin was disguised as Ethriel, with false manacles on his wrists. Jeremiah, disguised as an elf, was on Amartin's right side. They waited, hearing shouting inside the gates. The gates opened slightly, and guards came out, swords bared. Ethriel looked up and saw archers on the wall.

"Who are you?" one of the guards asked.

"Jemial," Jeremiah answered. "You don't know me. I'm my Queen's man, though, and I snuck into the rebel encampment to find out what I could. It was easy. Saw the chance and took it, and caught me a fake king." He grinned and shoved Amartin forward. "Brought my Queen a present. Hope she likes it."

The guard frowned slightly. Then he nodded. "And your friends?"

"My brothers," Jeremiah answered.

"This way," the guard turned and led them toward the gates. Ethriel glanced at Jeremiah. Surely it wasn't going to be this easy?

They passed into the courtyard, and Ethriel tried to look around without making it obvious he was doing so. There weren't nearly as many guards as he'd expected.

"Getting an eyeful, boy?" one of the guards said.

"Yes, sir," Ethriel answered, looking down, trying to act ashamed. "Sorry. Nowhere's ever been so fine."

"That one, he's never been off the farm before," Jeremiah said. "He's not a good thinker, if you take my meaning. But he's good with horses."

"I like horses," Ethriel added, smiling broadly. "Jem, are there horses here?"

The guard chuckled. "I see. Well, if the Queen allows, we'll see about finding him a place in the stables. Yes, lad, there are horses here."

"I like horses," Ethriel repeated. The guards laughed and stepped back, and Ethriel stepped closer to Fantiel. Fantiel smiled and took Ethriel's hand. He coughed, and nodded, and Ethriel turned to see Siobhan had come out of the Palace. She walked over to them and stopped, smiling broadly.

"Well, this is a pleasant surprise," she said, then laughed as 'Ethriel' surged forward, only to be caught and held by the guards. "A very pleasant surprise, indeed." She turned to Jeremiah, who bowed.

"My Queen," he murmured.

"How did you succeed where my own forces have failed?" Siobhan asked. "You may rise."

Jeremiah straightened and smiled. "Played it cunning. Knew that I'd only get the one chance, so we joined his men, told them we wanted to join his fight. Back... I dunno. How long, Fan?"

"A moon, maybe?"

"Full moon, Danu's eye, watching us," Ethriel muttered. "Good or ill, She watches us." He looked down at the dirt, and saw the hem of a fine gown appear in front of him. He looked up, his eyes wide, feigning surprise as Siobhan studied him.

"What's wrong with him?" she asked.

"He's been like that his whole life," Jeremiah said. "He's good with animals, but... well, we can't leave him alone. Promised our mother I'd take care of him."

Siobhan turned away, clearly dismissing Ethriel. "We'll find him a place in the stables. And for the rest of you? I think there's a place in my guard for such loyal men." She turned back to Ethriel. "Let me see... I don't think I'm going to kill you, nephew. I have a better fate in store for you." She looked at her guard. "Take him and bring him to the throne room."

"And us, my Queen?" Jeremiah asked.

Siobhan nodded. "Take them to the barracks. The other... take him to the stables and put him to work." She turned, and Ethriel looked at Jeremiah. They hadn't planned on being separated. Jeremiah nodded. He took a deep breath and made a throwing gesture toward the now-closed gates.

The gates crumbled into sawdust, and the army that had been concealed outside rushed the courtyard. Ethriel saw a moment of terror on Siobhan's face, right before she turned and fled back into the Palace. Ethriel reached up over his shoulder and pulled the Henry free of the back scabbard they'd fashioned for it; as it came free, the illusions that Jeremiah had crafted fell.

"Take the Palace!" he shouted. "Bring me the traitoress!"

A surge of his men passed him, heading into the Palace. He heard shouting, the sounds of metal on metal, felt magic flaring around him. He raised the Henry and fired, ran the lever and fired again, picking off archers on the walls, until there was no one left. Then he stepped back into a corner and started to reload.

"Three!" Avorn raced up to him. "Inside or out?"

"We'll go in, once the Palace is secured," Ethriel answered. He turned and shook his head, watching as his men swept through the courtyard like a wave. "Which won't be much longer. She has barely any men left."

A few minutes later, he started hearing voices shouting, "Clear!"

"Courtyard, clear!"

"Stables, clear!"

"Curtain wall, clear!"

"Guardhouse, clear!"

He stepped forward and nodded. "Right, into the Palace," he shouted. "Parties of six, clear each section. A bonus to the person who brings me Siobhan, and a bigger bonus to the one who finds John!"

The first wave entered the Palace. A few minutes later, the second wave followed. Then Ethriel nodded.

"Jem!" he called. "Are you needing a nap yet?"

Jeremiah laughed. "Not even winded. Are we going in?"

"Yes. You, me and the Boys." He looked around. Avorn was with him, and Fantiel with Jeremiah. "Where are Mar and Glee?"

Jeremiah looked around. "I... don't see them," he said. "Mar was with us. Glee was with Granddad and Sir Kestriel. Do we wait?"

Ethriel frowned and looked around. He saw Kestriel near the Guardhouse, and headed that way. Kestriel saw him and waved.

"Hurry!" he called, and Ethriel went cold. He burst into a run.

"What is it?" he demanded as he reached Kestriel. "What happened?"

"Parse," Kestriel said in a low voice. "Fioriel and the boys are with him, but..." he shook his head. "He took a spear in the guts. Saved Glethin's life."

"Mother Danu," Fantiel breathed.

"He's asking for you, Ethriel," Kestriel added. "And you, Jem."

Ethriel looked over his shoulder at the Palace, then nodded, following Kestriel into the guardhouse. Fioriel was standing at a table, and Ethriel could see Parciviel was on his back. Amartin and Glethin were both on the other side of the table. Glethin was covered in blood. He looked up, saw Jeremiah, then hurriedly looked away. Jeremiah rushed around the table and hugged Glethin.

"It's not your fault," Ethriel heard him say.

"Fioriel?" Ethriel put the Henry down near the door and moved to stand next to the big smith. "How bad?"

"Bad enough that I'm amazed he's not dead yet," Fioriel answered. "I think he was waiting for you."

Ethriel nodded and moved closer as Fioriel stepped back. "Parciviel?" he said. "I'm here."

Parciviel opened his eyes and groaned. "My... my King..."

"Easy, Parciviel," Ethriel said softly. "I'm here. Jeremiah is here." He took Parciviel's hand. "My faithful Parse."

Parciviel took a shaky breath. "Have... have I atoned?"

Ethriel swallowed a sob. "You have. And you are forgiven."

Parciviel smiled slightly. "Jem—"

"I'm here, Granddad."

"Tell your mother..." he coughed, and blood stained his lips. "Tell her I love her. Love you."

"I love you, too, Granddad," Jeremiah answered, resting his hand on Parciviel's shoulder. "Thank you, for being my grandfather." He looked at Fioriel. "There's nothing more you can do? That we can do? If it will help, you can drain me dry."

"There's nothing more we can do," Fioriel answered. "It pierced his bowel. The poison is already in his blood. All we can do now is give him peace."

"Ethriel."

"I'm here, Parse," Ethriel said.

"Tell John... sorry. Didn't see him..."

"He'll understand, Parciviel," Fioriel said. "Now, let's do something about the pain."

A few minutes later, Parciviel was still, his labored breathing shallow. Ethriel leaned down and kissed his forehead.

"Go gently, my faithful Parciviel," he whispered. He wasn't at all sure if Parciviel could hear, but it didn't seem to matter. His labored breathing stilled, stuttered back to a start, then finally ceased completely. Fioriel looked around, then went and took a cloak off a hook on the wall and used it to cover the body.

Ethriel swallowed and closed his eyes. "I need to go into the Palace now," he said, amazed that his voice didn't shake. "I need to find her. She needs to pay for this. For all of this."

"I'm coming with you," Jeremiah said. "Glee?"

"I want her fucking heart," Glethin croaked. "I... Three—"

"I hate her, too," Ethriel said. "And if you get her before I do, then I won't fault you. She'll be dead whichever of us does it."

Glethin nodded. "I saw crossbows. I want one."

"Can you use it?" Fioriel asked. "It's not like a long bow. Kicks like a mule, or like that battle pipe of Ethriel's."

Glethin nodded. "I can use one."

"Go get yourself armed. Meet us in the courtyard." Ethriel turned and headed out the door, picking up the Henry as he went. He stood in the courtyard and reloaded it as Jeremiah came to join him.

"What happens to him?" Jeremiah asked. "Is there a funeral? Burial?"

"A funeral, yes. Then ritual burning, and the ashes are taken to Danu's forest, where the elves were born." Ethriel frowned as several of his men came out of the Palace. "Is it clear? Do you have her? And did you find John?"

"Dungeons are empty, Sire," one of them answered. "And we've taken the Palace and shook it, but we haven't found her yet. And... well, you need to see what we found. It's..." He shook his head. "You need to see."

Ethriel looked at Jeremiah, who reached out and touched Ethriel's shoulder. His skin started to tingle again.

"Thank you," Ethriel said. "Get the Boys. Tell Glethin this might be his chance."

They followed the men into the Palace, and the Boys surrounded Ethriel, with Jeremiah following behind them. Ethriel kept the Henry ready, but they saw no one but his own people.

"Were there no servants?" he asked.

"A few. Not nearly as many as I'd have expected," one of the men answered. "We've taken them off for now. When Mage Jeremiah is available, we'd like him to inspect them."

"Tomorrow, if that's all right," Jeremiah said. "Let's find Uncle John."

They turned, and Ethriel realized where they were going — the throne room. There were more of his men at the double doors, and they saluted and opened the doors, allowing Ethriel and the others to enter.

The first thing he saw were the statues — a row along each wall, and one in the center of the room. The one in the center... he knew that form.

"John," he breathed, and moved out from the center of the group. He walked around the statue, staring. It was John's very image, but the pose — his wrists were chained, and they were raised in a defensive posture, protecting his face. "What is this?"

"Do you like my work?" Ethriel spun, running the lever as he raised the Henry. Siobhan stood by the throne. She smiled. "It's a pretty bit of spellcasting, isn't it?" she added. "He's quite decorative, I must say. I rather enjoy looking at him." She smiled. "Now, if you were going to tell me it's all over, I'd suggest you think again. You see, he's in there."

Ethriel went cold. He looked back at the statue, then at his aunt. "What have you done?"

"Imprisoned him in stone, like a butterfly in amber. Except that he's very much aware of what's going on." She smiled. "Now, if you surrender, I'll release him."

"You'll release him, and you'll surrender," Ethriel snapped. "And I might let you live. But there's another claim on your life, woman." He looked at Jeremiah. "Jem, you and Glee can draw straws—"

Siobhan sighed theatrically. Ethriel saw something bright flare out of the corner of his eyes, saw the alarm on Jeremiah's face. He started to turn, and saw Glethin fire his crossbow just as Jeremiah made a wild throwing gesture. Siobhan screamed. There was a heavy thump, and the light faded.

"Oh, no," Jeremiah breathed. "Oh, damn. Terensiel told me I needed to be careful with that one."

"What was it?" Ethriel asked. "What did you stop? What was she doing?"

"A death spell. I've read about them. It's more forbidden magic. She was going to kill everyone in this room."

Ethriel turned and blinked. "And...what did you do?"

"It's... I created this one. It's like a magical explosive," Jeremiah said. "Like the grenades that Uncle John told us about from the war."

"The ones that didn't work?" Ethriel asked slowly. "The ones he said were a bad idea, and should never be used in war?" He looked at where Siobhan had fallen. "The ones that he told us were a horrible thing? You went ahead and made a *magical* version?"

"I never said it was a good idea!" Jeremiah protested. "Terensiel told me that I put too much power into them, and they were too dangerous—"

"And you're never using them again," Ethriel said softly. "Ever. I want this knowledge forgotten."

"What knowledge?" Jeremiah asked. "Ethriel, I'm sorry—"

"She was dead anyway," Ethriel murmured. "We just could have been more civilized about it. Now... I need to get her to release John." He waved the others off, walking over to the dais steps.

Siobhan lay on her back, broken and bleeding, both of her arms gone at the elbow. She spat as she came closer. "Are you happy?" she gasped. "You've killed me."

"Your life was forfeit," Ethriel said. "Release John, and I'll see you in the hands of my healer. He's very good—"

Siobhan's laughter cut him off. "There's no release. I crafted that spell to hold him alive and aware until he knows you are dead. My final revenge on you both."

Ethriel went cold. He looked at the statue.

"Jem?"

"I'll find a way," Jeremiah said. "I'll break it. If it's the last thing I do, Ethriel, I swear it."

Ethriel nodded. Then he looked back at Siobhan. He ran the lever and raised the Henry, aiming at her eyes, which widened as he spoke.

"Jacob Wraith sends his regards."

CHAPTER EIGHTEEN
Snippets

"She said you're in there. That you can hear me. I'm not sure I believe her." Ethriel pauses, and I hear him taking a deep breath. *"The other statues that were in here, her other victims, they all crumbled when she died. I don't know if you knew that. If you can see as well as hear."* A pause. *"If you can see, I should put something more interesting on that wall."* He sighs. *"I'm getting distracted. I apologize. I'm tired. We don't know who they were, or if they were all elves. We took the dust to Danu's forest all the same."* He pauses again. *"Parciviel is dead, John. And he told me... well, he confessed. I forgave him, at the end. Jacob Wraith is dead, too. Or at least, if he isn't yet, he will be soon. He said he was sorry he didn't get to... what was the word he used? Oh, yes. Wrangle. He was sorry he didn't get to wrangle with you again."* Footsteps, moving around the room. *"I sent the Boys off to bring Roshara and the others out of the camp. The Boys... they're my friends. My brothers, they told me. Avorn and Fantiel are a pair. That's Avi and Fan. Then Amartin and Glethin are brothers. We call them Mar and Glee. You'll like them. Once they're here and we're cleaned up, there will be a coronation."* He stops moving. *"Jeremiah says he'll break this spell. He'll find a way. I just need him to do it soon. I need you."*

"And... he can hear me?" The squeak in Roshara's voice is amusing.

I wish I could laugh.

"Siobhan said he was aware," Ethriel answers. *"That he can hear us. I've been talking to him, telling him my plans. It feels—"*

"Ridiculous?" That's an unfamiliar voice. A man's voice. Who is that?

"Avi, if you're going to make fun, you can go." Ethriel sounds so cold. He should never sound like that.

Avi. I know now. That's Avorn. One of the ones he calls his Boys. He told me about them.

"*I'm sorry, Three,*" Avorn says. Three? Does he mean Ethriel? When did that happen? "*It's just... are you sure? She could have been lying.*"

"*I don't know,*" Ethriel answers. "*I can't know. Until Jeremiah breaks the spell, I won't know.*"

"*Ethriel.*" Another unfamiliar voice. "*What if he can't? Have you given that any thought?*"

Ethriel snorts. "*Of course I have. If Jeremiah can't break the spell, then I'm not the Shining King, and there will be no peace during my reign.*"

What? No!

He doesn't hear me. He can't hear me.

THE CORONATION IS HAPPENING. Part of it is happening elsewhere. Someone speaking in slow Elven tells me his name is Mathiri, and tells me that they will begin their ceremony in Danu's forest, and will return to the Palace after. I appreciate the telling, although I have to work to translate. It's been a time since Ethriel last came to talk to me. I think. There is no way to judge the passing of time. I'm not sure how long I've been like this. How long since Ethriel came. How long since he last talked to me.

I hear the sounds of celebration, the sounds of a jubilant crowd coming closer. They surround me, and I heard someone talking about me. A man. I don't know his voice, and what I can translate is about Ethriel's false hopes. About his madness in believing Siobhan's lies. The voices die away, and another voice rings out. I hear Ethriel's name.

"*John,*" a man's voice, speaking English. "*I'm Fantiel. Three asked me to translate for you.*"

He does, and tells me everything, right down to how many buttons are on the doublet that Ethriel is wearing, and the number of brilliants on his collar. He tells me how Roshara is dressed, and that the particular shade of blue of her gown was chosen to set off her eyes. That the coronet she wore as Ethriel's second consort was ornamented with sapphires. That there was another coronet, studded with emeralds, resting on a table next to the throne.

"*That's yours,*" Fantiel says. "*Everyone knows that you're first consort, and the Undying One.*" He pauses. "*But not everyone believes that Jeremiah can break the spell. We all heard from the guards who were here when she did it, that she did turn you into a statue. And the guards who were here when she told Ethriel that you were still in there. But... not everyone believes her.*" He falls silent. "*I believe. I think I can feel you in there. So I'll keep talking to you. Ethriel says that you'd appreciate it if I came in and read to you. So I'll be doing that, too. Ori thinks I'm mad. Ori...that's Avorn. You wouldn't call him Ori. That's his pillow name, the way you call Ethriel Ethan.*" A soft laugh, almost drowned out by a commotion. "*Oh, he's about to be crowned! I've been prattling and not telling you what's happening. Let me see. Danu's priest just raised the crown—*"

He continues, telling me how Ethriel took the crown from the priest and crowned himself. He would, my wonderful, stubborn Ethan. He did this himself, got this far all on his own. It was his right to crown himself.

I wish I could see it.

THEY HOLD MEETINGS here, where I can hear them. I am starting to understand spoken Elven more, starting to be able to translate faster. And when the meetings are over, and the counselors all leave, Ethriel talks to me. More to get his own thoughts in order, I think, since I can't answer him. He talks, and tries to fill in the answers, and invariably, he does the best thing. Not always what I would have suggested, but always what turns out to be right. He always comes up with an answer. Except in one matter...

"*They want me to marry Roshara, to name her my wife and not my consort,*" he tells me. I know that. I've heard him refusing. I've heard Roshara refuse as well, and heard her when she comes to me and tells me that she will never take what should be my place. They hold fast to each other, my dearest ones, and are always aware of the space I would fill if I could.

"*I can't,*" Ethriel says. "*I promised you a long time ago that I would not betray you. She is my consort, and we've agreed that won't change.*" He takes a deep breath. "*They tell me it will help bring peace. It won't. I know it won't. The old noble line of the Mountain folk, they won't accept it. And they're still angry at me for killing Siobhan, for all that she was a traitor and a murderer. They've claimed I should have handed her over to them for justice, because she was a daughter of their line and I wasn't king yet. Marrying Roshara won't placate them, for all that she's a seer and a diviner, even though she can't see at the moment.*" He pauses. "*John, there will probably be war before the seasons turn again. They'll come down from the mountains by the time summer rolls around. I'm certain of that. And I'm scared. I don't know what to do anymore. Especially since I'm fairly certain that the man leading them is my grandmother's brother. Not that it matters to them. They deny the bloodline. They cast my father out. That's final among my people.*" He pauses again, and his next words shake me to the core. "*John, there's another reason I'm scared. Roshara is pregnant. She told me this morning. That's why she can't see. I didn't know that, but apparently, a female seer loses their gift when they're pregnant. Her father knows, but we're not telling anyone else. Not yet. I just... I don't know how to be a King, and I really do not know how to be a father. I thought I'd have you to help me. I thought I'd have you and Parciviel and Kestriel. But Parse is gone, and... you're not here. Not really. Kestriel does his best, but he keeps reminding me that he wasn't born to the nobility, and he doesn't understand politics. He's a guard, and he prefers it that way. And Mathiri... well, I'm fairly certain that he thinks I'm insane."* He sighs. *"Jeremiah says he's not sure what else he can do. He's tried. I've watched him. He thinks that the spell was laid using something of mine. Hair, probably. Buach probably saved some of my hair. Jem doesn't know how to break the spells without hurting either of us. He says he'll think on how he can work around things while he's gone, but he'll be leaving court for a time. We had word from Lightning Tree. Nathaniel has taken ill, and Avriel asked Jeremiah to come. So he and Lilith have gone back through the portal. I'm honestly not sure what he'll look like when he gets back. It's been..."* His voice trails off. *"When the letter came through from Avriel, the date on it was September 23rd, 1900. It's been twenty-five human years since we left Midsummer."* He took a deep breath. *"I need to go and meet with the Mountain emissary, and try not to strangle them. Fantiel tells me that he has some new poetry to read to you. He'll bring it later. I love you. I miss you."*

"So, it's war," Ethriel says without preamble. *"They waited until my head mage was gone, and they attacked the villages at the base of the Spires. I'm told there were no survivors. The emissary of the Mountain tribes has been expelled from court, but it's too late. He's already let them know that Jem is gone, that we're magically underpowered. None of Jem's apprentices are ready to take up the reins."* He laughs, sounding bitter. *"Now I know I'm not the Shining King,"* he said. *"If I were, there would be peace."* He pauses. *"If I were, you'd be at my side. I wonder, which of my descendants will be the one?"* He pauses again, then makes a rude noise. *"Maybe I shouldn't think too hard on*

that. I'm leaving at dawn, John. I've appointed Roshara Regent in my absence, and she will hold the Palace while I'm gone. So she will bring you the news as she learns it. Wish me luck, my love."

ROSHARA COMES OFTEN. It's been weeks since Ethriel left, she tells me, and there's no end in sight. She brings reports and letters, and asks my opinions. It strikes me as strange, but she often comes to the same conclusions I would have. She reads her letters aloud as she writes them, and tells me how she misses him. How she misses me. She's with me when she feels the baby move for the first time, and there is nothing I can do to share her joy or wipe away her tears. One of her maids comes and takes her out, leaving me alone again.

I don't know how long it is after that when the wailing starts. I can hear it, but no one comes to tell me what is happening, or why.

Until Roshara comes, her face streaked with tears. And I know. I *know*.

"*John*," she sobs. "*He's dead.*"

No.

No!

No!

ROSHARA TURNED FROM the statue, her mind in a fog. She wasn't sure what she needed to do next, what had to happen. Mathiri would know, and her father would be returning soon with the surviving guard. She needed—

"...lah..."

The voice was harsh, creaky from disuse, and she turned back to the statue to see it had vanished. In its place, there was a man on his knees on the ground, his chained wrists raised, his face buried in his hands. His dark hair had gone almost completely white.

"Lah," he repeated, and she wasn't sure what he meant. But the pain in his voice, that she understood.

"John?" she whispered, and went back, getting awkwardly down to her knees next to him. "John?"

He shuddered, then looked up. "Rose," he whispered, and held his hands out. He said something, but in no language she knew.

"I don't understand, John," she said, then repeated it in English. "I don't know what language you're speaking."

He frowned. Blinked. Then he nodded. "Help me," he said in English. "I... no, he can't be. He can't." He met her eyes and crumpled, and she wrapped her arms around him.

"Mathiri!" she shouted, as John wept in her arms. "Mathiri!"

"My lady? What... Great Mother Danu!"

JOHN PAID NO ATTENTION to the people, or to where they took him. There were servants who unchained him, who took him from Roshara, who brought him food. They helped him undress and put him to bed, and he wept until he passed into fitful nightmares where Ethriel died alone, with John's name on his lips. He woke, and wept again, and at last slept without dreaming.

When he woke, the sun was streaming through the wide windows, and Roshara was sitting next to the bed. She was dressed all in brown, and her face was pale.

"Tell me what happened," John said. "And come sit here with me. I need to be touched." He sat up against the multitude of pillows, and helped Roshara sit down next to him. As she arranged herself, he looked around. "Where are we?"

"This is your suite," Roshara answered. "It was set aside for you the first night, and it's been kept for you. Ethriel never doubted that Jeremiah would break the spell, given enough time."

John took a deep breath, marveling at the sensation of air filling his lungs. "Tell me what happened," he repeated, putting his arm around Roshara. She leaned against him, a comforting weight and warmth, and he turned to breathe her in.

"Are you all right?" she asked.

"Just... I've been starving for so long," he said. "For touch. For scent. I could only hear you. I couldn't see or feel." He closed his eyes and buried his face in her hair. "You don't know how much you need contact until you don't have it."

She took his other hand. "What we know," she said. "They were ambushed, on the road over the Amethyst River, above the falls. I don't know all the details of the attack, but I was told there was a mage, and something went wrong. The road collapsed beneath them, and Ethriel and part of his guard ended up in the river." She shivered, and he hugged her more tightly to his side. "They found Damask's body caught on a snag near the top of the falls. They haven't found..." She stopped.

"Who brought the news?" John asked, sitting up.

"Avi," Roshara answered. "Avorn. He and Fantiel made it out of the river. They're the ones who found Damask. We're not sure about Mar and Glee. They haven't been found, either."

"Amartin and Glethin," John said. "I know their voices."

"Avi brought the Henry back. They found it on Damask's saddle." Roshara turned to look at John. "What do we do?"

John closed his eyes. "I..." He shook his head. "I don't know." He took a deep breath. "The only thing I do know is that I will take care of you. And of his child." He winced, realizing what he'd just said. "I... seem to be good at raising my lover's child."

"Oh, John." Roshara turned her face against his shoulder. "It's not fair! You were supposed to have forever! We were supposed to have forever!"

John wrapped his arms around her and held her tightly. There wasn't anything he could say to answer her.

JOHN SAT ACROSS FROM Roshara at one end of the long table. The empty chair at the head of the table nagged at him, and he tried not to look at it. Instead, he looked down the table at the others. Sir Kestriel, seated as Master of the Palace Guard. Mathiri, the Seneschal. Jeremiah sat as Head Mage; he had returned from Lightning Tree with his mother and sister, and he now looked older than John. There were other men and women, but John wasn't sure of their names or their voices.

"There must be a Regent named," one of the men said. "Someone must hold the throne until the heir comes of age."

"Roshara is Regent," John said. "Ethriel told me that he'd named her."

"The documents he signed named her temporary Regent only," Mathiri answered. "For the duration of the war. We want this to be unchallengeable. That means we must name a regent to hold the throne until the unborn heir comes of age." He nodded. "It must be someone we can all agree on. Someone with the experience of age, and who will hold the throne in honor of Ethriel's memory."

"Someone who will care for Roshara and her child as his own," Kestriel added, and John immediately knew what the man was going to do. And Mathiri, damn him, was in on it!

"Sir Kestriel—"

He didn't even get the words out. Kestriel continued as if John hadn't spoken. "I put forward Tiarna John, first consort, to act as Regent."

"No." John rested his hands on the table and sat up straight. "I refuse."

"John—"

"Mathiri, I'm not an elf," John interrupted. "There are things about your people and your ways that I will never understand. It's not fitting that I rule. Not alone." He looked at Roshara. "I'll stand with Roshara. But I will not stand alone."

Roshara looked thoughtful. "Co-regent?"

John nodded. "Co-regent."

CHAPTER NINETEEN
Resurgence

John stood at the window and looked out over the snow-covered fields outside the Palace. He could see more dark patches than he had the day before, and when he'd walked the ramparts at dawn, he could taste spring in the air. Not a moment too soon — it had been a hard winter, and he and Roshara had struggled to make sure the people were safe and fed. The only blessing of the heavy snow was that it blocked the mountain passes, forcing a temporary peace.

"What have we heard about spring planting?" he asked without turning. "Is it still too soon?" He heard paper rustling behind him.

"The southern lands are reporting that they've started planting," Avorn answered. "The danger of frost has passed there. Here... I think we have another moon before we can stop worrying about frost and start planting."

John nodded and turned. Avorn looked up from the writing desk, wiping his pen nib and laying the quill aside. The elf had appointed himself John's secretary. And, according to his new husband, Fantiel, John's keeper. John didn't mind — he liked them both. Avorn didn't know much more than John did about Elven politics, but he was quick, and his advice was usually sound.

"John, it's been quiet, but I know that won't last," he said. "How long before the attacks start again?"

John looked out the window. He could just make out the distant mountain peaks. "How long before the passes open?" he asked, turning back.

Avorn looked thoughtful. "Perhaps... two moons?" he finally answered.

"Then no more than two moons," John answered. "They're preparing to march as soon as the passes clear. Mark me on that."

He frowned, folding his arms over his chest, feeling the quilted velvet of his doublet sleeves under his fingers. He'd ordered the young slave Wat freed, and hired him as a valet. Without being told, Wat seemed to understand that John needed the reassurance of touch, of texture, and had made sure that all of John's clothes reflected that. The tactile sensations were calming, and John stroked the nap as he thought. "We've relocated the people who live in the areas around the passes, and along the most likely routes. We've burned those fields, cleared the land there. Cleared away all possible cover. There's nothing more we can do but watch and wait."

Avorn nodded. "Which is the hardest part," he said, and came to stand at the window by John. "Speaking of waiting, is there any news?"

"Not yet," John answered, smiling slightly. Roshara's labors had started late the night before, and John had been firmly told that he was not allowed anywhere near the birthing room. "They'll come and tell me."

"You're very calm," Avorn said.

"I'm sure Avriel will take good care of her," John said. "I could wish that the midwife had believed me when I told her that I've attended more than one birth."

"She probably did, but it's still not our way," Avorn said. "Birth is a woman's mystery."

John nodded, turning back to the window. There was movement on the ramparts. "Avi, look," he said. "They're heading for the main gate, aren't they?"

Avorn unlatched the window and leaned out. "They seem to be. I can't see why, though." He closed the window and looked at John. "Are we heading for the main gate?"

John walked over and picked up the fur-lined robe he'd discarded in the warmth of the office. "We are."

THE WIND CUT THROUGH John's robe as he and Avorn came out into the courtyard. The stones had been swept clean of snow, and servants hurried here and there. There was a small crowd gathered near the open gates, and John started walking that way, hearing Avorn behind him. As they got closer, John saw Sir Kestriel among the throng.

"Kes!" he shouted. "What is it?"

Kestriel turned. The crowd parted, and John stopped in his tracks.

Ethriel.

Thin. Dirty. Wearing a rifle-green kepi over auburn hair cropped short. His left leg was splinted from ankle to thigh. He was leaning heavily on the shoulder of another elf, and had a rough-hewn crutch in his left hand.

"Mar!" Avorn gasped. "That's Amartin!"

"Is it?" John stammered. "And... wait. We don't know. We... wait." He paused, swallowed. "I know. I know how to be sure." He stepped forward and raised his voice, calling in Aramaic. "Is it really you?"

Ethriel jerked as if he'd been struck. He turned, staring in wonder at John, and the first words out of his mouth were, "What happened to your hair?"

In Aramaic.

For a moment, time stopped. When it started again, Ethriel was in John's arms, laughing and crying and repeating a single word.

"How?"

John silenced him by kissing him, and time stopped again.

"John, we should bring him inside," he heard Avorn say. "John, he needs to be seen by a healer. I've sent for Fioriel."

John nodded, then bent and picked Ethriel up. He weighed barely anything, and John sighed.

"Oh, Ethan, we need to put some meat back on your bones," he said.

"How?" Ethriel repeated. "How are you free?"

"How are you alive?" John countered. "Because the last I heard, you were dead. They found Damask, and the Henry. We thought you went over the falls and we'd never find your body."

"John!" Avorn sounded insistent. "Inside. Let Fioriel see to him first. The answers will still be there once he's warm and fed." He stepped closer, and John saw the tears on his face. "Ethriel, I need to know, too. But I'm a bit more patient than this one." He rested his hand on John's shoulder. "Inside. Now."

Ethriel laughed. "John, you can put me down."

"No."

They entered the Palace, and Avorn ran on ahead. John didn't ask where he was going — he just carried Ethriel up the stairs and through the halls to the doors that he'd been told led to the royal suite. His own rooms were next door, and Roshara's were on the far side.

"Where's Rose?" Ethriel asked as John settled him into a chair. He shifted and winced.

Amartin came in and flopped into another chair and closed his eyes. "Will there be food?" he asked. "Soon? I can't think when we last ate."

"Yesterday," Ethriel said. "We ate yesterday. I think. John, where's Rose?"

"Rose is a little busy at the moment," John answered. He knelt down next to Ethriel's chair. "What happened? All we knew was that you went into the river. Rose came and told me you were dead."

"And that broke the spell," Ethriel murmured. He reached out and touched John's face. "I can't believe that."

"Is it true?" John turned to see Jeremiah in the door. "Holy Mary, Mother of God, it is true. Ethriel!"

Ethriel sat up straighter in his chair. "Jem? You look so different! How long was it? On the other side of the portal?"

"It's been over twenty-five years," Jeremiah said. "You all warned me that the time could catch up with me if I went. But I was there when my father died. Mama and Johanna are here now. You'll see them later."

Avorn brushed past Jeremiah. "Fioriel is on his way. And so is food." He smiled. "Lots of it."

"Oh, huzzah," Amartin muttered. "Now, Three, do you want to tell them or should I?"

"I'll tell what I can, and you can tell the rest." Ethriel reached for John's hand. "I'm not sure why the road went out from under us, but we all ended up in the water. Before I could get out of Damask's saddle, she ran up against a rock." He nodded toward the splint. "That's what happened to my leg. Mar got me out of the water, but there were Mountain elves all around, so we hid."

"Did Glee make it out?" Amartin asked. "I heard him calling me, but I never saw him."

"We never found him," Avorn answered. "Fan and I, we looked all up and down the banks. We found Damask, but no signs of anyone."

Amartin closed his eyes. "I thought as much. I think I've known he was dead. This whole time, I think I've known."

"Mar got me away, and hidden," Ethriel continued. "He did the best he could with this leg, but... I was out of my head with fever before too long."

"This is where I take it, then?" Amartin asked. He sat up and rubbed his face. "We found a shelter. Coal burner's hut, maybe. I don't know. But I covered it with branches and vines to hide it, and we stayed there. There was water near, and I set snares. There were a few times I thought Mother Danu was going to win." He looked at Ethriel and grinned. "But Three is more stubborn than anyone ever should be. He wouldn't die."

"Too much to do," Ethriel said. He rubbed his thumb over John's knuckles. "By the time the fevers broke, it was snowing. And I wasn't going anywhere on this leg in snow up to my hips." He frowned and looked around. "What's Rose busy with?"

John laughed and brought Ethriel's hand to his lips, kissing them. "She's having your son. Or daughter. We're not sure which."

Ethriel stared at him. "I didn't miss it?" he breathed. "Mar, I didn't miss it!"

"That's why he was so insistent on getting here before the snows melted," Amartin said. "He wanted to be here to meet the baby."

Someone knocked on the door, and Fioriel came into the room. "Well," he said. "I can't say I've ever worked on a dead man before." He laughed. "Let's see what's to be done about that leg. John, Mathiri is looking for you. Says the accounts are waiting for your approval?"

"They can keep waiting," John said. "I'm busy."

"John, the accounts can't wait," Avorn said gently. "Let's let Fioriel work, and let Ethriel get washed up and get some food into him. We'll come back in an hour."

John looked up and scowled. "Avi—"

"One hour," Avorn repeated. "I'll get the hourglass."

John looked back at Ethriel, who smiled and reached up to touch his face again. "I can't believe you're really here. You're really free. I don't understand how."

"I do," Jeremiah said. "And it's so simple. She said it herself, and I heard her, and I never realized how important it was."

"What?" Ethriel asked. "What did she say? I don't remember."

"She said the spell would break when John knew you were dead," Jeremiah answered. "It didn't have anything to do with if you really were. He just had to believe that you were. If I'd realized that... I'd have tried to trick him into believing it ages ago! Uncle John, I'm sorry!"

John took a deep breath and let it out. The sensation of breathing was still a marvel to him. "I'm not angry," he said. "Not with you, Jem. I do wish I'd had a chance to say goodbye to your father. And to Parsons. I wish I'd had a chance to meet Glethin." He looked back at Ethriel. "But I have my miracle. I have you back." He leaned forward and kissed Ethriel, then drew back. He could feel how tired Ethriel was. "One hour. No falling asleep while I'm gone."

Ethriel smiled. "I'll try not to. But no promises. Once I've eaten, I think I might have to sleep." He laughed slightly. "But wake me when the baby comes. I want to know."

Fioriel put his big hand on John's shoulder. "All right, John. Let me work."

John leaned in and kissed Ethriel again, then got to his feet. "I'll be back in an hour," he promised, and followed Avorn out of the room.

"HONESTLY, JOHN, YOU might as well not have come down," Mathiri scolded. He shook his head and smiled. "But I understand why. After all this time..."

"I'll try to focus," John said. "But between the wonder of having him back, and a baby at any moment? I'm amazed I can put two words together and have them make sense!" He looked down at the papers. "What else is there?"

"Have you given any thought to the spring?" Mathiri asked.

"I was talking to Avorn about the spring planting today," John answered. "And to the possibility... no, the probability of attacks once the passes are open. We've done everything we can, I think, to protect the people?"

Mathiri nodded. "That's good farmland, though," he said. "We'll have another hard winter if those lands aren't tended to this year."

"And if we do plant, then the Mountain troops will either raze the crops or steal them," John countered. "Better to let the fields lie fallow." He leaned forward to look at the map. "Didn't we plan to clear land here?" he asked, pointing. "I seem to remember ordering that last autumn. Did it happen?"

Mathiri went through his pages of notes, then nodded. "It did."

"Good. It's more defensible there. We can offer the land to some of the villages that were displaced, get them settled in time to start plowing once the danger of frost is gone." He frowned and looked at the map. "What about fishing? Do you remember me telling you about fishing?"

"I remember, but what of it?" Mathiri asked. "We've never had fishermen. Not the way you've described."

"We're going to," John said. He reached for paper and a pen, making notes and writing instructions. "I'll have to teach them how to weave nets, but it's not hard, and the rivers and the lakes will be full of fish."

"If you say so," Mathiri sounded skeptical, and John looked up at him and grinned.

"My family did this for hundreds of years, Mathiri. My father was a wealthy fisherman, with a big house and servants. This is something I know in my bones. And it's something we can do in the winter." He laid down his pen. "We'll need volunteers, and I'll need cord. I'll have to describe what I need, because I doubt— Johanna?" John looked past Mathiri to the young woman in the doorway. He smiled, realizing what it had to mean. "And?"

"And Mama says you should come," Johanna answered.

"Tell her I'll be there shortly," John answered. He clapped Mathiri on the shoulder and hurried out of the seneschal's office.

Avorn was waiting with Fioriel outside the door to Ethriel's suite.

"We heard that there's news. Ethriel is asleep," Fioriel said in a low voice. "We got him bathed and fed, and I took a look at that leg. And he fell asleep in the middle. Amartin is asleep in there, too."

"How's his leg?" John asked.

"It was a bad break," Fioriel said. "And it healed badly. And it doesn't help that he's been walking on it — he's been breaking it and rebreaking it for however long they were walking here. Now, I can break it again and try to straighten it, but that might not make anything better. We'll discuss options once he's stronger." He glanced at the door. "And after the fighting is over. We might not have time before the first assaults come from the mountains, and he's going to want to be out there."

John nodded. "I think he needs to be out there. Now that we're together? The Shining King and the Undying One? The war won't last much longer."

"Here's hoping that Danu's listening," Avorn murmured. "Now, are we waking him?"

"I think he should be there to meet his firstborn, yes," John answered. He opened the door and let himself in.

Ethriel was asleep in the same chair. He was clean, and wearing fresh clothes that hung loose on him. His leg was freshly splinted, resting on a cushioned stool. John went to his side and leaned down to kiss him. Ethriel hummed softly and opened his eyes.

"I'm not dreaming," he murmured. "You really are here. And I really am home." He looked around. "If I am dreaming, don't pinch me."

"I wasn't planning on it," John said. "Are you up for a walk?"

"Where?" Ethriel asked. His eyes widened. "The birthing room?"

John smiled. "Avriel sent for me. I don't think anyone has told them about you being back yet." He helped Ethriel out of his chair, and slid his arm around Ethriel's back. "There. Lean on me. Let's go."

They made their slow way through the halls to the birthing room, where Johanna was waiting outside the doors. She gaped at Ethriel.

"I... you're alive?" she gasped. "You..."

"Ethriel, do you remember Johanna?" John asked. Ethriel laughed.

"The last time I saw you, you were a baby!" he said. "Who let you grow up beautiful?"

She blushed, and knocked on the door. Avriel opened it, looked out, and clapped one hand over her mouth; she stepped out into the hall and hugged Ethriel.

"I don't know where you came from or what prayer brought you back, but thank any god who is listening," she gasped. "Oh, Ethriel!" She stepped back. "Come inside." She opened the door, and Ethriel looked at John.

"I need to do this on my own feet, love."

"I'll be right behind you," John answered. He followed Ethriel as he limped slowly into the room. Inside, he could see a narrow bed, and a wider one. The wider one was where Roshara was ensconced, holding a small bundle in her arms, looking both tired and radiant.

"Ara?" Ethriel whispered. She looked up, and her jaw dropped.

"Ethan?" she gasped. "Ethan? How? How... you're alive?" She blinked as Ethriel limped closer. "You're hurt?"

He smiled. "Yes, I'm alive. Yes, I'm hurt. And yes, I'm here." He stepped closer. "Ara, I'm so sorry. I never meant to leave you."

"You're forgiven," she answered. She looked down, then back up. "My King, my love, come and meet your son."

THE NEXT TWO MOONS were quiet. Ethriel recovered, slowly gaining weight, slowly gaining more mobility as Fioriel did more work on his leg. By the time Fioriel said he could do no more, Ethriel could ride without pain, but he would never again walk without a limp, or without a walking stick. His first excursion from the Palace after his recovery was to Danu's forest, where he formally acknowledged baby Cathail as his son and heir. He threw himself into governance, with John and Roshara by his side, offering safe harbor to Mountain elves who were willing to swear themselves to his banner. And when the passes opened and the Mountain lords attacked, Ethriel planned the defense, and he rode out at the head of the army with John by his side.

"Are you ready for this?" John asked. "I could lead this—"

"The prophecy says the Shining King and the Undying One together bring peace," Ethriel said. "Together. Not that the Shining King sends the Undying One to do the hard work." He grinned. "Besides, I've only just got you back. I'm not letting you out of my sight."

John grinned back at him, then looked out over the field. "You're sure about this?"

Ethriel nodded. "See the one in the gold armor? That's Lord Farathir."

"Oh, I know that name," John said. "Even more than what you told me. I didn't think he ever came down from the mountains."

"He came for the coronation. And now he's come down because he thinks this is the last battle. Which it is, but not the way he thinks." Ethriel glanced at John. "What's that monster in the mythology? Jeremiah told me, but I can't remember. You cut off the head?"

"A hydra?" John asked. "You cut off the head, two grow in?"

"That's the one. And if you cauterize the wound, then none grow. And there's one immortal head." He nodded. "Farathir is the immortal head of the hydra behind all of the strife. He's the last scion of the Mountain noble line. Tirgana is gone. Xanthe is gone. Siobhan is gone. Maniel and Buach are both gone."

"But you and Cathail are of the Mountain line," John murmured.

"Through my father," Ethriel agreed. "So if we cut Farathir off, that army will fall apart. And then... once they realize I'm the last adult male of their precious noble line, they will hopefully fall in behind me." He looked out the field. "The information we've gleaned from the Mountain elves who've sworn to us is that Farathir is so certain that I'm not really me, and that you're not the Undying One, that he's come down to prove it. I'm all for proving him decisively wrong." Ethriel reached down, took the Henry from his saddle, and passed it to John. "You're the sharpshooter. Do you think you can make the shot?"

"From here?" John looked at his target and laughed. "Ethan, give me a challenge next time, will you?"

"No," Ethriel answered. "Make this shot, and there won't be another challenge like this."

"Promise?" John raised the Henry. He aimed and ran the lever.

The Henry roared.

EPILOGUE

As Ethriel predicted, the army of the Mountain elves fell apart when Lord Farathir fell. There were some small skirmishes, some raids by men desperate and leaderless. But Ethriel rode out and took control, letting the people see him. He never once announced what he'd told John – that he was the last scion of the Mountain elves. They did it for him, and Ethriel, son of Cathail was named as the leader of the Mountain tribes by nearly unanimous acclaim. By high summer, quiet had settled over the land, and the official peace accords were signed.

The celebrations that followed went on for days; fairs and festivals that finally culminated in a great feast at the shining palace by the sea. There was music and dancing, and the halls were filled with flowers and laughter, just as the stories said. John sat on Ethriel's right on the dais, leaning on his elbow to look across to where Roshara sat on Ethriel's left. She had Cathail on her lap, and the baby was trying to catch a shining pendant that Ethriel was dangling in front of him. Cathail's delighted laughter set off ripples of answering mirth throughout the crowd. John shifted in his chair, taking a deep breath, happy in his bones for the first time in far too many years.

"Sire!" Amartin's voice rang out, and the herald came through the crowd. "Sire, I apologize, but we have a petitioner. She seeks sanctuary."

Ethriel sat up, catching the pendant in his hand and tucking it away. "Now? Amartin, bring them forward."

Amartin bowed, stepping back and letting the guards part the crowd and escort an older woman toward the dais. She led a little girl by the hand. The pair of them were clearly exhausted, their once-fine clothes dirty and torn, and the child's face was tear-streaked. The woman stumbled, and John jumped up, coming down the dais to catch her arm and support her the rest of the way forward.

"Amartin, a chair for the lady," he called. She looked up at him and he smiled. "It's all right, Mother. You're safe."

She looked up at him and shook her head. "I claim sanctuary for my little lady," she said in a shaking voice. "Sire, please, the child—"

"Mother, who is this child?" Ethriel asked. He picked up his cane and rose, coming slowly down the steps. "You are safe in this court; I promise you that. Tell me. Who are you, and who is this child?"

"I am Amina," the woman said. "And... my charge is the Lady Sarai, daughter of Lord Farathir."

"Sarai?" John repeated, feeling as if someone had hit him from behind. "I..."

"John?" Ethriel came closer. John looked at him, then walked over to stand with him. Ethriel looked as stunned as John felt, but it couldn't be for the same reasons. "What is it?"

"Joshua's daughter was Sarai," John answered. "It's a name I wasn't expecting to hear again."

"You told me Sarah," Ethriel said. "Or is it the same name?"

"Same name, over time."

Ethriel nodded, and stepped closer, bending so that he could be on eye level with the girl.

"My little kinswoman," he said. "We're cousins, you and I. You are welcome here. And you are safe." He paused, then straightened. "A moment." He turned back to the dais, catching John's arm as he walked. They went back to where Roshara sat with Cathail.

"She's kin to me," Ethriel murmured, "There's going to be pressure for me to adopt her. That's our way. But if I do, we start the cycle all over again. There will be those who say that since she's older, she should supplant Cathail as my heir. I can't put our people through another war. And I won't let an innocent become a pawn in anyone's political machinations. So what do I do?"

"Find someone we trust to adopt her?" Roshara suggested. "Avriel, perhaps? Or Jeremiah and Lilith?"

"Me." The word was out of John's mouth before he realized he'd said them. But the moment he did, he knew it was right. He glanced back at the little girl. Did she look like Sarai? He couldn't remember.

He'd never have a child of his body. And she wouldn't be the first child of his heart. But he wouldn't have to watch her grow old and die.

"John?" Ethriel sounded as if it wasn't the first time he'd said John's name. "Are you sure?" He looked over at them, then said in Aramaic, "You did kill her father, John."

John nodded. "I know. And quite possibly, she knows it, too. But if I adopt her, she's part of our household, but she's not in the line of succession. You can watch over her with me, but still protect Cat's inheritance." He looked back again. "And... I have experience raising little girls named Sarai."

Ethriel rested his hand on John's shoulder. "If she agrees, I give my blessing."

John smiled and leaned in to kiss Ethriel's cheek. Then he went back to where Amina was now sitting. Sarai had crawled into the woman's lap, clinging to her. John went to one knee in front of them, and saw the child frown.

"You're not like us," Sarai mumbled.

John smiled. "I'm not. My name is John, and your people call me the Undying One."

Her frown deepened. "You're the one who killed my father. Is that right?"

"It is," John said. "I won't lie. I killed him, because he wasn't going to stop. He was going to hurt a lot of people."

She nodded. "My father was a bad man. He hurt people." She paused, then shifted in Amina's arms and looked up at the woman. John almost heard the unspoken words, and met Amina's eyes. She nodded, and her arms around the child tightened. Sarai didn't seem to notice the interaction. "So you're going to live a long, long time, like me?" she asked. "And not ever die?"

John nodded. "A very long time, yes. And I can die, but I always come back."

She giggled. "That must feel terrible!"

"It's not pleasant," John said. "And I really don't like it." He made a face, and she giggled again. When she stopped, John shifted to sit on the floor, resting his hands on his folded legs. "I'd like to ask you something, but first I need to tell you something. May I?"

Sarai nodded.

John folded his hands. "A very long time ago, I had a little girl. She was my adopted daughter, the daughter of someone I loved very much, and her name was Sarai."

Sarai sat up in Amina's lap. "Like me? What happened to her?"

"Like you," John agreed. "And what happened to her? She was human. She grew up. And grew old. She died a very long time ago." He rubbed his hands over his linen trews. "Sarai, you're safe here. And you can stay here. Ethriel has called you his family, and he'll protect you. But... if you'd like, if you agree... I can adopt you. You'd be my little girl, and I'd take care of you and protect you."

She scowled at him. "And if I said no?"

"If you said no, then I'd hope we could still be friends?" John answered. He shifted, looking down as he moved to get up. So he was completely caught off guard when a small girl landed on him, bowling him over backwards. He sprawled on his back, the breath knocked out of him, then wheezed and looked up into brilliant green cat's eyes.

"You mean it?" she demanded. "I get to *choose*? If I say no, you'll *listen*?"

John nodded. "May I sit up?" She shifted off of him, and he sat up. "Sarai, you are old enough to know what you want. If you don't want to be my daughter, we'll find someone who you'll like, and you'll take care of you and look after you. And who won't hurt you." Behind him, he heard Ethriel hiss, heard Cathail start to fuss. But he didn't turn. Didn't look.

"And you promise you won't..."

"I promise," John said solemnly. He held his hand out. "Is it a deal?"

She bit her lip, then ignored his hand to throw herself at him and wrap her arms around his neck before bursting into tears. John closed his eyes and hugged her as tightly as he dared. Then he slowly got to his feet, still holding his new daughter.

"Amina, will you stay?" John asked.

"Thank you, my lord," Amina said, getting to her feet. "If you'll have me?"

"Yes, please?" Sarai murmured.

"Then come with me, and we'll see you settled and comfortable." He looked around, saw Mathiri smiling at him. "Sire, if I may be excused?" He turned to see that Ethriel and Roshara had both come down from the dais.

"You're excused, John," Ethriel said. "Go see to your daughter." He smiled and reached out to rub Sarai's back. "Welcome to the family."

John turned to follow Mathiri out of the hall, and softly, as if at a great distance, heard a familiar, wonderful laugh.

"*One last gift. Have a good life, Yohanan. I'll be here at the end of it.*"

John smiled, looking back at his loves, then looking down at his daughter. "*Thank you.*"

<<<<>>>

Endnote

THAT RIFLE ON THE BOOK cover? That there is the Escher rifled barrel muzzle loader. Takes a Minié ball, and you can get off a whole three shots a minute if you know what you're doing. It even fires around corners! It is recommended that you use powder from a cartridge instead of a powder horn, though. You don't want to see one of those get tipsy...

Seriously, though? The images that were originally used on the Kindle Vella covers did not translate well to being put on the actual book cover – my designer and I went through seven or eight revisions because we tossed the idea of continuity and went with the hourglass, rifle and roses, which I really do like. However, the rifles are... something else. First, they're not Henrys. I imagine that the designer couldn't find images of a Henry from the time period, so what they used are muzzleloading, not breechloading. And they bend space, which I have never seen as an option in a Civil War era firearm.

I opted to leave the space-bending rifles because they amused me, and I wanted to see how many people noticed.

So... did you notice before I pointed them out? Let me know!

Don't miss out!

Visit the website below and you can sign up to receive emails whenever Elizabeth Schechter publishes a new book. There's no charge and no obligation.

https://books2read.com/r/B-A-KGBH-GJCDC

BOOKS 2 READ

Connecting independent readers to independent writers.

Also by Elizabeth Schechter

Heir to the Firstborn
Worlds Begin
Written in Water
Forged in Fire
Bones of Earth
Wings of Air
Visions in Smoke
Children of Dreams

Rebel Mage
Counsel of the Wicked
Haven's Fall
Where Home Lies

Swords of Charlemagne
Hidden Things
The Lady and the Sword
Ashes and Light
Table of Stone
Swords of Charlemagne: The Complete Series

Standalone
The Rape of Persephone
Fools Rush In
Her Captive
To Market
Infernal Machine
Chains of Light
The Chronicles of John Zebedee

Watch for more at elizabethschechterwrites.com.

About the Author

Elizabeth Schechter has been called one of the top erotica and alternative sexuality writers in the world. Her writing credits include the award-winning steampunk erotic romance *House of Sable Locks*, the Celtic fantasy *Princes of Air*, and the dystopian fantasy *Rebel Mage* trilogy. Her shorter work has appeared in anthologies edited by D.L King (*Carnal Machines*), Laura Antoniou (*No Safewords*), and Cecilia Tan (*Jingle Balls*; *Like a Prince*).

With *Written in Water*, the first in the *Heir to the Firstborn* series, Elizabeth is exploring new ground, with her first new adult romance that was written entirely in real time on Patreon.

She was born in New York at some point in the past. She is officially old enough to know better, but refuses to grow up. She lives in Central Florida with her husband and son.

Elizabeth can be found online at http://elizabethschechterwrites.com, or on Facebook at https://www.facebook.com/Elizabeth.A.Schechter. You can also find her on Patreon, at https://www.patreon.com/EASchechter.

Subscribe to Elizabeth's newsletter at https://www.subscribepage.com/k4u7k2

Read more at elizabethschechterwrites.com.

www.ingramcontent.com/pod-product-compliance
Lightning Source LLC
Chambersburg PA
CBHW060212030726
47499CB00004B/1012